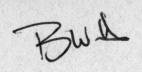

ARMED AND READY

Welsh drew back the slide of the Beretta to be sure there was a round in the chamber. He was okay now: the flip side of terror was adrenaline, and he was riding a pump so powerful it felt like he could rip the door off its hinges. The pistol felt right in his hand. He whispered, "Now!"

Scanlan yanked the door open. Anyone waiting to blow Welsh's head off would look for it to appear at normal height. He squatted down and bobbed it out low, using the doorjamb as cover, searching for targets right and left.

There was no one outside. Welsh was surprised, but the bad guys had done everything else wrong so far. Then he reminded himself that they had to be lucky once.

WILLIAM CHRISTIE

MERCY MISSION

LEISURE BOOKS   NEW YORK CITY

For Ruth E. Christie

A LEISURE BOOK®

August 2000

Published by

Dorchester Publishing Co., Inc.
276 Fifth Avenue
New York, NY 10001

Copyright © 2000 by William Christie

ISBN 0-8439-4753-5

The name "Leisure Books" and the stylized "L" with design are trademarks of Dorchester Publishing Co., Inc.

Printed in the United States of America.

ACKNOWLEDGMENTS

I would like to express my thanks to:

Joan, as great a reader as she is a friend, who slowly and carefully nudged me toward the right ending. My brother The Bull, who kept goring me until I got this finished. JAD and Peg, for basically the same reasons, along with friendship above and beyond the call. And Nelson and Donna, for proving that truth really is stranger than fiction. Also the Zooman, Rick, Erich and Vicki, and Ské. Jim and Beth King, for everything. Jason Gast, Ella Cowan, and Mary Gilbert, my rabid, self-appointed, and definitely unpaid promoters. My family members, too many to mention individually, but fanatics one and all. And last but not least, my agent, Jake Elwell of Wieser and Wieser. Only Jake and I know what we had to go through.

Chapter One

There were four Marines drinking beer. They were United States Marines, though the imbibing took place on a late summer Saturday afternoon in Guatemala City.

That Marines might be found having a few brews in the capital of Guatemala was not so unusual. Every U.S. diplomatic mission around the world was protected by a Marine Security Guard detachment, as few as six Marines or as many as fifty, depending upon the size of the post.

With the prospect of travel and life in a foreign city, being a security guard sounded like a great deal. But the first thing every Marine learned was that every great deal had a catch. In this case the catch was that after screening and a six-week training course at Marine Security Guard Battalion Headquarters in Quantico, Virginia, a security guard spent only half of a three-year tour of duty in an "easy" post, which in South America might be Buenos Aires or Mexico City. The other half had to be served in a "hardship" post. Guatemala City was a hardship post.

The Marines were taking their ease at a sidewalk table of a restaurant in Zone 10, the southeastern corner of the city. Guatemala City was divided into fifteen zones, ostensibly to make it easier for visitors to find their way around. However, the practice of giving streets in different zones the same names and numbers effectively canceled out any advantage to the system. Zone 10 was the upscale part of town, with the fanciest homes, luxury hotels, restaurants, and the U.S. Embassy.

The sidewalk tables were mainly occupied by the Marines, obvious groups of tourists, and only a few hardy Guatemalan families. Most Guatemalans preferred to leave open-air dining to their visitors. It wasn't just the rampant street crime, which made U.S. cities seem safe by comparison. Guatemala City's air pollution was considered to be far worse than Mexico City's, which meant that it was only slightly better for the lungs than standing downwind from a fire in an auto-tire storage yard.

The temperature was in the mid-seventies, a benefit of the 4,900-foot altitude. Guatemala City sprawled across a mountain range and precariously contained a population of nearly two million. It didn't have the residual architectural charm of many Central and South American capitals, since over the years most of the Spanish colonial buildings had succumbed to a series of earthquakes. Concrete was the order of the day.

The Marines had stopped at the restaurant to map out their Saturday itinerary, and it was thirsty work. Their table was littered with empty bottles of Moza, a good dark Guatemalan beer. Their waiter had grown increasingly nervous at the prospect of handling drunken, shaven-headed gringos, even though the Marines were quite docile and made no complaint about bottles of beer that arrived warmer than room temperature. After the fourth round, he worked up his courage and presented a bill with each order. This was highly unusual for a Guatemala City restaurant, but the Marines kept paying and drinking.

Sergeant Perkins, Sergeant Wentzel, Corporal Costa, and Corporal Richardson were busy discussing their plans for the evening, which basically revolved around getting laid. Since the State Department picked up most of the tab for the Marine Security Guard program, and was not eager to pay for moving and housing families that were not its own, Marines below the rank of staff sergeant were required to remain unmarried during their tour of duty. The effect of this policy was to unleash packs of twentysomething single American males, brimming over with semen, upon the unknowing citizens of the world. In diplomatic circles the Marine House and Marine bar in every U.S. Embassy compound was known as the place where taxpayer-subsidized booze and a major-league party could be found virtually every night. The Marines' collective inability to keep their flies zipped was just as well known. In the past, this had led to sexual compromise by foreign intelligence services, or much more frequently, run-of-the-mill sexual scandals that resulted in the culprits being court-martialed and sent home.

As the Marines sat drinking, the sidewalks were filled with pedestrians. South American pop music was pounding out from somewhere. Horns were blaring on the street. A city bus packed solid with passengers and sporting no window glass or paint job, with smashed lights and most likely no brakes, rumbled by, leaving a cloud of noxious black smoke in its wake. The Marines coughed and cursed.

Then something caught Corporal Costa's eye. "Check it out," he said to the others.

Two young men were making their way down the

street. One carried a guitar, the other a tattered black porkpie hat. The sound of loud, enthusiastic, and utterly incompetent guitar-playing reached the tables. It provoked an undertone of angry voices.

The Marines listened attentively. "Jesus," Sergeant Perkins exclaimed. "This guy sucks."

"What the hell is he playing?" asked Corporal Costa.

"I doubt it he knows," said Sergeant Wentzel.

"It sounds like they found the fucking guitar in a shit-can on the way over here," said Corporal Richardson, who tended to become touchy and ill-tempered after too much to drink.

Corporal Costa, a born peacemaker, tried to defuse his friend's mood. "I don't know, I feel sorry for the poor bastards."

Sergeant Wentzel made the decision for all of them. "We'll throw a little coin their way when they come over."

"If they make it in one piece," said Sergeant Perkins. "I think they picked the wrong crowd."

The two minstrels were having little success, other than at annoying the natives. Just as Americans were easily identifiable when abroad, these two had the unmistakable angular shabbiness of Englishmen far from home and down on their luck. Both were in their early twenties. The guitarist was dressed in black jeans and T-shirt. He twirled on his heels and thrust the guitar to and fro, his face to the heavens, eyes closed, completely caught up in his performance. It looked much better than it sounded. The one with the hat, obviously the brains behind the operation, bowed grandly from table to table, soliciting funds in terrible Spanish. He closely resembled the later, ascetic John Lennon, including the wire-rimmed eyeglasses.

The two Englishmen proceeded through the tables, collecting only angry looks and traditional Spanish insults. The Marines, by now no strangers to the ways of Latin America, waited tensely for the panhandlers to respond to one of the challenges. This would provoke the inevitable explosion of machismo, and all the men in the vicinity would begin dueling each other with their table utensils for the honor of killing the two troubadours.

But the Englishmen took no offense, the one in the hat thanking everyone profusely. Except for the music, which wore on the nerves, the two were so blissfully placid that they gave no excuse for violence. There was still tension in the air, but the restaurant patrons and passing pedestrians now chose to completely ignore the minstrels' existence.

The minstrels reached the Marines' table, and the guitarist broke into what could have been a flamenco. His comrade offered the hat around. It held a few lonely *centavo* coins obviously thrown in to salt the claim.

Sergeant Wentzel, as senior in rank, took charge of the situation. He held up a hand, and the guitarist obediently halted in mid-chord. "We'd like to hook you guys up," Wentzel told the one with the hat.

"Many thanks, my friends," the Englishman replied, offering him the hat. The guitarist stood by silently, trying to feign artistic detachment, but a little too desperate to pull it off.

"How much," Sergeant Wentzel inquired, "for you guys to hit the road?"

"I'm not quite sure I follow," the Lennon-esque one replied.

"He wants to know," Sergeant Perkins added helpfully, "how much money you want to go someplace else."

"Like another restaurant," added Corporal Costa.

"Across fucking town," said Corporal Richardson.

"Well, now," the one with the hat said brightly, trying to calculate an obtainable amount that would not alienate his benefactors. "What say one hundred twenty *quetzals*?" It was slightly over twenty dollars.

"What say we ram that guitar up your ass?" Corporal Richardson offered.

"Then I imagine whatever you could spare would be more than generous," the Englishman replied with a tentative smile.

"Sixty," Sergeant Wentzel decided, to groans from the others.

"Are you kidding?" Corporal Richardson demanded.

"Get it up," Sergeant Wentzel growled. "Fifteen each."

Grumbling, the Marines dug in their pockets and tossed money into the hat.

The Englishman scooped out the notes, folding the wad carefully before placing it deep into the pocket of his jeans. He dumped the *centavos* into his hand, put the hat on his head, and tipped it to the Marines. With good reason, since they now had enough money for a steak that, even though it might be a little tough, would still be the size of a car hubcap. The guitarist slung his instrument behind his back, eager to leave and eat.

"You might want to think about pawning that guitar," Sergeant Perkins suggested. "No offense, my man, but the way you play it, you could wind up getting hurt."

The guitarist pouted, but his friend smiled broadly and tipped his hat once again. The two Englishmen turned and strolled from the square. The nearby tables applauded the Marines for getting rid of them. The Marines laughed and took a few sitting bows. Everyone smiled in cheerful good fellowship. Except Corporal Richardson.

"They're probably laughing their balls off right now, calling us suckers," he said sullenly.

"For Christ's sake," Sergeant Perkins said wearily,

"would you just pull the bug out of your ass? Can't you even enjoy a nice day and a few brews?"

The others clearly agreed with Sergeant Perkins, but said nothing. Corporal Richardson grumbled something unintelligible and slunk down in his chair.

The shrieking noise of yet another motorbike without a muffler was nothing out of the ordinary. The Marines were really too drunk to be cautious, and too young to worry much about it. The only took notice when everyone around them began to scatter in a screaming crashing of tables, glasses, and chairs. Two motorcycles had pulled up to the curb, and the four riders in crash helmets and tinted visors were pulling submachine guns out from under their jackets.

The Marines stared dumbly at the bikes for a very long moment. Then, as if on cue, they turned back to each other, expressions of absolute amazement on their faces.

Corporal Costa was looking across the table at Sergeant Perkins. There was an explosive puff an instant before the sound, and Perkins's face split apart like a balloon blown up too fast. Beside him, Corporal Richardson screamed, and the white of the table splashed red. Costa pushed himself backward and rolled out when his chair hit the ground. He was showered with broken glass. A string of piercing cracks split the air just above his face, so close that he could feel the shock waves. He'd pulled enough targets on the rifle range to know that these were bullets breaking the sound barrier.

The drivers of the motorcycles sat atop their machines, covering the action. They fired short bursts over the heads of the crowd and into the nearby buildings. Not much more was needed to create the desired level of hysteria. Their passengers had dismounted, and were advancing together on the Marines' table, firing as they came.

Costa's backward momentum took him across the sidewalk and close to the restaurant entrance. He scrambled along on his hands and knees. All he could hear was screaming and the relentless *bap-bap-bap* of automatic-weapons fire. Then the sound suddenly closed off inside his head. The elemental instinct for self-preservation took him over, and demanded flight. In the firm grip of panic, Costa plowed through the swinging door and into the restaurant.

The customers and staff were lying flat on the floor. Their white-faced, wide-eyed gazes matched Costa's own. Unable to see past the tables, Costa lurched to his feet and whirled about, looking for escape. He caught sight of the service door to the kitchen. A burst of fire came through a window and Costa dropped back to his knees, scrambling like a beetle for the service door. Each heaving intake of breath came out, "Ah . . . ah . . . ah." The rough wood floor ripped both his trousers and the flesh of his knees. He didn't even feel it.

Through the swinging service door, Costa sprang up and sprinted across the narrow kitchen. He burst right through a screened wooden door, tripping and landing in a reeking, garbage-strewn alleyway. The sound of gunfire was loud and clear from the end of the alley leading back to the square. Sobbing, Costa regained his feet and lurched the other way. He was positive the shots were getting closer, that the killers were right behind him. If he broke stride to look they would surely catch him, so he ran even harder. Thirty yards down, the end of the alley was blocked by a seven-foot cinder-block wall.

Sprinting, Costa launched himself at the wall. He got a grip on the top, but all the strength in his arms had drained away. He dug at the wall with his feet, but couldn't get a toehold.

Back on the street, the two gunmen were right on top

of the Marines. Corporal Richardson was still alive, trying to crawl away an inch at a time and leaving a wide track of blood behind him. A long burst at point-blank range cut his chest open like a saw. The other gunman started into the café after Costa, but halted when the first one shouted. His partner took a photograph from his jacket and hurriedly compared it to the faces of the three corpses. He nodded, and both backed toward the motorcycles, firing in the air as they went. When their magazines ran out, they dropped the submachine guns onto the cobblestones and pulled pistols from their belts, brandishing them to discourage any intervention. They boarded the bikes, fired a last few shots, and sped out of the square at high speed.

In the alley, Costa hung limply from the wall, moaning loudly. Then the pistol shots spurred on a last spasm of effort. An uneven joint in the cinder block gave him enough leverage to get both arms over the wall. Broken glass cemented into the top slashed his forearms. Costa felt the impact of the glass, but no pain. He swung his hips, hooked a leg on top of the wall, and scrambled over, ripping his pants and shirt. He dropped heavily to the other side, forced himself to his feet, and broke into a frenzied, limping run.

Costa ran aimlessly down the narrow streets, bleeding from his legs and arms, clothes spattered with the blood of his friends, not knowing where he was, but only that he would surely die if he stopped.

A Guatemalan military police patrol found him two miles from the restaurant.

Chapter Two

At 10:00 in the morning, in an office suite on the third floor of the Richard B. Russell Senate Office Building in Washington, D.C., Richard Welsh sat at his desk fighting to keep the expression of polite interest on his face. Seated on the other side of the desk was a lobbyist representing one of the nation's largest aerospace corporations, pitching away with all his might.

Welsh was the legislative assistant for military affairs to the Honorable Warren Anderson, junior United States Senator from Kentucky. He was meeting with the lobbyist for the simple reason that the lobbyist's firm had paid enough in campaign contributions to rate a meeting, but the Senator didn't want to attend. Like all politicians, the Senator only enjoyed talking to people he could say yes to. Or who would say yes to him.

Albert Wozluski was a very large, pink, apple-cheeked gentleman closing in hard on retirement age. He was a longtime Washington lawyer who had gotten his start with the Chicago Machine. It was said of Albert, as he was known to everyone in town, that he would lobby for the Devil himself as long as the Lord of the Flies' check cleared promptly. A point of view that few on Capitol Hill found out of the ordinary.

Albert was there because the system of defense against nuclear missiles once known as Star Wars had experienced shifting fortunes in recent years. The expense had grown so horrific, and the results so negligible, that even the Pentagon had become nervous about taking responsibility for it. But no program involving that much money could ever die in Washington. Every time the Iranians, Indians, Pakistanis, or Chinese tested a new missile, the contractors and those members of Congress who belonged to them came roaring out of the gate to get the funding increased.

It didn't take Albert long to get into his pitch. A hazard of the lobbying game was that you never knew when you were going to be either interrupted or asked to leave.

As it happened, Welsh did interrupt him. "Now, Albert," he said reasonably. "You know that Senator Anderson was against the old program. So why waste your time dancing with me when you could be getting lucky with someone easier?"

Albert tried out the world-weary tone of the disregarded prophet. "Rich, don't you want your children to be able to sleep with a peace that mine have been denied since the beginning of the nuclear age?"

That brought a smile to Welsh's face. Secretly, he thought Albert was a hell of a lot more fun to deal with than the other species of the lobbying family. At the top of the food chain were the impeccably groomed lawyer offspring of the old political chieftains, whose cynicism and moral ambivalence was so pure that they made French politicians look idealistic, and whose ability to unlock a hundred grand in campaign contributions with a casual wave of their manicured hands guaranteed their influence with both parties. Then there were the humorless whiz kids who barraged you with carefully prepared and utterly persuasive statistics predicting the end of civilization if their legislation was not enacted immediately. And feeding on the bottom were the direct-mail hucksters with perfectly capped teeth who had made the step up from selling kitchenware and hair-in-a-can on local cable. Dealing with them was like being trapped in a room with a small, frantic dog who refused to stop trying to hump your leg.

No, Albert was one of the last of the dinosaurs. In any case, Welsh was immune to the sentiment. "Albert, since 1962 we've spent about a trillion dollars on missile defenses. It cost less to go to the moon. And, if you'll recall, we actually got to the moon; we still don't have any missile defenses. If your employers could ever manage to make one of their gizmos work, we might have something to talk about."

"Rich, in years past the technology wasn't advanced enough to handle the mission. Now it is. A nuke is bound to get out of Russia sooner or later, and just look at all the unstable countries who can't wait to get their hands on one. You can't deny it's a threat we'll be facing very soon, and we need to be prepared to defend ourselves."

"Albert, ballistic missiles with nuclear warheads are designed to *deter* countries who also have them, or threaten ones that don't. If you were the dictator of your typical outlaw nation, would you spend billions building ICBMs knowing that if you ever worked up the balls to launch one at the U.S., thirty minutes later the entire land surface of your country would be a skating rink of radioactive glass? I think not. You'd build yourself a nice, big, crude, dirty nuclear weapon. Then you'd stick it into a packing crate, slap on a few postage stamps, and ship the whole thing air freight to the United States, through a third country. The 747 lands in Los Angeles and the bomb goes off. All the evidence is vaporized, and we'd never know who did it."

"A real nightmare scenario," Albert conceded. And then, with a twinkle. "But we still have to worry about the missiles. At least we can fix that part of it."

"You're probably right, Albert," Welsh said wearily. "Because while the Pentagon spends billions on missile defenses, the Defense Intelligence Agency cut the number of analysts working on counterterrorism for budgetary reasons." He stood up to signal an end to the meeting. "But don't think this hasn't been fun, Albert. Who knows, the Senator might even change his mind."

Albert gave off a dispirited chuckle as they shook hands. "Rich, don't piss down my back and tell me it's raining."

"You know me, Albert," Welsh replied with complete sincerity. "I would never tell you it was rain."

Welsh didn't have a lot in common with his fellow Senate military aides. They were generally senior staffers older than his thirty-eight years. They held the obligatory Ph.Ds. in International Relations or Political Science, while Welsh only packed a humble bachelor's. They were usually adjunct professors at the local universities, self-anointed experts in defense issues, and in their learned pronouncements on everything from weapons technology to future force structures, almost always wrong.

Welsh had gotten his national security education the hard way, on the ground as a Marine Corps infantry officer. He'd been with the reinforcements sent to Lebanon immediately after the 241 Marines and sailors of Battalion Landing Team 1/8 were killed by a terrorist truck bomb.

He resigned his commission a short time later. Unusually, he didn't blame the politicians for the Lebanon fiasco. Their advisors—the professors with their theories, as Welsh contemptuously called them—were always going to come up with idiotic schemes. Positive they knew it all, they never knew any better. It was when the generals and admirals, who ought to know better, acted either like neutered little lapdogs, or worse, politicians themselves, that the troops always ended up dying.

He briefly worked as a Congressional aide, then went to the Pentagon as a civilian employee in the office of the Assistant Secretary of Defense for Special Operations and Low Intensity Conflict.

Lebanon had been like waking up. Welsh liked to say that once you've been shot at as the result of screwed-up national policy, it's hard to be detached about it again. At the Pentagon his frequently expressed opinion, that outstanding special operations troops were hamstrung by lousy intelligence support and a conventional military establishment that nearly always misused them, hadn't gone over well with the senior military men and civilian political appointees in his office.

The fact that the Panama invasion and Operation Desert Storm had largely borne out his views didn't win him any friends. It was even worse when the U.S. suffered a series of terrorist attacks. A universal concept in every bureaucracy is that it is better to be wrong along with the herd than right all by yourself. A skill Welsh had never been able to get the hang of.

Senator Anderson had rescued him from the terrifying possibility of law school with an offer to join his staff. Though interested, Welsh pointed out that he didn't have the usual credentials. The senator replied that he'd had a bellyful of the professors too. He wanted a smart grunt with common sense and experience, who would tell him the truth and not let the Pentagon get away with any nonsense.

The military affairs post did have its interesting aspects. Welsh considered himself an advocate for everyone who packed a rifle or flew a plane, and worked hard to stay on top of things. He had a ready-made network of moles in the military, and knew all the Pentagon tricks.

After walking Albert out to the hall, he headed back to his desk. There were six offices in the suite. The Senator and his chief of staff each had their own. Everyone else—the press secretary, the legislative aides, the Senator's personal secretary, the other secretaries and receptionists, the office assistants and summer interns—all roomed together according to the office hierarchy. Welsh worked with only two others, a major step up. In the Pentagon he'd shared an office with over twenty people.

Phones were ringing, visitors were being evaluated as to their relative importance, and TVs everywhere were broadcasting C-SPAN. Not for the first time, Welsh was spooked by how much it reminded him of both the Marine Corps and the Pentagon. Always too much work that had to be done *right now*; smart, conscientious people having to spend all their time and attention on just getting it *done,* with not a spare moment to consider whether *what* they were doing was necessarily the best, or even the right, course of action.

He'd almost made it back through his door when he ran into his fellow aide Jeannie Lamonica.

"I just had a great meeting with a constituent," she announced brightly. "What was yours about?"

"Star Wars," Welsh replied. Jeannie had a funny look on her face, so he asked cautiously. "What about you?"

"Pig penises," she said.

Welsh banged the heel of his hand against the side of his head, as if there was a little water in his ear that needed to come out. "Excuse me, Jeannie, I could have sworn you just said pig penises."

"I did."

"You're not usually so vulgar," Welsh observed. Jeannie was the type of person who wouldn't use the word *shit* even if she were standing in a vat of it and trying to describe the experience.

"Constituent service will do it to you every time, Rich."

Welsh was trying to keep from laughing. "Okay, so what position does our constituent want us to take on pig penises?"

"He doesn't want them green."

"I'd tend to agree," said Welsh. "Now, I'm no authority, but wouldn't it have been better to consult a veterinarian before bringing the problem to his Senator?"

Jeannie finally started giggling. "Maybe I ought to break it down for you."

"You *have* piqued my interest," Welsh admitted.

"This man's company buys pig penises from packing houses," Jeannie explained.

"I suppose it's a job like any other," said Welsh. "But still, why would anyone other than the original owner want the article in question?"

"They sell them as pet treats."

"I'm trying not to vomit. Go on."

"They had approval for this from the Department of Agriculture. Then the USDA started dyeing them green."

"I presume you're talking about the penises."

"That's right. And in the words of our constituent: 'The discoloration rendered them unusable.' "

Now Welsh couldn't keep himself from laughing. "And you kept a straight face through the whole meeting?"

"Of course, he's a contributor. But it was very interesting. He's a man in love with his work."

Welsh could just picture Jeannie sitting there in her conservative suit like a good Junior Leaguer, hands folded in her lap, not a hair out of place, as the guy went on and on about pig dicks. But there was something he was curious about. "Why *are* they dyeing them green?"

"No one seems to know. That's why he wanted our help."

"You know, Jeannie, ordinarily I'd think you were pulling my leg, but no one could make up something like that."

"Wait," she said. "You forgot to ask me the name of the company."

"Okay, I can tell you've been waiting for this."

"Su-ey, Incorporated."

Welsh laughed so hard he almost swallowed his tongue. He had to lean a hand against the wall to support himself.

Jeannie smiled sweetly and moved on to tell someone else.

Then one of the secretaries called out, "Rich, the Senator wants to see you."

The Senator's office was as large as all the others combined, but more cluttered. Hunting prints hung from the walls, along with the usual grip-and-grin photos taken with everyone who *mattered*. Portraits of the Senator's family were prominently displayed on the mantel, and political mementos were packed into every other open space. Welsh walked in and took a seat, still chuckling.

The Senator was sixty-three years old, and a first-class weave was responsible for that distinguished thatch of silver hair. "All right," he said at the sight of Welsh. "What's all this about?"

"Jeannie will kill me if I don't let her tell you," said Welsh. "But don't be surprised if a letter dealing with

27

pork penises comes across your desk for signature one of these days."

"What the hell?" the Senator exclaimed. Then something clicked in that formidable memory of his. "Oh, *that* guy! Now I remember. I met him at a fund-raiser and it was all he talked about. He wouldn't shut up. I almost had to have a state trooper mace him just so I could get out of there."

Welsh started laughing all over again.

"Did you have any trouble getting rid of Albert?" the Senator asked, getting back to business.

"I hardly even mussed his tail feathers," Welsh said weakly, wiping his eyes and finally regaining his composure. "But we haven't heard the last of it."

"All the contractors and pressure groups come pounding on your door," the Senator pontificated. "And everyone who's against them just sits home and expects you to do the right thing."

"If they can swing it," said Welsh, "their next move will probably be to give some company in Lexington a twenty-million-dollar contract for widgets, and you'll have to vote for the program."

"I probably will too," the Senator admitted cheerfully. "I don't think a principled stand on the issue would be appreciated by any of my constituents whose jobs are riding on the contract. But that's what I like about you, Rich. Unlike a lot of the young people around here, you don't turn into an opera singer whenever I have to practice some politics."

Senator Anderson frequently enjoyed acting like the old film version of the cracker-barrel country lawyer in the rumpled suit, though Welsh knew he'd been on the Law Review at Harvard. He was as much a fatuous windbag as the rest of his colleagues, but would shut the hell up and listen every now and then. As Welsh explained to his friends, you weren't talking about a normal human being: it was a *politician* for crissakes.

The Senator was halfway through his first term after winning a special election to fill the vacant seat of his predecessor. A vocal champion of family values, the predecessor had suffered a massive heart attack while being punished for his sins by a professional dominatrix known as Mistress Helga. Mistress Helga displayed both Teutonic efficiency and professional discretion by phoning the late Senator's chief of staff instead of 911. The two of them managed to clothe and transport the mortal remains from Mistress Helga's dungeon to a less compromising location before rigor mortis set in.

Even so, the story got around. There wasn't a dry eye during the funeral, as several coincidentally accurate remarks made during the eulogy caused those in the know to weep tears of laughter.

"Are you familiar with what happened to those Marines down in Guatemala?" the Senator asked, changing the subject with his usual blinding speed.

"I've read about it."

"What's your take on these killings?"

Welsh's face darkened. "It's happened before. I'm sorry for the poor bastards, but from what I know about Marines, I'm sure they went to that restaurant all the time. So whenever someone needed to kill a few Americans to make a point, there they were. I'm also sure, being typical Americans, they never for a minute imagined anything like that could ever happen to them."

"You may be right," the Senator said. "What some might call just a touch insensitive, but probably right. In any case, I want you to find out exactly what happened."

Now Welsh was puzzled. "Isn't the FBI handling that?"

The Senator handed him a thick binder. "They just came back from Guatemala, and this is the preliminary report. It also includes the report of the Guatemalan National Police investigation."

"Then I don't understand, sir. Why do you want me to cover the same ground?"

"One of the Marines who was killed, Corporal Thomas Richardson, was the son of the party chairman of the largest county in the state. And a good friend of mine."

"I'm sorry, sir."

The Senator waved it off. "Bill Richardson called me yesterday. He's not at all satisfied with what the Marine Corps has told him, and he asked me to look into it. So now I'm asking you. As I recall, you speak some Spanish, and of course I can count on you to do your usual thorough job."

Welsh hated stroking of any kind. Just cut the shit and tell him what needed to be done. "You don't have to scratch behind my ears, sir. You pay me good money."

The Senator thought that was funny and chuckled heartily. "Go over the report with a fine-tooth comb, talk to anyone you need to. Drop everything, give this your full attention. I also want you to go down to Guatemala."

"Do you really think that's necessary, sir?" Welsh asked, a touch of desperation in his voice.

"Yes, Rich, I do."

Welsh understood. It was necessary to the party chairman of the largest county in the state. He could picture the Senator telling the kid's father that he had a top aide on it exclusively, was even sending him down to Central America. Going through those motions was far more important than actually finding out what had happened. Well, it was the way things worked, and he was going to Guatemala. "I'll get right on it, Senator, but there's something I'd rather ask you than anyone else."

"What's that, Rich?"

"How did the son of such a successful man come to

be a corporal in the Marine Corps? You'd think he'd go in as an officer." Actually, Welsh thought they sounded like that class of people who would rather see their son become a Moonie than a U.S. Marine.

"Thomas's father planned on him taking over the family law practice. The boy loved computers and things like that. He wanted to study engineering. Bill Richardson refused to pay for it, and couldn't grasp the fact that his son was as hardheaded as himself. So Thomas went to college on his own, but it didn't work out. He left after two years and joined the Marines."

"I see."

"Rich, if you can do this without having to bother the boy's parents, I'd appreciate it."

Welsh took that as an order. "Not a problem, sir."

"I'm flying home for the funeral this weekend, and I'd like to be able to tell the boy's father you've started."

"I just started, sir."

"Thank you, Rich."

Chapter Three

After spending the rest of the day researching both the killings and Guatemala, and being increasingly disturbed by what he found, Welsh took the Metro back to his apartment. It was in a building in Arlington, Virginia, on a hill within walking distance of Key Bridge. Just one bedroom, and it continually mystified him that no matter how many things he bought, the place always looked unfurnished.

Since he was expecting a guest, dinner was a little fancier than usual. A personally modified variation of a dish he'd had in Benidorm, Spain. Chicken cooked with whole vegetables and a wine-based sauce in a clay dish. It was already prepared and waiting in the refrigerator; he only had to chuck it into the oven and set the table. Of course he was in the shower when the doorbell rang.

Carol Bondurant was a petite, mostly serious brunette in her early thirties. She and Welsh had worked together in the same Pentagon office, and engaged in a continuous friendly flirtation that always hovered around the edges of mutual sexual harassment. They'd become lovers just before he left the Pentagon. She was currently working as a staffer for the Senate Foreign Relations Committee.

Welsh cracked open a bottle of wine while the chicken cooked.

"I got to shake hands with the Dalai Lama today," Carol announced.

That put a grin on Welsh's face. No one was more susceptible to celebrity-itis than political operators. And Carol was still an idealist after working so long in Washington. Even though he enjoyed making a little sport of it on occasion, Welsh admired her for it. There was so little passion around, other than for shopping. "Yeah," he said. "That whole mob was clogging the halls all day. Any actors left in Hollywood to make movies, or were they all getting face time on Capitol Hill today?"

"Now don't be like that. He's a true holy man, a great spiritual leader, and spokesman for non-violence."

"*He* may be, but just don't put your hand in your coat around those nice Tibetan boys who surround him all the time. They were all packing heat, or my name isn't Welsh."

"Your cynical side is showing again."

"My realistic side, Carol."

"Say what you want, but the Chinese occupation of Tibet is a tragedy. When the Tibetans named a seven-year-old boy as the reincarnation of the tenth Panchen Lama, the Chinese threw him into prison. He's still there. A little boy."

"Funny thing about that," said Welsh. "The Dalai Lama didn't smuggle the kid out of Tibet and then proclaim him the Panchen Lama. He proclaimed him the Lama first, practically daring the Chinese to put him in the bag. They did, and it was great propaganda. So don't think only the Chinese know how to be ruthless."

"That is too cynical even for you."

"Don't worry, if things get too rough, the kid can just hop back on the Wheel of Life and go for another rebirth."

"Rich," Carol warned.

"Hey," Welsh protested. "I'm sure that's the way the Dalai Lama looked at it."

"There are some things that shouldn't be joked about."

"Those are the things I can't help joking about."

The buzzing of the stove timer kept Welsh from any further sacrilege.

Between forkfuls Carol said, "Rich, this is delicious. Now don't get me wrong, but how did an ex-Marine become a good cook?"

Being an ex-Marine was like not having opposable thumbs. "Well, I like to eat, and I haven't been able to find a family of elves to come and cook my food for free."

Carol let that fly past without shooting at it. "Oh, by the way, Rebecca asked me if I could baby-sit for her this weekend. Of course I said yes. Her little girl is so adorable!"

Welsh had once witnessed an eight-man section of extremely pale and hairy British Royal Marine Commandos strip balls-ass naked and, like the Rockettes from Hell, perform the legendary Zulu Warrior dance. As a finale, they segued into the Elephant Walk, which can be visualized by anyone who has seen a group of circus elephants moving in single file, connected trunk-to-tail. Not a sight for the faint of heart or politically correct, and even the unshockable military audience was deeply impressed by the performance.

And Welsh would rather be forced to watch the lads pound out an encore with all his paternal aunts in attendance than spend any time at all, let alone an entire weekend, in close contact with the little yuppie monster in question. His first impulse was to smash his face down on the kitchen table to wipe off the deer-in-the-headlights look he knew was there. But he didn't do it fast enough.

"Okay," Carol said in a strained tone of voice. "I'll give you a call sometime next week."

"It's just this project I've been working on," Welsh said feebly. "I've got to become the duty expert on Guatemala before I go down there. And I still have to talk to some of the boys in the special operations community; I can only catch them on the weekend."

"That's okay, Rich. Your feelings on children are well known."

Welsh did feel that if you were ambivalent about children, then it probably wasn't the best idea to have any, at least until your feelings changed. But all honesty had gotten him was a reputation as some kind of mutant because, as everyone knew, every last idiot who came down the pike ought to become a parent. Which pretty well accounted for the state of the world, as far as Welsh was concerned.

They did the dishes together, then finished off the bottle of wine. Later, on the way to the bedroom, Welsh said, "Do we have to leave the drapes open again?"

"You know I love to watch the stars."

"But I might get performance anxiety."

"Hasn't happened to you yet."

Welsh had nothing against exhibitionism, especially within the confines of a locked apartment. It was just that he'd lived in a high-rise dorm in college, and had once been introduced to a fellow resident with a powerful telescope and an encyclopedic knowledge of the sexual habits of everyone in a five-block radius. Thinking about it tended to affect his concentration. "Will you be sitting at your usual spot on the windowsill?"

"Probably."

Well aware of his matchless gift for unintentionally saying the wrong thing to women, Welsh shut up and dutifully followed Carol into the bedroom.

Chapter Four

"I've told this a story a thousand times," Corporal Costa said sullenly after Welsh introduced himself.

A Marine kicked a lawn mower into life just outside the window of the conference room at Marine Security Guard Battalion headquarters at Quantico, Virginia. Welsh moaned quietly and massaged his temples. He'd driven down from Washington the previous evening for Sunday dinner with his old friend The Bull, a Marine major and student at the Marine Corps Command and Staff College at Quantico.

When they finally ate dinner it was too late; the food never managed to catch up to all the beer.

Welsh regained consciousness at six in the morning, seriously disoriented, on The Bull's living room couch. There was just nothing like a good half hour's sleep. He opened his eyes to find The Bull's three-year-old son Larry staring at him from less than a foot away. The child obviously had little experience with such sights;

his expression was the same as if he'd awakened to find an enormous garden slug snoozing on the family sofa. Imagining what he himself looked like, Welsh could sympathize.

Then The Bull's six-year-old daughter Jill joined them. "Hi, Rich," she said cheerfully.

"Hi, Jill," Welsh croaked.

With brisk feminine efficiency, Jill grabbed Larry by the arm and dragged him off. "Leave Rich alone, Larry," she commanded. "He and Daddy tied one on last night."

From the mouths of babes, thought Welsh. He crawled to the bathroom. After a violent purging of the system, followed by a quick infusion of fluids and aspirins, his condition improved to the point where he only felt like shit. But he was capable of traveling.

"Man," The Bull informed him at the breakfast table, "you look like shit."

Welsh's vocal cords still weren't fully operational, but better now than before. "Thanks, Bull, I like my appearance to match my mood. It may be that I'm nearly blind, but I wouldn't say you were looking your best this morning either."

The major groaned. "It's going to be a great day at Command and Laughs. We've got a history seminar, and the instructor's already pissed off at me."

"What did you do this time?" Welsh demanded.

"Oh, the last seminar he was going on and on about the campaigns of Frederick the Great, how old Fred won fifteen and only lost two, or some such shit. All full of himself, the instructor asks: 'And what do you think about that, Major?' So *I* said: 'It's a hell of fine record, sir, but if he was coaching for Dallas he still would've gotten fired.'"

Welsh shook with laughter, then had to grab his head tightly to keep it from snapping off his neck.

The Bull joined in, then had a sudden attack of vertigo

and nearly fell from his chair. "Next time be a pal and come for *Saturday* dinner. I could use the recovery time."

"*You* invited me," Welsh said accusingly. "Not like the good old days when we got back to the ship five minutes before curfew, is it, Bull?"

"They've got to be making the alcohol stronger," The Bull replied.

Joan, wife of The Bull, stood in the center of the kitchen shaking her head. "I've been watching this scene like *Groundhog Day* for over ten years now. You've both grown old and weak. Deal with it."

They looked at each other through red and bleary eyes, and laughed at what they saw. "She's right," Welsh said affectionately. He loved her like his own sister. "Joan, you've been a saint all these years. A *saint!*"

"Don't I know it," she replied.

Welsh made it to MSG battalion headquarters just in time to cool his heels for an hour in a poorly ventilated conference room reeking of industrial cleanser. The last time he'd been there was as a student at the Infantry Officer Course. They'd landed by helicopter on the nearby athletic field and practiced the evacuation of an embassy. The two gunnery sergeant instructors who'd played State Department Officers had really gotten their rocks off on being called "sir" by a whole platoon of second lieutenants. Welsh had been the platoon sergeant for that exercise. With all the exercise "civilian" role players either freaking out, pulling guns, or taking hostages, he remembered having to shoot more people than he processed for evacuation.

The Security Guard Battalion staff officers he encountered treated him with an obsequiousness usually reserved for generals. No one with ambitions to higher rank wanted any trouble with a member of the Senate Armed Services Committee. That was one of the nice things about working for a senator. Sometimes those magic powers were transferable. Welsh used the long wait to fortify himself with a succession of cold drinks from a vending machine.

When Costa finally arrived, he was accompanied by a major who was going to be the command's watchdog for the interview. Welsh knew the game. Costa wouldn't say shit while the major was there; that was the whole idea. Welsh's head couldn't take a prolonged argument, so he suggested they walk down the hall to the colonel's office so he could call Senator Anderson. The major left.

Having cleared all those obstacles out of the way, Welsh was more than ready to get down to business with Costa. Unfortunately, the corporal had brought an attitude along with him.

Welsh had once prided himself on his ability to size up Marines; he'd been doing just that from the moment Costa walked through the door. The corporal was a short, pale, thin American youth of about twenty-two, with dark hair and civilian eyeglasses. His haircut was long, for a Marine, just on the fine edge of regulation. Costa also sported a sparse and wispy mustache. Nothing, Welsh thought, a little extra testosterone couldn't cure.

Welsh tried to find the right word to describe Costa's overall manner. Mild. Definitely mild. Welsh's experience was mainly with the infantry. Grunts had many different looks, ranging from piercing to no-one-at-home, but never mild. He pictured Costa as one of those who joined the Marine Corps to prove something to himself. A smart middle-class kid who tried to look and act tough, but didn't really pack the gear for it.

Welsh was sure Costa had been coached by any number of officers on what to tell, or not to tell, the Senator's aide. He'd save the important questions until he got some sense of the kid. "This won't take too long," he said reassuringly.

Costa gave him a cocky shrug.

"Okay," Welsh said. "Let's start off with your career field. What did you do for a living before you became a security guard?"

"2542."

That was cooperative. His hangover hadn't left him in the best of humors to begin with, but Welsh managed to keep an amiable smile on his face. "Exactly what is that in the communications field?" he asked calmly.

"Communications Center Operator," Costa informed him.

"Did you work on a staff?"

"Yeah."

What would have been a completely innocuous reply by a civilian was deliberately provocative coming from a Marine. In Marine Corps etiquette, "sir" and "ma'am" were mandatory when speaking to superiors and all civilians. And "yeah" instead of "yes" was not only inappropriate, but disrespectful.

Welsh could feel the muscles of his face tightening up. "Where?" he asked.

"Two MEF."

The 2nd Marine Expeditionary Force was the umbrella command for the 2nd Marine Division, 2nd Marine Aircraft Wing, and 2nd Force Service Support Group.

"The G-6?" Welsh asked. That was the communications-electronics section.

"Yeah."

In a way, Welsh was almost nostalgic; it reminded him of those days as a new second lieutenant when all the troops tried you out. The root of the problem was that kids like Costa started out working in big staffs, and got promoted solely because of their technical and ad-

ministrative skills. Their staff NCOs, who ought to be
providing leadership and discipline, were also technical
weenies and couldn't lead the proverbial horse to water.
The troops walked all over them. The officers were too
senior and too busy.

Marines like Costa knew how they should behave, but
like most American youth, would act like snot-nose little
punks if allowed to get away with it. In Welsh's experience corporals, non-commissioned officers, simply did
not pull that kind of shit.

He leaned forward and turned off his tape recorder.
With both palms planted on the table he gave Costa the
coldest, fiercest look he could summon up. He didn't
yell; that would have made it too easy to take. "Okay,
slick, now clean the fucking wax out of your ears and
listen up."

Costa's eyebrows shot up into his hairline.

"I did not come down from Washington to listen to
your bullshit," Welsh continued. "And I don't feel like
hearing any more of it. In case someone didn't fill you
in, you are here to answer my fucking questions. You
will tell me whatever I want to fucking hear, as many
times as I want to hear it. You will tell me the complete
fucking truth, and include every fucking detail. You will
use proper military courtesy and you will cease breaking
my balls, or I will fucking dance all over yours. Now,
do you understand me?"

Costa's mouth hung open a good inch and a half. His
face had the bright, clear, totally amazed look of someone who had just accidentally stepped out of a plane at
ten thousand feet without a parachute. Then, in an automatic reaction that would have warmed the depths of
any drill instructor's icy heart, Costa snapped into the
sitting version of attention, his upper body rigid, his eyes
focused on the wall directly over Welsh's head. "Yes,
sir!"

Welsh sat back in his chair. His face was expression-less, but inside he was smiling like a crocodile. It was nice to know he still had the touch. Now it was time to be firm but sympathetic; Costa had just needed to have the rules explained to him. "Good. We got off on the wrong foot because you decided not to act like a pro-fessional Marine NCO." He turned the tape recorder back on and softened his voice. "Now relax, take your time, and tell me exactly what happened that day in Gua-temala City."

Corporal Costa told the story of his escape com-pletely, without emotion, and without looking Welsh in the eye. When Costa finished, Welsh knew he'd heard everything.

They looked at each other in silence. Costa took out a handkerchief and spent a long time cleaning his glasses.

Welsh picked up his tape recorder and went out into the hall to give Costa a few minutes alone. When he came back in he brought the corporal a soda from the machine.

Costa seemed surprised by the gesture. He thanked Welsh, quickly drank half the can, and then made an abrupt statement. "You know, sir, they all blame me. For running away. Nobody says anything to my face, but I know they all talk about it."

Welsh nodded. It was the favorite indoor sport in the military, second-guessing some other poor bastard from the comfort of your office. The thought of all the hairy-chested assholes dumping on the poor kid because he hadn't taken on four machine-gun-toting killers with a broken beer bottle made Welsh feel like crying. Despite what he'd thought earlier, Costa wasn't a turd. The kid put up the bluster because he couldn't deal with con-stantly having to describe what he thought was his own cowardice.

"Look," Welsh said gently. "I was a grunt, and I was in Beirut. Believe me, I know what I'm talking about. There was absolutely nothing you could have done, except die along with your friends. But you made it; it wasn't your time yet. You can either wallow in the guilt, or you can look at your life as a gift your friends gave to you. Concentrate on living it well. Don't pay attention to the opinions of people you wouldn't respect anyway."

Costa absorbed it very solemnly.

Welsh thought he had gotten through. "Tell me about Corporal Richardson."

As Welsh had calculated, Costa seemed pathetically grateful for the change in subject. He thought for a moment, as if trying to give an especially good answer. "Well, sir, I thought he was an okay guy. But you probably heard that everyone else thought he was a major pain in the ass. A lot of times he was really hard to get along with."

"How do you mean?" Welsh asked.

"Sir, he was really sensitive, you know? He couldn't take any criticism. I always used to wonder how he got through boot camp. If anybody gave him any shit, you know, just the usual friendly harassment, he always looked like you killed his mother. He never gave it back like everyone else, he just clammed right up." Costa rattled on, as if he thought he wasn't describing it properly. "If he got the idea that somebody burned him on something—duty, whatever—he'd never have anything to do with them after that." Costa shook his head. "And in a small detachment, that can be kind of rough."

"How did you become friendly with him?"

"Sir, he was a buddy, but we weren't that close, you know, like really best friends. He just latched onto me." Costa looked helplessly at Welsh. "I guess you know how it works, sir?"

Welsh nodded. "I sure do."

"I guess it's because I never gave him any shit, sir."
Costa frowned. "I never liked to do that anyway, not the
way some guys do. I don't know what else to tell you."
He thought some more. "I definitely know he couldn't
drink. That's one of the reasons nobody in the det really
liked him."

"You mean he couldn't hold it?"

"Yes, sir. A few beers and Rich turned into a real
asshole. That's the only time he'd give it back. He'd
slam on everybody except me. Act like a real asshole.
And in the morning, everyone he ran into the night before would be pissed off, and Rich wouldn't remember
a thing. That really got old after a while. We'd go someplace, and he'd get fired up and want to fight everyone,
you know? I'd have to threaten to bail out on him to get
him to calm down."

"Somebody told me once that your real personality
comes out when you're drunk," said Welsh.

Costa grinned. "Then I guess he really was an asshole."

They laughed together, too long and loud for the thin
humor, but it drained off some of the tension.

Then some instinct told Welsh to ask a question. "Was
Richardson friendly with anyone else down there? I
mean not in the Marine detachment."

Costa didn't say anything, but he looked very uncomfortable.

Welsh knew he'd have to be very careful. "I need to
know what happened. If it's something that's not on the
record, maybe you should get it documented now, for
your own protection. Nobody's going to get hurt from
this," he added, hoping it was true. He hit the pause
button on his tape recorder, and made sure Costa saw
him do it. "Remember, I haven't advised you of your
rights under Article 31 of the Uniform code of Military
Justice, so nothing you say to me is admissible in a

court-martial." Welsh wanted information. Hanging people was someone else's job.

Costa seemed impressed. "I guess there's no harm, sir," he said grudgingly. "Especially since Rich is dead. And right now I don't really give a shit if they throw me out of the Corps or not."

Welsh looked quickly to make sure the recorder was running, and there was enough tape left on the cassette.

"There was this guy, sir," said Costa. "An American. Claimed he was a retired sergeant. Army," Costa added with a Marine's distaste. "Rich and I ran into him in a bar one night."

Welsh broke in. "You remember the name of the bar?"

"No, sir."

Welsh could have slapped himself for breaking Costa's rhythm. "Tell me about the guy."

"He picked us out as Americans right away. Tall, skinny guy, Southern accent, kind of old. Acted tough but friendly, you know; real country. He said his name was Brock, Tim Brock. I don't know if he was telling the truth or not. He came over to our table, introduced himself, and bought a round."

Costa seemed to be running out of steam. "He want to know anything?" Welsh asked.

"Just if we were in the Marine detachment." Costa rubbed his head and smiled ruefully. "We both had high and tight haircuts. It wasn't too hard to figure out."

"Did he ask you anything else?"

"Nothing he shouldn't ought to know," Costa said defensively. "He just bought us beers."

"But you thought there was something funny about him," Welsh said quietly.

"Rich really liked the guy," said Costa. "Which, to be honest, surprised the shit out of me. They hit it off, and Brock invited us out to dinner the next day."

"Did you go?"

"No, sir."

"But Richardson did?"

"Yes, sir."

"Did he see Brock again?"

"Yes, sir, a lot."

"Meals, beers?"

"Yes, sir." Costa looked slyly at Welsh. "You see, sir, Brock had spent a lot of time down there. He had money, knew a lot of people. A lot of bar girls," he added. "Real fine ones too."

"And he got Richardson laid," said Welsh, helping him along.

"Yes, sir." Costa seemed glad he didn't have to draw Welsh a picture. "Rich had never gotten a lot, you know, sir? He wanted it, but back here in the U.S., whenever the time came to close the deal he was too hostile, you know, usually drunk. He scared the ladies off."

"What about in Guatemala City?" Welsh asked. Now they were just a couple of jarheads shooting the shit.

Costa screwed up his face. "Nobody wanted AIDS, and the bar whores were nasty, I mean really foul. That didn't bother some of the guys, but I was always real careful."

Welsh smiled sympathetically. "And what about Richardson?"

"Before he met Brock, no. But like I told you, sir, the pussy Tim had on hand was really a cut above."

"Did you ever get invited along?"

"No, sir, not after I stayed away those first few times."

"And you never said anything because he was your buddy."

"Yes, sir."

"Didn't the detachment have a rule about going anywhere on your own?" It was the first thing Marines learned when going out on liberty. Especially in a foreign country.

"Oh, yes, sir, buddy system all the way."

"But it was kind of nice to have Richardson out of your hair."

"I guess so, sir," Costa said sheepishly.

"Richardson used to go off alone to see this guy Brock? A lot of times, you said?"

"Yes, sir. After a while I got a worried and told Sergeant Wentzel."

"Why?" Welsh asked.

"That guy Brock wasn't right, sir. It was making me nervous. I talked to Sergeant Wentzel and he was going to talk to Rich." Costa looked like he wanted to cry. "That's one of the reasons we all got together that day. We were going to relax a bit, and then Sergeant Perkins and me would go cruising and leave Sergeant Wentzel with Rich."

"You went to your sergeant hoping he'd handle the whole thing unofficially and keep Richardson out of trouble. Save him from a court-martial and getting sent home."

"That's it exactly, sir. But if I'd handled it earlier, maybe we wouldn't have been at the cafe that day."

"You were taking care of your buddy," Welsh said forcefully. "You don't know what would have happened."

Costa shrugged.

"Tell me if I'm wrong," said Welsh, "but Richardson sounds like one of those guys who's always trying too hard. You know what I mean."

"Yes, sir. In everything. He used to study books on electronics and computers on his free time. His locker was full of catalogs."

"You called him Rich," said Welsh. "But his first name was Brian. What's the story, didn't he like it?"

Costa smiled. "We gave him that nickname. He was always buying these investment magazines. And the way he acted. You could tell he didn't exactly grow up poor, if you know what I mean. He always had money."

"I never knew a corporal that wasn't always broke."

"He was funny. In most things he was really cheap. He used to drive me crazy; whenever he wanted to buy something he'd spend like this incredible amount of time shopping for the best price. But sometimes he just threw his cash around. If I needed a couple of bucks until payday he always let me have it, sometimes more than I wanted."

"His dad was loaded, right?"

Costa seemed relieved that Welsh hadn't directly asked the question that was probably on both their minds. He stared at the table, and said, "Yes, sir, but he told me once that his old man cut him off when he quit college and joined the Corps."

"It's okay." Welsh was smiling, and his hangover had all but disappeared. "I think we're finished here."

"Am I in trouble, sir?" Costa asked.

"Not from me," Welsh told him honestly.

He waited until he got off the base, then called the office from a pay phone. To his great surprise, he got Senator Anderson right away.

"How did the interview go, Rich?" the Senator asked.

"Fine, sir," Welsh replied. He didn't want to give the Senator any details until he'd put the whole thing together and was sure he was right. "But I have a question I need you to ask Corporal Richardson's father."

"What question would that be, Rich?"

"Did Mr. Richardson sever all personal, and particularly financial, contact with his son after he left school and joined the Marines?"

"I don't need to call about that, Rich. I know for a fact that he did. And I can't begin to tell you how guilty he feels about it now."

The Senator had to make a quorum call, so Welsh

hung up. Richardson's father wasn't the only one feeling guilty. If anyone wanted to call him a manipulative son of a bitch for the way he'd handled Costa, Welsh wouldn't have argued with them.

As he walked back to his car, Welsh was thinking that his few remaining illusions about an easy, relaxing, straightforward investigation had just gone right out the window.

Chapter Five

Welsh drove back to Washington, and as always it took a little longer than expected. You could reach the District to Columbia at 3:00 A.M. and still run into a traffic jam.

There was a thick stack of pink telephone message forms waiting for him in the office. Following his usual routine, Welsh shucked off his jacket, loosened his tie, opened his collar, put his feet up on the desk, and only then began sorting through the messages. Five were from the same person. The name didn't ring a bell.

The only information was the name and number.

Welsh strolled over to Marie, Senator Anderson's large, middle-aged, imperious, deceptively jolly private secretary. Marie had worked on Capitol Hill forever, knew everyone, and took shit from absolutely no one. But what made her so valuable to the Senator was that she never went around looking to give any either.

She protected Senator Anderson from both himself and others, maintaining good relations with everyone who was important to him. But if you made a habit of giving either of them any static, then God help you. One high-ranking legislator, whom Welsh considered an egomaniacal prick of the first order, used any number of elaborate excuses to conduct his business with the Senator outside the office, such was his terror of running into Marie.

There was a persistent rumor that her inviolable position came from being the Senator's first love. Few things were beyond the realm of possibility in Washington, but Welsh seriously doubted it.

He showed her the messages. "Marie, who is this guy?"

"I don't know, Rich. He wouldn't give me any information. He said it was personal. I really hate that," she said emphatically. "That you're-just-a-secretary attitude."

"I hear you," said Welsh. He turned to go back to his desk, but Marie was staring at him expectantly, as if waiting for him to say something else. For the life of him, Welsh couldn't imagine what that might be. He just stood there grinning nervously, totally embarrassed. "Ah, was there anything else, Marie?" he finally asked.

"No," she replied, as if she found the question surprising.

Welsh blinked a couple of times to reset his gyros, then slunk back to his desk. That happened a lot with Marie. He had no idea whether she was fucking with him or there really was some kind of psychic communication lag between them. No matter. His curiosity aroused, he picked up the phone and dialed the number on the messages.

After three rings the line clicked open. A secretarial-sounding female voice said, "482–1100."

Welsh was startled. Shit, he thought. There were very few organizations who answered their phone that way, but he knew of one. He gave the extension. "Thomas Kohl, please. Richard Welsh calling."

Evidently it was good enough. "One moment, please," the voice requested.

The phone clicked again. "Hello, Mr. Welsh, this is Thomas Kohl. Thank you for getting back to me."

A voice with a little New York edge to it, thought Welsh. Rough, but smooth. Or maybe slick was a better word. "What can I do for you, Mr. Kohl?"

"I'd very much like to speak with you on an important matter, in person. Will you be my guest at lunch? Either tomorrow, or whenever it's convenient for you?"

"What would we be talking about?"

"If you don't mind, I'd prefer to discuss that in person."

"Then perhaps you can give me some clue as to who you are. My mother doesn't like me to go out with strange men."

There was a rich chuckle on the other end of the line. "Forgive me. I'm a friend of Ed Howe."

Howe was the Central Intelligence Agency's head of Congressional liaison. The CIA were also the people who greeted you with their telephone number when you called. "Then I assume you work for the same organization. I mean, other than the federal government as a whole."

"That's correct."

"Then am I also correct in assuming that Ed will recognize the name you gave me, if I call him?"

"He will. And that is my name, Mr. Welsh."

A little testy, thought Welsh. Nice touch of arrogance. Must have some rank. "Thanks for the invitation, Mr. Kohl. I have a call on another line right now; would it be all right if I called you back in about ten minutes?"

There was a pause. "That would be fine," Kohl said politely. He rang off.

Welsh didn't have a call on another line, as Kohl had known very well. He called Ed Howe. "Ed, I need to establish someone's bona fides."

"What are you up to now, Richard?" Howe asked indulgently. He was one of the last of the old-fashioned CIA patricians, having survived all the Company's purges only to be put out to pasture in Congressional liaison.

"Now, Ed, you guys never tell anyone anything, so why should I?"

Howe laughed. "All right, Richard, what do you need to know?"

"Is Thomas Kohl a colleague of yours?"

"What would make you think so?"

Welsh groaned. Howe was such a Secret Squirrel, he probably kept his golf handicap on a need-to-know basis. "I ran into him, and it's important to know if he's who he says he is. Also, he dropped your name."

"It's high time you broadened your horizons, Richard."

"Then he is one of the boys?"

"He's an old friend."

Welsh knew that was as much as he was going to get. "Thanks a lot, Ed."

"Any time, Richard." Howe hung up.

By this time Welsh was ready to start checking his #2 pencils for hidden microphones. He called Kohl back and set a lunch date for the following day. Then he made another call.

After work he drove to the Fredericksburg, Virginia, home of a friend from his days at the Pentagon. At that time Lieutenant Colonel Michael Longenecker, U.S. Army, had been assigned to a unit called Intelligence Support Activity, or ISA.

During the Iranian hostage crisis, the Army created a unit it called the Forward Operating Group (FOG) out of frustration with the CIA's complete inability to put agents on the ground to support Delta Force's planned hostage rescue. Although the attempted rescue was a fiasco, the Army decided to retain the unit. They wanted to develop their own intelligence-gathering capability and agents, convinced that the CIA had neither the desire nor the capability to supply them with the detailed intelligence needed to mount special operations. As FOG expanded, it was given the name ISA.

ISA originally operated without the knowledge of the CIA, White House, or House and Senate Intelligence Committees—which is to say, in clear violation of the law. In 1983, several years after its establishment, President Reagan finally gave them official sanction.

That same year several scandals blew up around ISA. The unit was accused not only of exceeding its charter in several operations, but violating federal law by conducting intelligence gathering inside the United States. Three officers were also under investigation for fraud and diverting unit funds to personal use.

From ISA's point of view, they were so effective that they made the rest of the intelligence community, and particularly the CIA, look bad, thereby inviting jealous retaliation.

The CIA's opinion was that ISA were a mob of green-suited amateurs who operated with no oversight, controls, or sanction. And in the end, they got what they deserved, since the few who weren't out-and-out embezzlers at least padded every expense voucher they ever filled out.

In the end the CIA won. When the dust settled the three ISA officers underwent courts-martial, and the Activity was reined in and put under the thumb of the Defense Intelligence Agency.

For Welsh, the moral of the story was never to sneer

at rumors of intelligence agencies no one had ever heard of.

Lieutenant Colonel Longenecker currently worked for the Army Intelligence and Security Command. He was marking time until he could finish out his twenty years and retire.

He was also an old Central America hand. ISA had been deeply involved in the Sandinista-Contra war in Nicaragua, the civil war in El Salvador, and Guatemala.

They sat on lawn chairs in the colonel's back yard, under the protective shade of the trees. Longenecker cracked open two beers, and Welsh related the day's phone conversations.

The colonel was a blue-eyed blond Viking whose hair, no matter what he did with it, always stuck up in a Dennis-the-Menace cowlick. He was of medium height; one of those people who appear somewhat thin and frail until you see how much weight they can bench-press. He listened to Welsh solemnly and asked, "What are you working on now?"

Welsh told him about his assignment, but not what he'd found out so far.

"Kohl was the CIA Chief of Station in Guatemala," said Longenecker. "He's back working at Langley right now."

"Doing what?" Welsh asked.

His friend smiled and shook his head at such a stupid question.

Welsh held a Sensitive Compartmented Information security clearance, which was above Top Secret, but Longenecker wouldn't give him anything he didn't need to know about. It was one of the many things Welsh liked about him. Of course, the reason he needed Longenecker and others like him was that the Pentagon and CIA would only give him the absolute minimum, no matter the clearance. "Okay, Mike, then what do you think they want from me?"

Longenecker gave him a look of exasperation. "To know what you're doing, of course. What the fuck else?"

"But why?"

"Rich, I don't know. And that's no shit; I haven't heard anything. They must have some kind of interest in your investigation."

"Duh," Welsh said impatiently. "Okay, so you don't know. So what do you *think*?"

"It could be a lot of things. Guatemala's been the CIA's private preserve since the fifties. But since the Berlin Wall came down, the wind's changed. Nobody cares about keeping the Commies from taking over the world anymore. Now they care about human rights violations, torture, and mass murder. The Company's had so many scandals involving Guatemala lately, maybe they want to make sure you don't come up with another one."

"When I was doing research, I read about that guy Scanlan."

Longenecker shook his head. "Guy joins the Peace Corps, serves in Guatemala, falls in love with the place. Fine. But he gets married and flies back with his wife to set up some kind of model organic farming cooperative. Guatemala. In the eighties. Guerrillas running around assessing war taxes. Army body-counting anything that moves. Real good place to settle down, especially out in the bush. Very swift."

"Like an American moving to Lebanon to farm the Bekaa Valley," Welsh said in agreement.

"So one day he's driving back from picking up supplies and gets stopped at an Army checkpoint. The soldiers search his truck, drink his beer, and hack him to pieces with their machetes."

"The troops went to jail, right?" Welsh asked.

"Only because the guy's family wouldn't let it go. The Embassy had to demand it. But no Guatemalan troops, no matter how drunk, are going to have the balls to tag an American without orders. And a few years later, it turns out the colonel who gave the order was on the CIA payroll. Which isn't exactly a revelation, since every officer in the Guatemalan Army above the rank of second lieutenant is on the CIA payroll."

"Unfortunately," said Welsh, "the CIA knew what the colonel did as soon as it happened, and just plain forgot to mention that fact to anyone."

"Like what the fuck are they going to do?" Longenecker demanded tiredly. "Say: 'Okay, Colonel, please stop violating human rights. And by the way, what's the latest news in the Army?' What the fuck do people think intelligence assets are? Noble foreigners in love with American democracy?"

"More like scumbags who betray their countries for money," said Welsh.

"Or sex and money or blackmail and money or excitement and money. And the CIA says: 'Hey, it's a dirty business, but our job is to gather intelligence, not be Amnesty International.' "

"Of course," Welsh countered, "that attitude, however realistic, sometimes leads the local intelligence assets to believe they can, with impunity, cut the head off any American citizen who gets in their way."

Longenecker lowered the beer from his lips. "Wouldn't be the first time, I tell you that."

"Why would the Guatemalan government want a bunch of our Marines dead?"

"What makes you think it's the government?"

"It was a textbook professional assassination, but when it was done, and under no pressure at all, the killers just dump their submachine guns on the ground and drive off? Guerrillas love their automatic weapons better than their children. No way they give them up when they don't have to. But with the weapons in hand, the government has no trouble saying they traced them to the guerrillas."

"You're not as stupid as you look," said Longenecker.

"But then on the other hand, I don't see why I should suspect the government since—"

"Since it's a nice, democratically elected government anxious to right all the wrongs of the last forty-plus years," Longenecker said, finishing the sentence. He grunted down the rest of his beer. "On a good day the current government of Guatemala controls a fair chunk of Guatemala City, and that's about it. They only think they control the Army and the intelligence services. So don't say 'government' like it's all one team under one manager. Any half-assed official with a couple of grand and either a scheme or a grudge could have set up that hit."

"And you can't narrow that down for me?"

"No. But good government doesn't pay all that well. The Army's out a lot of money if they can't hire their troops out as security for the big ranches or drug-runners' airstrips, kill union activists as a favor to manufacturers, or clear-cut the hardwood forests for hard currency. All the cops who got dismissed from the police force are still doing the same strong-arm and kidnapping they used to do in uniform. And they've still got their uniforms."

"You're trying to tell me there's a lot of incentive to upset the apple cart," said Welsh.

"Ordinarily, but Guatemala is one of those countries where, like it or not, if the U.S. raises a finger, the economy collapses. If the Army overthrows the government and the U.S. says, 'We don't like that,' then the troops go back to their barracks and the generals catch the next flight to Spain to see if they can make do with what's in their Swiss bank accounts. So anyone who wants to change things has to think about the U.S. first."

"But the Army did go along with free elections and a peace treaty with the guerrillas," Welsh said doubtfully.

"That's because a new generation of smart military leaders came in to replace the old Nazis. They looked at El Salvador and saw that they could make peace and still dominate the guerrillas—but politically instead of militarily. A hell of a lot better for business and relations with the U.S. and Europe, not to mention less chance of getting yourself killed. Their main problem now is that a lot of the old cavemen are mightily pissed at the way things have changed. And there's another wild card. In exchange for a peace treaty the Army got total amnesty. But they're turning up Indian mass graves in the countryside, and the Archbishop who came out with a human rights report accusing the Army of genocide got his brains bashed in in his garage. Genocide's not covered by the amnesty."

"And the guerrillas?" said Welsh.

"The leadership are good Marxists, which means now that Moscow and Havana aren't paying the bills anymore, they've decided to become Social Democrats, join the system, and get their patronage jobs by running for office like everyone else. The lower level are just bandit gangs with guns. Take away the ideology and they'll still keep kidnapping people and extorting businesses. It's a good living, hell of a lot better than most in Guatemala these days."

"You should always brief after a few beers," Welsh marveled. "I mean, the content might be the same, but the extra flourishes would bend some people's minds."

Longenecker slowly extended his middle finger.

"Why would the CIA come to me through Kohl?" Welsh asked. "Why not use a guy I know, like Ed Howe?"

The colonel gave him an irritated smile. "Because then they'd have to tell Howe what it's all about, dick-head."

"Jesus!" Welsh exclaimed. "You fucking spooks. You'll put me on some shrink's couch yet."

"I'll tell you a little about Kohl. Don't let him fool you; he's been around. Spent most of his career in the field. And really good, from what I've heard. Done his share of dirty work, but always avoided taking the blame."

"For what?"

"For anything. Everybody wants the dirty work taken care of, but nobody wants to give the order. If something blows up in someone's face, which it nearly always does, then the guy who actually did the job gets the blame. Kohl was always smart enough to never take the blame, which is the real art."

"In everything," Welsh agreed, even though it was another skill he had yet to master. "Hey, Mike, I need you to run a name for me."

"Because if you do it the CIA will find out, right?"

"You're not so stupid yourself. The survivor of the attack gave me a name that he didn't give to the FBI. Tim Brock. American. Lives in Guatemala. Claimed to be an ex-Army sergeant."

"FBI has no sense of humor about that shit," Longenecker warned. "They'll ram some obstruction of justice up that kid's ass before he knows what hit him."

"No one has any plans to tell the FBI just yet."

"Then you better pucker up your asshole, 'cause you might just get yourself obstructed too."

Welsh handed Longenecker an index card with Brock's name and the details Corporal Costa had given him.

"How does this guy fit in?" Longenecker asked, studying the card and then handing it back to Welsh.

"He might have been trying to recruit some Embassy guards for someone. He might have set them up for the hit. Or maybe he had nothing to do with anything. Can you check him out without putting your name on any requests?"

"I didn't just fly in on the noon balloon."

"Sorry," Welsh replied.

"When I get something, I'll call Mr. Welsh about some samples."

They both laughed at that.

"Can you stay for dinner?" Longenecker asked.

"Thanks, pal, but that military family of yours rates some time alone with you." Welsh picked up his empty beers and rose to leave. "I really appreciate this little talk."

"No problem, for a guy who can keep his mouth shut. You know how that Scanlan story came out, don't you?"

"Yeah, a State Department guy read the Top Secret files and thought it was a little sick that the CIA not only knew that one of their informers ordered the killing of an American, but had every intention of covering it up. So he leaked the information to a Congressman."

"And the CIA got his security clearance pulled for divulging classified information. And without a clearance he had to give up his career at State, which he did."

"Revealing the name of an intelligence source being an infinitely greater sin than covering up a murder."

"Another good lesson for whistle-blowers, though," said Longenecker. "Do the right thing and get fucked for sure."

They walked down the driveway.

"You going down to Guatemala?" Longenecker asked.

"That's right."

"If they're worried about what you might find down there, knowing how the Company operates, I wouldn't be surprised if Kohl asks you to join the team."

"Because once I'm on the team I keep my fucking mouth shut, right?" said Welsh. "Or else."

Longenecker nodded solemnly. "And heads up, because sometimes they don't bother to ask, if you know what I mean."

"Great," said Welsh. "That was just what I needed to hear. Just fucking great."

"One other thing," said Longenecker.

"What's that?"

"Don't believe a goddamned thing anyone tells you down there, unless you check it out three different ways. They only thing they love more than spreading rumors is selling them to gullible government employees like you."

"Okay."

"And don't trust anyone. Americans included."

"I already came to that conclusion," said Welsh.

Chapter Six

The lunch took place at an upscale Washington steak house. The dark wood-paneled decor practically screamed WASP establishment; that is, if the WASP establishment had ever been in the habit of screaming. It was a little too tight-assed for Welsh's taste, but in a way he was relieved.

He'd been dreading having to eat at one of the precious high-end restaurants infesting the Washington area. The squiggles of sauce, chosen for color, not flavor, cascading around the plate; the chef wielding his squeeze bottles like Jackson Pollock. The food, carefully harvested before maturity from pygmy animals and vegetables, artfully arranged on the plate to appear as even less. Being forced to eat the floral arrangement in order to stay alive long enough to conclude your business and go get a pizza.

Kohl was waiting for him in the bar. Before Welsh even had a chance to look around, a well-dressed gentleman in his early fifties suddenly popped up and grasped his hand.

"Mr. Welsh," he announced confidently, "Thomas Kohl."

Welsh wasn't wearing a name tag, so the idea that Kohl had studied a photograph of him didn't seem far-fetched. "It's nice to meet you, Mr. Kohl. You make me feel as if we know each other. Or at least one of us does."

Kohl pointed out their table with a vigorous thrust of one hand, and nodded to the maitre d'. Then, in the most polite and unobjectionable way possible, he took Welsh's arm, led him over to the table, sat him down, and motioned for a waiter. Everything, Welsh thought, except tuck the fucking napkin in his collar.

Kohl's hair was steel gray and cut short. A beautifully tailored Italian suit covered the stocky, densely packed frame of a man who had never stopped lifting weights. Welsh couldn't help but admire the body language and psychology; Kohl was out to establish control over the meeting. It told Welsh that he wasn't dealing with an intelligence analyst or bureaucrat. This was a case officer: a recruiter and agent runner. An honest-to-God spy, which were actually a small minority within the CIA.

A waiter appeared. Welsh counterattacked by insisting that Kohl order first. Kohl chose a vodka on the rocks. Welsh declined to take the hint. Quietly amused with the way things were going, he had a club soda.

After the waiter left, Kohl began with basic chitchat. He asked Welsh about the Marine Corps, and brought up mutual friends at U.S. Special Operations Command in Tampa. In each case he deferred to Welsh's opinion. Welsh was very impressed. He could easily picture Kohl as gravel-voiced and hard-assed in a blue-collar bar, or sipping white wine and chatting about the early Impressionists with the wife of a Foreign Minister. And if you didn't watch yourself, you'd end up telling him your whole life story.

It was all so charming that Welsh's first impulse was to throw a little burr under the man's saddle. The more Kohl put up with, the more he'd want from him. But then Welsh decided that the smartest move was just to sit there and be courted. After all, *he* wasn't paying for lunch.

So he just kept his face buried in the menu and remarked conversationally, "A lady friend of mine would have something to say about all this red meat. Just looking at a menu like this is enough to make the cholesterol go up."

"It's ironic, isn't it," Kohl replied, "that we've come to the point in our history where the greatest threat to our lives is our own lethargy?"

"That's a very interesting observation," said Welsh.

"And perhaps I should stop imposing on your good nature and come to the point?"

"Only if you feel like it. *I'm* enjoying myself."

"You're planning a trip to Guatemala, as part of your investigation into the deaths of those three Marines."

"I didn't hear any question there."

The conversation stopped when the waiter reappeared. Kohl ordered crab cakes. By now it was quite obvious that Kohl wasn't on his own, and Welsh had skipped breakfast in anticipation of eating out on Uncle Sam. He asked about the lobsters. Unfortunately, all they had were one-pounders; too small for his taste, all shell. The look on Kohl's face, though, was priceless. Welsh ended up ordering the largest porterhouse on the menu, medium-rare, with pomme frites and a salad. And it was a damn shame he had to keep his head clear; the wine list was really nice.

When the waiter left, Kohl continued. "You have a reputation for discretion. May I count on it?"

Welsh finished swallowing his bread roll before answering, "I always say absolutely, up to the point where what I hear puts me in jeopardy of felony conspiracy."

"Fair enough. We have an ongoing operation in Guatemala. And we're very concerned about your trip having an unintended impact on it."

Welsh's antennae sprung out. He was fairly sure that Kohl was lying. After so many years with the CIA, Kohl would have found it easier to breathe underwater than tell the truth to a civilian. Especially about an ongoing operation. But Welsh thought if he listened carefully, he might find a jumping-off place to the truth. "Would you care to give me any more information?" he asked politely.

"I'm sure a professional like yourself will understand why I can't."

"Are you suggesting I not go to Guatemala?"

"Absolutely not. We wouldn't want to interfere with your work in any way. But we are worried about our operation. We'd appreciate, as a courtesy, if you would keep us informed as to what you're doing."

Welsh thought you couldn't get any clearer than that. Informed, as in informer. "I'm afraid I'm going to have to have some more details." He paused. "So I can make an *informed* judgment."

"All right," Kohl said gravely. "It's a joint operation: CIA and Drug Enforcement Administration."

The food arrived. Welsh ate while Kohl talked.

"The multi-agency aspect of the operation is why we're giving it such importance. As you know, the Congress wants us to act jointly," Kohl said pointedly.

Welsh nodded.

"I really can't tell you any more."

Now Welsh was sure it was a bullshit cover story. If there really was a joint operation that sensitive, a spook like Kohl would have cut his tongue out before saying even that much. Besides, the CIA and DEA working together in harmony sounded as feasible as carrying a cobra and a dog around together in one bag. The drug aspect was interesting, though. The DEA might be doing something that Kohl would anticipate him bumping into. Welsh shook his head. You could go nuts trying to figure this shit out.

"What do you think?" Kohl asked.

"I'm sure Senator Anderson would regard it as a conflict of interest."

"You misunderstand me. We wouldn't dream of compromising you. This would be, in effect, normal liaison, but through back channels. We would also be in a position to assist you with your investigation. And to help out with any problems that might come up in Guatemala."

"I don't think I'm going to have any trouble, Mr. Kohl." Welsh paused then, as it occurred to him. "That is, unless someone down there starts saying bad things about me to certain people. You don't know anyone who'd do a rotten fucking thing like that, do you?"

Kohl didn't seem to have heard; he was concentrating on his crab cakes.

"Is this the point where I name my price?" Welsh asked.

Kohl didn't go so far as to wink, but his expression was enough to extend the invitation.

Inside Welsh was churning, but he tried to keep a poker face. "You know, this reminds me of when I was in the Marine Corps." He paused. "You don't mind if I tell what's known as a Sea Story, do you?"

"Not at all."

"I was a new second lieutenant, going through the Infantry Officer Course. The major who ran it was this classic Marine Corps hard-dick kind of guy, loved to impart his own brand of homespun infantry philosophy.

He used to say that if you kissed ass, even if you only did it once, then you'd be an ass-kisser the rest of your life." Actually, the major had referred to a different part of the anatomy than the ass, and a different act than kissing, but it was a public restaurant.

"I don't think I understand you," said Kohl.

"Oh, I think you do," said Welsh. "It's a typical Marine Corps metaphor, crude but pretty clear."

"I was told you're in the habit of speaking your mind, Mr. Welsh. I was also told that you didn't think much of the intelligence community, but I didn't believe it until now." Kohl said it with more regret than anger.

"Anyone who was in Beirut," said Welsh, "or worked with Special Operations Command, or was around during Desert Storm would feel the way I do. If you can name one significant event that's occurred in the world since 1950 that didn't catch the U.S. government completely by surprise, then I'll kiss *your* ass. Of course, you boys always word the analysis so perfectly that no matter what happens, you can claim to have called it; it was just a goddamned shame no one listened."

Welsh had lost a little of his cool there. He wished he could stop doing that. He expected Kohl to be livid, but the man still wore that same pleasant expression, and there even seemed to be amusement in his eyes.

"You're very sure of yourself, Mr. Welsh. But you're still a young man. As you age, you'll find you're not capable of that same certainty."

The waiter appeared to inquire about dessert. Both declined, Welsh only because he was full. He would have loved to make Kohl sit there and watch him eat. Then again, after running his mouth like that, he'd probably get stuck with the check.

Kohl signed the credit card slip. "I really wish I could convince you to help us, Mr. Welsh. It would be to everyone's advantage, especially yours."

Now Kohl sounded like he was passing a kidney stone every time he called Welsh "Mister." Welsh knew this wasn't the end of it, so he thought he ought to add a final note. "Did you ever hear what Lucky Luciano said about U.S. Senators?"

"No." Kohl was no longer pretending to be all that interested.

"He said, 'A U.S. Senator can make more trouble, day in and day out, than anyone else.' "

"That's very interesting."

Leaving the restaurant, Welsh reflected that it was true only if the U.S. Senator happened to be in your corner.

He was going to have to do some more research on Kohl. The CIA was one institution you didn't want to have anything on you. You could only buy someone who wanted to be bought. And you could only blackmail someone with something to hide, or something he wanted that you could take away. Welsh didn't think he fell into any of those categories, but there was one thing he knew for sure. If he ever did, Thomas Kohl would be the first one knocking on his door.

Chapter Seven

Welsh spent the rest of the week pinned to his desk, trying to get ahead of the paper before he had to leave for Guatemala. As usual, no matter how hard he bailed, the water kept lapping up around his ankles.

On one of those days, the phone rang just before lunch. He pinned the receiver into his neck almost without pausing at the computer keyboard and announced, "Rich Welsh."

"Is this Richard Welsh?" a voice asked.

The ex-Marine in Welsh wanted to say, "Didn't I just fucking say that?" But Welsh the Senate aide patiently replied, "Speaking."

"Yes, Mr. Welsh, my wife and I are remodeling our home, and we'd like to talk to you about doing our interior decorating."

Now Welsh recognized the voice, and it brought a smile to his face. "I'm sorry, sir, I think you have the wrong Richard Welsh. I'm not a decorator."

There was a pause. "You're not?"

"No, sir."

"Well, do you know any good decorators?"

"Sorry," said Welsh, stifling a belly laugh.

"Okay." The other party broke the connection.

Welsh left the Russell Building and went in search of a pay phone. With Washington, D.C., the way it was, and in the era of the cellular phone, it took him a while to find a working one. He set his notebook on the metal counter, dropped in some change, and dialed the number of another pay phone.

"Are you sure you don't do interior decorating?" Michael Longenecker asked in lieu of saying hello.

"You've seen my apartment," said Welsh. "What's up?"

They weren't just playing cloak and dagger. In Washington telephone calls went through secretaries, and secretaries filled out phone logs and message forms. And if someone opposed to a stand you had taken wanted to find out who was telling you the things you weren't supposed to know, it was easy enough to wander through your office and read what was lying on the desk. It happened every day.

"You ready to copy?" Longenecker asked.

"Go."

"Tim Brock is one of the known aliases of Thomas Allen Booker. Joined the U.S. Army in 1967. Volunteered for Airborne school, then Special Forces. Vietnam-era Green Beret, you know what I mean?"

"Got you," said Welsh. During the Vietnam War the Army went for relative quantity as opposed to quality in Special Forces. A lot of guys got in, right from boot camp, that wouldn't have either before or after the war.

"Special Warfare School, qualified as a communications specialist," said Longenecker. "Seventh Special Forces Group, Fort Bragg. Then 5th Group, Vietnam.

71

Two months with 1st Mobile Strike Force Command, Da Nang. Then the rest of his tour with 5th Group Headquarters, Saigon."

"Well, which was he?" Welsh demanded. "A wounded stud or a couldn't-cut-it dickhead who got himself shitcanned from the Mike Force?"

"Special Forces has its turds too," said Longenecker. "Just not as many. No Purple Heart or any other combat award. Somebody did give him his Combat Infantryman Badge. And an Army Commendation Medal from 5th Group; the green weenie. No V for valor on that. From Nam back to Bragg, 6th Group this time. Reenlisted 1971. Then a parachute accident in 1973. Must not have liked it much, 'cause five years in Special Forces and he was only a senior jumper."

"Help out a miserable 'leg,' " said Welsh. "How many jumps do you have to make for senior wings?"

"Thirty for senior. Fifty-six for master. He got a medical discharge for that last jump. Hundred-percent disability. He shows up in Guatemala in 1979. Buys a cattle ranch in the northeast part of the country, the Petén. He does some favors for the Guatemalan Army, mainly training advice and letting them use his ranch. That's normal for anyone who wants to do business and prosper down there. There's also a report that he helped train one of the local death squads on his ranch."

"Army *and* death squads?" Welsh asked.

"Usually not much difference between the two," Longenecker replied.

"Okay, go on."

"Drug Enforcement Administration had some questions about the small planes he was letting use the landing strip on his ranch. But they didn't pursue it."

"Why," Welsh asked.

"The file I'm quoting from is Defense Intelligence Agency. There's a recruiting hands-off notice, which leads me to believe that Booker kept the CIA informed about what he was doing with the Guatemalans. Standard operating procedure south of the border. You become a source for one agency of the federal government to keep all the other agencies off your back. Good insurance policy."

"It sounds like this guy is connected down there."

"Damn straight. And if he was, or is, refueling drug planes on their way up north, then he'd have to be kicking back a piece to the local chiefs."

"Army or government?" Welsh asked.

"At least Army. They run the show in the Petén. But probably both."

"This is great stuff," said Welsh. "Anything else?"

"That's it. Just keep in mind that ninety percent of what's in intelligence files is rumor, gossip, and conjecture. So give this guy the benefit of the doubt."

"Even though he sounds like a total creep?"

"Even though he sounds like a total creep. God knows what your file says. And don't bother asking me for it."

"Don't worry," said Welsh. "I could give a shit. Hey, buddy, I owe you another big one."

"I know," said Longenecker. "It's already recorded in my black book of favors owed."

Welsh went back to the office, carefully memorized the notes he'd taken, and just as carefully fed the notebook pages into the office shredder.

Chapter Eight

Welsh was lying on his back, in the dirt. He kept trying, but he couldn't move. A man stood over him, pointing a gun. Welsh was so frightened he was hyperventilating. Just as the man was about to fire, something yanked him out of the way. Then he was sitting up in bed and Carol was hanging onto his arm.

"Rich, you were having a nightmare."

Welsh let out a deep breath. "Damn! I sure was. Thanks, Carol." Sweating and clammy, he flopped back on the pillow. The last time something like that had happened was during a high-stress no-sleep week of negotiations over the defense appropriations bill. He'd had recurring dreams of being back in high school. It was a toss-up which nightmare was scarier.

"Are you all right?"

"I'm okay. Just a bad dream."

Carol leaned over and turned the light on. "Rich, please tell me what's wrong."

"Nothing. Really."

"Something's been bugging you all week," Carol persisted. "I've never seen you like this."

Welsh didn't say anything. What could he do, tell her what his so-called routine investigation was turning into?

"It's what you're doing, isn't it? We used to talk about everything; why won't you talk about this?"

"Carol, I can't."

"You don't trust me, is that it?"

Welsh fought off the impulse to sigh out loud. "I do trust you. When I can tell you, you'll understand, but right now I just can't."

They were both quiet, and Welsh was hoping to get back to sleep. Then Carol said, "I want to talk."

"Carol, I told you—"

"Not about that. About us."

Welsh looked up at the ceiling. Of course it had to be today. Thomas Kohl would be nothing compared to this. He would rather charge a machine gun than have an emotional confrontation with a woman. It already felt like someone inside his stomach was trying to chop his way out with a hatchet.

"Carol, couldn't we talk over breakfast? It's not even dawn and I'm flying out today."

"I want to talk now."

It was said in the sort of tone that didn't allow for any debate. Welsh put his hands behind his head and waited for it.

"I've been thinking about this for a while," Carol said. "I'm thirty-four years old. I feel like I'm getting too old for dates and coming over here for sex three or four times a week."

There was just no escaping gravity, Welsh thought. Whatever went up always had a way of dropping back down on you.

"I'm tired of my life the way it is," Carol went on.

"I'm tired of living in an apartment. I'm tired of being alone."

Welsh's face gave him away.

"I don't think what I want sounds so terrible," Carol said angrily.

"I've always been honest with you," said Welsh. "You know how I feel." He'd given up lying to women in his early twenties. It made life both easier and harder, but was worth it.

"Why don't you tell me, Rich? Why don't you come right out and do it?"

"Okay," said Welsh. "I'm sorry, but I like apartments. I hate houses and mowing lawns and puttering around. I like having everything I own fit in the back of a rental truck. I'm not domestic. Neither was my father, but I won't put a woman and kids through what he did. That's the plain truth."

"It sounds more like a preplanned speech for when anyone gets too close to you."

"It's not. I'm just telling you the way I am. I won't pretend to be anything else."

"I know you're a lone wolf; I've known that all along. But I can't believe that alone is the way you always want to be."

"You're not mad because of the way I am. You're mad because it's not what you want." Welsh had yet to meet the woman who regarded him as anything other than the raw clay on which to shape her vision of the ideal man. He didn't consider himself perfect, or even normal, not by any stretch of the imagination. But if he knew one thing, it was that you cannot change people. You can love them, hate them, tolerate them, sometimes influence them, or ideally, even accept them for what they are. But you cannot change them.

"You know, Rich, there's something I haven't been able to figure out. Is it that you can be one cold bastard on command, or is it that you really are a cold bastard?"

Welsh kept silent. He'd heard of men winning arguments with women, but he had no personal experience of it.

His silence only made Carol angrier. "Okay," she said, "this is the point where I say, 'You really don't love me, do you?' So let's get it over with."

"Not enough to give you what you want, Carol. Enough to not want to hurt you."

"Great. That makes it all fine then. Richard no-hard-feelings Welsh." Now Carol was up and charging around the bedroom, collecting clothes.

Welsh just lay there, wanting to pull the covers up over his head but not having the nerve.

When Carol slammed the door behind her, Welsh leaned over, opened up the drawer of the night table, and took out a small stainless-steel revolver. He followed her down the stairs and waited by the door, watching to make sure she got to her car safely. When she drove off, he walked back up the stairs. The first light of dawn was just breaking.

Welsh let himself back in and set the pistol down on the coffee table. How the fuck did that happen? He felt rotten. He felt relieved. He felt ashamed of himself for feeling relieved.

Going back to sleep was out of the question. He had to do something. So he decided to finish packing for his trip to Guatemala.

Since he hated dragging a lot of stuff around in his travels, it didn't take long. All his suits were tropical-weight; he took a dark blue and dark gray. A couple of dress shirts, ties, and polo shirts. Because he didn't know how far out of town the investigation would take him, a pair of black ripstop cotton trousers and a featherweight but mosquito-proof long-sleeve cotton shirt. Because nothing else could hold up as well, a pair of well-broken-in jungle boots. And because it was Central America, the well-stocked first-aid kit he always took backpacking, along with mosquito repellent and water-purification tablets. Even brushing your teeth in the local water was enough to tie the pampered North American digestive system into a knot. It all fit into a carry-on bag and a small day pack.

Then an envelope full of cash and traveler's checks, and a leather dress belt. A hidden zipper opened up the inside of the money belt, and Welsh carefully slotted the checks in one side, dollars in the other. He'd been to quite a few places around the world where the locals fell on their ass laughing when you asked where you could cash a traveler's check.

As he worked, a thought kept turning over in his mind. What the hell was Carol's reason for slapping him with an ultimatum at 4:50 in the morning on the day of his departure? Could it be that she wanted out and wanted an excuse? It might be yet another rationalization, but Welsh found it comforting nonetheless.

Comforting enough to try for a little more sleep. He was careful to set his alarm.

When it went off two hours later, he felt worse than if he'd stayed up. His bags were by the door, the cab was called. Then, just as he made a final circuit around the apartment to see what he'd forgotten, Welsh noticed his Ruger revolver still lying on the coffee table.

Swearing to himself, Welsh snatched the pistol off the table and trotted to his bedroom closet. Dropping to his knees, he moved a cardboard file box and a pile of sneakers out of the way. He grabbed the section of molding facing the open door, and pulled it up off the tongue-and-groove tracks he'd mounted on the wall. Then he slipped a finger into the small hole the removal of the molding had revealed in the wall panel. Welsh pulled, and the entire panel swung open, hinged on one side, and revealed a small safe.

One day he'd been trying to drag some files out of the closet and nearly kicked through the panel by accident. After a little curious messing around with a screwdriver, he discovered that the space behind it had been left open to accommodate the bathroom water pipes.

Then it was a just a matter of a weekend's work. The safe was a small fireproof model, but with a plate on the dial to make it hard to punch. He'd bolted it to the floor studs, and then scored the edges off the bolts.

Welsh opened the safe and set the Ruger SP101 on the top shelf. Already inside was his Glock 21 .45 automatic, ammunition, birth certificate, and other hard-to-replace documents.

Everything else in the apartment was insured, and therefore not worth worrying about. He closed the safe, replaced the panel and molding, and returned the closet to its usual disorder.

Then, satisfied that anything else he might have forgotten was insignificant, Welsh threw his bags out into the hallway and locked the door behind him.

Chapter Nine

As the flight from Miami thumped and bounced its way through the mountain clouds toward Guatemala City, the well-dressed Guatemalan matron seated next to Rich Welsh leaned over and confided in English, "You should use the bathroom before we land."

Welsh didn't think he could have heard that right. "I beg your pardon?"

"The bathroom. Use the bathroom on the plane."

Welsh flashed back to his mother's usual admonition before long car rides as a child. Maybe he'd brought out this lady's maternal instinct. Maybe she was some kind of nut. But he still had to ask politely, "Why?"

"You do not wish to use the bathrooms in the airport."

"Ah," said Welsh, finally getting it. "Dirty, or dangerous?"

"Filthy," the lady assured him. She shuddered involuntarily, as if even the memory was too hard to bear. "Filthy."

"Thank you very much," said Welsh as he got up to take care of business. When someone went out of their way to give you unsolicited advice like that, you'd best take it.

It was 7:20 P.M., local time, when Welsh stepped out onto the air stairs of Aurora International Airport. He'd gained an hour, but that didn't help much after a day spent in airports and on planes.

The arrival/departure area was guarded by a few indolent policemen who carried their Beretta submachine guns every possible way except professionally. Welsh judged them worse than useless. In an event of an emergency, two thirds would doubtless drop their weapons and run for their lives, while the rest would go berserk and shoot anything that moved, friend more likely than foe.

Welsh got in the line at the Banco de Guatemala booth to change a few dollars into *quetzals*. Only a few, because changing them back was a hell of a lot harder. Welsh's rule was no black-market money exchanges when on government business, even though he figured he was about the only U.S. government employee who felt that way. The line was correspondingly short.

Immigration was next. Welsh couldn't help noticing an official-looking gentleman standing behind the immigration officers. It wasn't just the pistol bulge in the suit jacket. The sunglasses were a little much in a reasonably well-lighted terminal.

Customs was the last stop. The inspector was about twenty two and looked like some politician's otherwise unemployable nephew. But that wasn't much different from the Department of Motor Vehicles back home. Welsh had gone to the trouble of traveling in a suit, something he didn't normally do. The more important you looked, the less likely some petty bureaucrat would risk screwing with you.

But before Welsh could unzip the pockets of his bag, another Guatemalan in a suit too nice even for a secret policeman showed up and asked, "Mr. Welsh?"

"Yes," Welsh replied, hoping it would be good news. He had absolutely no desire to be strip-searched.

The man stuck out his hand. "I am Roberto Esguerra, representing the Foreign Ministry. Allow me to welcome you to Guatemala."

Welsh shook the hand. "My privilege, sir," he said in Spanish.

"Representatives of your Embassy are awaiting you," Esguerra said. "If the Foreign Ministry can render you any assistance during your visit, please call on me."

Welsh accepted the offered business card. "I thank you for your courtesy."

The Customs inspector was listening so intently to the conversation that it took an elbow in the ribs from Esguerra to get him to release Welsh's bags. The kid wielded his stick of chalk like a blunt instrument.

Exiting Customs and trying to figure out how to handle his bags without getting chalk all over his suit, Welsh was approached by an athletic North American male in his late twenties, wearing slacks, a short-sleeved madras shirt, and a khaki Banana Republic photographer's vest.

"Mr. Welsh?" he asked, extending a credentials case.

"Yes."

"I'm Ted Alonso, one of the Embassy security officers. Welcome to Guatemala."

Welsh checked the credentials carefully and then shook the man's hand. Now he knew what was both in and under the vest. "Nice to meet you, Ted. Call me Rich." He was a little surprised. All the Diplomatic Security Service guys he'd ever met wore polyester suits and the kinds of haircuts favored by retired military men:

a bit too long for regulation, but still too short and chopped to look like a normal civilian.

Alonso went to pick up Welsh's bags, but Welsh got there first. "I'll carry them," he said. "You keep your hands free." He grinned. "Unless you want me to carry your piece."

Alonso looked relieved. "Finally, someone who knows the drill. Most of the time we get treated like bellboys, and we just have to swallow it."

They headed out of the terminal.

"So how was the flight?" Alonso asked.

"Other than being packed into a seat with no legroom, fed garbage, and generally treated like shit, it was fine."

"So, in other words, a typical airline experience?"

"Exactly."

"I figured you'd want to crash," Alonso said tentatively, "and hit the Embassy tomorrow?"

"Sounds good to me."

"If you're hungry we can stop someplace."

Welsh shook his head. "No, thanks. I'm just a little tired."

They shoved their way through the mob of porters fighting for the arriving passengers' bags. Then the unlicensed "taxi" drivers who, for a very reasonable fare, would drive you not to your destination but someplace quiet, relieve you of your luggage and valuables, and if you were very lucky, leave you to walk back to town in your jockstrap.

Outside the terminal there was a chill breeze and crisp, thin, high-altitude air. A black Jeep Cherokee with another American behind the wheel was waiting at the curb. The thickness of the window glass and the obvious weight the tires were bearing told Welsh it was armored.

Alonso took the front seat and Welsh the rear. "Rich Welsh," Alonso announced, "Mike O'Brian."

83

Welsh leaned over the front seat to shake hands with the driver, a large, beefy Irishman who seemed more than a little surprised by the gesture. O'Brian was dressed the way Welsh had expected.

"He's not one," Alonso told O'Brian.

"So I see," the driver replied.

"One what?" Welsh asked.

Alonso looked at O'Brian. They both shrugged, and Alonso said, "An asshole." They both turned to check out Welsh's reaction.

Welsh laughed loudly. "I try not to be whenever I possibly can," he said, to more laughter from the front seat. "I guess you see your share, though."

"More than our share," said Alonso. "They expect us to do everything up to and including wiping their runny noses."

O'Brian pulled out into traffic.

"Remind me not to complain about my job then," said Welsh. "How did you happen to get into this line of work?"

"I was a platoon leader in the 82nd Airborne, and then I made it to the 1st Ranger Battalion. I missed Panama and Desert Storm, and the chances for any action seemed a little slim, so I bailed on the Army and hooked up with State. I speak Spanish, so here I am."

You had to be very good to make it to the Ranger battalions as an officer. "West Point?" Welsh asked. He thought he recognized the ring.

"That's right," Alonso replied.

"Enough action for you?"

"I'm up to my ass in action," Alonso replied, not unhappily. Welsh had given everyone the signal to relax their language. "Guerrillas, death squads, narcos, professional kidnappers, organized and disorganized crime, assorted freaks, bombers, arsonists, you name it."

Welsh thought he had Alonso pegged. A genuine American enthusiast. He'd known more than his share. Eagle Scout, class president: Give them a goal and they'd charge it like a rhino. In the military they were painfully earnest but prone to disillusionment. They loved the work, especially all the dangerous toys, and never could understand why the troops weren't as enthusiastic. But the perfect man for this kind of job. Not a lot of introspection required, just continuous and perfect attention to detail. Welsh wondered how long it would take before he burned out.

"I suppose I ought to tell you," Welsh said. "Back at immigration I was getting eyeballed by a Guatemalan spook who liked to wear his sunglasses indoors."

Alonso didn't seem surprised. "Local intelligence. Just checking you out. You pick up any kind of surveillance, though, be sure to let us know."

"So what's the straight skinny on Guatemala?" Welsh inquired. Screw the Ambassador. These guys were the sources you wanted to cultivate.

"No one in this country pays any attention to the rules," Alonso said.

O'Brian groaned. "Don't get him started."

Welsh smiled warily. "The rules?"

"Sure," said Alonso. "Which countries in the world have the most successful multinational corporations?"

If someone was about to go on a roll, you just broke their rhythm if you answered their rhetorical questions. Welsh just nodded for Alonso to go ahead.

"U.S., Japan, and Germany, right?" said Alonso.

Welsh kept nodding him along.

"And what do they all have in common?"

"I'm waiting for you to tell me," said Welsh.

O'Brian chuckled loudly from the front seat.

Alonso ignored him. "Everyone obeys the rules."

"The rules?" said Welsh.

"People wait their turn in line," said Alonso. "They stop at traffic lights, even at night when no one else is around."

"You haven't been to New York City in a while, have you?" Welsh asked.

O'Brian started laughing again. Alonso got a little frustrated. "I'm not saying everyone back home. I'm just saying that in successful countries most of the people follow the rules of law, the rules of business, the rules of society."

"So no one follows the rules in Guatemala?" said Welsh. He was remembering trying to get on a Paris bus once; he'd thrown fewer elbows in a college rugby game.

"There are no rules in Guatemala," said O'Brian.

"There are rules," said Alonso. "Instead of only outlaws breaking them, here only suckers follow them. Or the next worst thing, someone poor who has no choice."

They went a quarter of the way around a rotary, down the Avenida Reforma, and two blocks later pulled up in front of the Hotel Camino Real.

O'Brian stayed with the vehicle. Alonso accompanied Welsh as he checked in. It was a well-appointed, top-quality hotel; little different from ones in the U.S., except for the extra uniformed guards. On the way up in the elevator, Alonso said, "You requested the seventh floor?"

"A car bomb would have to be big enough to drop the whole building to get you that high," said Welsh. "But it's low enough that a hook-and-ladder can get you out. Too much angle if someone wanted to take a shot at your window from the street. But don't worry, I'll stay off the balcony and keep the drapes shut anyway."

"I see you know your personal security measures. This

is a place you want to practice every one of them. When you first come down, you don't know what to sweat and what to ignore. So my general rule of thumb is to sweat everything. It's much safer that way."

The room was carpeted, with hardwood furniture, an unobjectionable pastel decor, and prints of the local countryside on the walls.

"Very nice," said Welsh. "What's the word on Guatemala City water?"

"It's not bad, but I'd still stay away from the tap. No matter what you eat or where you eat it, you'll be a little loose for a few days, but that's just part of the local charm. Don't eat anything off the street vendors."

Actually, it was Welsh's experience that it was better to eat mystery meat smoking hot from a street vendor than in a well-appointed restaurant where no one washed their hands, but he didn't say anything.

Alonso handed him a piece of paper. "Phone numbers and procedures. You've got an appointment with the Ambassador at ten tomorrow morning. But if you feel like coming in earlier, we can have breakfast and I'll show you around."

"Breakfast at the Embassy canteen?" Welsh said unenthusiastically. "Why don't you come here for the breakfast buffet and we'll charge it to the room?"

"I'd like to, but I can't swing it."

Welsh sighed. "Okay, the canteen it is then. What time is breakfast?"

"I guess eight-thirty would give you a chance to get some sleep. Is that okay?"

"Fine with me."

"The Embassy number is on the list. Give me a call when you're ready and I'll send a car. This is a nice part of town, but be careful anyway. It's not the U.S."

"I didn't relax in Lebanon," said Welsh. "I won't relax here."

Chapter Ten

Welsh woke a little before 5:00 the next morning, tried to roll over for some more sleep, and couldn't. The hotel had U.S. TV via satellite, but it was too early for anything other than the news. He cursed himself for going to bed so early. While brushing his teeth, he got the idea to go for a run.

He spread his Guatemala City street map out on the coffee table. A little planning was in order for a jog in one of the most dangerous cities in the world. Even more so than Washington, D.C. But he needed to take a look around anyway, and running somehow seemed better than walking or taking a cab. And it was the right time of day to explore a strange town. The criminal night shift would be finishing up, and the daytime crowds not out on the streets yet. Even if anyone was watching the hotel, he could be out and back before they had time to get on the phone and arrange something.

Deciding on a route, Welsh slipped his passport and

a few *quetzals* into a nylon traveling wallet worn around the neck. A street map of Guatemala City went in a pocket. Since Guatemala was a country where the wearing of shorts was frowned upon, and the early morning mountain temperature was quite cool, he'd packed a pair of lightweight cotton sports pants to run in. Not being the usual Bermuda-shorts-and-Hawaiian-shirt-wearing Yankee tourist had always paid off.

By the time he finished stretching and reached the lobby, the sun was coming up. He took a moment to admire the hotel gardens in the soft first light. Based on the looks he was getting from the staff, Welsh guessed that his act had some real novelty. He couldn't blame them. All gringos were crazy, of course, but some were truly deranged.

Welsh headed north at a slow pace up the Avenida Reforma, pausing at each intersection to check for vehicles that might be following him. Everything looked clear. The traffic was light. A few laborers were heading to work, and a few dedicated partyers were staggering home.

The fronts of all the shops were protected by heavy steel security shutters. The businesses became a little less exclusive as he went north. In the doorways and alleys the street children slept on filthy slabs of yellow foam packing, huddled together in mounds for warmth and a small degree of protection.

Welsh spotted a colorful poster attached to a utility pole, and almost tripped over a curb and face-planted onto the concrete trying to read it. No, he told himself, that couldn't have been right. He must have mistranslated it. But there was the same poster on the next block, placed too high up on a pole for a kid to reach. Sponsored by a local business association, the poster called for the physical extermination of all street children in the capital.

Welsh was struck by a fast, perverse impulse to grab one of the posters as a souvenir, but he just as quickly abandoned the idea. It would be too hard to explain outside its own natural environment. Not to mention the fact that any civic organization publicly advocating the mass murder of juvenile beggars and thieves probably had some pretty definite views on sign theft.

Welsh ran on. Even so early, there was a haze of pollution that left a harsh taste in the back of his throat. It was very cool, and the thin air was making it feel as if there were lit matches in his lungs.

After he'd run a half hour, Welsh stopped to consult his map. He was careful to take a different route back to the hotel. The streets were much more crowded now. The children were up and hustling, and the sidewalk peddlers were laying out the mats on which they'd sell their goods. Welsh was provoking a few double takes as he went by, but quite a few friendly waves too.

A couple of the street kids ran along with him for a while, half for sport, half sizing him up. Welsh gave them body language to keep their distance, and they picked right up on it like young wolf cubs sensitive to every danger. He remembered being on liberty in Rome and watching a couple of Gypsy kids just like these strip the wallet and camera bag off a tourist and vanish in about a second. The kids only lasted a block or so before falling out. Welsh hadn't missed the angry red encrusted upper lips that came from glue sniffing. It killed the pain.

He was about twenty yards away from a crowded bus stop, debating whether to cross the street, when a group of men, poorly dressed and grinning in anticipation of a little fun, spread out to block his path. A confrontation was not in order, and the cars on the sidewalk were parked so close together that it was impossible to walk between them. Welsh side-vaulted over the trunk of a Fiat and cut a diagonal route across the street and in the opposite direction. Brakes squealed and horns blew; a little Honda had to swerve to miss him. He made the other sidewalk and picked up the pace. Two of the younger ones tried to chase him while the others yelled insults, but Welsh had a good lead and pumping adrenaline to compensate for the altitude. One block later they gave up and collapsed against a light pole. Welsh shot them the finger over his shoulder. As far as he was concerned, lifting weights was fine, but the ability to run your ass out of trouble was a priceless advantage.

Feeling he'd pushed his luck just about far enough, he headed straight back to the hotel at the fastest pace he could manage.

By the time he finished his shower, both the adrenaline and the cockiness had worn off. Sitting on the couch guzzling bottled water and reading the newspapers, he decided that he'd been pretty stupid. The best that could have happened was being beaten like a drum after trying to explain that it wasn't customary to carry a lot of money while jogging. The worst case, other than being dead, was ending up eating rice and beans in some tiger cage until his kidnappers discovered the true market value of a U.S. Senator's aide.

And he hadn't even approached the periphery of those parts of Guatemala City that, according to the U.S. Government country reports, should only be ventured into both fully armed and with an extreme spirit of adventure.

After his few long months in Beirut, Welsh always kept an eye out for it everywhere he went. Always looking for how near or far a society was from that moment when the invisible whistle blew and whatever social compact there was dissolved. People waking up one morning and deciding that they hated each other so much they just had to burn down everything standing. Guatemala wasn't that far away, he decided.

The lobby called when his ride showed up. It was

another armored black Cherokee, with two Guatemalans in it. The one in the front seat said, in halting English, "Mr. Welsh?"

Welsh nodded, making no pretense about keeping a heavy pillar between himself and the car.

"Summertime," said the guard.

That was the code word of the week, on the paper Alonso had given him. If he didn't hear the word, these were the wrong two guys, and it would probably be a good idea to start running like a bastard. Every bad guy in town had police or security credentials.

The Embassy was only a few minutes away. Merchants were beginning to open up their shops. Practically every one was covered by a couple of private security guards in blue uniforms wielding shotguns and automatic rifles.

The Embassy windows facing the streets were covered with steel mesh to prematurely detonate any rocket-propelled grenades fired at them. A line of Guatemalans waiting to apply for visas was already queuing in front of the visitors' entrance. The modern-day scriveners who filled out the forms for a fee were setting up their manual typewriters under umbrellas on the sidewalk.

After the Cherokee passed through the security screen, the driver parked, and the bodyguard led Welsh through the Embassy grounds to Alonso's office.

Welsh had to stifle a grin as he walked in. The room had a definite Army Ranger motif. There was a Ranger scroll nameplate atop the desk, and on the wall was an Airborne Ranger poster and a 1st Ranger Battalion plaque. Alonso's Ranger School diploma hung next to his West Point sheepskin. "Reminds me of Hunter Army Airfield in here," Welsh observed.

Alonso, at his desk, smiled a little self-consciously. "Right on time," he said. "You want to look around first, or have breakfast?"

"Breakfast," said Welsh. "I'm starving."

In the cafeteria Alonso loaded his tray with waffles, eggs, sausage, toast, milk, and a jelly doughnut. Welsh resented people with hummingbird metabolisms. He forced himself to be content with cereal, juice, and fruit.

They picked an empty table and Alonso immediately attacked his food. Welsh nearly laughed out loud. You could always tell an ex-infantryman. They ate faster than most people breathed. It took a long time, if ever, to break the habit.

Alonso took a short break, eyed Welsh for a few moments, then said cheerfully, "I'll bet you're anxious to see the Ambassador and kick off your investigation."

Welsh finished swallowing before he said, "Look, my man, you may be right and I *may* not be an asshole. I also try my best not to be an idiot. There's no way I'm going to spend a quick week sleuthing around Guatemala and find out who killed those Marines. Every official I talk to is just going to jerk me off like a pro and patiently wait for me to fly home. If I'm lucky I might get invited to cocktails. All I can hope is the word gets around I know how to keep my mouth shut. I don't take notes, name names, write cables, or talk about sensitive matters on the telephone. So if anyone wants to whisper something in my ear, get something off their chest, no one will ever be the wiser."

Alonso gave him a look of fresh appraisal and rammed his doughnut into his face. "Sounds like you've got the right handle on the job," he said while he chewed. "Good luck."

Chapter Eleven

Nicholas Marshall, the United States Ambassador to Guatemala, had previously been one of the bright lights of the New York City financial scene. Marshall, Big Nick to his acquaintances and the tabloids, liked to say that the millions he'd accumulated could in no way match the pure satisfactions of public service. Welsh had heard in Washington that Big Nick had exponentially increased his contributions to the party in power after the Securities and Exchange Commission began inquiring into some of his deals. He'd decided that a change in scenery might do him good, and his ego settled on an ambassadorship.

Welsh would have paid good money to be in the room when the President called to tell Big Nick where he was going. Even now, months later, the Ambassador was said to wear the stunned expression of a man who had cut a very large check only to find out that it wasn't large enough to buy what he wanted. And not realizing that in politics there were no money-back guarantees. A shark in one game might be just a bait fish in another.

Big Nick was one of those guys who left your hand still shaking even after he'd released it.

"Great to meet you, Rich," he told Welsh. "I've heard a lot about you."

"My pleasure, sir," Welsh replied, fighting off a perverse desire to wipe his hand on his trousers.

"Be sure you give the Senator my best," Big Nick ordered.

"Consider it done," said Welsh. He decided to drop the sir. It only brought out the worst in these guys.

"I can't tell you how broken up we were about the Marines," said the Ambassador. "My wife took it even harder than I did. It was like losing our own sons."

Welsh only nodded, tempted to wager Big Nick a hundred dollars that he couldn't remember the Marines' names.

Coffee was served, and after they were comfortable, Big Nick leaned forward in his chair and asked confidingly, "Tell me, Rich, what's the prospect for a change in the capital-gains tax law?"

They wouldn't want to waste the whole morning talking about dead Marines, though Welsh. "You mean a *further* cut?"

"No, no, I mean that eighteen-month rule. It's nothing but a crimp on the average investor."

Average investor, my ass, thought Welsh. Once Congress had dropped the top rate, the very rich, like Big Nick, had promptly arranged to take most of their income in stock instead of paying a much higher income tax. But the law also required them to hold an equity to quality for the low rate. If you were in the market that deep, you wanted to be able to sell as fast as your broker could hit his "enter" key. Pretty soon the bastards would be demanding freedom from all taxation and the right to

95

flog their servants in public. Not that Congress wouldn't give it to them. "I wouldn't count on a change very soon," said Welsh.

"What a fucking shame," said Big Nick.

And the rich guys really loved to swear, Welsh had noticed. Marines did it just to make themselves understood. But for the rich guys, it was a way of announcing that no one else had the weight to make them watch their language.

The Ambassador's phone rang, and he picked it up. "Yes," he grumbled. "Is it?" He looked at his watch. "All right, all right." He turned to Welsh. "Rich, I'm sorry, but I've got to run. I've got a signing ceremony with the Minister of Agriculture."

"I didn't know we'd negotiated anything to do with agriculture lately," said Welsh.

The Ambassador mumbled something unintelligible.

"I'm sorry?" said Welsh.

"It's a joint screw-worm fly-eradication program," Big Nick said eventually.

Welsh must have given off some kind of involuntary wince, because the Ambassador said, "Hell, I really don't mind that stuff. What I can't stand are these cables I keep getting from the Vice President. I average about one a month, telling me to tell the Guatemalans to stop cutting down the rain forest."

Welsh knew that the Vice President, besides having a lot of time on his hands, was an ardent environmentalist. Especially with the environments of foreign lands, where there was no political price to be paid for a unambiguous moral stand.

"When I bring it up to the government, most of them have the good manners to just smile and say they're working on it," Big Nick continued. "But once in a while you run into one like the Minister I was talking to last time. He tells me that since we in the U.S. logged all our old-growth forests when we industrialized, just who the fuck are we to tell Guatemala what to do? Harvard-educated little prick."

It struck Welsh that Big Nick hadn't quite gotten the hang of international diplomacy.

On his way out the door, Big Nick said, "Oh, you need anything?"

"Just a car and a driver." Welsh didn't drive in foreign countries if he could help it, especially ones with Latin driving habits. Or no rules, as Alonso would say. He'd learned that lesson a long time ago.

"Jeez, we're a little short," said Big Nick. "Budget, you know. Chairman of the Foreign Relations Committee loves to squeeze our balls."

"He doesn't think the taxpayers' money should go to foreigners or anything to do with them," said Welsh. "Just tobacco farmers." He paused, and then, as if it was an afterthought. "It's just that it might be embarrassing if I rented a car and anything happened to me."

Big Nick processed that information. "Arrange it with Alonso."

"Thanks." Welsh had always believed that with the right lever, and the right timing, you could move the world.

Big Nick started moving again, then stopped abruptly. "By the way, we're having a reception. Make sure my secretary gives you your invitation."

Chapter Twelve

The embassy offered to arrange a meeting between Welsh and the Minister of Defense. Welsh didn't see what that would accomplish besides the opportunity to drink more coffee and listen to the Minister tell him that of course he knew none of the details but was sure the investigation had been carried out properly.

He knew he was going to have to talk to someone official on the Guatemalan side, if only to check off that box on his report. But he hoped it might be someone at least fairly interesting.

As it turned out the Guatemalan government had already contacted the Embassy and scheduled Welsh an appointment with an Army lieutenant colonel who they said was currently supervising the murder investigation.

At Army headquarters, Lieutenant Colonel Armando Gutierrez kept Welsh waiting in his outer office for nearly thirty minutes, a little comment on their relative status. While Welsh waited, he was given excellent coffee and the opportunity to take note of the lack of activity. Welsh was already feeling a little over-caffinated, but of course he couldn't refuse. The low-energy office was more interesting. There were no ringing telephones, no aides bearing urgent documents. It was all quite relaxed.

A captain finally ushered him into the colonel's office. A highly polished wooded desk and padded leather chair. The typical display of framed diplomas from military schools and courses; plaques presented by previous units or as tokens of visits by other military forces. A guerrilla flag with a few dramatic bullet holes was mounted on one wall, with a brace of captured AK-47's alongside. A crucified Christ so realistic it made Welsh rub his palms hung on the opposite wall. Placed prominently on the colonel's desk was a blue-steel Smith and Wesson .44 magnum revolver, the Dirty Harry model with the six-inch barrel. One of those, Welsh thought. The Smith had been a favorite of militia psychos in Lebanon. The revolver was positioned so the barrel was pointing directly across the desk at Welsh's chair.

The colonel was a small man. Welsh had some experience with short guys in the military. For the best of them, that enormous chip they carried around on their shoulders meant that only perfection in the performance of their duty was acceptable. Not only were they always up for anything, but they'd rather die than let it be known that they left you hanging. But for the worst, the uniform and authority were all they were about, the most back-stabbing, brown-nosing, careerist weasels imaginable.

Colonel Gutierrez was dapper in dark green service dress with flashy outsized filigreed insignia. He brusquely shook Welsh's hand and announced, "We speak no English here," in perfect U.S. Army School of the Americas English.

Welsh took a seat, slightly surprised. Not at the sentiment, since foreigners who had been educated at U.S. military schools almost always ended up disliking the United States. It was just that he'd been expecting a seduction, an attempt to get him on their side. He'd been so sure of it that the only question in his mind was whether it would be subtle or crude. Then again, maybe the stick before the carrot was seduction Guatemala-style. Poker-faced, Welsh reached across the desk and shifted the .44 magnum so it was pointing at a neutral wall. He noted that the pistol was loaded.

Then, though not quite sure how well his by-the-book Castilian would hold up under hard use, he said in Spanish, "Then we will speak Spanish."

The colonel nodded brusquely and dismissed the captain, who had stayed to translate, with a flick of his wrist. "Your Spanish is quite adequate, Mr. Welsh."

"The colonel is too generous."

The colonel swung his chair around and picked up a submachine gun from the table behind him. He passed it across the desk to Welsh. "This is one of the weapons the Communists used to kill your Marines."

It was a run-of-the-mill Israeli Uzi. Not new, the bluing almost worn away, but Uzis didn't have to be new to work. Out of pure weapons-handling reflex, Welsh removed the magazine, pulled the bolt to the rear, and inspected the chamber. The weapon had been cleaned and oiled recently. So much for the preservation of evidence. As he replaced the magazine, his eye fell upon a photograph on the colonel's desk. An extremely voluptuous woman wearing a bathing suit, a beauty contest sash, and a tiara. The picture was so incongruous in that setting Welsh couldn't help staring.

"You think she is beautiful?" the colonel asked.

Welsh was about to answer frankly, but something in

the colonel's voice made him stop. He looked up quickly.

"You are attracted to her," the colonel stated. He was smiling, but there was a wild gleam in his eyes.

"No, no, no," Welsh quickly insisted, shaking his head for emphasis.

"You do not think she is attractive," the colonel demanded, now even more upset.

"I meant that she has a great dignity," Welsh said, backpedaling as fast as he could. "A purity, like . . . a Madonna."

The colonel calmed down instantly. "Do you really think so?" he asked, reaching over the desk.

For a second Welsh thought the little wacko was going for the pistol and, since the distance to the door was too far to run with any reasonable hope of making it, almost lunged across the desk to club him with the Uzi.

But the colonel picked up the picture. "This is my wife."

"My respects," Welsh said weakly, not daring to wipe the sweat off his upper lip.

The colonel had already forgotten about it. He carefully replaced the photo and sat down behind his desk.

Welsh remembered the Uzi in his hands, and passed it back to the colonel.

"You know weapons," the colonel said. "Let me show you my favorite."

Anything to change the subject. Welsh dutifully followed him across the room. The colonel handed him a compact assault rifle. Once again Welsh pulled the charging handle to the rear to make sure there was no live round in the chamber. He was amazed, because the rifle was an M-4A1, the short-barrel, sliding-stock carbine version of the standard U.S.-issue M-16A2. What had been called the CAR-15 in the Vietnam era. Welsh knew that the Bush Administration, suspending an arms embargo of many years, had provided twenty thousand M-16's to Guatemala in the late eighties, then resumed the embargo in 1990 after an American civilian had been killed by the Army. But this weapon was brand-new. Some U.S. special operations units hadn't yet received the A1 version of the M-4.

"You are familiar with the model?" the colonel asked.

Welsh nodded.

"We have obtained these through your Drug Enforcement Administration," the colonel said, answering Welsh's question.

Welsh found the news disturbing; the reason had to do with Guatemala's recent history.

In 1954 the President of Guatemala, Jacobo Arbenz Guzmán, after winning a free election in which he was supported by both Guatemala's Army and tiny Communist Party, committed the enormous sin of promoting land reform. In particular, the 42 percent of Guatemala's land owned by the United Fruit Company, a large, politically well-connected U.S. corporation used to having its own way in Central America.

The United States government's response was to sponsor a coup, executed by the CIA. In Guatemala, it was not regarded as a coincidence that Allen Dulles had been United Fruit's counsel before he became the Director of the CIA.

The coup succeeded only by accident, and would be remembered today as a piece of sheer comic opera buffoonery, except that it snuffed out every hint of democracy in Guatemala for two generations.

The military took over the country, and not too surprisingly land reform went out the window. Constitutional guarantees were suspended, and the left was crushed.

In 1960 there was an internal military revolt over the CIA's ham-fisted appropriation of the country as a training ground for the Bay of Pigs invasion force. Inspired by the example of Cuba, some rebel officers took to the mountains and began studying Marxist-Leninism, laying the seeds of a modern guerrilla movement. The U.S. helped the government out with Special Forces advisors and military aid.

While guerrilla movements are almost always led by middle-class sociopaths, the rank and file are almost always peasants. It took a lot of governmental abuse for peasants to leave what little they had and head for the hills. A simple end to the abuse, along with schools and clinics to give people a stake in the existing government, would have gone a long way toward ending the guerrilla problem, or a least rendering it ineffective.

But the status quo was just fine with the families that made up the Guatemalan elite, and whom the Army officer corps worked for. They were doing just fine, and weren't keen on getting along with any less.

After carefully studying the U.S. experience in Vietnam, they decided that the answer was more My Lai massacres, not less.

In the cities, anyone with a left-wing affiliation, like university students, trade unionists, or teachers, got disappeared by right-wing death squads. That is, you were killed, but your body never turned up. In the countryside, anyone suspected of dealing with the guerrillas was killed, and villages in guerrilla areas were either wiped out or moved en masse.

Historically, such tactics always resulted in more vengeful recruits and new guerrilla supporters than actual guerrillas killed by governments. But the Guatemalan military was so spectacularly, extravagantly brutal that a large percentage of the population was cowed. And though the government and Army were despised, the guerrillas destroyed things, like power lines, that made people's lives a little easier; when they stopped buses to collect war taxes, they were holding up the poor. It was a classic stalemate. The guerrillas and whatever sympathy there was for them among the population wouldn't disappear, but they could make little progress against the government.

The cost was 100,000 dead, forty thousand disappeared, 250,000 children orphaned, and a million people driven from their homes, out of a population of only ten million or so. At the height of their power there were never more than 7,500 guerrillas.

Now, after more than thirty years of guerrilla war, and an elected government that had dragged the military kicking and screaming into signing a cease-fire with the guerrillas, in Welsh's opinion any action by the U.S. that would make the Guatemalan military stronger was pure and simple madness.

But it was the latest trend in the War on Drugs to turn to the militaries in the producing and trafficking countries, on the theory that soldiers were less corruptible than the police. This was only true to the extent that since armies usually had no role in enforcing drug laws, the traffickers hadn't bothered to corrupt them.

And in the case of Guatemala, where some of the military leadership were already allegedly involved in protecting cocaine traffickers and marijuana cultivators, getting them further involved in law enforcement was criminally stupid.

But the Drug Enforcement Administration was only responding to the "just do something" school of fighting the war on drugs, and it was always easier to do something in foreign countries than at home. Welsh often despaired at how often the really smart people in his government instinctively did the wrong thing.

"We need the M-16," the colonel told him. "Our Israeli Galil rifles are good, reliable weapons, but the range is less than the M-16's used by subversives. The Galil bullets fall off too soon."

Welsh knew that difference in range between two weapons of the same caliber was negligible, especially at the short effective range of a small assault-rifle cartridge, but imagining that the enemy's weapons were somehow superior to yours was as old as warfare. "I thought the M-16's were to fight drug traffickers, not subversives," he said.

"The traffickers are protected by Communists," the colonel replied smoothly. Then: "Your mission in our country is to investigate the deaths of your Marines, is it not?"

"At the request of my Senator," said Welsh, the scare over the picture having sharpened his senses.

The colonel leaned back in his chair and folded his hands over his belly. "You have been provided with the official report?" he asked blandly.

"Yes, of course," Welsh replied. "I have only a few quest—"

"The report carries the seal of the President of the Republic," the colonel informed him abruptly. "The report is clear. The report is complete."

"Certainly," said Welsh. "But—"

"You must tell your Senator this," the colonel commanded. "The Communists have killed your Marines. Perhaps now you in the United States will see their true nature. They attempt to use this peace to win a victory that they could never win from us in battle. Perhaps now you will see that the subversives are as much a threat to you as to us."

Jesus, thought Welsh. That was a bolt out of the blue. Either the colonel was both insensitive and unwilling to pass up an example to hammer his point home, or the implications of that statement were enormous.

"You are a military man," the colonel added, "not a

diplomat. I know that with you I may speak as a soldier."

Nice of him to tell me how much he knows about me, thought Welsh.

The colonel glanced at his watch. "You must excuse me now, Mr. Welsh. I have much work to attend to."

Welsh was a little annoyed at being given the brush-off, but it was no time to get bitchy. "Perhaps we may meet again?"

"Perhaps. And please, Mr. Welsh," the colonel said, in a soft, solicitous tone that raised the hairs on the back of Welsh's neck. "As you go about our country to ask your questions, please do so with the greatest care. I regret that Guatemala is very dangerous at the present. The subversives have little love for North Americans."

Welsh finally realized that the reason he was there was so the colonel could give *him* a good looking-over. Colonel Gutierrez was obviously G-2; the popular name for Guatemalan intelligence was the traditional military staff designation. Welsh supposed he ought to be grateful that the interview hadn't been held at the squat concrete military intelligence headquarters with the American-supplied satellite dishes and antennas crowding the roof. It was a building that historically far more people entered than left. Alive, that is.

But Welsh was impressed. The little bastard was more subtle than he'd given him credit for. The point of the whole conversation was to let him know that the U.S. government had enough invested in Guatemala, whether an interest in stability or the trouble-free continuation of the war on drugs, that the deaths of a few Marines or an unpleasantly accusatory report from Welsh might upset the apple cart for all of a day and a half—if it was a slow news week. Then it would be back to business as usual. And if he made too much trouble, taking Welsh out in a failed mugging or rigged guerrilla assassination would be the easiest of things to arrange. He'd heard there was even a special section of G-2 that specialized in killings made to look like accidents.

"I thank the colonel for his concern," Welsh replied. Then, on his way out door, he turned and said, "And if you threatened me before without my realizing it, my apologies."

Lieutenant Colonel Gutierrez, sitting calmly in his padded chair, smiled ever so slightly.

As soon as he left the building, Welsh loosened his tie and opened his collar. He needed a cold beer badly.

Climbing into the Embassy Cherokee, he gave Hernando, his stoic Guatemalan contract driver/security man/spy for whomever, some new directions.

Hernando drove him to the restaurant in Zone 10, and parked ostentatiously up on the curb. The diplomatic plates rendered them immune from the traffic laws. Welsh had been watching all day. They'd been followed by at least two cars, periodically switching off.

Welsh stood on the sidewalk for a while, just looking. The bloodstains had been washed off the concrete. There were new chairs and tables, and the bullet holes in the walls were puttied up and painted over. You wouldn't know that three Marines had died there.

He went inside and had a beer. It was too late for lunch and too early for dinner; only a couple of grizzled regulars were inside. Welsh bought them a round, and they were more than happy to tell him the story as if they'd been there that day, which they probably hadn't. The proprietor looked on in horror; every retelling probably cost him business.

Welsh finished his beer and left. He would have liked a couple more, but the Ambassador's reception was that night. He was going to have to keep his wits about him and watch his mouth, and that was hard enough to do sober.

Back at the hotel he discovered that his belongings

had been searched. He'd left a gap in the zippers of his luggage too small for someone to fit their hand in, and measured the gap exactly. The distance was different now, but nothing had been removed or repositioned. Not taking notes was looking like a good idea, but it wasn't just the memory work that was making his head hurt.

Chapter Thirteen

The best thing about diplomatic receptions was always the food, since for reasons of national prestige no country wanted their spread to show up badly against anyone else's. The worst thing about diplomatic receptions was the crowd. They tended to be a bit stiff, for much the same reason.

It took Welsh a while to actually get into the Embassy. Security was heavy because no one wanted a repeat of the takeover of the Japanese diplomatic compound in Peru.

He caught sight of Ted Alonso in the main banquet room, standing near the doorway to the kitchen. Alonso was resplendent in tuxedo and Motorola walkie-talkie radio. Welsh ambled over and inquired, "What time are the armed guerrillas scheduled to arrive?"

"That's what's known in the security trade as a joke in very poor taste," Alonso replied. "Besides, didn't you hear? The country's at peace."

"My mistake," said Welsh.

"And how did you and Colonel Gutierrez get along?" Alonso asked.

"Just peachy. He threatened to kill me—not in so many words, of course."

"He does that a lot; he catch you staring at his wife's picture?"

Welsh was stunned speechless for a few seconds. Then he managed to blurt out, "You have *got* to be shitting me!"

"Oh, it's happened before," Alonso assured him calmly. "Hell, a couple of weeks ago they were in a restaurant and he pistol-whipped a guy he thought was staring at her too hard. You ought to check her out in person. Miss Guatemala runner-up. A real hammer."

"I will the next time I get a death wish. The picture was bad enough."

"They'll probably be here tonight."

"Then if you see me wearing sunglasses, you'll know why."

Alonso looked around quickly to see if anyone was listening. "That's not a bad idea. Gutierrez doesn't look like much, but he is one dangerous little son of a bitch. For real."

"You mean in the bush with an M-16?" Welsh asked skeptically.

"More like knocking on your door at midnight," Alonso replied. "And no one ever sees your ass again."

"I figured that was the deal," said Welsh.

Alonso's radio crackled. He held it up to his ear, and then spoke into it. "He's right here," he said. Then, to Welsh: "The Ambassador would like to have a word with you."

"Me? What does he want?"

"No idea, but I have to get back to work anyway. Enjoy the party."

"Yeah, I can't wait for you guys to get liquored up and start shooting glasses off the bartenders' heads."

Chuckling loudly, Alonso disappeared into the kitchen.

Ambassador Marshall and his wife were preparing to mingle. Amanda Marshall was an ex-model, prominent New York socialite, and reputed plastic-surgery junkie—if you were credulous enough to believe the New York tabloids. But she did spend more of her time in Manhattan than in Guatemala City supporting her husband's official duties.

She was the sort of person who would never call Welsh Rich. "It's very nice to meet you, Richard," she said.

"My pleasure," Welsh replied, shaking the offered hand.

Without further ado, or an excuse-us, Big Nick threw an arm around Welsh's shoulder and dragged him out of earshot.

Welsh made a gesture of apology, and Amanda Marshall nodded sympathetically, as if she were used to it.

"Rich," Big Nick said, "I want to ask you a favor."

"And what would that be?" Welsh replied. Never agree to anything unconditionally. Unless you wanted to be sorry.

"Margaret Scanlan is here tonight."

"Scanlan? Scanlan?" Welsh knew the name, but he went into momentary brain lock and failed to make the connection.

"You know, the farmer who got killed down here? Michael Scanlan?"

"Oh, right. Right."

"She's going to want to talk to you, and I'd appreciate it if you'd give her some time."

"His wife?" Welsh asked uneasily.

"No, his sister. Lives in Chicago. Did very well for herself in commodities, I hear."

"What does she want to talk to me about?"

"She's trying to get to the bottom of this, find a little closure."

"Well, aren't the troops who did it in the slammer?"

"Yeah, but the colonel who supposedly gave the order, Dominguez, the base commander at Santa Elena—no one can find him."

"And no one's looking all that hard, I imagine," said Welsh. With the colonel unavailable, the rest of the Army command was sealed off from any blame.

"Look, just talk to her, promise you'll help, whatever. Just so she gets out of my fucking hair sometime." Big Nick stopped for breath, and his pleading took on a harder edge. "Like what am I supposed to do? I'm trying to make this peace treaty take. The last thing I need is to start a new ruckus with the Army."

Welsh didn't feel the need to contribute anything to that. Big Nick's conscience was his problem.

"So you will talk to her," said Big Nick, trying to close the deal.

"Sure," said Welsh.

"Thanks, Rich." Big Nick locked his arms around Welsh's shoulders in a sort of pseudo-macho New York hug. Then, having gotten what he wanted, released him and was gone.

It was a black-tie crowd. Welsh was one of the few wearing a suit. The diplomatic community was fully represented, and Guatemalan notables made up the rest. There were some high-ranking officers in uniform, and even a few of the playboy-polo-player types, proving that stereotypes were sometimes accurate. The women were in designer gowns, gold, pearls, and diamonds.

Then Welsh had to look more than twice, because there was one Guatemalan beauty who absolutely stood out. She couldn't have been over twenty-five, and her body was so spectacular that she was either a 1 percent genetic anomaly or the product of a crack surgical team. This was readily apparent because she was wearing a gown cut down to her navel in front and the top of her ass in the back. And . . . she seemed to be staring at him.

Certain it was a mistake, Welsh looked over his shoulder, but there was no one there. He looked back and she was still giving him the eye.

Normally Welsh would have strolled over and given it the old college try, but she couldn't have come alone. And it was Guatemala. The men tended to be dedicated practitioners of machismo like Colonel Gutierrez. Hell, she might even be his niece. The way the women were being watched, Welsh had the idea that becoming too familiar would cause the husbands or fathers to order their bodyguards to drag you outside and forcibly extract all your teeth. So he only smiled, and nodded, and made a mental note to keep an eye on her for the rest of the evening.

He reached the bar, which was packed with guests getting their predinner drinks. Finally catching the bartender's eye, Welsh said, "Beer, please."

The bartender stared at him as if he were a card-carrying lunatic.

The little shit probably wouldn't have batted an eye if he'd demanded a chichi with an extra cherry and an umbrella in it. Welsh gave the bartender a Clint Eastwood narrowing of the eyes, and growled, *"Cerveza, por favor."*

The bartender had to rummage around to find a brew and a suitable glass, if only to keep Welsh from drinking out of the bottle.

Welsh had only gotten down a single large, refreshing swallow before a hand touched his arm and a female voice said, "Mr. Welsh?"

Welsh turned and found himself looking almost eye-to-eye with a tall woman in her mid-thirties. Her straight black hair was worn short. She was tanned, with intelligent dark eyes and strong features. Though her face had an unforced pleasantness, he could see her frankly sizing him up. He would not have described her as conventionally beautiful, but then neither was he. In contrast to his across-the-room flirtation earlier, which had been a case of pure animal sexual attraction, this was fascination. Welsh was smitten. He looked: no wedding ring. Then he set his beer back down on the bar and made a quick check to be sure his mouth wasn't hanging open.

"Mr. Welsh, I'm Margaret Scanlan."

Even that didn't take the shine off the fascination. As warmly as he could, he said, "My pleasure, Ms. Scanlan. I know about your brother. I'm very sorry."

At that she lost her smile. "Everyone is."

"And after they say they're sorry, they blow you off, right?"

Her eyes widened in surprise; then the smile made a tentative reappearance. "Right."

"What can I do for you?"

"You can help me pry some information from our government and Guatemala's."

"I'm investigating *three* murders. On behalf of a U.S. Senator. And I'm having the same lack of cooperation." He didn't mention that Senator Anderson didn't really give a shit whether he found out anything or not.

"So you're saying that you're blowing me off too."

"I'm saying, hit me with a specific request, and I'll see what I can do for you. What I'm trying to tell you is that my influence is limited."

"You know, Mr. Welsh, when the Administration forced the CIA to release all its documents on human rights abuses in Guatemala, it was a media event down here. TV even covered the documents being unloaded

114

from the plane and driven downtown. And when the nearly six thousand documents were examined, practically everything except the punctuation marks was blacked out."

"That's the way the CIA does it," said Welsh.

"Colonel Patricio Dominguez ordered his soldiers to kill my brother. Dominguez was selling information to the CIA, and they knew what he did. The only reason anyone knows this is because Mr. Nordstrom of the State Department broke the rules and let it out. And for his trouble his career was destroyed."

Welsh knew that Nordstrom was currently working as an aide to the Congressman he'd given the documents to. "He did the right thing, and he paid the price. That sent a message to everyone else. For the most part, people only act in their own best interest. It's in no one's best interest to talk to you; or to me, for that matter. The trick is to find someone who feels that it's in their best interest, for whatever reason, to spill the beans."

"Have you found anyone like that?"

"If I did, I wouldn't tell you. And if *you* do, I recommend that you don't tell a living soul. At least until you get out of the country."

"This is the point when I usually get told to go home like a good girl and forget all about it."

Welsh didn't mind her tone. If he were in her shoes he'd be a little scratchy too. "I'll tell what I think is the real deal instead, and you make up your own mind. Take a look around this room. Same kind of crowd you'd see in any first-class country club back home, right? Well, these people *run* this country, the same way people like them run most of the countries on earth. They have their own private armies and they do whatever the hell they want. If you get in their way they don't sic their lawyers on you. They have you killed. Your brother got in someone's way. Now who do you want: the man who gave the order to kill your brother; the man who gave him the order; or the man who gave *him* the order? If for some reason you do manage to get close to them, they'll have you killed too. They've been doing it and getting away with it for a very long time. And the cemeteries are full of people who thought that being a U.S. citizen would protect them."

"I'm not going home until I get some satisfaction. I only had one brother and he's dead."

The line between gutsy and stupid was usually imperceptible, but Welsh still admired her. "I stand by the offer I made. Come to me with anything specific, and I'll do whatever I can for you."

She offered her hand and Welsh took it. "I'd better find my table," he said.

"You're sitting at mine," Scanlan replied. "I'll show you."

Welsh followed her, thinking that the Ambassador wasn't such a bad guy after all.

They barely had time to sit down and greet their table mates before being called up to the buffet line. Joining them was a Roman Catholic priest, Monsignor Avilla. Then Connie and Bob, two Americans whose last names, as usual, immediately floated out of Welsh's head. They ran an environmental foundation and had come down to save the place. Connie was as abrasive as any professional activist. Bob was a baby-faced guy with a ponytail and obviously the patience of Job. Welsh had always been an environmentalist, but these were the kind of tie-dyed tree-huggers that gave the other side of the issue all the ammunition they ever needed. Finally, there was Raul, a professor of history at the University, and his quiet wife Maria.

At the buffet, waiters carried their plates and loaded up on everything requested.

Welsh checked out the offerings carefully, and his eye

116

fell on one particular pan. "Saltimbocca?" he asked the server.

"Yes, sir," was the reply.

"With prosciutto?" was Welsh's next question.

"From Italy," the server replied proudly.

Welsh motioned for him to pile it on, leaving just a little room on the plate for some asparagus.

On the way back to the table, the waiter nearly buckled under the weight of Welsh's plate and salad. All Welsh carried was a glass of white wine, and he was middle-class enough to feel guilty about it.

He sipped his wine until everyone else was seated, politely bowed his head while the Monsignor said grace, then picked up his fork with anticipatory relish. And just then Connie, sitting at his left, said, "You're eating veal?"

Welsh was already pissed off by her manner, not to mention the walk back from the buffet, where he came close to spilling his wine every time she tripped over her native sandals and the long skirt matching her brightly colored embroidered Maya *huipiles* blouse. He took a large forkful, leisurely chewed, and swallowed before replying, "In case you were wondering, there's nothing wrong with your eyesight."

She opened her mouth to educate him into submission, but Welsh didn't give her the chance. "I want the animal dead and cooked properly," he said. "I really don't care if it grew up in a bad home."

There were a few chuckles from around the table. Welsh figured she wouldn't let that one go, but Bob, who must have been used to it, quickly asked Raul the professor if he had any work in progress.

"I am currently working with the Project to Recover Historical Memory," Raul replied. He was soft-spoken to a degree that made him seem painfully shy.

"This good work is sponsored by the Church's human rights office," the Monsignor said.

"We are interviewing the survivors of our thirty-six years of civil war," said Raul. "To produce a comprehensive record of what occurred."

"Has the project been going on long?" Bob asked.

"Since 1995," said Raul. "Before then, compiling the modern history of Guatemala was work so dangerous that few would attempt it."

"Yes," said the Monsignor, "but now we are entering a new chapter in the history of our country."

"The work is now simply dangerous," Raul replied softly but firmly. "And there are no new chapters in history."

Welsh would have cried, "Bravo!" but his mouth was full. When he was able to talk, he asked, "Then where is Guatemala today, in the context of history?"

Raul thought for a while before he spoke. "The colonial period and the Cold War froze us in time. Africa, Asia, Eastern Europe, the Americas outside the United States and Canada are today like Europe one hundred to three hundred years ago. Continuous tribal and religious wars. Corrupt dictators, greedy and selfish elites, brutalized peasants. Enormous poverty but also enormous potential. Guatemala is different only in that our wars are between classes and races: the Criollos of Spanish descent, the mixed-race Ladinos, and the Maya Indians who are the majority of our population and whom we have always repressed."

Welsh had been expecting the usual left-wing/right-wing ideological bullshit you'd get from an American historian, but that was about the neatest and most concise piece of historical analysis he'd ever heard. "But what broke Europe out of that pattern was colonialism, wasn't it?"

"Excellent," Raul said, really animated for the first

time. "Yes, it allowed the European countries to direct their aggression elsewhere, and the wealth they looted led to modern industry and prosperity. That option does not exist for us today. And, I am sorry to say, contrary to the belief of the United States government, free elections do not make a democracy. Democratic institutions, which do not currently exist in Guatemala, are essential."

Welsh hadn't heard anything he totally disagreed with. "But perhaps a people who become used to standing up for their rights and demanding justice will be *your* first step," he said.

"Perhaps," Raul said noncommittally.

Welsh raised his glass in a toast. "To a fellow skeptic."

"Life makes them," said Raul.

"*History* makes them," Welsh replied.

Raul's wife Maria hadn't said a word until then, but something had obviously been rubbing away at her and she couldn't hold it in any longer. "Your pardon, Señorita Scanlan, but I have seen your story in the newspapers and on television, and I must ask you a question."

"Certainly," Scanlan replied.

"We have all of us lived through a civil war in which the two sides made war on all the rest of us. Now they have passed an amnesty law in which they have pardoned themselves of all their crimes. All Guatemalans are asked to accept this, for the sake of peace. So why should your case be different? Because you are a North American?"

Judging by the length of time it took Scanlan to frame a reply, Welsh thought that had hit pretty close to home.

"I only want to know what happened to my brother," she said.

"We all want to know what happened to our brothers," Maria said relentlessly. She ignored the restraining hand Raul had placed on her arm. "You already know more than most."

The Monsignor tried to keep the situation from deteriorating even further. "Perhaps . . ."

"May we have your opinion, Mr. Welsh?" Maria asked. "You are after all an official of the U.S. government."

"Mr. Welsh is not," Raul corrected her. "He is an aide to a U.S. Senator, which is entirely different."

Maria waited until Raul was finished, and then said, "May we hear your opinion anyway?"

Later, Welsh admitted to himself that there was no way he could blame a sip of beer and two glasses of wine for his failure to mouth a few safe platitudes and then shut the hell up. But he had tried. "I understand all the good political reasons why an amnesty had to take place. Just like El Salvador, Chile, and South Africa. Realistically, you have to forgive those with the guns because they still have the guns, and you don't."

"Is this how you feel personally?" Maria asked.

"As an outsider, I would encourage anyone to forgive those who killed a member of their family. For the sake of peace. But if they killed a member of my family, I would want to see their heads mounted on sticks." Welsh didn't turn his head, but he could practically feel Margaret Scanlan's eyes on him.

Now the Monsignor weighed in. "Vengeance is mine; I will repay, saith the Lord."

"Paul to the Romans, Chapter Twelve," Welsh replied automatically. Now everyone was staring at him, so he shrugged and added, "Sunday School."

"Then what you said before was academic," said the Monsignor.

"I think Paul gave some excellent advice to the members of a tiny, persecuted minority religion in its first century of existence," Welsh replied.

"Is Christian forgiveness not also good advice today?" the Monsignor demanded.

"I speak personally, meaning no offense," said Welsh. "But I believe that the concept of unconditional forgiveness is what allows evil to flourish in the world." He flashed a glance to his right, and found himself staring straight into Margaret Scanlan's eyes.

"Then what do you believe in?" Maria asked.

"Justice, punishment, and if necessary, vengeance," said Welsh.

Raul nodded thoughtfully. "They can be very time-consuming obsessions, to the exclusion of all other good things in life."

Welsh certainly wasn't going to presume to lecture him. "I spoke personally."

"You must have faith in God's justice," said the Monsignor.

"With all respect, that is something I have yet to witness."

"His justice is not of this world, Mr. Welsh."

"That's exactly what I meant."

"Were you raised a Christian, Mr. Welsh?" the Monsignor asked.

Implying that he was obviously no longer one, Welsh thought. "Episcopalian."

The Monsignor nodded solemnly, as if everything was now explained.

That was the high-water mark of the dinnertime conversation. Just like the dinner tables of Welsh's youth, once everyone sensed that the topic of discussion had been taken too far, by mutual consent the subject matter immediately moved to the level of sports, the weather, and gardening.

For Welsh the evening headed even farther downhill. When, after dessert and coffee, he returned from a trip to the men's room, Margaret Scanlan was gone. And before he'd even had a chance to offer her a ride home, and thereby unintentionally discover where she was staying.

But the evening wasn't over yet. Welsh said his good-byes, exchanging cards and phone numbers only with Raul and Maria, a really formidable pair.

Back at the hotel, he was just stepping out of the shower when he heard a knock at the door. Dressed in his hotel robe, Welsh took a look through the peephole. There, standing in the hallway in her evening gown, was the Guatemalan goddess he'd exchanged meaningful glances with at the reception.

Rich Welsh had sorrowfully limited experience with beautiful women stalking him back to his hotel room. And while his ego was as large as anyone else's, it didn't reach the heights of personal vanity that would regard the visit as his rightful due.

The best move might have been to just go to bed, but arrant curiosity *was* one of his many faults, so he did open the door.

She tried to push by him into the room, and ran into Welsh's outstretched forearm.

She pressed her breasts into his arm and purred, "Don't you understand? I want to be with you."

Her English was rudimentary, but no doubt her proficiency wasn't in the language arts. Welsh laughed, because it even sounded rehearsed. And the breasts were plastic. No doubt about that. They were like two elbows poking into his arm.

She tried to push by him again and, peeved at being thwarted, put her hands on her hips and impatiently tapped a high heel on the carpet. "What, you queer?"

Welsh chuckled again. "I've heard that all over the world. It must be on page one of the international prostitute's handbook."

"You don't have to pay," she said, as if that was what was hanging them up.

That only meant someone else was. "You can go back and tell whoever did that I didn't just fall off the turnip truck," Welsh said pleasantly. "And it didn't just back over my head."

"What?"

He'd lost her. "Just tell them. You can leave now."

She didn't move.

"You can either get out of the doorway on your own," said Welsh, "or we'll see how far I can throw you."

She stomped back down the hall, scorching the air with a loud chorus of: "Bastard! Son of a whore! Faggot!" in Spanish.

The door across the hall opened cautiously, and a businessman bursting from his underwear like an overfilled sausage peered out through the crack.

"There goes my one chance at true love," Welsh told him. "Sorry to disturb you."

The door slammed shut.

Welsh closed his, and threw the chain and dead bolt. The world's two oldest professions, prostitution and espionage, had always worked comfortably together. There were many variations on the game. A screaming outraged "husband" could appear pounding on your hotel room door, threatening a public scandal. Then friendly "officials" would show up to mediate the dispute. More guys got into really bad trouble letting Mr. Penis do their thinking than by any other way.

Personally, Welsh had no interest in sex with a woman who didn't care whether he was alive or dead, except that if he was dead it would be easier to steal his wallet. But maybe that's what turned a lot of people on.

As he went to bed, and reality gradually sunk in, his feeling of near-amusement grew much colder. Someone wanted some leverage on him. So far they'd started off light, but if they persisted, it was bound to get heavier.

When he was finally able to get to sleep, Welsh was thinking about Margaret Scanlan.

Chapter Fourteen

Welsh spent the next day interviewing the Embassy Marine detachment. He didn't learn anything new. Half the detachment hadn't even been in-country when the other Marines were killed. As for the rest, no one felt like sharing anything beside the fact that none of them had particularly like Corporal Brian Richardson.

On the way back to the hotel Welsh was giving some serious thought to how to get in touch with Margaret Scanlan without having to go through the Embassy. But that turned into the one thing he didn't need to worry about, because she was waiting for him in the hotel lobby.

She rose from her chair and blocked his way, as if he might not want to talk to her, something Welsh couldn't understand.

"It's great to see you again," he said, shaking her hand. "I'm sorry I missed you when you left the Embassy." Don't gush, you asshole, he thought, mentally slapping himself.

"Mr. Welsh, I really need to talk with you," she said quickly.

"Business?" Welsh asked, more than a little disappointed.

"Yes."

"Do you have a car?"

That threw her off stride. "Why can't we talk here?"

"Is there any way that the best international hotel in the city isn't wired for sound by someone? No, no way."

"You're kidding?"

"Want to bet your life on it?"

"No," she said, giving it some thought. "I guess I convinced myself I was being pretty careful. I have a rental car, but wouldn't a cab be better?"

"In a country like this, every cab driver works as a part-time informer for the police, some domestic or foreign intelligence service, or all of them at the same time."

"Okay, that was lesson two. My car is in the parking garage. Is there any place in particular you'd like to go?"

Welsh thought she looked even more magnificent than the previous night. But he cautioned himself not to let his glands do any thinking for him. If past history was any guide, their common sense was very limited. "Lesson number three. We should go to a place neither of us has been to before. That way there's less chance someone will be there waiting for us, or show up along the way."

She gave him an amused look. "All right, lead on."

Welsh pulled his guidebook from his pocket and consulted it. "I think we can find someplace in the Zona Viva. You drive, and I'll navigate."

The Zona Viva was the several blocks surrounding the

Hotel Camino Real. High-end dining, bars, and nightclubs. The places on the outer edge of the Zona were less exclusive and the prices more reasonable. Even though it was only a few blocks from the hotel, at night driving was safer than walking in Guatemala City.

As they drove, Welsh watched for a tail, but didn't see one. At night all you could make out were headlights, so it was much harder to pick out anyone following.

Scanlan said, "Now, what I wanted to talk to you about was—"

"Don't talk business in a car," Welsh interrupted. "Easiest thing in the world to bug."

"Are you being a little extreme?"

"Could very well be," Welsh admitted. But all the case studies he'd ever read on intelligence and industrial espionage proved that, on a scale of relative naiveté, Americans were the country bumpkins of the world, and taken advantage of accordingly.

They drove past the bar Welsh had chosen from the guidebook. From the outside it looked reasonably crowded and well lit.

A parking place miraculously opened up less than a hundred yards away.

The bar wasn't a highbrow place, or overly decorated, but it had a nice, friendly vibe. Welsh had had to back out of a few bars in the course of his travels, and it was something he'd learned to recognize.

He picked a table in a corner where he could sit with his back to a wall and watch the entrance. They were right beside a frosted-glass window that overlooked the street. A marimba band was playing loud enough to almost guarantee a private conversation.

"Do you want anything to eat?" he asked when they were seated.

Scanlan shook her head. "I'd rather talk now, if there aren't any more lessons for me to absorb."

But a waitress showed up and cut off the conversation. They ordered two bottles of Gallo, or in English, goat beer.

When she left, Welsh said, "Okay, what do you want to talk about?"

"I've had some information come into my possession," she said. "About the murder of those Marines."

"You don't say?"

"Some elements in the Army killed them. Pinning it on the guerrillas was just a setup."

The waitress returned with the beer. Welsh sipped from the bottle, not wanting to disturb the slumber of any bacteria in the accompanying glass. The Guatemalan Army killed her brother, so she wasn't about to be neutral where they were concerned. "Is there some proof of this?"

"I have proof," Scanlan said.

Welsh happened to glance up just in time to see two Guatemalan men in their twenties enter the bar. They looked around carefully, stared directly at him, and nudged each other. Uh-oh, Welsh thought to himself. They were between him and the exit, so there was nothing to do but wait and see what happened.

The two pushed their way through the crowd, heading directly toward the table. One was a real gorilla, only about six feet tall or a little less, but close to three hundred pounds with a power-lifter's chest and arms. Everything but the knuckles dragging the ground. The other one was shorter and leaner and less well-muscled. They were dressed in flashy leather jackets and gold chains, like successful young punks.

Welsh said quietly to Scanlan, "We may have to get out of here in a hurry, so be ready."

Startled, she looked over her shoulder as the two approached. They came right up to the table.

The gorilla, standing to the right of Welsh in his chair, smiled and said cheerfully, in English, "Hey, Americans! Buy us a drink."

No one had any trouble picking out Americans abroad. That didn't bother Welsh. Neither did buying a round. It was a great way to break the ice in another country. Of course, as the designated rich American, it was also a great way to assume an open-ended financial obligation for the rest of the evening. Welsh did not like being told what he had to do, but none of that had any bearing on the situation. These guys were looking for trouble. Welsh's stomach tightened up into a cold hard painful knot.

"No," he said flatly.

"What's the matter, gringo?" the big one replied. "You don't like us? We not good enough to drink with you?"

This was how the verbal portion of the event usually began. The equivalent of the New York "You talkin' to *me*?" From the playground on, these guys always had to run their mouths before getting around to business. They loved it if you tried to reason with them. If you said anything at all, it only let them know how scared you were.

Welsh fought to keep all expression off his face. While the other side was still talking, he looked across the table at Scanlan, shrugged ruefully, and at the same time raised his right ass cheek from the chair and snapped off a hard kick straight onto the side of the gorilla's kneecap. Welsh felt the knee collapse; there was a loud pop and an even louder scream as the man went down.

The gorilla's friend stood shocked and immobile, as frequently happens when something you've counted on going according to plan doesn't. Launching out of the chair, Welsh grabbed his beer bottle and whipped it into the guy's face. The bottle hit but didn't break. Using the time he'd gained, Welsh grabbed the back of his chair with both hands, letting his momentum carry him forward. His opponent's hands were still up to his face when Welsh brought the heavy wooden chair down like an ax onto his head. The force of the blow shivered through Welsh's arms; the other guy lost control of his muscles and dropped like a limp sack.

Welsh pivoted and swung the chair like a baseball bat, catching the gorilla, who was still on the floor screaming and holding his kneecap, square in the face.

Now the whole bar was awake to what was going on. Welsh dropped the chair, picked their table up by the base so the top was aimed like a battering ram, and threw it right through the frosted-glass window.

He kicked the glass shards away from the new exit he'd created, then turned, thinking he'd have to grab Margaret Scanlan and drag her along. But she was up already, standing with her back to the window and emptying a can of pepper spray into the path of anyone who might be inclined to follow them. Then, before Welsh could let loose with the bellow he was readying, Scanlan was through the hole.

He was right behind her. When he hit the sidewalk he slid on the broken glass and went down on one knee before he caught himself. Welsh picked up a big piece of glass as a weapon, and found himself in the midst of a group of startled pedestrians. They immediately stampeded when he came up off the ground brandishing the glass.

Scanlan was already halfway to the car. Welsh broke into a sprint. The engine was roaring when he got there. He checked back down the street for any pursuers, but there were none. Welsh dove into the car and tossed the piece of glass out the window.

"Let's go back to the hotel," he said, breathing hard but trying to keep his voice as even as possible.

"Damn!" Scanlan exclaimed as she stomped the gas pedal onto the floor.

Welsh's head ached, and his stomach was twisted with the sickening exhilaration that always followed him through a fight. His hands shook as the adrenaline subsided and let him down. "Slow down," he said, noticing the streetlights shooting by. "Hey, slow the hell down!"

"Who were those guys?" she demanded.

Welsh held a finger up to his lips.

They got back to the hotel and parked in the underground garage.

"Do you have a flashlight?" Welsh asked.

"No, not with me."

"Wait here." Welsh walked to the attendant's booth and told him that his girlfriend had lost an earring. He waved his room key, and the attendant let him borrow a flashlight.

He trotted back to the car and without a word disappeared underneath. He rummaged around, and when he crawled out Scanlan was understandably curious.

"Let's take a walk in the garden," Welsh suggested.

On the way out he returned the flashlight to the attendant.

"Okay," Scanlan said when they reached the hotel gardens. "Now, can we talk here?"

"Sure," said Welsh.

"What was the deal under my car?"

"Those two guys came into the bar looking for us. Since I didn't see anyone following on the drive over, I was wondering how they found us. There's a bird dog on your car."

"A what?"

"A homing transmitter. A black box about the size of a paperback book. All you have to do is attach it to the frame and align the antenna with the front of the car. It transmits to a receiver in another car. So while you're driving the wrong way down one-way streets trying to lose a tail, the guys following you are a couple blocks back, watching you on a screen and laughing their asses off. It's state-of-the-art for law enforcement nowadays."

"How did the Guatemalans get it?"

"Probably bought it right from the manufacturer like everyone else. Either that or the DEA gave it to them, just like their M-16's. I was wondering why I always picked up a tail in my Embassy car, but didn't in yours. The answer is that the Embassy vehicles get screened for gadgets like this when they come back to the motor pool every night."

"And rental cars don't."

"Hell, if you've got enough time you can even wire a bird dog into a car's electrical system, so the batteries don't run down. Yours is."

"So is it the government?"

"Government, death squad, anyone rich enough to afford the equipment; no way to tell."

"Then what were those two guys in the bar after?" Scanlan demanded.

"That I don't know either," said Welsh. "Just the two of them . . . the street wasn't covered . . . they moved on us in the bar instead of outside in the dark. Doesn't make sense. I'm thinking maybe they were just supposed to throw a scare into us." He smiled grimly. "And maybe I overreacted."

"Just as well. I was scared enough the way it happened." Scanlan surprised him by giggling. "You know, not only did we destroy that bar, we didn't even pay our bill."

"Don't worry," said Welsh. "The management didn't let those two hammerheads into the ambulance until they squared the damages."

131

"Poetic justice. Do you mind if I ask why we had to go out the window?"

"If two Guatemalans strolled into a cowboy bar in Oklahoma and kicked ass on a couple of the locals, how easy do you think it'd be for them to leave peacefully, never mind who started it?"

"I see your point. You made up your mind pretty fast."

"If you move before the other guy decides what he's going to do, you win."

"I think what I heard about you was right, Mr. Welsh. You know how to handle yourself."

Welsh really wanted to, but decided not to ask from whom or exactly what she had heard about him. "You're no slouch yourself, Ms. Scanlan. Now you've seen what you're up against, why don't you pack it in? It's only going to get worse."

"Why don't *you* go home?" she said angrily.

"I intend to. As soon as possible."

"Run away?" she challenged.

"Hell, yes! If there'd been a way to do it back in the bar, they'd have been eating my dust."

"Before you go, you might hear what I have to say first."

"I've been trying to," Welsh said patiently. "But we keep getting interrupted. As I recall, you were saying something about proof."

She lowered her voice. "I've met a man who says he can tell you who killed the Marines."

"What does he want?"

"To meet with you, face-to-face."

"No money, or anything like that?"

"He won't discuss it with me."

"Can I talk to him on the phone?"

"No, he doesn't want that."

"Of course he doesn't," Welsh said angrily. "The best-case scenario is that this guy is a simple con artist who

132

wants to sell me the informational equivalent of the Brooklyn Bridge."

"And the worst case?" she asked, angry at him for doubting her, but also half curious.

"I get recorded on videotape with some agent provocateur. Or get kidnapped, which I understand has replaced soccer as the national sport. Or just get shot, which is an oldie but still popular."

"You're sounding a little paranoid."

"Are you kidding?" Welsh found it hard to keep his voice down. "I'm *feeling* a little paranoid."

"I know what you're thinking. I'm the biggest Midwestern rube who ever got off the plane, right? But this guy is genuine. Make no mistake about it, he's crooked as the day is long. But he *is* genuine. I'm telling you, Welsh, this is the guy you were talking about last night. The one whose best interest is to spill the beans. He gave me this to give to you." She handed him a cassette tape.

That took a little of the air out of Welsh. "What the hell does he want?"

"He won't tell me. Only you."

"You've met him then?"

"Just once in person. After that he insisted we talk on the phone. Pay phones. He told me to tell you his name, and that you shouldn't use it in any communication. He's just like you that way, paranoid about being bugged."

"It's not paranoia if you're really being bugged. And this guy's name is . . . ?"

"Booker. Tom Booker."

It was like a jolt of electricity, because Thomas Booker was the name Mike Longenecker had given him. From the alias Corporal Costa had given him. The well-connected ex-U.S. Army scumbag who showed such an interest in Corporal Brian Richardson. This put an entirely different spin on things. Not that Booker wasn't trying to set him up the same way he'd probably set up the Marines.

"You haven't left this lying around or anything, have you?" Welsh asked, fingering the plastic cassette case. "In your room or your car?"

"If it's not in my pocket it's under my pillow when I'm sleeping," Scanlan replied.

"How do you get in touch with this guy?"

"Like I said, pay phones. A different phone and a different time for every day of the week. He calls a number every day, and if I don't want to talk to him I just don't go to the phone. He uses something electronic to disguise his voice. But it's the same fake voice each time."

That made Welsh feel a little better. Only someone in fear of their life would go to such lengths. If it was a setup, he thought it would be much simpler.

He came to a decision. "I've got to make some arrangements. Tell him that I'll set the conditions of the meeting. I'll give him the day and the time, but he won't get the place until right before we meet, with just enough time to get there."

"He won't like that. He's a control freak too."

Welsh ignored the jab. "That's tough. Then we don't meet."

At that she smiled. "Okay, I get it. The side that *has* to make a deal is always at a disadvantage. Let's see how desperate he is."

The conversation halted there, and they both stared at each other. "Any more business to discuss?" Welsh asked.

"Yeah, what are we going to do?"

"I'll let you know before we do it."

"You don't trust me, Mr. Welsh?"

"No," he said. "I trust your guts, but I haven't known you long enough to trust your judgment. Don't take it personally. I recommend you don't trust me either—I might leave you hanging. Oh, and please call me Rich."

She laughed and shook her head in bewilderment. "You're a strange guy, Rich, but I've already made my mind up about you. Oh, and you can call me Maggie."

"How about some dinner, Maggie? I'll put it on my official U.S. Government American Express Card."

"You're hungry?"

"Sure."

"Thanks, Rich, but I'm not."

Welsh gestured toward the hotel. "A drink then?"

"I appreciate it, but it's been a busy night. I'd better head back to my hotel."

It was just business then, Welsh thought with genuine regret. Too bad.

They exchanged hotel telephone and room numbers, and she agreed to meet him the next day. He walked her back to the garage.

"Aren't you going to take that thing off my car?" Scanlan asked.

"If we do that, they'll just know we're on to them and try something we might not like. Don't worry, we'll make good use of your bird dog."

"And you'll tell me how when the time is right."

Welsh nodded.

Shaking her head again, Scanlan got in her car and drove off.

Quite a woman, Welsh thought. If he wasn't really, really careful, she'd probably get him killed.

Chapter Fifteen

With Margaret Scanlan's tape in hand, Welsh had need of a portable tape player. He didn't own one, feeling that it wasn't too bright to go jogging though a city without being able to hear what was coming up from behind.

So on the way to his room he stopped by the hotel gift shop and bought himself a cassette player, earphones, and a couple of packages of batteries.

The purchases were assembled by the time the room-service pizza arrived. Welsh flopped down into a chair, inhaled a slice of pizza, and washed it down with a soft drink, not a beer. He felt he no longer had any margin for stupidity, and at least he could do something about the chemically induced kind.

A deafening blast of white noise had him fumbling for the volume dial. Then a voice came through. It had that echo-chamber quality and the background sounds that usually indicated a listening device. The voice was speaking English with a Guatemalan accent.

"He is dead!" the voice said emotionally. "Dead! The little son of a bitch!"

Then another voice came in. Native English speaker, but there was a reason why Welsh couldn't be sure. Also pissed off, but not emotional. "You're planning to kill him, and you brought me here just so you could tell me about it? *You're* the son of a bitch!"

Now the first voice dropped to a more soothing tone. "Don't be like that, my friend. If a decision concerns you, of course I have to tell you about it."

"And make sure I'm involved. Don't insult my intelligence. You people always think you're going to take care of loose ends by killing someone, and all you do is attract a lot of attention. You never learn."

"It is a national failing, to be sure," the first voice said coolly.

"Pay him some more money, shut him up, and close out the operation."

The first voice became hotly passionate again. "I'll shut him up. After what he has done? After betraying me? Never again!"

"Bring him in and have a talk with him."

"Impossible. He is stupid enough to threaten me, but not that stupid. He will not come near us now. He goes nowhere alone. He is dead."

"He's trying to put the arm on us—we can put the arm on him just as easily. We can get him in as much trouble as he can us. Make him aware of this, give him a final payment, and close this out quietly. If you kill him, the problems could never go away."

The tape hissed for a while. Then the first voice said, "No. But do not worry, my friend. We will take care of everything. You need know nothing about it."

The second voice mocked him. "I need know nothing about it. So I can read in the newspapers after you cowboy it and leave the streets full of bodies. No, thank you. You put me in this, now you'll listen."

"Of course, my friend," the first voice replied soothingly. "When have I not?"

That was the end of the tape. Welsh thought that if it wasn't for the movies, the tough guys of the world wouldn't know how to talk.

The first voice was that of his old buddy, Lieutenant Colonel Armando Gutierrez. The second had been electronically distorted, as if the tape had been run through a personal computer mixing program. Probably by Booker, the guy who gave Scanlan the tape. Why? Maybe because the voice belonged to an American.

As proof of anything, it was useless. But as a teaser, it was damned effective.

Well, what was it going to be? Get the hell out of town, or take it all the way? And if he took it all the way, he could end up dead even if he didn't make any mistakes. What did he owe three dead Marines?

In everything he'd encountered thus far in his professional life, the absolute guiding principle had always seemed to be the avoidance of responsibility. And it had always made him sick to his stomach. Which led to an even better question: Are your principles worth dying for?

Welsh got out his Guatemala City street map and started putting a plan together.

Chapter Sixteen

Welsh was standing in front of his hotel on the Avenida Reforma looking at his watch. Margaret Scanlan pulled up in her car, and he got in.

It might have been the expression on his face that prompted her to say, "You're one of those guys that's never been late for anything in his life, right?"

"Never when my life is on the line," Welsh replied curtly.

"Sorry about that," she said. Then, as if trying to lighten the mood, she exclaimed, "But my goodness, isn't it a lovely day for sightseeing?"

He'd told her to talk for the benefit of any microphones that might be in the car along with the beacon, but now it was irritating. It was fine to joke around before and after, but when you were doing something dangerous you put your game face on and *focused,* so you didn't miss a thing. She was either some kind of adrenaline junkie, or unable to appreciate what she was getting into. Neither boded well.

With his map on his lap, Welsh navigated them into north Guatemala City. He was glad he wasn't driving; it was the worst he'd ever seen, Naples, Italy, being the previous titleholder. There was a near-universal disregard for all signs, traffic laws, and normal standards of human conduct. All the traffic lights did was slow down the cars speeding into the intersections from all four directions at once.

The spirit of the place had obviously infected Scanlan. Welsh thought she might as well have been driving a tank the way she charged right into the thick of things.

When she horsed her way through a four-way horn-honking jam that he wouldn't otherwise have thought negotiable, a quiet but audible groan escaped from Welsh's lips.

"Hey," she announced. "I'm from Chicago, the city of big shoulders . . . and sharp elbows."

From then on Welsh resolved to keep his eyes on the map as much as possible. To add to his unease, Scanlan also cheerfully employed a full repertoire of the cruder Spanish adjectives and hand gestures. As they drove through the land of the macho, Welsh waited for one of the locals to come unglued at being dissed by a woman, grab his piece, and start blasting.

Finally they reached their destination, a well-guarded parking lot recommended by his guidebook. The space he chose couldn't be seen from the street; someone would have to come looking for it.

They left the car without comment and set out from the parking lot on foot.

Welsh had run his eye over the local clothing styles and gone shopping. You could pick a foreigner out of a crowd just by their clothes. But covering his local garb was a long cheap plastic raincoat. Scanlan had listened to him and done the same.

They walked for a block and casually strolled into a large office building. They got on an elevator alone and got off on the second floor—after Welsh pushed a half-dozen buttons for the higher floors. They walked down the stairs and left the building by a rear fire exit that had no alarm, emerging onto another street.

Welsh removed the raincoat, crammed it into a paper bag, and threw the bag in the trash. Scanlan did the same.

They used the side streets and put some distance between themselves and the building. They came up on a bus stop, which in Guatemala City was usually identified not by a sign, but by a newspaper and candy stand and a group of locals hanging around for no obvious reason.

"Now I get what you meant about using the beacon on my car," said Scanlan. "The people following us are probably back at the parking lot scratching their heads."

"Or running into the office building trying to figure out which floor we got off on," said Welsh. "Our next move is to get the hell out of here before they can get enough help to check the whole area."

"It really is kind of nice not knowing in advance. You don't get nervous at all."

It was a conveniently short wait before a bus appeared and creaked to a stop at the street corner. They climbed aboard and grabbed a seat.

"Very smooth," Scanlan said.

"It ought to be. I spent the last two days rehearsing every step we took." Welsh didn't say so, but was relieved not to have run into the real professional surveillance he'd planned for. He knew he didn't have the skills to pick out a first-class team with several vehicles, radios, and a lot of followers constantly changing outfits.

He and Scanlan were separated on the bus's bench

seat by a mass of naked protruding springs. And God only knew what it would have smelled like if a defective tailpipe hadn't been blowing burnt diesel back into the passenger compartment.

As the bus rolled south, Scanlan said, "You know, I've been wanting to ask you. What did you do to that bruiser back in the bar? Before you hit him with the chair, that is."

Welsh looked around before answering, but there was no one within earshot. "Kicked him in the kneecap."

"Why?"

"*Why?* Because your Mom was wrong, violence does solve everything."

"No, really, I think it's great learning all this stuff. Tell me, why the knee?"

"Are you kidding?"

"No," she insisted, laughing nervously. "This is all new to me, and I really want to know."

Welsh looked into her bright, shining eyes and thought: adrenaline junkie. Nice American girl, business professional, she'd had a little taste and now she was hooked. Most military officers, by contrast, weren't. The emphasis was always on how to get the job done in the least dramatic fashion without getting yourself or your people hurt. He moved in close, so he was talking right in her ear. "Hit a three-hundred-pound goon in the ribs with a baseball bat and watch him laugh at you. Take out a knee and his career is over. And if I hadn't got my hands on a chair, I would have smashed their testicles, fractured their larynxes, or ripped out their eyeballs. That's why they're in the hospital getting fed through straws instead of us."

"Hey, don't get mad."

"I'm not getting mad. I just want you to wake up and realize what the fuck's going on. Compared to what the

Guatemalans can throw at us, those two were fucking Mouseketeers."

"I am taking this seriously. If you recall, I'm the one who had the pepper spray."

"Then I could just as well ask you *why* you had the pepper spray?"

"Because the men down here never learned to take no for an answer."

Despite his best efforts, Welsh felt a smile creep onto his face. He filed that away for any time the word no might come up in conversation.

Every time the bus stopped, Welsh checked everyone who got on and off. Soon there were all new faces, which was exactly what he wanted to see. He and Scanlan got off in south Guatemala City.

They walked three blocks to another modern office building. The lobby was an open atrium that could be observed from balconies circling the inside of the second and third floors. Welsh had the name of a company ready for the security guard who challenged them.

He looked at his watch. "Go ahead and make the call," he told Scanlan.

"Me calling him," she said. "You should have heard the screaming when I sprang that on him."

"But he went for it."

"He went for it. He's desperate to meet you." Scanlan picked up the pay phone and dialed. When she was done, they went up to the second floor to watch the entrance.

"We're not so much looking for him," said Welsh, "as guys in good physical condition who'll arrive either before or after him. They'll be in twos and threes, and in a hurry. Maybe flashing badges at the security guard."

"And what do we do if they show up?"

"Get the hell out of here."

"And leave Booker?"

"Damn straight. We showed up clean. They'll be his

143

problem." Welsh turned to look at her. "That's the way it's played."

"Okay, okay."

Welsh kept one eye on the entrance and the other on his watch. About fifteen minutes after the call, a lanky middle-aged man carrying a briefcase came through the doors and almost sprinted across the lobby to the elevators.

"That's Booker," Scanlan said.

Welsh waited for another fifteen minutes. No one who entered the building made him suspicious. "Okay," he said. "Let's go up and meet the man."

They took the elevator to the top floor, and then the stairway to the roof.

It was his second trip up, and Welsh still thought the stairwell smelled like the rats held a dance there every night. The roof door was normally locked. On his visit the previous day, Welsh had jimmied the lock. The movies might delight in depicting high-tech burglar tools, but the true thief knew there were few things a crowbar wouldn't open. Welsh arranged for the bolt to stay retracted into the door with the help of some super glue and a small-denomination coin as a shim. After that the door only looked locked.

Welsh knocked twice, paused, and then knocked twice again. The door opened an inch, and then a little wider as the man behind it looked Welsh over. Then it opened all the way and they both walked up, squinting in the bright sunlight.

The truth be told, Welsh had been expecting Booker to be wearing a tailored linen safari suit, solid gold Thai bhat chains, and mirrored sunglasses. But he turned out to be a bald, skinny redneck in his early fifties, dressed in blue jeans, expensive cowboy boots, and a flashy silk shirt. He did have the gold Rolex, though. Booker was one of those bony guys with angular shoulders, arms that hung down to his knees, and absolutely no ass. But he was also pointing a Colt .45 automatic very confidently at Welsh's head.

"Friend," he said to Welsh. "I hate to get off on the wrong foot, but I'd appreciate it if you'd take out your passport, real slow so's I don't have to blow your head off, and put it down in front of you. Then lace your fingers together behind your head and take a couple of steps back."

Welsh did what he was told.

Keeping his pistol on them, Booker checked the passport. Then he reached into his jeans pocket and took out a small plastic box smaller than a pack of cigarettes. He extended a thin antenna with his teeth. "Real sorry about putting you to all this trouble," he kept saying as he aimed the antenna up and down at Welsh and Scanlan. Satisfied, he closed the antenna and slipped the box back in his pocket.

"This is the second time he's done that to me," Scanlan said to Welsh. "And he won't say why."

Welsh knew, and it wasn't a bad opportunity to let Booker know he wasn't dealing with a putz. "He was checking to see if we're wired. His little box is a bug detector. The kind of wire microphone you hide on your body transmits a signal. The box detects a radio frequency field. That's what his apology was for, to make any voice-activated bug transmit. The bias oscillator in a tape recorder emits a detectable energy field too. The box is a little more civilized than having us strip down to our skivvies."

"I'm a civilized fellow," said Booker. "And you're a right smart young man."

"Of course," said Welsh, "I'm sure the fact that there are self-powered bugs smaller than a dime, which you might miss in a search, had nothing to do with your decision."

Booker engaged the safety on the .45 and slid it back into his belt. "Okay," he said, as if it was the most natural thing in the world. "No hard feelings. I knew you wouldn't screw me, Maggie."

"Thanks," Scanlan said dryly.

Welsh was keeping an open mind, but there was nothing about Booker that he liked so far.

"Now, Maggie," Booker said. "I'd be eternally grateful if you'd go over and watch the stairs while I have a few minutes alone with this young fellow."

"Now wait just a minute," Scanlan said. Welsh hadn't seen her that angry, and in a perverse way it was kind of amusing.

"Right next to the door," said Booker, leaving no room for argument.

Scanlan went over to the stairwell, talking under her breath. Welsh couldn't quite make it out, but it sounded neither clean nor complimentary to the male gender.

Booker led him over to some noisy shade beside an air-conditioning unit, checking him out all the way. "You look good," he said. "You look just like a tall Guat."

"How long do we have to talk?" Welsh asked, sitting down.

"Hell, all day," Booker said gleefully. He gestured toward his open briefcase.

Welsh took a peek inside. He'd seen that piece of equipment before, being used by Marine Corps radio battalion reconnaissance teams. It was an AR-3000 communications receiver, a handheld unit that scanned the communications spectrum and picked up every radio set transmitting within range. It was connected by cable to a notebook computer. Spanish voices could be heard through the notebook's speakers. "Looks to me like someone out there is talking on encrypted radios, your computer is set up for their cryptographic software, and

146

it's breaking today's key setting so you can listen in."

"Didn't I say you were smart?" said Booker. "Been listening to your surveillance talking to each other all morning. And you were just slicker'n snot on a doorknob. They still aren't sure whether you lost them on purpose or they lost you by accident. They're on the other side of town right now, trying to figure it out."

Booker had one of those rumbling Southern smoker's voices, pure phlegm. Welsh thought it sounded as if he might cough up a lung at any moment. "They weren't very good," he said.

"They weren't expecting you to be. But next time they'll be ready. So don't let your guard down."

"I won't."

"Say, you and Maggie must have hit it off; she seems to have taken quite a shine to you."

Welsh didn't know what the son of a bitch was fishing for, but he wasn't going to indulge him. "How did you happen to meet her?"

"She came nosing around a while back, and I thought I ought to get in touch with her."

"Why?"

"She wants to know what happened to her brother, and I want to get the fuck out of Guatemala. She's some pretty nice tail, isn't she? You gettin' any of that?"

The guy was an asshole, but he'd finally come to the point, and it wasn't the time to talk about manners. "So why don't you go catch a flight?" Welsh asked.

Booker's smile had thinned out considerably. "If it was as easy as that, I would."

"Well, what's the problem?"

"The problem, Rich—you don't mind if I call you Rich, do you?" Welsh didn't respond; Booker took that as a yes. "The problem, Rich, is that if I tried to leave, the people I work with would get the idea I was going to fuck them."

"You just described your problem," Welsh said calmly. "And why I probably shouldn't be here talking with you. So why don't you give me a reason to stay here and chat?"

"You don't strike me as the timid type. And I can help you out."

"Out of the goodness of your heart? What a guy."

"All right now, I'd expect you to help me out in return."

"But I'm just a Senator's aide. Why don't you try the U.S. Embassy? The State Department is supposed to help Americans in trouble overseas, even though I've never heard of them actually doing it." Despite the situation, Welsh was almost enjoying himself.

Booker maintained his equanimity. "Rich, it just so happens that a Senator's aide is exactly what I need."

"I'm all ears, Tom."

"Your Senator is hot to know who killed those Marines. Not only can I tell him who, but I can give him proof."

"And you'll provide all this service in return for a plane ride home?"

"And immunity from prosecution," Booker added.

"Immunity from being prosecuted for what?" Welsh inquired.

"Let's say anything that might have happened during my years down here in Guatemala."

Welsh just started laughing.

"Hey, Rich, that's not nice."

"Maybe not," said Welsh, "but it was funnier than shit. You want a free ride on all your death-squad work and drug trafficking on your ranch?"

Booker's face dropped about a foot. "How the fuck do you know all that?" he screeched.

"Not to mention the murders of three Marines," Welsh added. "Your high-speed code-breaking computer system just put it all together for me, Tom. I read the record book of your drinking buddy, the late Corporal Brian Richardson. His MOS was 2631, uncommon enough for me to get curious and look it up in the military occupational specialty manual. He was a Non-Morse Electronic Intelligence Intercept Operator/Analyst. Which means the Corps trained him to intercept communications, just like you're doing right now, with equipment you didn't buy at Radio Shack."

Booker's hands were trembling. He shook a cigarette out of a pack, and it took two matches to get it lit. His face was sunburned and deeply lined; his forehead was scored horizontally, and the crevices on each side of his mouth looked half an inch deep. "Okay, Rich," he said glumly. "What's the deal?"

"How can I tell you what it's worth until you tell me the story?" Welsh asked reasonably.

"Dam-nation," Booker exclaimed. "The Guats think you're some shithead gringo college boy. Rich, you're a fucking shark. But you know what? That makes me feel good. I think you're nasty enough to get me out of here." He peered up innocently at Welsh. "Say, who else knows what you know about me?"

"It's not public knowledge," said Welsh. "But if you think your problems are over if I have some kind of fatal accident, you're sadly mistaken."

"That's not what I meant," Booker protested.

"Sure," said Welsh.

Booker smiled for the first time in a while, and Welsh was nearly blinded by the sun flashing off his dentures, definitely not a product of U.S. dental technology. "Nasty," Booker said. "I like that. Okay, Rich, I'll tell you the story."

"Try to keep any self-serving bullshit down to a minimum. I don't give a shit what you did or why. All I'm interested in is accurate information."

149

"Whatever you say." Booker's initial cheerfulness had pretty well evaporated. "This used to be a hell of a country, Rich," he said without a trace of irony. "All the shit that was going on in the U.S. when I left, they weren't about to let it happen down here. And you could live like a king on an Army pension." He shook his head. "The Guats ran the place as they damned well pleased, and as long as the Russians and Cubans were running around making trouble, they got away with it. Even if they went a little wild and Congress hit 'em with an arms embargo, the CIA was still here no matter what. Whatever they couldn't supply under the table they arranged for the Israelis to take care of.

"Then things changed. I mean, the U.S. always talked human rights, but now it looks like they fucking *mean* it. Maggie's brother gets killed and the Ambassador says someone has to go to jail. First time Army officers ever went on trial for *anything*. CIA starts taking it up the ass for everything they did down here. You know, Rich, the Guats never could stand us, thought we were a pain in the ass, but they knew they couldn't get along without us."

Welsh was preparing to intervene if Booker didn't get to the point.

"So I was out drinking one night, and I run into Richardson. The kid's drunk, and he gets to blabbing about what he does in the Marine Corps. I was a communicator myself, so I know what he's talking about. We hit it off; the kid likes to brag. I'm thinking, maybe some people I know down here would like to meet him. They're worried about the way their own government is going. They're worried about the U.S. leaving them hanging, or worse. Maybe they did a little business with some Colombians, just as a sideline. And the CIA turned a blind eye because making sure the country didn't go Communist was the main thing. And now that's not the main thing anymore, are they going to get double-crossed; you know, grabbed by the DEA and flown north? The U.S. supplies all their communications gear, which means the U.S. listens in whenever they want.

"I talk to the Guats. They're interested. Then I talk to Richardson. He's interested. It wasn't like I had to twist his arm," Booker said defensively.

"Was it just him, or were there others?"

"Just him. We didn't need anyone else. Richardson's specialty was intercepting people's communications. What made him valuable was that he knew exactly what the U.S. could do. And he knew what kind of equipment the Guats needed to stop that, and where to get it. Unlike in my day, it's all software now. You can buy Russian encryption software, unbreakable stuff, right off the street in Moscow. Integrate it with the right hardware, wire everything into your radios and cell phones, and no one is going to be listening in when you're talking. The kid made himself a real nice piece of change."

"And they killed him to shut him up," said Welsh.

"No," Booker insisted. "Nothing like that."

"But he did get killed," Welsh pointed out.

Booker shrugged, as if those things sometimes happened. "The kid was a crooked Boy Scout. Now, you can be crooked, or you can be a Boy Scout, but a combination is always trouble. Richardson was willing to help the Guats put together a communications system the U.S. couldn't break into. He did. They loved it. But then they wanted him to help them break into U.S. communications. Not the Embassy or CIA traffic to Washington, you understand; they knew that was impossible. But Embassy, CIA, and DEA cell phones and walkie-talkies. He wouldn't do it. They wanted him to bug the CIA and DEA offices in the Embassy. He's a security guard, walks around all night with the keys, right? No way.

"The Guats are not people who take no graciously. Now, you understand, I'm being honest with you, Rich. I was getting damned worried. I brought the kid on board. He goes over the falls, maybe he takes me with him."

Welsh felt unable to generate any sympathy.

"Okay," said Booker. "I knew right from the start how the Guats operate, and that we needed to protect ourselves. So when Richardson rigged up their phones and radios, he also bugged them."

"He what?" said Welsh.

"When he put the scramblers on the cellular phones he did something that turned the whole fucking phone into one big microphone. So if you had the right equipment you could record the phone calls *and* what everyone was saying in the room. And you could do it from a long way off. Even if the phone isn't turned on, the bug is. The battery doesn't last as long, but you'd never notice that."

Welsh didn't have to be a rocket scientist to figure out where Scanlan's sample tape had come from.

"It was a perfect deal," said Booker. "We were covered all around. Then Richardson gets too smart for his own fucking good. He'd already held the Guats up for more money than they ever intended to pay him. Then he decides he'll sell the tapes from the bugs back to the Guats. No matter we'd both listened to the tape where they talked about killing him if he kept pissing them off. He did it without telling me, Rich. Kid was crazy; thought he was going to make enough to retire. Two days later he was dead."

"And the other Marines?" Welsh asked.

"They just happened to be in the way."

So it hadn't been some kind of meticulously planned strategic-level covert operation to restart the civil war or influence U.S. policy, thought Welsh. Just a grubby little piece of minor-league treason for money to help a few people cover their asses; it must have seemed like nothing but a money-making opportunity without consequences to Richardson. "Don't take this wrong, but why are you still alive?" Welsh asked.

"Let's say I managed to convince them that I didn't know what Richardson was doing. I just introduced them, took my commission, and that was that."

"And they bought it?" Welsh exclaimed. "That's a little hard to swallow."

"They didn't buy it. But maybe they made a mistake in hitting Richardson so fast. They don't have the tapes, and nobody's shown up trying to sell them yet. If Richardson had an accomplice, it's me. So they keep an eye on me and make sure I don't get out of Guatemala City. They figure sooner or later I'm going to have to make a deal with them."

"You're lucky they haven't blowtorched you."

"They call it the *capucha*. They stick a latex rubber hood over your head and tighten a string around the neck of the hood to shut off your air. They would have done it, no regrets at all, except they don't know how many copies of the tapes there are, and how many friends I have. I disappear, and someone might mail a package to the FBI. So what we've got is a kind of a Mexican stand-off. Except in Guatemala!" Booker cackled.

Tough talk, thought Welsh, but those shaking hands gave him away. Booker was probably lighting candles every day, praying the Guatemalans didn't run out of patience.

"Your story is great," said Welsh. "But let's break down the cast of characters. 'Guats' is a little too inclusive. I've already met Lieutenant Colonel Armando Gutierrez, the star of your teaser tape."

"He's the man in charge," said Booker. "They're a bunch of military intelligence types. They work for the government, but they also work for themselves, if you know what I mean."

"Making sure their retirement plans are fully funded in case they get canned by the new government?"

"That's it exactly. Damn, you're one smart guy, Rich."

"Yeah, right. Now, about the American on Scanlan's tape. The one whose voice you electronically disguised to tease me."

Booker stopped and gave that some thought, as if he wasn't sure he wanted to answer. But he gave it up. "CIA guy. Getting a little worried about the Company hanging him out to dry, blaming him for all the things that went on down here. Maybe that made him get a little closer to Gutierrez and his boys than he would've otherwise."

"I'm still waiting to hear a name."

"The Chief of Station himself."

"Thomas Kohl," said Welsh. It was just like a brick dropping onto his head.

"Very good, Rich."

Just then something dawned on Welsh, which he thought he'd better address. "Back to the teaser tape. Richardson didn't hear it, did he? The bugs transmitted to a central base station with a bank of tape recorders— an apartment somewhere in town. You picked up the tapes, and Richardson walked into the ambush."

"Didn't happen like that," Booker said, too fast and too nervous for credibility. "You're right about the base station. I closed it out and got rid of the equipment *after* the kid got killed. When I heard the tape for the first time, he was already dead. Nothing I could do."

"Whatever," said Welsh, not believing a word of it. "Just don't think you can play me like that. Before *I* go over the falls I'll get your name out, and you'll be right behind me."

Booker smiled grimly and massaged his stomach with both hands. "And I can't even threaten you back. One whisper that we'd met and you'd be out of the country by the time they finished working me over. I'm screwed, Rich. You got me right by the balls. It's you or nothing."

"Yeah, and they wouldn't kill *me* if they found out I'd talked to you. Can't threaten me back, huh?"

"Well, maybe just a little. Can we make a deal now?"

"What do you want?"

Booker hunched over and dropped his voice to a conspiratorial whisper. "Keeping everything real quiet, your Senator sends the FBI down here. They put me on a plane back to the States. No DEA, no Customs, and absolutely no CIA. And not a word to the Guatemalans." Booker drew back and smiled triumphantly, as if the deal was already done.

"That's it?"

"That's it. He wants me to testify, I'll testify. Of course, I'll have to have immunity—and a spot in the witness protection program."

No money, thought Welsh. Or not enough to mention right then. Booker probably had enough salted away. He just needed a way out and a new identity. "If the tapes are as good as you say, I don't see a problem."

"Being honest again, Rich, I'm afraid if I give you the stuff you'll go back home and—no fault of your own, you understand—the people there will enjoy listening to it and then forget all about me."

"There's no way I could persuade anyone to make a deal without it," Welsh said flatly. "Being honest again, Tom. Bring just your word and that story back to Washington with me? People would say you're in trouble down here, and you'll promise anything to save your ass."

"Now, Rich, I'm really going to have to think about that."

"Do it quick," Welsh said coldly. "We're not having any more face-to-face meetings in Guatemala. Give me the tapes and I'll get you out of here. Don't, and I walk off this roof, catch the next plane home, and forget I ever met you. Oh, and I want the original tapes. Nothing edited or altered. No more teasers. That's the deal."

"Not like I got a lot of choice," Booker grumbled. "Okay, Rich, it's a deal. But there's just one little problem."

"What?" Welsh said in exasperation.

"I can't get you the tapes. You're going to have to get them."

"What?" Welsh repeated in a much harsher tone.

"The Guats are on me too tight. I stashed the tapes, but now I can't get to them."

"Where are they?"

"The Army base at Santa Elena."

"Why the fuck did you put them there?"

"Couldn't stash 'em on my ranch. Couldn't even travel around with 'em to hide 'em anyplace good. Put 'em there right before Gutierrez told me he wanted to see me in Guatemala City. I figured they'd never think to look right under their noses. Haven't been back since."

And couldn't trust anyone else to go get it. The worst part of it, from Welsh's point of view, was that Booker had to be telling the truth. Any plot to kill him could be arranged just as easily for Guatemala City as Santa Elena. Oh, it was an easy investigation. He didn't have to dig anything up, just rap with people and lay back while they dropped hand grenades in his lap. "Are all the tapes hidden there?"

"There's hundreds of tapes," said Booker. "This is the greatest-hits collection."

"Where exactly on the Army base."

Booker told him.

"And you figured a Senator's aide would be the perfect gringo to get on the base without a lot of heartburn?"

Booker only shrugged again and lit his fifth cigarette. Some of his old cool was back, though his hands still shook. "What do you say, Rich, we got a deal?"

"Yes," said Welsh. "But I still have to get to Santa Elena, get the stuff, and get out of the country alive."

"I know you'll fox 'em, Rich."

"You got a cell phone number? One that you're going to have for a while?"

Booker nodded, and told him the number. Welsh memorized it. "Someone will call you and ask for Mr. Martinez. You tell him he's got the wrong number, hang up, and get your ass down here to this building. The FBI will pick you up either in front or in the lobby."

Booker held out his hand. "I know you'll do it, Rich."

Welsh ignored it. "Does Scanlan know any of this?"

"No way. My business with her is private; my business with you is private. You be damn careful who you tell this to, especially in Washington. I already know you don't put nothing on paper. Drove the Guats crazy when they tossed your room. Matter of fact, why don't you relieve Maggie on stair watch. I've got to thank her before you go."

Welsh liked that about as much as Scanlan had. His last words to Booker were: "Don't fuck anything up until I'm out of the country." He walked over to Scanlan. "He wants to talk to you."

"About time," she said.

She came back over a couple of minutes later. "What did he tell you?" she asked.

But Welsh was already halfway down the stairs. "Let's get the hell out of here first."

Chapter Seventeen

On the bus back to the parking lot, Margaret Scanlan said, "What did you think of—?"

Welsh had cut her off with an upraised hand. "We don't want to mention that name again. But to answer your question, not much. I've met some real amoral scumbags in my time, but I think he just shot to the top of the list."

"He is a creep, isn't he? And what makes it worse is that he thinks he's the most normal and reasonable guy around." She paused for a moment. "So what did he tell you?"

Welsh just smiled and gazed out the window.

"You still don't trust me, do you?" Scanlan said.

"No," Welsh replied, still pleasantly. "What did he have to tell *you*?"

Now it was Scanlan's turn to smile and say nothing.

"See?" said Welsh. He offered her his hand. "No hard feelings?"

Scanlan took it and gave it an exaggerated shake. "No hard feelings."

"Anyway," said Welsh, "that was very interesting, especially since it seems we've survived it. I hope you got what you wanted in exchange for putting us together."

"I hope I did too," she replied.

"Nicely enigmatic," Welsh complimented her. "How about lunch at my hotel, instead of just dropping me off?"

"Okay."

All right, Welsh thought.

They retrieved Scanlan's car from the parking lot, and Welsh braced himself for the ride back to the hotel.

They hadn't gone a block when two marked police cars with lights flashing showed up.

"Maybe I spoke too soon," said Welsh.

"Do you think they know where we were?" Scanlan asked, her head darting back and forth from the road ahead to the rearview mirror.

"No. This is how they react to not knowing."

"What do you want to do?"

"Nothing we can do but pull over and keep our mouths shut, no matter what happens. They've been told what to do. Don't give them any excuse to exceed their orders."

Scanlan pulled over, and the two police cars pinned them in front and back. The policemen sat immobile in their vehicles. Welsh knew they were trying to make him nervous, and it was really working beautifully. He could feel the pulse pounding in his throat.

Guatemala's police were brutal and corrupt, as were many of their counterparts all over Latin America, and for many of the same reasons. They had so little training that reporting a crime to the police and expecting them to solve it was almost an act of eccentricity. They were so underpaid that choosing not to be corrupt was to literally risk their family's well-being. They were authority in a country where brutality and authority had come to have the same meaning.

Being a cop in Guatemala was having a license to do almost anything you wanted. They kept the population of street kids down by taking them out to the jungle and shooting them. Three officers of the anti-kidnap squad formed to combat the brutal rings plaguing the capital had recently been arrested on a charge of kidnapping.

Four policemen finally walked slowly up to the car. They were dressed in the khaki drill of the new, allegedly revamped police force. All were wearing mirrored sunglasses, and two carried Uzi submachine guns.

"Keep your hands on the wheel," Welsh murmured. Even if the cops didn't intend to use them, automatic weapons being brandished just increased the chance of a stupid accident.

A sergeant, obviously in charge, came up to the open passenger's window. He had a round, pockmarked Indian face that appeared indifferent to everything. The brim of his cap was pulled all the way down to the sunglasses. He slowly looked Welsh over, then said, "Out."

Welsh obeyed, very carefully. They didn't put their hands on him, but the submachine guns probably had something to do with backing him up against the side of the car. He heard Scanlan's door open, but didn't want to take his eyes off the sergeant. One of them gave Welsh a hard, thorough frisk. He was glad he'd destroyed Scanlan's tape right after listening to it. Sometimes paranoia was healthy.

Two of the cops began searching the vehicle, while the one who'd done the frisk kept his Uzi aimed at Welsh's belly. The sergeant did all the talking. "Papers," he said.

Welsh noticed that the Uzi selector switch was all the

way forward to full-auto, and the cop's finger was curled around the trigger. One twitch and there would be five or six 9mm slugs in his guts, just another tragic weapons-handling accident. Welsh knew tensing up his stomach muscles wouldn't do any good, but he couldn't help it. He brought his wallet out very slowly, and the sergeant examined the passport and driver's license with great deliberation.

He paid particular interest to the letter from the Minister of the Interior, requesting all police agencies to extend Mr. Welsh, aide to a United States Senator, the utmost courtesy and cooperation. The sergeant read the letter carefully, mouthing the words. Then he raised his head so Welsh could see himself in the sunglasses and methodically ripped the letter into small pieces, letting them fall to the ground. "Get out of Guatemala," he said. "Gringo son of a bitch. You'll end up dead."

The other cops were waiting for the sergeant to give them a cue. But the sergeant was finished talking. Welsh had no questions.

When the cops drove off, Welsh slumped back against the car door and let out a deep breath. He looked back over his shoulder, and Scanlan was in the identical position. "You okay?" he asked.

"Yeah."

They got back in the car. The contents of Scanlan's bag and the glove compartment were scattered all over the inside. The seat cushions had been slashed open.

Scanlan sat staring through the windshield.

"You okay?" Welsh asked again.

She nodded.

"What did they do?" Welsh demanded.

"Felt me up a little," she said tonelessly.

Welsh felt his fists clenching. "Want me to drive?"

"No." Scanlan started the car and pulled into traffic.

She didn't say a word until they got to the hotel. Then: "I'm sorry, but I don't feel like lunch now."

"I understand."

"You're getting out of town, aren't you?"

Welsh nodded. "Seems like a good time for it. You?"

"I don't know yet," she said slowly. "But I am appreciating what you've been trying to teach me. It goes against my basic personality, but I appreciate it now."

"Most people like us, this kind of thing has no relation to anything in their experience. So they either don't deal with it the right way, or they don't deal with it at all." Welsh paused. "I admire your courage."

"But I'm still making a mistake in pursuing this."

"Who am *I* to say?"

Scanlan sighed. "Well. Thank you for your help."

"I don't think I was that much help to you." Welsh passed her a card. "Office, fax, e-mail. And my home phone number. Call on me if you need me."

"Thanks again." Scanlan threw her arms around Welsh's neck and hugged him tightly.

She released him before he could reciprocate. Then they both stared at each other with some embarrassment. Not knowing what else to do or say, Welsh got out of the car.

Scanlan waved and drove off.

Welsh stood in front of the hotel entrance and shook his head. Not a clue. Anyone who thought they knew what was going on in another human mind was a fool.

162

Chapter Eighteen

"You're traveling to *where*?" said Alonso.

"Santa Elena," Welsh repeated.

"Why?"

"I don't figure I'm going to get any more trips down here on Uncle Sam's dollar," said Welsh. "And I'm sure as shit not going to come back on my vacation time. So before I go, I thought I ought to see the Mayan ruins at Tikal."

"Investigation is over then?"

"Yeah, I'm done," said Welsh.

"Find out anything?"

"Just like I told you at the beginning. Jack shit."

"Too bad. You said you wanted some maps?"

"Yeah, have you got any good Defense Mapping Agency topograhics of the Petén region?"

"Sure, you want large or small scale?"

"If you've got it, 1:50,000 scale would be great. The

infantry platoon commander's disease; I can't be in the woods without a map in my hand."

"Make sure you get on a tour group, though," Alonso warned.

"Is that a State Department travelers' advisory?" Welsh asked with a smile.

"Damn right," said Alonso. He had his back to Welsh as he rummaged through a file cabinet for the maps. "One thing about peace. It means there's a lot of fighting men on both sides who don't have jobs anymore, but still have weapons. There's an epidemic of highway banditry all over the country. They love setting up roadblocks and hijacking tourists in the Petén. If you're going to Tikal, hook up with a tour agency. They run buses with security guards. The better hotels down there will arrange it for you. Whatever you do, don't rent a jeep and drive yourself, and stay away from the fly-by-night tour vans at the airport. Oh, and fly Aviateca, they use jets. Otherwise you might find yourself on some turboprop held together with duct tape and chewing gum." He handed Welsh a pile of maps. "Here you go."

"Thanks," said Welsh. "And I really appreciate all the travel advice."

"Tikal's an amazing place," said Alonso. "Reminds you that there was a real civilization here once."

"As opposed to now?"

"I've probably been here too long," Alonso admitted.

Chapter Nineteen

Welsh had made no reservations, and purchased his ticket at the Guatemala City airport just before the regular 7:00 A.M. flight departed. Even so, when he exited the 737 at Santa Elena, two Guatemalan Army officers were waiting to greet him.

A major and a captain. They weren't holding up a piece of cardboard that said, "Rich Welsh," yet there they were blocking his way.

Welsh stopped, dropped his bags, and waited to take his medicine, not that there was any other option open to him.

"Welcome, Mr. Welsh," the major said in perfect English. "I am Major Esteban, representing Colonel Mendes, commander of the Santa Elena garrison. This is Captain Garcia. We are at your service."

After shaking hands all around, it seemed polite to reply in his much less perfect Spanish. "Thank you very much, gentlemen. I am honored to make your acquaintance."

"Colonel Mendes would be honored if you would accept his hospitality for the duration of your visit," the major said. "Quarters on our base have been prepared for you."

Well, that would get him on base, but also put him under their thumb. "Thank you, Major, but I will only be here for a day or two, and I have already made hotel reservations. I plan to visit Tikal before I fly home."

"And you will enjoy it," the major replied. "But you must join the officers of the garrison for dinner tonight."

"It would be my privilege," Welsh said quickly.

"Excellent," said the major. "Now, may I offer you transportation?"

Another driver to keep an eye on him, thought Welsh. "I have a rental car waiting," he said.

That exhausted the major's resources, so after firming up the time and directions to dinner, he and the captain took their leave.

Then Welsh had to deal with a rental clerk in a state of high nervous agitation. His Yankee client was obviously friendly with high-ranking soldiers; the Petén region of northeast Guatemala was still frontier country, and soldiers ran the show there. When Welsh asked him to make sure the Suzuki jeep was equipped with a winch, as requested, the poor man actually ran outside to check, leaving Welsh standing at the counter wondering where the hell he'd gone.

Welsh's hotel was a just a short drive from the airport, right on the eastern edge of Santa Elena. And that was a lakeshore town of unpaved streets that left the air filled with dust—whenever it wasn't raining. Drainage ditches lined the sides of the roads to handle the rain and sewage runoff. The lake was Petén Itzá. Five hundred yards into the lake, connected by a causeway and built on an island, was the departmental capital of Flores, a smaller but less ramshackle town than Santa Elena.

Welsh picked up his tail as soon as he left the airport. They were a little less high-tech out in the sticks; not that there was a lot of traffic, or even a lot of streets, to lose a tail in.

The hotel was concrete and stucco; thirty-six rooms, a pool, and a restaurant. It was across the street from a cemetery, but had air-conditioning, not all that common among the area inns. But needed; it was much warmer and more humid at four hundred feet of elevation than in the five-thousand-foot mountain air of Guatemala City.

The room was a little musty, but Welsh jacked up the air and stood in front of the vent, flapping the bottom of his polo shirt to cool himself off. There was a private bathroom with a shower, a TV, and even a minibar. But the first priority was shopping for some necessities in town.

He jiggled the handle to make sure his door was locked, turned to his left, and ran right into Margaret Scanlan going into her room two doors down.

Welsh was so shocked that he failed to find the power of speech for a second or two. Then, like some kind of involuntary reaction, he blurted out, "What the fuck are you doing here?"

"My sister-in-law still lives near El Remate," she said levelly. "What the fuck are *you* doing here?"

"Wanted to see Tikal before I left," said Welsh—he thought convincingly.

Her expression was plainly disbelieving.

"Your sister-in-law is in El Remate," Welsh went on, as if he was confused, "but why are you staying *here*?"

"I'm going to do some shopping for her before I drive to the farm tomorrow."

It was a standoff. Neither bought the other's story, but

if they called each other on it, they'd have to do some unwanted explaining.

"I'm also on my way to do some shopping," said Welsh. "Want to carpool?"

"No, thanks, but are you free for dinner?"

"The first time you make the offer, and I have to decline," he said regretfully. "I'm already committed."

"Oh, anyone interesting?"

"The officers of the Santa Elena garrison."

That turned her face to stone. "Have fun."

"It wasn't my idea; it won't be fun, but I still have to go."

Scanlan gave him an ironic little look. "Well, if I don't see you, have a good time at Tikal." She stepped inside her room and closed the door.

Damn, Welsh thought. Her being there could really screw things up.

Chapter Twenty

Though Welsh hadn't expected to, the former Marine Corps officer found the dinner that night more familiar than not.

Besides the stuffy formality of no one wanting to do anything to annoy a commanding officer, there was the same clannishness. All the Guatemalan officers of the same units sticking together in their tight little groups.

Welsh could even recognize the pathology of a defeated army. Years before in the officers' club at Camp Lejeune, only wanting to drink a few beers and eat the Happy Hour munchies, he and a few fellow lieutenants had instead been compelled to listen to a Marine colonel give a twenty-minute extemporaneous oration on how the U.S. military had not lost the Vietnam War. Probably the same "the politicians stabbed us in the back" talk that a German Reichwehr colonel had given to a bunch of junior officers around 1932. And with the honest cruelty of youth, one of the fellow lieutenants had leaned over to Welsh and whispered, "If we didn't lose, how come they changed the name from Saigon to Ho Chi Minh City?" The Guatemalans felt they'd whipped the guerrillas to a standstill, and it was a serious humiliation to see the bastards not only walking the streets openly, but even running for office.

War had had made the Guatemalan officer corps feel indispensable. At a public symposium in 1987, they had all but told the country's leading landowners and businessmen that the rules of the game had changed: They were no longer the leg-breakers of the ruling classes but an equal partner in power. But they hadn't given much thought to the prospect of peace. Now they were just redundant public employees—the number of active-duty generals had been cut from twenty-three to eight. Welsh had been part of the post-Vietnam, pre-Desert Storm military, when no one even thought about wearing the uniform out in public.

He had no sympathy for them, not by any means, but recognized what made them tick. The feeling that they were protecting civilization from an enemy that was the "other." None of these officers were Indian, and it was always easier to wage war the way they did if you were convinced your enemies weren't quite human.

More than any reading, his tour in Lebanon had opened Welsh's eyes to the fact that war the way armies like Guatemala's waged it was the rule rather than the exception. If torturing and killing captives, destroying the enemy's homes and crops, and raping their women wasn't some dark instinctive part of human nature, then it wouldn't be such a bloody constant in the history of the species.

Welsh also followed his experience in not hanging around long after dinner. The tighter these events started, the looser they ended up. The alcohol flowed, inhibitions loosened, and some hot-blooded young stud who held the United States responsible for the current state of affairs might decide that the best way to articulate his frustrations would be to tee off on the only gringo present.

When he went over to take his leave, Welsh discovered that Colonel Mendes was already three sheets to the wind.

"No, you cannot leave!" the colonel protested.

"I have a very early day tomorrow," Welsh said regretfully.

Colonel Mendes threw his arms around him. "My friend," he said, his voice filled with drunken emotion, "how good of you to join us."

"I will not forget your hospitality," said Welsh, still stiffly wrapped up in the embrace. What the hell, it didn't sound as bad in Spanish. Someone better do something or they'd be tongue-kissing in a minute, he thought.

Welsh finally awkwardly patted the colonel on the back, and in the process managed to push himself away without objection.

He shook hands all the way out, and at the door heard. "Mr. Welsh, are you ready?"

"As I said before, call me Rich." Sometimes, at events like this, the duty officer had dinner and then went back to work. It wasn't hard to find the lieutenant, since they were the only two not drinking, and offer him a lift back to the headquarters building.

"Okay, Rich." The lieutenant was eager to practice his English. He spoke the following words one at a time, and very carefully: "Your speech was very good."

They crossed the parking lot and got into Welsh's jeep.

"Thanks," said Welsh. Called on to make a toast, he'd given the obligatory speech on the solidarity of men at arms. Strictly bullshit, and he'd received the usual bullshit round of applause in acknowledgement.

171

"Perhaps one day your Senator will visit us to discover the truth about Guatemala for himself?" Whenever the lieutenant became stumped for a word, he lapsed into Spanish.

"Perhaps." Welsh didn't have the heart to tell the kid that Senators generally restricted their taxpayer-funded fact-finding trips to areas vital to the national interest, like Paris, Hong Kong, or Tahiti.

Welsh stopped the jeep in front of the headquarters building. "Would it be all right if I came in and used the bathroom?"

"Of course."

The duty sergeant was hunched in front of a portable TV, totally engrossed in *Baywatch,* the world's most popular program. It was dubbed into Spanish, but the language of spandex bathing suits and bouncing breasts was universal. The lieutenant waited a bit, then cleared his throat. The sergeant sprang to attention.

The lieutenant let him stay there for a few moments, then said curtly, "Carry on."

"Your pardon," said Welsh.

The lieutenant pointed down the hall. "Go to the end there, turn left. On the left side."

"Many thanks." Welsh set off down the hall. The building was nearly deserted.

"It's hidden in the storage room right next to the men's shitter on the first floor," Booker said. *"It's the only one on that floor."*

Welsh turned the corner and found the bathroom. He tried the door to the storage room, and let out his breath in relief that it was unlocked. He slipped inside and closed the door as quietly as he could. The light was a naked bulb on a chain.

Pails, mops, and brooms stood in neat formation. One wall was filled with shelves of cleaning supplies. It was a suspended ceiling: fiber panels on metal tracks.

"Above the panel in the left rear corner of the room," Booker said. *"There's a big cast-iron pipe."*

Welsh pushed up on the panel. There was the pipe. He slid the panel aside and felt around. There was nothing there. Goddamn it.

"The stuff's in a box," Booker said, *"attached to the pipe."*

The pipe ran upward, and Welsh couldn't reach around it. He looked around and grabbed a metal pail, turning it upside down and stepping up very gingerly so it didn't scrape on the floor.

With the extra foot the pail gave him, he could slide his hand around the bend in the pipe. It hit something that didn't belong there. It was metal, and yielded slightly when he tugged it. A harder yank, and the box not only came off, but hit the pipe with a distressingly loud gonging noise. Welsh froze, then brought the box down gently.

It was an olive-drab metal ammunition can. A small one, about ten by seven by three inches, the kind 7.62mm machine gun ammo came in. They were tough, handy, and waterproof. The can had been attached to the pipe with four dime-store magnets. It was definitely not the time and place to open it. Welsh set the can down on the floor, then went back up and felt around some more. Nothing else in there.

He replaced the ceiling panel and put the pail back. Before opening the door he pressed an ear to the floor. There were footsteps coming down the hall. Welsh turned out the light and took a step back so he'd be behind the door if anyone opened it.

The clicking sound of leather soles on linoleum floor grew louder. Welsh concentrated on breathing quietly. His neck began to itch furiously, but he ignored it. The footsteps slowed. Standing motionless was giving him the feeling of involuntarily wobbling back and forth. Just a little vertigo, he told himself. Take it easy.

A loud boom echoed in the room. Welsh nearly crapped himself before realizing it was only the bathroom door slamming shut one thin wall away. He took a deep breath.

A toilet flushed loudly. Water ran in a sink. Welsh was so wired he heard the paper towel being ripped from the dispenser.

The door, pulled open, only squeaked this time. The footsteps trailed off down the hall. Welsh prayed it hadn't been the lieutenant or sergeant. After the last sound of steps, he waited a minute that stretched on and on. Peeking suspiciously around the door wouldn't be very bright. He walked out and darted into the bathroom, the ammo can tucked in his armpit under the suit jacket.

He checked, but there was no one in there. The bathroom was on a wall with an outside window. Welsh held the ammo can between his legs and quickly opened the window. It rattled and squeaked all the way up. Then there was a screen, painted shut.

Welsh unfolded his Swiss army knife and sliced the lower corner of the screen right against the wood frame. He peeled the screen back and took a look out. No one around. Then, grabbing the ammo can, he stuck his arm through the hole up to his shoulder to reduce the distance it would have to drop, and cringing slightly, let it go. It hit the grass with what seemed to be a very loud clank.

Welsh pulled the screen back into place and shut the window. He had to use the bathroom for real now, but he didn't want the can sitting out there too long.

He passed the duty desk with a casual wave and headed for the door. The duty officer shouted, "Rich! Rich!"

Welsh's stomach flipped over. He forced a smile onto his face before he swung around. Both the duty officer and the sergeant were leaning over the desk and motioning for him to come back. Welsh made his legs move. "Yes?" he said.

"Rich," the lieutenant said. "Before you leave, I must ask you a question. You have been to California, yes?"

Welsh felt as if he was having an out-of-body experience. "Yes, of course."

"Are there really women there," the captain asked, gesturing toward the TV, "who look like that?"

Welsh blinked his eyes twice to steady himself. That always worked with Marie back in the office in D.C. "In Los Angeles?" he replied. "Yes, they are everywhere. The most beautiful women in the world come to Los Angeles, to be on shows like that."

"Mother of God," breathed the sergeant.

Welsh hoped he hadn't done the wrong thing. From the look of the sergeant, he'd probably be striking out for the border before morning.

The lieutenant shook his head wistfully and gave Welsh a firm farewell handshake.

Welsh thought things over outside. The question was: foot or vehicle? He had to figure he was being watched. He climbed into the jeep and gunned it around to the back of the building. He jumped out, ran over to the bathroom window, snatched up the ammo can, tucked it under his jacket, sprinted back to the jeep, and was away.

As soon as he left the base a pair of headlights popped up behind him and stayed there all the way to the hotel.

Welsh locked his door, drew the blinds, and opened the ammo can. The rubber gaskets on the lid were very sticky.

Booker had done a good job. The can was lined with a heavy plastic bag and held packs of audio cassette tapes. No papers, nothing else but Styrofoam padding and bags of silica gel desiccant to absorb moisture.

Welsh repacked the can, closed it, and secured it inside his day pack.

His first impulse was to hop back in the jeep and blow town immediately. But he remembered Alonso's warnings about bandits on the road. It wasn't the country for a long night drive through the jungle.

Better to get a little sleep, and just before first light get on the highway west. Instead of branching north to the Maya ruins of Tikal, his cover story, keep going straight to Belize. With a little luck, a three-to-four-hour drive and he'd be across the border and home free.

Chapter Twenty-one

The noise brought Welsh off his pillow and up on one elbow to listen, but it was dead quiet. He almost went back to sleep. Then he heard it again. The subtle scraping of a key being inserted into the lock of his door.

He leaped out of bed. The door handle turned, and there was a muted jingling as the security chain came taut. A bent wire would be put through next to slip off the chain.

They were coming to kill him. Welsh was shot through with a bolt of pure animal terror. The body under great stress draws large amounts of blood inward to protect its core. Welsh's chest felt frozen, and his limbs were so heavy he literally could not move them. He couldn't even get any air to breathe.

He thought he was paralyzed, but his head was actually jerking back and forth: instinctively searching for the hole, the tree, any place to run, to just stop thinking and blindly run for.

He was almost lost to it when the bright clear thought punched through the panic that if he didn't want to die, he would have to save himself.

Fear is both emotional and chemical. Welsh fought it down with something even more powerful—anger. Standing at the foot of the bed, he clenched his fists and tensed all his muscles to force the blood back into them, channeling it into a pure rage at whoever was coming through that door.

The chain slid off and clinked against the door as it fell. The sliver of moonlight shining through the drapes allowed Welsh to see the inside of the room. A quick visual search for available weapons told him there was nothing he could get his hands on without making a life-ending noise.

The windows were to his right, the door to the adjoining room and the dresser were in front, and the narrow alcove leading out to his left. The bathroom was set in the alcove on the left-hand side, and the little open clothes closet a little farther down next to the door.

Welsh heard the door open, but no light came into the room. They must have disabled the fixtures outside.

He could think clearly now, and instantly decided on the only possible course of action. He stuffed both pillows under the sheet to approximate his form, then crept across the room and pressed his back to the wall at the corner where it angled into the alcove. He was wearing only nylon running shorts, not the most ideal combat dress. The door opened slowly; that meant they weren't coming hard and fast. Good. The door closed, and he knew they were in.

The bathroom door opened quietly, and someone went inside. Welsh was puzzled when he didn't see even the beam of a flashlight. Another set of footsteps advanced very slowly down the alcove. So there were at least two of them.

All Welsh had any hope of was to go down fighting. He was still shaking slightly, but the fear had coalesced into a murderous fury. He slid slowly and silently into a slight crouch to prepare himself.

The one coming down the alcove had almost reached him. They were only feet apart, separated by the corner. Welsh held his breath. *Don't hesitate, you fucker. Don't get suspicious. And don't wait for your friend.*

When Welsh saw the cylindrical end of what he immediately recognized as a sound suppressor slowly emerge from the alcove, he knew his opponent was about to make a mistake. Then more of the suppressor appeared. It was only a foot or so from Welsh's face; the man was staying close to the wall. Only the corner separated them. The guy was leading with his weapon, Welsh thought. Both hands were on that pistol, arms fully extended in a good tight firing position. And that was how he was creeping along, with that pistol way out in front of him. Wait, he told himself. Don't set yourself; don't shuffle and make noise getting ready. Don't move before you move.

Now the front sight of the pistol was visible. Welsh could hear the man's breath. He was still holding his. Just a little more.

Welsh drove himself forward. Both his outstretched hands grabbed the pistol. With all his strength he yanked the pistol back toward him, twisted at the waist, and drove his left shoulder forward into his enemy's wrists.

The nearest forearm broke like green wood against Welsh's upper arm. The man screamed, dropped the pistol, but Welsh lost hold of it too. Welsh violently shoved the man out of the way, and was startled by the sight of his face in the darkness.

Welsh bent over to try to recover the pistol. He heard a soft dry snap at the other end of the alcove, at the same time he felt the air pressure of a bullet pass by his hair. It was the other one. Welsh moved so fast it had to be instinct. He sprang across the alcove and hit the light switch.

The lights came on, and the shooter down the alcove shouted and threw his hands up to his face. Welsh picked up the pistol. It was an automatic, and he couldn't count on a round being in the chamber. He held the pistol sideways close to his chest, grabbed the slide with his left hand, and pushed the entire weapon forward with his right. A cartridge ejected, and he had the pistol on target as the slide snapped home.

It would be only too easy to miss. Welsh held the sights tight on the shooter's chest and fired deliberately. Nothing seemed to be happening; then the shooter suddenly folded at the waist and dropped to the floor. Welsh only stopped firing when the man hit the carpet and lay motionless. He had no idea how many rounds he'd fired or how many were fired at him, though he'd felt a few go by.

Then something crashed into his ankles and Welsh went down. It was the other one; the man had tackled him even with a broken arm. Welsh didn't fight it; he let himself fall backward, concentrating on holding onto the pistol and keeping his elbows tight against his body. He landed on his back, and the man lunged at him, reaching for the pistol. Welsh did a half sit-up off the carpet and shot the man in the face. He collapsed onto Welsh's legs. Welsh fired once again, point-blank into the top of the head directly in front of him. He was splattered with something wet and solid, and the grotesque sensation spurred him to furiously kick away the heavy limp body and struggle to his feet.

Welsh refused to repeat the mistake of fixing his attention on one adversary when there was another around. He took five quick steps forward, like marching in a dream, until he was standing in front of the other shooter. The man was slumped sideways against the door with his head down and his arms in his lap, and now Welsh could see the blood and the dark grouping of bullet holes in the center of his chest. He didn't know if the man was dead, but shot him twice more in the head to make sure of it.

Welsh stood motionless, breathing hard, the pistol clasped in both hands. Suddenly he had the idea that he should lock the door. He leaned over the body and then remembered that the door locked automatically when it closed. He slid the chain on anyway.

The room reeked of burned gunpowder and shit, the latter released by the two killers in extremis. Welsh was sure of that because he'd checked himself first.

He had to get moving. Still holding the pistol, he took a fast shower. That decision was first made irrationally, but when the cold water hit his face he realized it was the right one. He couldn't go walking around in public with blood and brains all over him. Then he got dressed with a speed acquired at Officer Candidate School. The day pack was all ready to go. Welsh looked at his watch for the first time: it was 1:06 A.M.

Then he took his first close look at the pistol. It was not only U.S. military-issue, but U.S. military-special-operations-issue. A Beretta 92F 9mm automatic, the M-9 in U.S. nomenclature, equipped with a Knight's Armament Company snap-on sound suppressor, an aircraft aluminum tube only five and a half inches long and weighing six ounces. Since the suppressor obscured the pistol's sights, there were front and rear sights mounted on top of the tube.

Welsh flicked the safety on and off to decock the hammer. Then he removed the magazine, furious with himself for not checking it before. There were only six rounds left, out of a possible fifteen in the magazine and one in the chamber. He'd fired more than he thought.

The ammunition was subsonic, which was why he'd felt rather than heard all those near-misses.

Mounted to the pistol frame beneath the barrel was a Sure-Fire 1 laser sight. It resembled a small flashlight, and projected an intense beam of laser light as an aiming point. This particular model operated in the infrared spectrum, so the laser spot would only be visible through the night-vision goggles each of the killers was wearing.

Welsh had seen the goggles when he'd pushed the first man away from him, and his experience with them in the Marine Corps accounted for what he'd done next. The goggles electronically magnified low levels of light such as stars, the moon, or infrared sources. But any bright light was also magnified. When he'd hit the alcove lights the blinding flash in the shooter's goggles had given Welsh enough time to pick up the pistol and fire.

Over-reliance on technology had turned unexpectedly lethal for them. As far as Welsh was concerned, a laser sight was just another complex piece of gear that could let you down in a tight spot. And the laser dot was a dangerous crutch; you ended up concentrating on it rather than the good shooting technique that was the only way to hit what you were aiming at.

"Should have used a flashlight, come in fast, and learned how to shoot," Welsh said aloud to the two dead men. He removed the laser sight and pressure-pad on/off switch from the pistol and tossed them away.

Having put it off long enough, he searched the corpses. The carpet was sticky with blood, and several times Welsh had to choke down bile at the sight of the damage he'd done.

The one piled up against the door had a small Motorola walkie-talkie radio stuck in his back pocket. It was turned off so an unexpected call wouldn't give them away. A radio meant there were others backing them up, inside the hotel or outside. Or both. Faster, Welsh told himself. You're wasting time. They'll get worried and the backup will come crashing into the room. Move fast, but don't move before thinking about it first, he reminded himself.

They had no wallets or ID, but each carried five hundred dollars in U.S. currency, hundred-dollar bills. Welsh was flattered. He'd heard you could get it done for a hell of a lot less in Guatemala. He stuck the money in his pocket. Their only other possessions were two hotel room keys, a folding-blade hunting knife, and two extra magazines of ammo each, in double-pocket leather belt pouches. They'd carried their pistols in leather belt holsters with openings in the bottoms for the suppressors to slide through.

Welsh inserted a fresh magazine into the Beretta that was now his. He removed the magazine from the other Beretta and kept that too; it was three-quarters full. He washed off his hands before threading both magazine pouches and a holster onto his belt, pulling out his shirt-tail to conceal them. He also took one of the knives.

Both men had short haircuts. The pistols were probably more Foreign Military Sales from the U.S. These two were either moonlighting, or had taken up higher-paying work after their hitches ended. In any case, they were second-raters who'd done everything wrong. Other than the terrible hatred that still remained, all Welsh felt was contempt.

As an afterthought, he took a set of the night-vision goggles and tucked them into his day pack. The one at the door had torn his off after being blinded, so they weren't covered with blood. The goggles were AN/PVS-7's, the U.S. military's latest model.

Then Welsh had a sudden inspiration. He took out his little 35mm pocket camera and photographed the two corpses and the room. He just might need proof that everything had happened the way he said it did. The exposed film went into the ammo can to protect it.

Then he sat down on the bed to give a little thought to how he was going to get the hell out of there. But his train of thought was interrupted by a fast series of small-caliber pistol shots. They were muffled but unsuppressed, and sounded as if they were coming from a few doors down. Scanlan's room.

Fuck, Welsh thought. She'd constantly insisted on shifting for her own self; maybe he ought to slide along and let her do just that. But the only trouble with making the easy decision like that was you had to live with it.

"Fuck," Welsh repeated, out loud this time. He unzipped the front pocket of the day pack, removed his Mini Mag-Lite flashlight, and twisted the lens to turn it on. He opened his side of the double door to the adjoining room, and kicked in the other one. The room turned out to be unoccupied, which saved a lot of heartburn. He crossed it, opened the next adjoining door, and put an ear to the second one that led to Scanlan's room. He couldn't hear anything.

Welsh backed across the room to give himself a running start. With the Mini Mag-Lite in his left fist and the pistol in his right, he sprinted across the room and hit the door with his shoulder. It cracked open, and his momentum carried him in. He landed on his right side, his hands crossed and the pistol aimed down the flashlight beam.

Margaret Scanlan was sitting on the bed, dressed only in a bra and panties, listlessly holding a small handgun. She slowly turned toward him.

"Whoa, Maggie, hold it!" Then he noticed that the slide of her pistol was locked back—she'd emptied the magazine. He got to his feet and stuck the flashlight into his pocket. A body was on the floor, a dark-haired male in his underwear, half a dozen bullet holes in his face and head. If he wasn't dead after that, Welsh thought, somebody better have a silver bullet. "Who's this?"

"Colonel Patricio Dominguez."

The guy who'd ordered her brother's death. Major payback. But the story was going to have to wait.

She was still sitting on the bed. Welsh realized she was in shock. He grabbed her by the arm, wrenched her to her feet, and shook her hard. "Get your shit together," he whispered fiercely in her ear.

"I'm all right," Scanlan insisted.

She was still way too sluggish for comfort. Welsh shook her again. "Listen to me. Did you have a plan for what you were going to do after this?"

"N-not really."

"I didn't think so. Get dressed and packed, right now," he ordered curtly. "One bag you can carry easy. Pack toilet gear, extra socks, rain jacket. Wear long pants, long-sleeve shirt, hiking boots if you've got 'em, sneakers if you don't. Leave everything else. We have to move fast, there's probably more of them nearby."

It worked; Scanlan was pulling on her jeans. "Then how are we going to make it out of here?" she asked.

"We're going to have to be smarter than they are," Welsh replied.

Chapter Twenty-two

Scanlan finished dressing. She'd pretty well snapped out of it, but was still moving much too slowly for a very anxious Rich Welsh. She noticed the pistol in his hand for the first time. "Where did you get that gun?"

"From one of the two dead guys in my room."

That stopped her in her tracks, which he didn't want.

"We'll talk about it later," Welsh said urgently.

"All right. What are we doing *now*?"

Welsh looked down at the body on the floor. "I think calling the police is a dead issue."

He hadn't even meant that, but it got her fired up nicely. "You think that's funny?"

"You shot the son of a bitch. Hurry up and finish packing."

Welsh went back to his room to get his day pack. The rest of the luggage was going to have to stay behind. His eyes happened to fall on the walkie-talkie on the bed. It gave him a very good idea. Most people could come to a decision, given enough time. One thing about the Marine Corps, they trained you to do it with no time.

Welsh returned with his pack on his back, carrying a metal wastebasket. Scanlan was ready. She had a travel bag with shoulder straps like a backpack.

"Okay," said Welsh. "If we go out the door or a window right now all we're going to be are two perfect targets. We won't get far on foot at one in the morning; we need a car. So we're going to utilize a little deception."

"Could you be a little more specific?"

"We'll get everyone in the hotel out of their rooms, to stir up a little confusion."

"How are we going to do that at one in the morning?"

"Start a fire."

Considering the situation, she surprised him by saying, "What if someone gets hurt?"

"They won't, and it's better than dying." Welsh quickly told her what he wanted her to do.

They went to the unoccupied middle room. Welsh picked up the phone and called the desk. "Fire!" he shouted in Spanish. "Call the fire department! Fire!" He slammed down the receiver.

They turned out all the lights in the room, and Scanlan stood by the door. Welsh took the walkie-talkie out of his pants pocket and turned it on. He pressed the talk button and rubbed his fingernail back and forth across the speaker while whispering urgently in Spanish, "He escaped, he escaped! Out the back window! On foot, heading east! Running into town!" Welsh released the button.

Scanlan had a look of admiration on her face. "You're a very devious person."

"The scratching makes noise like static, and everyone sounds the same when they whisper."

Voices erupted from the speaker, all fighting to get

through. "What did he say?" "Where did he go?" "The east, you idiot." "Where?" "The east, the east." "Roberto, come in." "What happened in there?" "How did he get away?" "Forget that, you idiot, get after him." "Shut up! Listen! Everyone, head east and cut him off!"

Scanlan shivered. "Well, we know they're around."

"It's going to be a real clusterfuck out there," Welsh said happily. "We'll give them a few seconds to start running in the wrong direction." He opened his bottle of alcohol-based aftershave and emptied it into the wastebasket. The basket was stuffed with a polyester window drape he'd sliced up with his newly acquired knife.

Welsh drew back the slide of the Beretta to be sure there was a round in the chamber. He was okay now. The flip side of terror was adrenaline, and he was riding a pump so powerful it felt like he could rip the door off its hinges. The pistol felt right in his hand. He whispered, "Now!"

Scanlan yanked the door open. Anyone waiting to blow Welsh's head off would look for it to appear at normal height. He squatted down and bobbed it out low, using the doorjamb as cover, searching for targets right and left.

There was no one outside. Welsh was surprised, but the bad guys had done everything else wrong so far. Then he reminded himself that they only had to be lucky once.

Scanlan set the wastebasket down on the concrete walkway and tossed in a complimentary hotel match.

The basket burst into flame, and they were off. They ran in a low crouch down the covered walkway, so they'd be concealed by the bordering shrubbery. As they went by each room they pounded on the door, screaming, "Fire! Get out!" in three different languages. Reaching the protection of an alcove at the corner of the building, they stopped and ducked in.

"God, look at all the smoke," Scanlan said.

"Those man-made fibers are better than a smoke grenade," Welsh replied.

People were beginning to stumble out of their rooms. Welsh couldn't remember ever seeing such a wide range of sleepwear. In particular, there was one admirably endowed lady who had only managed to escape her room in a filmy robe and spike heels. He must have been devoting particular attention to her difficulty, because beside him Scanlan muttered, "Oh, for crying out loud."

The hotel fire alarm went off with an earsplitting howl.

"Bingo," said Welsh. He snapped open a paper bag and slid it over the Beretta to keep from alarming the other guests. He could fire just as easily through the bag.

"Now?" Scanlan asked anxiously.

"Patience. Let the crowd get a little thicker."

Sirens could be heard in the distance.

"Okay," said Welsh. "Go."

They ran toward the parking lot, and by now they were just two of many people running around the hotel grounds. They reached a clump of bushes and Welsh pushed Scanlan down in between them.

"Wait here," he said. "I've got to scope out my jeep. It may take some time to make sure no one's around. Don't get impatient, don't come looking for me, don't stick your head out. Just wait right here until I come back."

"I understand English."

"Super," said Welsh. "Just do what I said."

He made a long, slow circle around the entire parking lot, slipping in and out of the surrounding trees. He didn't see anyone, but found it hard to believe they'd all run off and left the lot unguarded. He sniffed the air but there was no cigarette smoke, always a tip-off. He even took a chance by standing up in the open for a second or two, and didn't attract any undisciplined gunfire.

Then he caught the flare of a match in a car parked on the road just outside the parking lot exit. Welsh worked his way around behind the car and was able to make out two men inside, one holding a walkie-talkie up to his ear.

The fire-engine sirens were getting closer. The whole street would soon be blocked to traffic. A good plan violently executed was always better than a perfect one attempted too late. Welsh was moving so fast now, he barely thought about it.

He held the paper bag across his chest, with his right hand inside it gripping the Beretta. The safety was off, and he kept his finger away from the trigger. Both men in the car had their attention fixed on the parking lot and the fire trucks coming up.

Welsh walked quickly up the dirt road. Running would make too much noise. As he got closer he stayed in line with the driver's-side taillights so he'd be hard to see in the rearview mirrors.

He'd just passed the rear bumper when the driver heard something and stuck his head out the window to look. Welsh extended the paper bag and shot him through the ear. The paper bag blew open, and a stream of blood jetted from the bullet hole. Welsh was even with the window before the passenger could pick up the submachine gun in his lap. Even if Welsh trusted the stopping power of the 9mm round, which he didn't, you didn't shoot someone a couple of times and then stop to see if they could still pick up their weapon and kill you with it. Welsh fired until the man fell back on the door, then leaned in to put one more round in his head.

The driver's head was hanging out the open window. Welsh put his foot on it and pushed the head back in the car. He couldn't do anything about the blood and tissue that had run down the door.

He looked around, but everyone in the vicinity was concentrating on the fire trucks and the building with a pall of smoke hanging over it.

Running back into the parking lot, Welsh slapped a new, full magazine into the Beretta. He came up to the clump of bushes and hissed, "Maggie!"

Scanlan's head appeared between the branches.

"Let's go," said Welsh.

When they reached his jeep he tossed her the keys. "Drive it out the exit. I'll be waiting there."

As he watched the road, hidden beside the car containing two dead men, Welsh suddenly realized that if the Guatemalans had been even moderately thorough and wired a bomb to his jeep, he could shortly expect a very loud explosion. Too late to do anything about that now. He'd gotten her out of the hotel; now it was her turn to put her ass on the line for the team.

But there was no explosion. Scanlan drove up, the jeep shuddering each time she popped the clutch. She saw him, stopped, and slid over to let him take the wheel. "I'm not too great with a stick shift," she explained sheepishly.

"No problem," said Welsh. He pulled out into the road and hooked a hard right to stay away from the fire engines and police that were roaring up.

"Watch behind," he told her. He sped up and took several hard turns. He thought about another homing beeper, then dismissed it. The Guatemalans were there to kill him; they hadn't bothered to screw around with the jeep.

"We're not being followed," Scanlan announced. She sank back in her seat. "I can't believe it, we got away."

"Not yet," Welsh said curtly, keeping his eyes on the road.

"I assume we're going to Belize," she said.

"We are unless you've got any other business."

"No," Scanlan replied. "No other business."

Chapter Twenty-three

Inside five minutes they were past the airport and speeding east on Highway 13. Only two lanes, and narrow, but a hard-surface asphalt highway. There was a hunter's moon, nearly full. Welsh would have liked less light.

There hadn't been much conversation since they'd left the hotel. As they drove along, Welsh first heard a loud gulp. Then, right behind it, Margaret Scanlan said, straining, a word at a time, "Pull . . . over . . . quick."

Welsh whipped the jeep onto the shoulder. The door opened, and there was the sound of vomiting. Welsh had stashed a roll of paper towels behind his seat. He tore off a few sheets and passed them out through the door to her.

While she was busy, Welsh occupied himself in the cargo area of the jeep. He opened the case of bottled water he'd purchased in Santa Elena, and slipped a liter plastic bottle into the mesh pouch on each side of his day pack. Two more bottles went inside, followed by a bag of assorted purchases and his new machete, the handle sticking out the top. He put four more water bottles into her bag, and tossed a couple more into the front seat. By that time she was off her knees, back in the jeep, and getting her breath.

Welsh slid back into the driver's seat, uncapped a bottle, and handed it to her. "Here, rinse your mouth out with this."

She did, then sat back, shut her door, and put on her seat belt. "I'm okay now. Thanks."

Welsh pulled back onto the road.

"Sorry," Scanlan said. "I don't know what happened."

"Pretty common reaction, usually when the action's over. Difference between here and the bar in Guatemala City. Watching violence is exhilarating. Doing violence is sickening. Unless you do it often enough to get used to it. When you feel up to it, I'd like to hear how it went down."

Scanlan sighed and put her head back on the seat rest. "Colonel Dominguez was staying on a ranch to the north of here. Everyone knew where he was, but whenever you asked no one could find him. I couldn't get near there. So the word leaked out that I'd been able to buy some original Army documents, ironclad evidence he ordered my brother's death. The word is also that the high-level people who sold me the documents are ready to sell him out too.

"So, I've got the documents. I fly into Santa Elena. I check into the hotel. Colonel Dominguez dropped by to pay me a visit. He was going to rape me, kill me, and get the documents. I didn't know you were in the hotel, or even in Santa Elena, until I bumped into you. I'm sorry if what happened to you was part of it."

"Where did you get the pistol?"

"It's easier to buy a real gun than a toy one in Guatemala. My dad taught me to shoot."

"I'm curious," said Welsh. "I hadn't shown up, what were you planning to do?"

"Call the police and barricade myself in the room until morning. Then surrender, plead self-defense, and see if I could embarrass both the U.S. and Guatemalan governments for not moving against him when they had the chance."

"Great plan," Welsh said dryly. "They'd throw you in jail during the investigation, and someone would hire one of your fellow inmates to knife you. Or a couple of guards to hang you in your cell. You wouldn't have lasted a day." He paused. "And the word getting out? Was that Booker's quid pro quo for you putting me and him together?"

Scanlan didn't reply to that, which was good enough for Welsh. Instead she said, "What happened in your room?"

"I was asleep. Two guys let themselves into my room, and they ended up dead instead of me."

"Did you have a gun?"

"Used one of theirs."

"After all that, why did you come in to help me?"

"Because you're a woman."

That put a hitch in the rhythm of the conversation. "I beg your pardon?"

"Because you're a woman," Welsh repeated. "The same thing happened that's going to happen if they ever let women into combat units. It's not that women aren't as smart, or tough, or capable of violence as men. It's because men instinctively protect women. It's imprinted on our genes to ensure the future of the species. We do it without thinking . . . as we do most things," he added.

"You mean if I was a man you wouldn't have come crashing into my room?"

"And I knew him as little as I know you? Hell, no, I'd have been a half hour farther down the road, alone."

There was a moment of silence as she digested that. "Thank you for doing it anyway. And for being honest too. Even though I suppose I ought to be offended."

"Why? When I busted into your room, you didn't thank me for my concern and insist on handling the situation yourself. You came along for the ride."

"You can be a bastard, can't you?"

That only made Welsh chuckle out loud. "I very well may be one, but I only seem to get called it by women whenever I speak some truth they didn't enjoy hearing."

"Only women ever called you that?"

"Sure, when men call you names there's a fistfight." He stopped and regrouped. "Look, my intention here wasn't to start an argument. It was to make the point that we're in a major jam. So from here on we have to team up and play it straight all the way. No questions about each other's motives, no manipulation. Teamwork."

"All right." She put out her hand. Welsh took his off the stick shift and shook it.

"Why were those two guys trying to kill you at the hotel?" Scanlan asked. "It didn't have anything to do with Dominguez and me, did it?"

"I honestly don't know. They weren't carrying manifestos of explanation in their pockets."

"I know you got something from Booker too."

"That's right. And if it was just my ass, I'd tell you all about it right now. But other people's lives are on the line, so I have to be discreet."

"I'll try not to take it personally, you not trusting me."

"You shouldn't."

"By the way, we'll never get across the border checkpoint at Melchor de Mencos. Someone will have called ahead and they'll detain us on a murder charge, whether they can make it stick or not."

195

"Don't worry," said Welsh. "We won't be crossing the border at the checkpoint."

"So you've already made a plan for that?"

"Yup. Want to hear it?"

"No, not really. It's much easier on my nerves when you're close-mouthed and suspicious. When it's time, just tell me what I have to do."

"Okay, whatever you want. I want to warn you, though, if we run into any checkpoint or roadblock on the highway, I'm hitting the gas and going right through. So if it happens, duck your head below the windshield and hang on."

"And pray."

"I wouldn't rely on prayer exclusively, but feel free."

They drove steadily for the next half hour. Scanlan played with the radio, searching for news, but finding only some terrible Spanish rock and roll that kept fading in and out as they traveled through the rolling hills.

They passed through a number of small towns, just a few adobe or mud huts and the ubiquitous church clustered together along muddy streets. All dark, due as much to early rising as there not being enough money to keep a kerosene lamp lit. Welsh remembered reading an account by the legendary Army General Vinegar Joe Stilwell, who as a lieutenant in 1907 had spent six weeks traveling and spying in Guatemala. The Guatemalan, he wrote with characteristic frankness, would not work more than he had to. Not because he was lazy, but because everything he made was stolen by officials, landowners, or the professional classes.

At a town called El Cruce the highway branched. The asphalt portion continued north to the Tikal ruins, for the convenience of tourists. Highway 13 west to Belize was now just unpaved dirt—and mud. It was less than fifty miles to the border, but it would take three to four hours of very careful driving to cover that, depending on the conditions.

After an hour and forty-five minutes, the road ran into a series of winding turns and hills. Not knowing what was ahead, Welsh took them slowly. He came onto an open stretch, then suddenly, in the jungle ahead and off to the right, there was the flash and crack of a single rifle shot.

"Wha . . ." Scanlan began.

Welsh jammed the gas pedal down to the floor and killed the headlights. The vehicle surged forward. "Ambush right!" he shouted automatically. "Get your head down!"

The jungle lit up with muzzle flashes. A huge explosion went off just behind them, and the jeep was buffeted by the shock. Claymore mine, Welsh's brain told him. He thought he heard Scanlan yelling.

Welsh was flying through the gears, trying to get up speed. It was much easier than the hotel room, the suddenness allowing no time to get scared. Bullets punched through the sides of the jeep and blew by him like little gusts of supersonic wind, but most of the fire seemed to be going high. He began to think he'd succeeded in driving through the ambush.

Then a machine gun opened up from the bend in the road directly in front. The stream of red tracers from the first burst passed over the jeep. A classic L-shaped ambush, the gun anchoring the small leg of the L at the curve in the road. They were driving straight at it, and the gunner would only need another burst or two to get on target.

Welsh said, "Oh, shit." He yanked the steering wheel hard to the left, and they went off the road. Now Scanlan was definitely yelling.

They crashed through foliage, and the front wheels went out into empty air. The front end dropped, and

there was a sickening feeling of negative gravity. Welsh
thought it was over: a pile of burning metal at the bottom
of some canyon. Then all four wheels touched ground,
and the jeep was going downhill very fast. The slope
was steep and rocky. Welsh thought he could hold on if
it didn't get any steeper. He got off the gas and down-
shifted; he knew that if he hit the brakes they were
screwed.

The jeep kept running over things, and each time the
wheels left the ground. Don't roll, Welsh prayed silently.
He fought the steering wheel to keep going straight
down the slope. Any little twist and he knew they'd start
rolling.

He was doing it all by feel. The jeep scythed through
walls of foliage, and Welsh couldn't see anything
through the branches slapping at the windshield. He
couldn't risk looking over at Scanlan.

"Are you all right?" he shouted. There was no answer.
"Are you hurt?"

"I'm okay," came the shouted reply.

"Brace yourself on the dash!"

They kept going down. Then the jeep finally hit a tree
large enough to stop it. The front end buckled, and even
with his arms locked on the steering wheel, Welsh
couldn't stop himself from snapping forward. He took a
sharp blow as the shoulder safety belt caught him. Then
everything stopped, and he was sitting upright, still holding the steering wheel. The windshield was broken but
intact. He reached down and calmly shut off the engine.

Scanlan was hunched over in her seat. Welsh popped
his seat belt and felt for her arm. He gave it a hard
squeeze, and she shot up.

"Are you okay?" he asked.

"I think so."

"See if you can move your limbs and your neck."
Welsh felt around his waist; the Beretta and spare mag-

azines were still there. He hit the latch to open his door. It swung out about five inches and stopped. He kicked at it, but there was a sapling or branch in the way. "Get your door open and get out," he said. "But for Christ's sake check for the ground with your foot before you step off."

Welsh climbed over the seat into the back of the jeep. It was pitch-black dark under the jungle canopy, so he had to feel around for what he wanted. He found his and Scanlan's bags and tossed them into the front seat. Also one of the four spare metal gas cans he'd purchased and filled in Santa Elena. Scanlan was standing outside her door, as if unwilling to leave the security of the vehicle.

Welsh thought he could hear more firing coming from up the hill, though nothing was hitting anywhere near them. It was time to be gone. He popped the strap of his pack and took out the night-vision goggles. They're probably broken, he told himself. He slid them over his head and cinched the straps tight, like a baseball catcher's face mask. He flicked the switch, and the goggles went from solid black to lime green. He brought them into focus, and could see perfectly. You are still one lucky son of a bitch, he told himself. He snapped up the pack, then remembered the map. It was jammed half under the front seat. Everything else that had been lying around loose was scattered all over the inside of the cab.

He slid out Scanlan's door with both packs in his hands. It took him a moment to get reacquainted with the peculiarities of night-vision goggles. There was tunnel vision, like looking through a toilet-paper tube. And you couldn't look directly at the ground and try to walk, because the goggles offered limited depth perception.

The bottom of the draw was about twenty yards away, and there was a little stream, just a trickle a few inches wide, running down the length of it. "Take my arm," he said.

There was a high edge to her voice that she wasn't able to keep down. "I can't see anything."

"You'll get your night vision in a little bit. Just take my arm and follow me, we've got to get going." He led her down to the draw and dropped the two packs. "Put on your pack and wait right here, I'll be back in a second."

"No way!" said Scanlan, her voice completely broken by now.

"You've got to," Welsh said harshly. "No matter what happens, don't move from this spot."

He went back to the vehicle and grabbed the gas can. The cap was jammed, and he hammered it on the bumper until it came off. He poured gas inside, over, and under the jeep, making sure none of it got on him, and kicked the door shut.

He took off the night-vision goggles so he wouldn't be blinded, and struck his book of hotel matches. They flared up in his hand with an angry hiss. He threw the book at the jeep and scrambled down the hill as fast as he could.

The vapor caught even before the matches reached the jeep. There was a loud whoosh, and the jungle came alight. Welsh could feel the heat through his shirt, and the back of his neck felt like it was broiling. He had to touch his clothing to be sure he wasn't on fire.

Several shots snapped overhead, fired from up the hill. They were aiming at the burning jeep, but it was far and inaccurate. Welsh thought it would take them a while to get organized to come down.

He reached Scanlan and hurriedly put on his pack.

"Why did you do that?" she shouted. "Now they know right where we are."

Welsh spoke with forced calm as he cinched the

shoulder straps. "I gave them an excuse to wait around till morning to see if we burned up inside." He flipped the goggles back down over his eyes. "Grab one of the long straps on the back of my pack."

"Why?"

"Just fucking do it!" he snapped.

"Okay, okay, I've got it," she said quickly.

Welsh settled his voice down. "Now, I'm going to walk slow and easy. Hang onto the strap and follow behind me. Watch how my pack moves to see the shape of the ground, whether I'm going up or down. Feel with your toe to make sure you have good footing before you put your whole foot down. Don't say anything unless you have to, and then only in a whisper."

"God," she said, her voice quavering, "this is terrible."

"I'll go nice and slow until you get the hang of it," he assured her gently.

Welsh started walking. Scanlan wasn't able to go five yards without stumbling, but movement was the most important thing now. The bottom of the draw was the only open area around. Downhill was the direction they wanted to go, so he decided to follow the little stream until daylight. Then he could try to get his bearings from the map.

The jungle at night was almost unimaginably noisy. The insects blended their sounds together in a dull roar. The nocturnal animals made their way as easily as others did in the light. Animals lived, killed, died, and each act had its own screaming chorus. Though it had been a while since he'd walked a jungle in the dark, Welsh felt almost electrically confident. If they could put a little distance between them and the bad guys tonight, he'd worry about the rest in the morning.

Chapter Twenty-four

They walked all night. Welsh didn't make any rest stops, only because they were both hyper after the ambush, and the pace was such that fatigue didn't become a factor. He passed his water bottles back and they drank as they walked. Just before first light he called a halt, and they moved into the cover of the stream-side brush.

"Sit on your pack," he whispered.

"Better than sitting on the ground, right?" she said.

"More like something on the ground might object to being sat on," Welsh replied.

Scanlan pulled herself up onto her pack so no part of her body was touching the ground. She moved so fast Welsh felt the breeze.

He took off the night-vision goggles, handed her a bottle of water, and opened up his pack. It took a few minutes to get his night vision back. The canopy was thin over the top of the streambed, and quite a bit of moonlight came through.

Welsh filled the empty water bottles in the stream. Then he dug around in his pack and pulled out a bulky green nylon military Unit-1 medical bag. He unzipped one of the three pockets and found a small glass bottle. He shook two tablets out of it and dropped one in each water bottle. "Iodine tablets," he said. "They make the water taste like shit, but kill all the nasty bugs. Unless you want to die out here, drink no untreated water." He dropped the iodine bottle into his shirt pocket, felt around in the bag, removed two more items, and put the Unit-1 back in his pack.

One of the items was a plastic squeeze bottle. "Insect repellent. Cover all exposed skin except your eyes. When you're done, wipe your hands off by running them through your hair. Keeps the bugs out of it."

"I'm not complaining, you understand, but how come you have all this stuff?"

"My plan for getting across the border was to ditch the jeep short of Melchor de Mencos, walk around through the jungle, and flag down a bus on the Belize side. So I bought the basics for jungle travel and a night in the bush. Now it'll be a few more nights. You up for a short lecture?"

"How can I say no?"

"First, a little philosophy. Most people bumblefuck their way through life with their head up their ass. Which is fine, as long as there's someone to call 911 and a rescue squad to cut their hand out of the garbage disposal. Even in the military, if some idiot falls down a hill at night, you can always call a helicopter to medevac them. We're on our own out here. So, before you do absolutely anything, you have to think about it very carefully.

"First, don't touch anything without checking with me. Don't push a branch away as you go past, don't even rest your hand on the trunk of a tree when we stop.

203

There might be a snake, or a poisonous centipede, or fire ants. Out here even the caterpillars can fuck you up." He produced two pairs of light cotton gloves from the pack and gave her one. "Wear these all the time. Did you bring a hat?"

"I have a baseball cap."

"Put in on. It'll keep crap out of your hair."

"Two pairs of gloves?" Scanlan said.

Welsh thought he could hear a smile in her voice. "When I saw you at the hotel I got one of those feelings. Next thing. As we walk along you've got to watch your footing. We can't afford even a sprain, let alone a broken bone. If you get tired, I want you to let me know."

"I'll be all right," she replied briskly.

"That's another thing," he said. "In the jungle you've got to rely more on your good sense than your guts, or you'll never make it. When you get tired you make mistakes, you lose your coordination, and it's easier to get hurt. This kind of situation, people die more from stupid pride than anything else. Okay?"

"Okay."

"Great. Now, water. You have to drink and keep drinking. Don't ration water; let your body store it for you. In this climate, if you wait until you're thirsty to start drinking, your body is already a liter and a half low. That cuts both your endurance and your oxygen intake. And if you keep moving and losing water, you're looking at dehydration and then heat stroke, no matter how much you drink after that. If you feel woozy, if your skin feels dry and you stop sweating, if you get one of those metal-band-squeezing-your-forehead headaches, let me know 'cause those are the signs. You've got to constantly monitor your body. If you don't feel good, you stop and do something about it. You don't push on and try to gut it out. Okay?"

"Okay."

"You're doing just great. I had Marines, kids who grew up in the city, on their first night walk in the jungle they were so scared they nearly pissed their pants."

"Thanks for trying to make me feel better."

"You think I'm lying," said Welsh, "but I'm not. Last thing. The only stupid question is the one you didn't ask because you were too embarrassed. Just get in close like this and keep it down to a whisper."

"Okay."

He felt in her pack for a fresh water bottle. "Go ahead and fill your tank, then we'll move on." The last item on his lap was a Silva Ranger compass with a loop of green nylon parachute cord attached. He tied the cord to his shirt-collar button hole and used the luminous dial to take a bearing along the streambed they were following. About 8 degrees magnetic. The stream probably emptied into a small lake to the north. He'd been worried about the draw angling back toward the road. Now he could be sure.

Welsh slapped on some insect repellent, then put the bottle in his trouser pocket. "This is the ritual after each stop. Make sure all the buckles on your pack are secure, then put it on. Check the ground to see if you dropped anything. Then pat your pockets and make sure you've got everything you came with. Every piece of gear is irreplaceable, and we don't want to leave the bad guys a trail of bread crumbs."

The morning mist was thick, but Welsh could still make out a large hill to the northeast. It seemed like a good spot to check the map. They'd have to move into the canopy to get there, so he took a compass bearing. It was terrifyingly easy to get turned around in thick cover.

Primary jungle was tropical forest in its natural state, untouched by man. Trees grew to heights of up to two hundred feet, forming a mushroom of leaves at the very top. Smaller trees grew up and spread out below them in lower layers, creating a double or even triple canopy. Little light reached the jungle floor, so the vegetation there was mosses, ferns, and tough herbaceous plants. Endless varieties of fungi sprouted up on fallen growth, and vines twined up the tree trunks in an effort to reach the sun.

Even so, it was not as difficult to move through as secondary jungle, where man's clearing of trees allowed sunlight to reach the fertile earth and provoke an explosion of unbelievably tangled, practically impassable undergrowth.

In primary jungle the dead organic material falling to earth formed layers of decaying muck that could be up to a foot thick. With most of the sun blocked out, the air was slightly cooler, though dead still and chokingly, thickly humid. Primary jungle was swarming with raucous birds, monkeys, and two thirds of all the world's species of insects.

When they reached the base of the hill, Welsh circled three quarters of the way around before climbing up. The slope was so steep they had to use saplings for handholds.

"You told me to ask any questions I wanted," Scanlan said as they reached the top, drenched with sweat and gasping for breath.

"Go right ahead," Welsh said. "But remember, quietly."

She dropped back to a whisper. "Why climb up the steep part when the slope in front was a lot less?"

"Because this way we can walk over the top of the hill and watch the trail we made. If anyone is following our track we'll be able to see them. And while they swing around the back and break their balls climbing up, we slip down the easy way and gain some time."

"Very clever."

"Just experience. Now we have a seat, I try to find out where we are on the map, and you remove your underwear."

"I beg your pardon?"

"You can't wear underwear hiking in this climate, especially cotton. It gets wet and stays wet, chafes, and pretty soon you have a beautiful case of jungle rot."

Scanlan was clearly dubious. "What?"

"Burning, itching, inflammation, skin peeling off. Drives you crazy. Believe me," Welsh said earnestly, "I know what I'm talking about."

"This is no time to kid around."

"I'm not, cross my heart. You can step behind those trees." He just then remembered something. "I need to cover a couple of things before you go to the bathroom."

"I already know how to do that."

"In that case it'll be a much shorter period of instruction."

He led her into the trees and took out the machete. "Cut a circle in the turf, kind of deep," he said, demonstrating. "Pry it out with the blade, put it to one side, but keep the surface intact. Do your business in the hole." He handed her a roll of toilet paper in a plastic bag. "Put the paper on top, replace the circle of turf, press it down. You've left no trace of your presence."

"I was a little worried about the content of this lecture, but I can handle that."

"Also, when you're going, you need to check the color of your urine."

"Excuse me?"

"Clear means you're well hydrated. The darker it is, the more dehydrated you are. It's the best way to determine your fluid level."

"You can level with me now," Scanlan said. "This has just been a series of monstrously tasteless jokes, right?"

"I thought it would go over like a fart in church. But

who could make up something like that? And be frugal with the paper, I hate using leaves." After that there was nothing to do but walk away and leave her to it.

He grabbed his pack and crawled to the edge of the hill. Iridescent butterflies beautiful beyond words fluttered about the undergrowth. Lying on his stomach, out of sight, Welsh spread the map out on the ground.

Just then Scanlan reemerged from the trees. He gave her a mischievous grin. "Underwear come off all right?"

"Yes, thank you very much. That's what I get for being a child of the suburbs."

"I would have thought it was some kind of twisted wilderness initiation ritual too."

She grinned and nodded.

"Now I can tell you to take off your watch and loop the band through one of the button holes on your shirt."

"And why am I doing that?"

"In this climate anything worn next to your skin is going to irritate it. I'd say the same thing about jewelry, if you were wearing any."

"I don't wear jewelry; it's too much trouble."

Without thinking, Welsh said, " 'Who troubles himself about his ornaments or fluency is lost.' "

"Who was that?" Scanlan blurted out.

"Walt Whitman, prose introduction to *Leaves of Grass*."

"And you remember it?"

"Sure. It's one of the great influences on my life." He continued. " 'Re-examine all you have been told at school or church or in any book, dismiss whatever insults your own soul, and your very flesh shall be a great poem.' "

"Jungle survival and Whitman. I'm impressed."

"Yeah, well, you'll probably get the whole package before this is over. Now, pull up a chair and observe how we figure out where we are."

"It just looks like a bunch of squiggles."

"It's a 1:50,000-scale topographic map. One inch on the map equals fifty thousand inches on the ground. The squiggles represent the contours of the ground. And you have to learn this in case something happens to me."

"Do me a favor, make sure nothing happens to you."

"We take the compass, put it on the map, and twirl the map around so north on the map corresponds to north on the compass. Now we're oriented: What's in front of us for real is what's in front of us on the map." He pointed to a spot on the map. "We went off the road somewhere around there." He waved his finger around a section of amorphous green jungle on the map. "We're somewhere in here, but that's not good enough. So we look for prominent terrain." Welsh pointed out in the distance. "See those three peaks there?"

"Yes."

"They look just like these three hills on the map. Same location, same shape, same height. Now we resect."

"I can't wait."

Welsh picked up the compass and sighted in on the peak of one of the hills. "Okay, while I hold this, twirl the dial of the compass so the hollow arrow lines up exactly with the north needle."

She did it. "Okay, what now?"

"Read the number on the dial."

"Twelve degrees."

Welsh wrote it on the map in pencil. Then they did the same thing to the other two hills. They were 18 degrees and 33 degrees, respectively. "Now we add one hundred eighty to each of those numbers. That gives us the back azimuth, or the bearing we'd get if we stood on the tops of the hills and took a bearing down to where we are right now. We consult the map-conversion diagram to change the magnetic bearings to map grid bearings. Now, we go to the map. In the military they teach you to use a protractor, but we'll use the orienteering technique. We dial the bearing onto the compass, shift it until the north needle fits into the hollow arrow on the dial, and use the plastic straight edge of the compass to draw a line from the peak of each hill." Welsh did that with the pencil for each one of the bearings, and on the map the three pencil lines intersected on a single smaller hill. "Eureka, here we are."

"Wonderful," said Scanlan. "Don't let anything happen to you."

Now that he knew where he was, Welsh could plot a route to Belize with accurate compass bearings to follow. It wouldn't be direct; he first wanted to head north, away from the highway and deeper into the jungle, before turning northeast. When he was done he folded the map so the route was face-up, slipping it into a plastic ziplock bag.

Scanlan was looking over his shoulder. "How far is it to Belize?"

"Eighteen to twenty miles to the border, another eight or so to San Ignacio in Belize. That's as the crow flies. It'll be more walking."

"And how long will the walking take?"

At least she sounded willing. But she wasn't stupid, and there was no other way out. "Hmmm. In this terrain, and having to tippy-toe around so we don't get ambushed again? A good rule of thumb in primary jungle is a thousand meters an hour. So I guess between five and ten miles a day, depending on the breaks. Probably closer to five."

"So anywhere from four days to a week?"

"Maybe. But that's not the way to look at it. It'll take us as long as it takes to get there."

"Are you a Zen master too?"

"We've got a map, a compass, and some gear. But even if we were standing here naked we'd still make it.

210

Survival isn't equipment or knowledge, though they help. It's the right attitude. Set your mind to it, refuse to quit, and you can get through anything. Without mental toughness all the fancy gear in the world won't save you. So no matter what, we *will* make it."

Scanlan was watching him closely. Then she smiled. "Okay, if you believe it, then I will."

"Now we know where we're going, let's take a peek at where we've come from." They walked over to the other side of the hill. A blown-down tree at the edge of the slope opened up a good view. Welsh crawled up to the dead log on his stomach, and Scanlan mimicked his every move. He unzipped his pack's outer pocket and took out a pair of palm-sized binoculars. He braced himself on his elbows and focused on the streambed they'd come down.

"Binoculars too?" Scanlan asked.

"Bought 'em in Guatemala City. Handy for sightseeing. Good thing we didn't waste any more time up here."

"What do you mean?"

He handed her the binoculars. She looked carefully, and said, "Oh, my God."

A group of men dressed in military camouflage and carrying M-16 rifles were walking down the streambed.

"I counted at least ten," Welsh said matter-of-factly.

"Can you tell who they are?"

"They're dressed and armed pretty uniformly for hired guns. There's a Kaibil base at La Polorva, not too far away."

"The Kaibils are special forces."

"More like elite light infantry. I don't see a dog, so they've got someone who knows how to track. I figure we have a couple of hours head start."

"Why don't you sound as worried as I'm feeling?"

"If I was to start running around like a chicken with

its head cut off, you'd probably get a little panicky, wouldn't you?"

"Depend on it."

"Well, there you go. Besides, these people might be dangerous, but they're not very good. Otherwise they would've been able to ambush one lousy car driving down a road. And failing that, they would have been hard on our heels all night long instead of waiting for daylight to start. In the jungle two people can move faster than ten. We won't underestimate them, though; we'll act as though the very best were chasing us."

"So what are we going to do?"

Welsh took the map out again. "Drink all you can hold. We may not be able to slow down for a while."

They both drank, and Welsh packed up his gear. Now he had to urinate, and went behind a tree.

Scanlan had her pack on and was ready to go. "You still haven't told me what we're going to do."

"First we're going to run away," Welsh replied. "Then we're going to cheat. I'll explain it all as we go along."

They walked off the hill, and back into the jungle.

Chapter Twenty-five

Welsh was completely soaked with sweat. His sleeves were buttoned down to keep the bugs off, and the thin cotton material was so saturated it stuck to his skin like a wet suit. His legs and shoulders felt tight; unfortunately, the only way to get used to carrying a backpack across hills and jungle was to carry a backpack across hills and jungle.

Scanlan was following a few paces behind. She might have been a child of the suburbs, but she was in good shape and picking up the techniques of jungle movement very quickly. With the canopy overhead and the foliage up around your ears, it was easy to get claustrophobic. Every brush of a leaf felt like a big bug crawling down your back. If you panicked and tried to thrash your way through heavy cover, it would exhaust you and pull you under. Not to mention that you'd leave a trail like a highway. Using a machete was out for the same reason. You had to relax and feel your way through rough terrain. Welsh wasn't surprised that she seemed to have some natural talent for it. Women only had to get over those childhood-programmed phobias about dirt, crawling things, and the unknown. They were much more patient than men, and when confronted by obstacles more likely use their brains than their brawn.

Welsh stopped and looked back over his shoulder. The ground was so soft they couldn't help but leave footprints. He was going to have to do something about that soon.

Scanlan whispered, "I'm on my last water bottle."

"We should be running into a stream in about a quarter of a mile."

"You even know the distance?"

"You have to know how far you've traveled in order to navigate. Count off every time your left foot hits the ground. For my stride, I cover a hundred meters in sixty-two paces."

"And you keep all that in your head while we walk?"

"It just takes practice. Compass bearing, pace count, and matching the terrain with the contours on the map."

"I see. Please try not to let anything happen to you."

They continued on. Welsh was being careful not to follow a straight-line compass bearing. All his pursuers would have to do was plot the course on their own maps and extrapolate ahead to predict where he was going to be. So he made frequent zigzag and dogleg turns.

There was no blue line on his map, but the valley ahead was quite deep, which meant it was likely to be holding water. They walked downhill, and at the bottom of the steep slope was a muddy stream about five feet wide.

The undergrowth grew up in a thick belt along the banks. They walked outside it, parallel to the water, until Welsh found the spot he wanted. The valley narrowed, and there were exposed granite outcroppings extending from both opposing slopes all the way down to the streambed.

Welsh drew the machete and cut a long sapling to use as a staff. When he finished trimming, it was six feet long with the remnant of a Y-shaped crook on one end. Then he chopped a path through the brush along the bank all the way down to the water. No one could miss it. He tested the water depth with the staff; even small streams could be quite deep. About three feet. "Let's go," he said.

Scanlan held back. "Um, I don't want to sound stupid, but what if there are piranha in there?"

Welsh was already thigh deep in the brown water. "Not a native species in Guatemala."

Scanlan took the bait and stepped into the stream. "It's beautiful and cool," she exclaimed.

"Of course," Welsh mentioned, as an afterthought, "I'm not sure if piranha know where they're supposed to be found."

She splashed him.

He said, "Don't let any of this water into your mouth. It's bound to be loaded with all kinds of bad microscopic beasties. Keep it out of your eyes too, if you can. The little critters love to sneak in that way."

"I wish you'd stop giving me things to worry about."

"I will, when there's nothing more to worry about."

They walked down the middle of the stream, Welsh using the staff to check the footing before each step. When they reached the rock outcropping on the opposite side, he handed Scanlan his staff and told her to wait in the stream. He pulled himself onto a large rock, after first breaking down the tall grass growing beside it with his foot, as if by accident. He climbed the rocks up the hill, and near the top leaned off the one he was standing on and scraped a foot in the soft earth beside it, as if he'd slid off. Then he made his way back down and into the stream.

Scanlan gave him a questioning look.

Welsh pointed his thumb the other way. "We go back where we came from. But we stay on the rocks so we leave no sign. One slipup and we're screwed."

"Just tell me what to do."

Welsh gave her a boost onto a large, flat boulder that projected out into the stream. He handed up his pack, and she passed down a water bottle. They drank the bottles dry. Welsh refilled all the containers from the stream, liberally adding iodine tablets. He pulled himself up on the boulder and shook as much water off his clothing as he could.

It was a tricky climb to the top, and a few times they had to jump from rock to rock. At the top was a ledge that, although thankfully short, was nearly sheer. Welsh had to drop his pack and climb up by wedging his fingers and boot edges into a long crack in the rock. Scanlan handed up both packs. She had to grab his outstretched hand and swing up before she could push off with her feet. It meant temporarily hanging out over the edge. She scrambled over the top on her hands and knees. "I didn't like that," she informed him once again.

"I hate like hell to keep telling you this," he said. "But it's going to get worse."

"I don't doubt it."

The brush was thick at the top of the hill, just what Welsh wanted. "Why don't you wait here and catch your breath while I poke around?"

"Be glad to."

Welsh crawled on his hands and knees, using the staff to hold back the brush and hopefully come in contact with anything unpleasant before his face did. On one side of the hill a cluster of deadfalls had brought up some secondary growth. There was a beautiful thicket of thorn bushes and wait-a-minute vines, whose little hooklike thorns grabbed onto clothing and wouldn't let go. Welsh pushed a little path into the thicket and then went back to get Scanlan.

She followed him in, both on their hands and knees and their packs in front of them. Welsh hacked out a small space in the center of the thicket and stamped it down to leave a reasonably flat surface. "Have a seat on your pack and relax," he told her. "I've got to erase our trail."

"How long are you going to be gone?"

"Fifteen minutes or so. But don't move around or make any noise."

Welsh crawled down the tiny path until he was at the spot where they'd come off the rocks. Backing towards the thicket, he scattered forest duff on any gouges in the earth and repositioned branches and grass that had been bent down.

"What now?" Scanlan whispered when he returned.

Welsh pulled a green nylon tarpaulin from his pack and spread it on the ground. "We couldn't have kept running. They'd get an idea from our track where we were heading, and radio for other groups to be waiting out ahead of us. Even if they didn't, we wouldn't be able to stop, and eventually we'd get so hungry and tired they'd be able to run us down. This way, they're going to follow our trail down to the stream and lose it. They'll think we climbed up the rocks on the other side, or walked up or downstream in the water. I'm taking the chance that they wouldn't dream we'd stop moving, backtrack, and hide. And even if they did, they won't be able to find the trail we made into here."

"What about the water that dripped off us onto the rocks?"

"The sun will dry them off in a heartbeat. Tracking across rock is the ancient equivalent of mastering particle physics. If they have someone who can do it, we're screwed no matter what we do."

"So we just sit here?"

"That's right."

"How long?"

"As long as it takes."

"Oh, no, not Zen again."

"I've got worse news. Pretty soon we're not going to be able to speak or move. Not one single sound. You'll have to take five minutes to unscrew a water bottle."

"All right."

"Don't be so quick to say that. If an ant bites you, if a mosquito stings you, you can't move to slap it. Even rolling over could snap a twig and get us killed."

"What if I'm not able to do it?"

Welsh stared straight into her eyes. "Every time you feel you can't stand it one more second, just think about being raped. All ten of them. Because that's what'll happen if they catch us."

"I know," she whispered.

"Then we'd both spend an even longer time dying. I don't want that to happen, and I don't want to watch it happening to you. So whatever we have to go through to avoid that is worth it, isn't it?"

"Yes."

"I'm sorry to have to be so brutal about it," he said.

"I know you are," Scanlan replied. "If I don't get another chance to say it, thanks for everything so far."

Welsh rooted around in his pack again, found two small bundles, and handed her one. Mosquito head nets, worn over the whole head down to the shoulders, with a flexible hoop to hold the net away from the face. "Put this on, and tuck your pants legs into your socks. The bugs will be a little easier to deal with." He removed the Beretta from the holster, made sure there was still a round in the chamber, checked the sound suppressor, and flipped the safety off. "If you hear anyone come close, don't move a muscle and don't look directly at them. Hard to believe, but sometimes you can feel another person's eyes on you. They might walk right over us and not know it, so don't let them panic you into running. A situation like this, all that determines the winners and losers is they both wanted to give up but the winners held out just another minute more."

"So we sit here in the briar patch," Scanlan whispered.

"Exactly." He set the pistol on the ground next to his hand. If they were discovered it would be useless to have Scanlan run while he tried to hold them off. Where would she run to? Welsh had already decided that they weren't going to be captured. He'd kill as many as he could, and the last two bullets in the Beretta would finish it.

When everything was ready, they lay down on the tarp, side by side and very close together. Welsh knew they'd disappeared into the green thorns, and even if the bad guys did get on line and try to cut their way through, he and Scanlan would be invisible up to only a few feet away.

Three hours passed. At the beginning Scanlan had made several little movements, almost involuntary, and each time Welsh laid a warning hand on her arm. The tarp kept the ground moisture from soaking up into their clothing. The insects hovered about, but the head nets, gloves, and repellent were keeping them at bay.

At close to the five-hour mark Welsh began to smell cigarette smoke. Then he heard voices where they'd first gone down to the stream. One man was directing the others, and another was speaking very softly, with an unfamiliar Spanish accent. Then the voice trailed off.

Welsh strained to hear everything that was happening around them. The sound of voices grew louder; the men were coming down the stream toward the rocks. They were making a lot of noise. Unprofessional bastards. Then there was nothing but the sound of the birds. Hours before, Welsh had known they were well hidden when the birds settled down and began to feed. The jungle had resumed its normal rhythms around them. Only the arrival of these new intruders had sent the birds back into the air.

Welsh's chest and thighs, which he'd been lying on, were incredibly painful. Every unscratched itch escalated into something maddening. He fought to take his mind away from those internal problems, concentrating all his senses on what was happening around him. He periodically took sips of water, moving so slowly he used it as a game to occupy himself, and nudged Scanlan to remind her to do the same.

He tried to keep his eyes off his watch, but two more hours passed. Then it began to rain, a hard blinding tropical downpour where the moisture arrived before the clouds even began to darken. It was a fantastic stroke of luck. The rain would cool them down, and more important, wash away any mistakes he'd made in covering the trail.

The voices returned: louder, angrier, and more urgent. They knew they had to regain the trail before the rain obscured it. They were back on the near side of the stream now, then even closer. Backtracking, Welsh thought. Trying to see if he and Scanlan had gone down to the stream and then walked back up the hill in their own footprints, jumping off the trail somewhere along the line.

The brush crashed, and a loud harsh voice demanded, "Did you find anything?"

Scanlan jumped, and Welsh rested a comforting hand on her back. It was also there to hold her down if she panicked.

The soft voice with the strange accent replied, "I told you they did not backtrack."

"Then where is their trail?" the loud voice demanded. "I thought you Indians knew how to track."

Other voices laughed together in ridicule, as if it were now permitted.

That explained the strange accent. An Indian would not have learned Spanish as his first language.

"The man knows about tracking," the Indian replied, still softly. "He played a trick on the other side of the stream."

"I'll show him a trick," said the leader's loud voice. "I'll make him eat his own balls."

A third voice broke in. "But we'll give that woman something else to eat, eh?"

They all laughed. Scanlan was shivering, and Welsh didn't think it was only from the sudden chill of the rain.

Then Welsh thought he heard a very quiet sound in front of him. The grass began to move. He slowly raised the Beretta.

The grass parted, and the triangular head of a snake emerged. It was brown, with paler brown geometric markings. Fuck, Welsh thought. The shit just kept piling up. The snake was a fer-de-lance, the *barba amarilla* in Guatemala. A big bastard if the size of the head was any indication. They were so poisonous that if you got bit and didn't have any antivenin, you had just enough time to drink a beer before you croaked. Welsh didn't have any antivenin. He also didn't have any beer.

If he shot the snake, even using the sound suppressor, the bad guys couldn't help but hear it. And if it bit him in the face he was dead. Great choices. Welsh was glad Scanlan had her face in the ground and couldn't see it.

The snake stopped, about eight feet from Welsh's head. Welsh couldn't remember if the fer-de-lance looped its body before striking. The snake wavered back and forth for a moment, and flicked out its tongue to taste the air. The rain must have confused it, because when its sensory apparatus picked up the heat of two very large creatures, the snake visibly twitched and coiled itself. Welsh aimed carefully and took up the slack on the Beretta's trigger. Then the fer-de-lance, probably because all that large heat in front of it neither moved nor attacked, suddenly uncoiled and slid gracefully through the grass away from them.

Welsh let out his breath and got off the trigger. That's what happens when you get cocky, he told himself. They'd been incredibly lucky. The fer-de-lance was lethal, but its regional cousin, the much more aggressive bushmaster, probably would have attacked instantly.

Preoccupied with the snake, Welsh hadn't been paying attention to the voices. Now they were arguing.

"Why not wait for them to come out of the jungle?" one asked. "If they do not emerge, then the devil take them."

"We have people in the villages watching for them," the leader said. "And if you wish to go home, after failing to kill them on the road as we were ordered, then that is your affair."

"I will stay," the man replied sullenly. The others laughed at him.

"How will we find them now?" another asked loudly.

The Indian answered him. "They have walked in the stream to hide their tracks. We must search up and down, and find where they emerged."

"They had to go down," the leader decided. "Upstream leads back to the road."

"As you wish," the Indian said quietly.

The rain stopped, having gone from a downpour to nothing in an instant. The sun came out just as fast, and the heat made steam rise from the wet ground.

"There, you see," the leader told his men. "An omen."

Welsh felt the same way. Then the leader must have spoken to the Indian. "There will be no payment if you do not find them."

The Indian had probably started back to the stream, because Welsh could hear movement, and the voices, though still arguing, grew fainter.

Another two hours, and the voices didn't return. The shadows were beginning to lengthen. Welsh's extremities were completely numb, but he felt the warmth of pure satisfaction. Even, he admitted to himself, joy. Patience, self-discipline, mental and physical toughness had won the day once again, as they always did. And Scanlan. She had been simply magnificent.

Welsh leaned over and whispered very quietly in her ear. "How do you feel."

It made her jump. "Terrible," she whispered back hoarsely.

"No, you don't," said Welsh. "What you feel is alive."

Chapter Twenty-six

It took Welsh and Scanlan several minutes of hard and painful effort to work the blood back into their muscles. An obvious solution would have been to rub each other's extremities, but even if it had occurred to them, each declined to broach the subject to the other.

Scanlan whispered, "Please tell me I can go now."

Welsh handed over the machete and toilet paper. "Don't wander too far, and be as quiet as you can."

"I'll do my best."

When he was able to sit up, Welsh crawled in the opposite direction and urinated. When she returned, he asked, "Are you hungry?"

"Not a bite all day? I'm starving."

"Got any food?"

Her face fell. "No."

Welsh smiled and rummaged in his pack. He came up with a bulging plastic bag.

"Fig Newtons?" she said.

Welsh shrugged. "They're filling, hold up in the heat, and I happen to like 'em."

"Nothing else?"

"Hey, I only thought I'd be out in the jungle for a day or two. By myself, I might add."

"Forgive me for sounding ungrateful," Scanlan replied. "But what happens when we finish them?"

"We'll see what we can forage while we walk. But plan on being hungry for an indefinite period. The Guatemalan jungle weight-loss plan."

Scanlan shrugged. "I was a little worried about my thighs anyway."

Welsh was pleased with her attitude. If there was nothing you could do to change a bad situation, complaining was a miserable waste of time.

Scanlan consumed her cookies very slowly. Welsh popped his into his mouth one by one, chewed once or twice, and that was that.

"You don't seem concerned about making them last," she observed.

"I got used to going hungry in the Marine Corps. Out in the field, that is."

"Don't they feed you?"

"It's not that. The combat rations, MREs or Meals Ready to Eat . . . how should I put this? They really suck."

"You mean the taste?"

"Revolting."

"You know, Rich, I have a little trouble picturing you in a Senate office. Or an office anywhere."

"I do it for money, like everyone else."

Scanlan wrapped her arms around herself, and if the temperature hadn't been in the ninety-degree range Welsh might have thought she was cold. "God," she said. "I thought it was all over up on the road."

"That accidental shot saved us. Someone either

jumped the gun or got nervous with his finger on the trigger. An ambush has to begin with an instantaneous, massive volley of gunfire, and they just couldn't get it together. And at night there's a tendency to shoot high, especially when you're nervous. Everyone's first burst went right over the jeep. Then I threw off their aim when I stepped on the gas. The guy on the claymore mine didn't allow for the little electrical delay between squeezing the firing claquer and the mine going off. The machine gun on the bend in the road was textbook, though. That would have gotten us."

"If you didn't drive off the cliff."

"They should have picked a spot that was steeper, or mined the opposite side of the ambush."

"I never imagined there was that much to it."

"Even in the military, people think any moron can be an infantryman. You know, you were really great today," he said, looking her straight in the eye. "Very few people could have done it."

She was too embarrassed to meet his gaze for long.

Welsh returned the bag of Fig Newtons to his pack. When he turned around, Scanlan was on her feet and had backed up several body lengths. She seemed a little agitated. "What's up?" he asked.

She wordlessly pointed to where they'd been seated. A cockroach over six inches long was feasting on the few meager crumbs left over from their meal.

Welsh walked over and crunched it under his boot. "How about that?" he exclaimed. "All you'd need is a collar and a leash, and you could call it Fido and take it for walks."

"God," Scanlan breathed.

Welsh had two small plastic bottles in his hand. He popped a tablet into his mouth and handed one to Scanlan.

"What's this?" she asked.

"Multivitamin with minerals. You've got to replace the electrolytes along with the water."

She accepted the tablet and washed it down with a slug from the water bottle. "Thanks."

"Do you have an antimalarial drug?" he asked, opening up the second bottle.

"Chloroquine."

"Good. Don't forget to take it on schedule." He checked his watch. "In these parts it gets dark really fast. We'll sleep right here tonight." He checked the canopy above them.

"What are you looking at?" Scanlan asked.

"Making sure there aren't any dead branches. You probably won't believe this, but in the jungle you've got a better chance of being killed by a falling tree than just about anything else."

"Don't worry, I'm on the verge of believing anything. What else do we need to do?"

"Wrap ourselves up in the tarp and go to sleep."

Something was obviously bothering her. "Do you intend for both of us to sleep in this thing?" she finally asked.

"You don't have to," Welsh replied politely. "Pick any spot you like and curl right up on the ground."

They looked at each other, and all that could be heard was the buzzing of the insects.

"My sense of chivalry extends only so far," he said.

"Then I guess we share the tarp."

"It's light to carry and low-profile. Even using night-vision goggles, someone could walk right by us and never see anything. The British military use hammocks and make pole beds, but the last people they fought in the jungle were the Indonesians. The people who taught me fought the North Vietnamese." He handed her a water bottle. "Let's drink these up, and after dark I'll go down to the stream and refill them."

"Can I go with you and wash up?"

"The short answer is no," said Welsh. "The long answer is that you're bound to have a lot of little cuts and scratches, and washing in the stream would let every kind of disease vector into them. Second, better to leave a layer of dirt on to keep the bugs off, no matter what the cost to your morale. Third, no soap or deodorant. Someone used to the jungle can smell it on you a mile off, and if you walk through a stream, the soap film you leave behind has a noticeable scent that travels way downstream."

"I was afraid you'd have more logical explanations," Scanlan said dejectedly. "Can I at least brush my teeth?"

"Sure. I've got a container of salt in my pack."

"No toothpaste?"

"Nope."

"Oh, dear."

"I will rinse your socks out for you when I go down to the stream. Do you have any foot powder?"

"No."

He took out his first-aid kit. "Let me see if you have any blisters."

Scanlan removed her running shoes and peeled off her wet socks. Welsh examined her feet closely. "No blisters," he said with some amazement. "You've got very tough feet."

"They've never been very ladylike."

"Screw ladylike. They're worth their weight in gold out here." He began to massage her feet.

Scanlan leaned back against her pack, an ecstatic expression on her face. "Oooh, that's wonderful."

"Very important after a long march. Breaks down any edema."

"Do Marines do this?"

Welsh found the mental image absolutely hilarious.

"No, Marines don't sit around massaging each other's feet. Everyone does their own."

"Well, that's silly."

"Guys get a little tight-assed about that sort of thing." When he was done, Welsh dusted on foot powder. Scanlan slipped on new socks.

"Nothing like a fresh pair of socks to perk you right up, is there?" said Welsh.

"I never would have thought it, but you're absolutely right."

"You've got to be very careful with your feet in this climate. If they stay wet too long, the skin sloughs right off and you're crippled."

"Let me do yours."

"If you insist."

The steep trajectory of the sun near the equator caused night to fall with the suddenness of turning off a light switch. Luminescent click beetles as large and bright as small flashlights began dancing among the trees. Welsh used the night-vision goggles to climb down the rocks to the stream. Even so, he nearly fell and broke his ass twice.

After he returned he said, "We'll give the iodine a chance to work, drink these to get ourselves hydrated for tomorrow, and I'll go fill them up again."

"Is that really necessary?"

"Iodine taste getting you down?"

"Kind of."

"It's pretty foul, but better than dysentery. Kool Aid is good to cut the taste."

"That sounds great."

"It's a shame I don't have any," said Welsh.

They were sitting side by side on the tarp. He couldn't see Scanlan's face, but her tone of voice let him know she realized she'd been had again. "And here you went and brought everything else."

Welsh was glad she couldn't see him smiling. "I think we'd better lay low for another day. Even if the bad guys decide to fan out ahead and set up ambushes along likely routes, they weren't carrying packs, so I don't think they could sit still long before giving up. And they might even decide to come back this way. Sitting tight and relaxing in the shade, our water would last for the whole day."

"You won't get any argument from me. After the last forty-eight hours I think a little rest would be nice."

After he came back from the stream the second time, he reviewed what to do in case of trouble.

"If anyone comes up on us, stay frozen until I give the word. Then bail out, grab your pack, and wait. I'll tuck everything under my arm, and we'll bolt. Oh, and don't take your shoes, gloves, or head net off tonight."

"Okay."

"A lot of things are going to go bump in the night. Don't worry unless it's something really close. If I don't hear it, jab me with your elbow."

"Don't worry about that."

Welsh removed the magazine from the Beretta and ejected the cartridge from the chamber. He pocketed the cartridge, closed the slide, and reinserted the magazine. Better to leave the chamber empty and take an extra half second to jack in a round than risk shooting his balls off in the middle of the night. He tied one end of a piece of parachute cord to his wrist and the other to the lanyard ring of the pistol so he wouldn't lose it in the dark.

They lay down on one half of the tarp, and folded the other over them. Welsh tucked the open end under his body, and the bottom under their legs. They used their packs as pillows, and pulled the nylon over their heads.

"It's called a Ranger Roll," said Welsh.

"We'll sweat to death," Scanlan said desperately.

"Trust me, in a couple of hours it'll be the only thing keeping us from freezing our asses off."

"Can't we leave the top open until then?"

"Sure, but I won't be responsible for what might wander in."

"Forget I said anything."

Welsh immediately fell asleep. Scanlan didn't. Though she tried to gain some separation, it proved impossible to migrate anywhere all wrapped up. Even getting up to relieve the bladder couldn't be done without disturbing the other party. The simple act of rolling over was a nightmare.

An elbow jabbed into Welsh, and he shot awake just as he had in the hotel room. He automatically rolled out of the tarp and fumbled for the pistol. After a few frantic moments he managed to bring it into action, but couldn't acquire any targets in the early dawn mist. "What was it?" he whispered back to Scanlan.

She was sitting up and wearing an expression of pure outrage that was visible even through her mosquito head net. "That," she whispered fiercely. It seemed to be all she could get out. "That!" She was pointing down at Welsh's crotch.

Welsh sagged visibly. He sat down on the tarp and put the pistol on safe. "Jesus Christ," he said weakly, "I thought we were being overrun."

After taking a few moments to collect himself, he got up and walked into the brush to urinate. By the time he came back he was shivering in the morning chill and filled with the immaculate wrath of the falsely accused. "It was an involuntary reaction, for crying out loud."

"I'm sorry," Scanlan said, totally serious, "but I couldn't take it anymore. It was sticking right into me."

A chuckle forced its way out of Welsh. "Really?" he asked innocently.

"No, it . . . I didn't mean that . . . I . . ."

"Anyway," Welsh replied. "It was just an EMHO."

"A what?"

"An Early Morning Hard-On."

"Oh, please."

Considering the hour, he was almost enjoying the weirdness of it all. "Don't worry, it was harmless."

"That's not what my mother told me."

Welsh laughed so hard he had to gag himself with his shirt. Then Scanlan joined in. When it had run its course, he said, "Can I get back in the tarp now?"

"All right."

It was useless. Whenever one of them was about to drop off to sleep, the other would begin giggling uncontrollably.

They finally gave up. Breakfast was Fig Newtons and warm iodized water. Scanlan had kept a deck of cards in her bag, and they spent the morning playing blackjack.

Chapter Twenty-seven

Welsh carefully weighed the odds, then said, "Hit me."

Scanlan dealt a ten of clubs onto the poncho. "Twenty-two. Bust."

"Jeez," Welsh moaned. "Are you sure you're not a professional dealer?"

"Actually, I'm a commodities trader."

"Big Nick mentioned that."

"Big Nick?"

"The Ambassador."

"You know him that well?"

Welsh held his thumb and forefinger a quarter of an inch apart. "Are you kidding? We were that close to playing golf together."

"What stopped you?"

"I used to be a busboy at a country club. I hate golf; I hate country clubbers. Wait a minute, do you think that means I hate Big Nick? This is a real revelation."

"You seem awfully cheerful, considering our present circumstances."

"We're not dead, and we really ought to be. It could be ten below, and snowing, instead of a nice warm jungle with things to eat in it."

"Like what?"

"You better wait until we cross that bridge—I don't want to psych you out." Welsh paused. "So how does a commodities trader from Chicago come to a piece of hard revenge in Guatemala?"

Scanlan flinched, thought about it, then said, "I was the oldest of two kids. Old enough to remember how happy my dad was when my brother Michael was born. A son, a son. But my poor brother didn't turn out to be anything my poor dad wanted. He didn't like sports, he liked books. He didn't study business in college, he studied philosophy. He didn't go into the commodity pits, he joined the Peace Corps. When he got out of the Peace Corps, he moved back to Guatemala to start a model environmentally responsible farm." Scanlan shook her head. "My Irish dad."

"You went into the business," said Welsh.

"And played sports. And made my first million on the floor. But Michael didn't do it. My dad pushed, and Michael went in the opposite direction every time." Scanlan had been talking to the trees. She turned to face Welsh. "Huge tracts of this whole Petén region were given to senior Army officers as rewards, tribute, whatever you want to call it. National park, biosphere reserve, that was just a colored space on the map. They logged the mahogany and sold the parrots and macaws to pet shops in the States. If there was a Maya site they sent in *huaqueros*, grave robbers, to strip it, and the artifacts ended up in art galleries in New York. Marijuana was planted instead of food, and planes from Colombia landed and took off. My brother saw all that going on, and he thought he was going to do something about it. Got himself killed, is what he did.

"I can see it on your face, Welsh. He was a naïve North American do-gooder, and he practically begged to get himself killed. You know what? I agree with you. But he was my brother, and when he was murdered it killed my dad too. Heart attack."

"I'm sorry," said Welsh.

"I buried Michael, and I buried my dad, and I got my mom settled. I thought about going back to work, but what was the point? I came down here to see if I could get some answers. My sister-in-law is the sweetest woman in the world. Wouldn't hurt a fly. Forgives the men who killed her husband. No one here would talk to me. The Guatemalan government. The State Department."

"You've got to understand their job," Welsh explained. "The State Department, that is. They're smart people, but their job is to go to another country and get along with the host government. When you consider what most governments are, after a while kissing ass and turning a blind eye become institutional characteristics."

"Oh, I understand that. How many people have the character to risk their career on behalf of a stranger? I don't know if I would. Anyway, I had money, I spread it around, and I got answers. I thought about hiring a killer, I really did. But a colonel in the Guatemalan Army? Any hired gun would just take my money and disappear. So what happened is what happened."

"Fathers and sons," said Welsh. "Takes us men half our lives to get over our relationship with our fathers, and the other half to get over our relationship with our sons."

"You too, huh?"

"I understand how your brother felt." He decided then he ought to let her know everything Booker had told

235

him, and the contents of the ammo can. It was only fair, since they were sharing the same risk now, and if something happened to him she needed to know about the stuff. He even told her about the appearance of the snake the previous day.

The story left Scanlan with a satisfied expression on her face. "Now I see. What I first thought was a special talent for irritating me was just you trying to protect me. I understand why you thought you had to keep everything secret, and why Booker wouldn't tell me anything." She stamped her foot. "That dirty, rotten son of a bitch. He set this whole thing up to get himself out of Guatemala. The only reason he got in touch with me was to get to someone like you. Do you think he betrayed you?"

"That wasn't in his own best interest, unless he was hanging by his thumbs. I'm pretty sure he's dead."

"I suppose you're right. He was an evil man, but no one deserves what they must have done to him." She shivered. "And I'm glad I didn't see that snake. I hate them." She looked at him questioningly. "Were you scared?"

"Are you kidding? I was barely holding my fudge."

Scanlan's eyebrows shot up, and she started giggling. Then she dealt out another hand.

"Damnation!" Welsh exclaimed as she dealt herself a blackjack.

"I think you could say that a commodities trader counts as a professional gambler."

"If this keeps up I'll have to sign over my car."

There were a few seconds of silence, and then Scanlan said, "You mean you're not going to bring up that old line: unlucky at cards, lucky at love?"

That was out of the blue. Welsh didn't know if she was just being mischievous, or he was being tested. "I don't use lines," he replied. "For the only reason that I can't say them and keep a straight face at the same time."

"That's very interesting. So how do you manage un-solicited introductions?"

"I just walk up and say, 'Hi, I'm Rich Welsh, would you like to dance?' Or whatever's appropriate to the situation."

"So you dance?"

"Being objective, if you saw me in action you'd say to yourself: This guy is either having a seizure or he needs to enter a Twelve-Step Program for the rhythmically challenged."

"But you do dance."

"As long as women like to dance, I'll be out there. I not only have no sense of rhythm, I also have no sense of embarrassment."

"What would you have said to that girl at the Ambassador's reception?"

"What girl?"

Scanlan mimed an hourglass shape with her hands.

Welsh grinned. So she'd noticed the meaningful glances across the room. "Oh, her. I'd say: 'Hi, I'm Rich Welsh, may I have my penis back when you're done with it?' "

Scanlan clapped her hands over her mouth to stifle a shriek. When she recovered, she said, "If we get back to the States alive, all gambling debts are square."

"Fair enough."

She scratched a cluster of mosquito bites on her arm. "I'm itching like crazy. I think they got me when we were hiding yesterday. I didn't even feel them bite."

"Monkeys," said Welsh.

"Pardon?"

"North American mosquitoes don't have many prey able to slap them off. Humans are only a tiny proportion of the available species. So, if you're paying attention, you can feel them land and bite. But in Central America there's a lot of species, monkeys in particular, able to squash them. So evolution favored very quiet, sneaky mosquitoes with a light touch and an imperceptible bite."

"You're certainly a fountain of useful information."

"Or useless, as the case may be."

"But you do know your way around."

"I'm school-trained as a Winter Mountain Leader Instructor, ironically enough. True to form, having done that, the Marine Corps only sent me to jungles."

"Which jungles?"

"Northern Training Area, Okinawa. Southeastern Thailand. Fort Sherman, Panama, which used to be the U.S. Army Jungle Operations Training Center."

"I picked the right guy to get stuck in the jungle with."

"Listen, I could tell you horror stories about some of the whiners in uniform I had to drag through the jungle; you're doing just great."

"I've been meaning to ask you, shouldn't we be setting out snares or something?"

"All survival books show you how to make a snare, which is fine as far as it goes. But the snag is that animals chased every minute by nature's most perfect predators are not going to throw themselves into your trap out of deep concern that you're a human and happen to be hungry."

"Then they don't work?"

"Sure, they do. But you have to spend days finding the trails and routines of the local game. Then you have to set the snare at a game trail or water hole without disturbing the tiniest thing that would make these very alert animals suspicious. Then you have to hang around, getting hungrier and weaker, until something hits the snare. Maybe."

"I see. So what's the solution?"

"Plant foods are easiest. You can gather them while you move. Fish are good. If we didn't have to stay hidden I'd have a line in that stream right now." There were other things too, but Welsh still didn't think it was the right time to bring them up.

They spent the afternoon taking alternating naps, one sleeping and the other keeping watch. Welsh took the opportunity to clean the Beretta. A single day in wet jungle climate would start it rusting. He detail-stripped the weapon and magazines, spreading the parts out on the poncho. A twig and piece of handkerchief served as cleaning rod and patch. A tube of Vaseline was all they had for a lubricant and preservative. He applied it thinly and rubbed it into the external parts. He wiped the internal parts through his naturally oily hair.

The sound suppressor was easy to clean. At one end was a screw-in package of wipes: polyurethane disks like washers that allowed a bullet to pass through while slowing the propellant gases to below the speed of sound. The gases were what produced the noise of gunfire, that and the bullet breaking the sound barrier. The subsonic ammunition made for suppressed weapons had a light powder load that kept the bullet under that speed.

Scanlan woke up and looked over at the hole Welsh had dug several feet away. The dirt was piled up on the edge of the tarp. "What's that for?"

"We need to lighten your pack."

"What do you mean?"

"Did you bring any other extras, beside the cards?"

"What would make you think I have anything extra?"

"Your pack is bulging pretty well for what I told you to bring. Don't be offended; it's a normal human tendency. On the Bataan Death March guys refused to throw away useless possessions, even though it cost them their lives. Every extra ounce on your back makes for that much harder going. Especially in this climate."

"What have you got in *your* pack?" Scanlan demanded.

"Bar of soap, toothbrush, container of salt, and the

roll of toilet paper I swiped from the hotel. The tarp and mosquito net. Extra socks. First-aid kit, bug repellent, water bottles. The ammo can with the tapes. And a little aluminum cooking pot and a pie pan."

"Oh." Then she asked brightly, "Will we be having pie?"

"No. You'll see." Welsh gestured toward the hole.

"I'm doing this under protest."

"So noted. After a few days on the march you'll see why it had to be done. Remember, new toilet articles can be purchased once we reach civilization. As the old Ranger saying goes: Travel light, and freeze at night."

"I've already done that. And I didn't find it personally fulfilling."

Welsh gestured toward the hole again. Scanlan unzipped her pack and began firing articles into the hole. When she was finished he carefully replaced the topsoil he'd cut away and set aside. He rolled the excess dirt up in the tarp and scattered it well away from the campsite.

"I hesitate to bring it up," he said. "But there's something else we need to do while it's still light."

"Oh, I'm sure this is going to be good. Out with it."

"Tick check."

"What?"

"Tick check. Every time you go to the bathroom, you should run your hands over your whole body. Any little bumps are probably ticks, and since they're big-time disease carriers, they need to be removed. Most you can do yourself. You can't reach your back, so someone else has to check it."

"This time I'm not going to ask if it's a joke."

"Ever take a tick off?"

"No."

"I'm sure we'll find one or two to practice on."

Chapter Twenty-eight

The second night under the tarp passed much easier. Welsh's watch beeped them awake before dawn. He packed everything by touch and then, Beretta at the ready, waited for first light. It was known as a stand-to in the military, because one of the most favorable times to make an attack was out of the rising sun when it was just light enough to see. There was no attack. They had a few Fig Newtons for breakfast and began walking. Welsh was careful to first head upstream before looping back onto his preplanned route.

By the afternoon they had made just over five miles, about what Welsh had expected. To guard against ambush, they were forced to move very cautiously. Welsh hadn't needed that first day to teach him that in the jungle the stationary always have the advantage over the moving. He walked with the Beretta in hand and the safety off, and tolerated no unnecessary conversation. He would take a single step, sweep his gaze slowly left to right, listening all the while, and only then take another step and repeat the process. Along with a ten-minute rest break every hour, they stopped and sat silently for a minute or so every half hour, alert for unusual noises or even smells in the air.

The rules were simple. They never followed trails or paths, even those made by animals. They avoided all open areas like clearings and breaks in the jungle.

The only unscheduled stops they made were when Welsh spied a familiar vine growing up a tree. He chopped the stalk off low to the ground, careful not to leave a cut on the tree trunk, and yanked the vine down. Then he sliced off the end, stuck it in his pack, and threw the rest away.

"What is that?" Scanlan whispered the first time.

"I don't remember the name. But I first saw it in Panama. The green growing tip is edible."

"What does it taste like?"

"Chicken."

"Whaaat?"

"All survival food tastes just like chicken," he said, grinning. "Always remember that."

"Okay," she said with a laugh.

Despite the common belief that jungles teemed with life, they encountered few animals other than birds and insects. Most creatures knew to make themselves scarce when two large predators were in the vicinity.

But in that late afternoon, when the sun was at a low angle, Welsh's gaze happened to fall on one particular tree. A shaft of sunlight threw a circle like a spotlight on the trunk, about seven feet from the ground.

He turned to Scanlan and held a finger to his lips. He silently thumbed on the pistol's safety and holstered it.

Scanlan watched him sprint toward the tree and swing his staff like a baseball bat. When it hit the tree something large dropped off and writhed on the ground.

Welsh drove the staff at it like a spear. Then, smiling broadly, he motioned Scanlan over.

She came up and saw a large snake, a beautiful emerald-green tree boa, pinned to the ground by the crook on the end of the staff. The boa was very angry, striking at the wood while Welsh kept his weight on the other end.

"Dinnertime," he announced.

"Oh, no," Scanlan breathed.

Welsh whipped out his machete and pinned the snake's head down with the flat of the blade. He grabbed it just behind the head with his left hand, and sliced the head off with the machete. The snake's body, acting on the last message from its nervous system, kept writhing.

Still holding the headless snake, he shucked off his pack. "Maggie, would you take out the pot and pie pan?"

She handed him the small aluminum cooking pot. Welsh released his grip on the snake's neck and drained its blood into the pot. He counted off the seconds in his head, and didn't get to ten before she asked, "What are you going to do with that blood?"

"Cook it into a broth. Lots of salts and minerals."

"You mean we don't get to drink it raw?" she asked, feigning disappointment.

"It would be the badass thing to do," Welsh conceded. "But you'd also be drinking raw bacteria and viruses."

"In that case I'll wait for the broth."

"So you'll have some?"

"I might as well. If we survive I'll be able to dine out for years on the stories from this trip."

Welsh slit the snake's belly and scraped the innards out onto the ground. Then he made a circular cut, just through the skin, about four inches from the tail.

"Here's your chance to help," he said.

"Oh, great," Scanlan groaned.

243

He offered her the tail end. "Hold on real tight. Use both hands and dig your heels in for traction."

Scanlan grimaced at the touch of the snake. "Just what are we doing here?"

"Pulling his coat off." Welsh cut a little of the skin free from each side of the belly incision and got a firm grip on the two flaps of skin. He was facing Scanlan, as if the snake were the rope in a tug of war. He'd left her that four inches of dry skin for a good grip. "Got it?"

Scanlan gritted her teeth and nodded.

Welsh pulled the two flaps down and toward his body. The skin came away from the meat with a wet tearing sound.

"Oh, God," Scanlan moaned, looking off in the distance so she wouldn't have to see it.

Welsh kept pulling and backing up. The trick was to use just enough force to get the skin off but keep it in one piece, like the peel of a banana. The snake turned into a tube of light red meat, except for the four inches of tail skin Scanlan was holding onto. "You can let go now."

She dropped her end as if it was on fire.

"Wasn't that fun?" Welsh asked, wiping his bloody hands on a handful of leaves.

"Terrific. I can't wait to see what comes next."

"Your work is done." He trimmed the bark from some green sticks, sliced the snake into chunks, and threaded the meat onto the sticks. "Snake kebobs," he announced.

"I'm thinking of becoming a vegetarian."

"All the more for me then."

Welsh took the twelve-inch pie pan and filled the bottom with dirt. He gathered some wood, placing the largest piece in the center of the pan, and leaned the smaller twigs against it at an angle. "Let me show you the secret of making a fire with permanently damp jungle wood, and not waste twenty matches doing it."

"I used to love watching Daniel Boone on TV."

"He didn't have this." Welsh arranged a clump of the very smallest twigs in his palm, produced a butane cigarette lighter from his pocket, flicked it alight, and applied the flame to the twigs. The twigs smoked, and then caught. Welsh pushed the flaming clump into the center of the twig lean-to, and soon the whole thing was burning.

"No fair!" Scanlan protested.

"The continuous flame dries out the wood, then sets it on fire. Works no matter how wet. A candle works too."

"I still say it's not fair."

"The next time we have a day to kill, I'll let you try flint and steel or an Indian bow and drill."

When the fire burned down to coals, he laid the kebobs on top, the sticks supported by the outer lip of the pie pan. He peeled the vine tubers he'd collected that day, cut them into pieces, and buried them in the coals.

"Wouldn't it be easier to just build a fire on the ground?" Scanlan asked.

"It would leave a deep blackened ring, very hard to conceal. After I dump the ashes and dirt from the pan in the nearest stream, you'd never know there was a fire here."

"Very crafty. But I was hoping for pie."

"Some people are never satisfied."

While the snake cooked, he unzipped his first-aid kit and removed a U.S. military aluminum canteen cup. Inside the cup was a plastic bag that he put back into the pouch.

"What's in the bag?" she asked.

"Homemade survival kit. Wind and waterproof matches; water-purification tablets; a candle; a fire-starting flint and magnesium bar; fifty feet of parachute cord; a button compass; piano wire; fishing line, hooks, and split shot."

"Very handy."

"But a little anal-retentive, right?"

"What's that expression? It's not paranoia if you really have enemies? Well, it's not anal if you actually find yourself out in the jungle, needing a survival kit."

"I feel so much better about myself." Welsh extended the wire handles of the canteen cup, and dropped in a piece of Fig Newton saved from the previous day.

"What's all that about?" Scanlan asked.

"An experiment. You'll be the first to know."

"I'm getting to love these mysteries."

Welsh disappeared into the trees, returning without the canteen cup.

Despite her proclamation of vegetarianism, the smell of grilling boa constrictor had Scanlan hovering over the fire.

Welsh picked up a skewer, checked the meat for doneness, and handed it to her. "Sprinkle a little salt on it. I've also got a bottle of hot sauce if you need it."

"Hot sauce?"

"I always bring hot sauce to the field."

"You like your food hot."

"Not really. Enough hot sauce and you can't taste what you're eating. That can be handy in a situation like this."

Scanlan took a cautious bite of snake. Then more. "You know," she said with her mouth full, "it really does taste a little like chicken. How did you see it in the tree?"

"I didn't at first. I was looking at where the light was falling. It's a tree snake, but cold-blooded. It crawled down the trunk to catch the last of the day's sun."

They finished the snake, and then the tubers. The hot sauce went on the tubers. Welsh added some water to the snake blood, and put the pot on the fire.

"You know," Scanlan said, after a cautious sip this time. "It's really not that bad. I think it's because the *idea* of drinking snake's blood is just so gross that the actual taste is nothing compared to it."

"How about dessert?" Welsh asked, after rinsing the flavor of snake blood out of his mouth with a lot of water.

"Pie?"

"No, not pie." He disappeared into the trees and returned with the canteen cup. It was covered with a leaf and a piece of wood. "Promise me you'll keep an open mind?"

"What's in the cup?" Scanlan demanded, her voice reeking with suspicion.

Welsh set the canteen cup on the coals, and periodically banged the side with a chunk of wood. "It might be better to just give this a shot without actually knowing what it is."

"No way."

"Okay," he said. "They're ants."

"Ants!"

"Please lower your voice."

"All right. You're cooking ants?"

"Yeah, you have to cook them to break down the formic acid."

"I wasn't talking about the cooking, I was talking about ants."

"I saw them going into a rotten stump. Chopped it open, and it was loaded with big black carpenter ants. I dropped in the Fig Newton, they piled on, and I just scraped 'em into the canteen cup. In the jungle you've got to be careful, because fire ants or army ants would ruin your whole day if you tried to herd them into a cup. Black ants are the best eating, in my humble opinion."

Scanlan slumped back against her pack. "I'm so glad to hear that."

Welsh took the leaf off the top of the cup. "That was just to keep them from climbing out. They get a little agitated when you heat them up." He scraped around with his metal spoon. "Want to take a shot? They shrink down to little black balls. Not even any legs. Just the abdomen."

"Thank you, no."

Welsh helped himself to a spoonful. "Just like powdered sugar in a crunchy shell. Great for dessert."

"Don't feel you have to lie on my account. I'm not having any."

"Don't be chicken, you already had snake blood. We'll be eating a lot of things that'll either look or taste like crap. Might as well get started."

After an angry look, Scanlan took the spoon and jammed it into her mouth. She chewed quickly and with her eyes closed. "They are a little sugary," she admitted. "But just the thought of eating ants makes me want to puke."

"Think of them as Nature's little candies," Welsh suggested. "Bears love them."

She took the canteen cup, shrugged, and helped herself to a larger portion. "They are better than those vines."

"That's the spirit. If you'll permit me another quote, 'Hunger is the best sauce in the world.' "

"Okay, now who said that?"

"Cervantes, *Don Quixote.*"

"Do you intend to keep quoting from the classics?"

"Only when necessary."

"Yeah, ants were necessary."

After a short rest period for digestive purposes, they continued walking, away from the smells of food and smoke, until Welsh found a suitable bivouac site.

It was in thick brush on the side of a hill. On the chance, however unlikely, that anyone had caught sight of them, they walked right past along the base of the hill, waiting until it was completely dark to circle back, using the night-vision goggles to set up the tarp.

"We spent all day walking along the sides of hills until one of my legs is longer than the other," said Scanlan. "Do we really have to sleep on a slope?"

"The short answer is yes," Welsh replied. "But to keep you from getting pissed, I'll give you the long one too. Every road was once a human footpath. And every footpath was an animal trail first. Animals don't waste energy, they take the easiest route from one point to another. The easiest route is always along valley floors, the long axis of ridgelines, and streams and rivers. So, if you want to lay an ambush with a strong expectation of someone walking into it, those are the places you set up in. Therefore, those are the places we *don't* walk.

"Now, sleeping. If you're a bunch of guys after one or two, and you think you've got a good idea where they are, you put everyone on line and sweep through the area. Hard to do in regular jungle. Nearly impossible in thick brush or along the side of a hill. So there we are."

"You learn something new every day."

"Glad you feel that way. Make sure you sleep with your head uphill from the rest of your body. Otherwise you won't be happy when you wake up in the morning."

Chapter Twenty-nine

The next day they were traveling through a stretch of jungle so thick that the light only came through the canopy in tiny shafts, creating a continual twilight. They'd already gone about two miles out of their way, forced to detour around a large swampy area. Welsh couldn't make out the contours in the terrain, so he followed a straight compass bearing. He was pushing his way through the greenery, stepping carefully with one eye on the dial and the other on the ground ahead, when he heard a low-pitched humming. He stopped and raised the pistol.

"What's that?" Scanlan whispered.

The sound grew louder, and suddenly Welsh's brain made the connection. "Run!" he yelled.

Behind him Scanlan shouted, "What?"

"Fucking run!" Welsh bellowed.

The humming evolved to an angry whine, and the cloud of bees enveloped them. Welsh felt white-hot needles driving into his face and neck and hands. There didn't have to be an allergy; enough stings and you died. That spurred him to run even faster; legs pumping, hands shielding his eyes, blindly breaking a path with his body. All the hollering in his ears told him that Scanlan was right behind.

They crashed down a small hill. At the bottom Welsh saw a scattering of grass hummocks and launched himself in between them. He belly-flopped onto the greasy wet mud and felt it envelope him. The Beretta was still in his right hand, and he managed to keep the muzzle out of the mud. He felt Scanlan hit with a splat right beside him.

When his breath ran out, Welsh very carefully shoved his left hand above the surface of the muck. Nothing stung it, or at least he didn't think so. The little bastards had gotten him so many times, he wasn't sure if he could even feel another sting. He stuck his head out. The bees were gone. The mud had a fulsome aroma of rotting vegetation, and his first move was to spit it out of his mouth.

Scanlan popped up a few seconds later, also spitting mud. As soon as she could see, he took her arm and they waded the short distance back to dry ground. "What an indignity," she exclaimed, grabbing a handful of grass to wipe the mud off her face and neck.

Welsh only grunted. He set the Beretta down in the dry grass and pulled off his muddy and sodden pack. He tore it open, hunting in the first-aid bag for tweezers. He could feel the venom surging through him like burning oil; it was making his arms and legs shake.

Scanlan was really swelling up. He began removing stingers from her face, neck, and arms. Even after the mud bath some of the little venom bags were still attached, and still pumping away.

"Are you allergic to bee stings?" he asked, trying to make the question sound unimportant.

"No, but I feel cold, and a little sick to my stomach."

"That's okay. Any trouble breathing?"

"No, but my tongue feels a little thick," she replied, the slight lisp to her speech confirming it.

When he was done he rolled over on his back, completely exhausted. Scanlan took up the tweezers and went to work on him. "God," she moaned, "I can't remember anything hurting this much. My skin feels like it's on fire."

"We'll be swollen up like soccer balls pretty soon." Welsh touched one of his throbbing ears; it felt like a bunch of grapes. "Not very sanitary, but cool mud probably isn't the worst thing to have on us right now."

Poised over him and busy plucking out stingers, Scanlan said, "Hey, amigo, were those the South American killer bees?" She used a broad Spanish accent, and a goofy smile was accentuated by her mud-slicked face and hair.

Despite the pain and his general mood, Welsh had to chuckle. She really was priceless. Almost anyone else, male or female, would have been either completely hysterical or else withdrawn into a tight sullen cocoon. "I didn't get a chance to check their dog tags, but I think so."

"They certainly were pissed off."

"We got too close to their hive and they attacked. These Africanized strains are really territorial. Run your ass down and keep stinging until you're dead."

"Not like those easygoing North American bees?"

"Nope. No sense of humor at all."

Scanlan tapped him on the shoulder, then grimaced at the pain it caused her swollen hand. "Rich, what would you do if I were allergic to bee stings."

"Unless you had one of those allergy injectors, all I could do is try to keep your airway open."

"If something like that ever happens," she said seriously, "I want you to leave me behind."

"Don't be melodramatic. This was just a nasty lesson in how fast the jungle can turn on you. We'll be more careful, keep hanging together. We'll be all right."

Welsh dispensed Benadryl antihistamine capsules from the first-aid kit, and after a short rest they got moving. By the time they found a stream to wash in, the mud had dried, brown and hard and scratchy like plaster. It made the bee stings even more painful, if that was possible.

The stream was slow-moving and about ten feet wide. There was practically no bank; the trees grew right down into the water. After finding a sharp bend where they couldn't be easily seen, Welsh stood guard while Scanlan rinsed herself off.

He was very anxious about being even that exposed in broad daylight, and rested on one knee with the pistol ready. When she was through, he dunked himself and his pack in the stream. They went back into the trees and slumped down on their packs.

Welsh was livid, mainly with himself. "After everything that's happened, to be ambushed and fucked up by bees!"

Scanlan reached over and gently took his hand. "Are you sure you're all right?"

Welsh put his other hand on hers, very gently. "I think I'm having a bad day. You want to bag the rest of it?"

"I was really hoping you'd say that." She paused. "By the way, what's for dinner tonight?"

He smiled through swollen lips. "We could go back and get some honey?"

"God, that's really funny," she said without enthusiasm.

"Okay, I see some water lilies growing in the stream.

We'll boil up the tubers. I'll throw in a line, see if there's any fish."

"Great," she said, again without enthusiasm.

"Hey, if you've got a better offer, take it."

"I'm not being ungrateful . . . yes, I am being ungrateful, and I apologize. I was just thinking back on that snake with more than a little longing."

"The jungle version of Murphy's Law. When you don't want snakes around, you're up to your ass in them. When you're ready to start eating, they're nowhere to be found."

They made camp a short distance away, and both felt sick the rest of the afternoon, and would until the venom passed through their systems.

To take his mind off it, Welsh opened up his survival kit and began putting together a fishing rig. He cut a piece of monofilament fishing line as long as the width of the stream. Every six inches along the line he tied an overhand knot loop. To each of the loops he tied a shorter leader line with a hook on the other end.

"I've never seen anything like that," said Scanlan.

"Probably because it's illegal any place with fish and game laws. It's called a trotline—a poacher's rig."

Welsh dug around with the machete for worms and grubs to bait the hooks. When he had enough, he took the whole rig down to the stream. He tied a sizable rock to one end of the long line and tossed it out into the water. The other end was tied to a strong sapling on the bank.

"With the rock sitting on the bottom the hooks hang at varying depths," he explained. "Much better chance of something biting. And since we can just leave it there, I don't have to sit on the bank like Huck Finn with his cane pole, in full view of anyone who might happen by."

He checked the line every so often, but nothing bit. So it was stewed water-lily tubers for dinner. Welsh diced in the earthworms left over from the fishing bait. Worms were high-quality protein, he explained to Scanlan, with most of the essential amino acids. He really thought she'd draw the line on that, even after all his fast talking. She ate it, but withheld comment. She was as hungry as he was.

During the flight from the bees, the nylon upper had come apart from the sole of one of her running shoes. Welsh contributed some tough nylon threads from a piece of parachute cord, and the big needle he used to puncture blisters. Scanlan did the jury-rigged sewing job.

In the predawn darkness Welsh found three small catfish on the trotline, and the shredded remains of several more that something larger had taken the opportunity to feast on. He grilled the fish over a quick fire, and then, swollen and hurting on top of everything else, he and Scanlan continued on their journey.

Chapter Thirty

By the sixth day in jungle they were pretty ragged. Their clothes were torn, even with corrective stitching every night. Averaging a meal a day, not always large, was only enough to keep them going, not maintain their weight. Welsh soon noticed his ribs protruding. Scanlan's clothes seemed to be hanging looser by the day. And the only good thing about their general lack of cleanliness was that being outdoors they could smell neither themselves nor each other. They were constantly wet: from the daily rains, the draining heat, or just walking through the damp foliage. It was like wearing a second skin of sweat and grit.

Just moving through the jungle brought endless scratches and insect bites. These were carefully tended every night, because in that climate small wounds boiled up into serious infections terrifyingly quickly.

After being subjected to the elements, a marginal diet, and the ordeal of movement in difficult terrain, it didn't take long to reach that level of fatigue where you found any number of excellent reasons for not moving at all.

From hard experience in the Marine Corps, Welsh understood this perfectly. He strictly adhered to a daily schedule. Scanlan occasionally grumbled at his fanaticism, but he went by the Marine Corps maxim that it was time to worry only when the troops *stopped* bitching. From the first day in the jungle it had been clear that Margaret Scanlan would walk until she dropped rather than concede that she was incapable of keeping up with him. Everyone found their determination in a different place.

On the afternoon of that sixth day they were out of water, but Welsh wasn't really concerned. If they couldn't find a stream or pool, he'd go to low ground and dig. Water nearly always bubbled up into the hole. Wait for it to clear or strain it through a piece of cloth.

Before it came to any of that, some noise attracted his attention. "Hear that?" he said.

"What?" said Scanlan.

"Listen."

"All I hear are birds."

"That's it. You know what brings so many birds together?"

"Stop teasing."

"Fruit trees. As you've noticed, the jungle isn't carpeted with fruit trees. The few there are attract a ton of birds. And even if the fruit is high up in the canopy, they knock a lot on the ground."

"What the hell are we waiting for?"

"My thoughts exactly."

They followed the noise, and it was a longer walk than expected. As usual in the jungle, they didn't see what they were looking for until they were right on top of it.

"Wild plantain trees," said Welsh. "A nice little grove of them."

Scanlan audibly smacked her lips. "Bananas."

"Plantains. More starch than sugar."

"Look," she said. "Up there."

Welsh shaded his eyes with his hand. Tiny forms were flitting about in the canopy and adding to the general din. "Spider monkeys. Not as noisy as howlers, but less shy."

"Aren't you going to shoot one?"

Welsh smiled. "Don't have anything against eating your ancestors, eh? I'd just waste my ammo trying to hit something that small that high up. And if I only wounded one, we'd lose it in the brush."

There was still some fruit hanging. Welsh knocked a bunch down with his staff. "Everything spoils so fast in this climate," he said. "We'll just take tonight's dinner."

He bent over to pick up the fruit. There was a tugging at his pack. He turned around. Scanlan was pointing. Two large male monkeys had whipped down a tree, touched ground, and were advancing on them, screaming and gesturing wildly.

The snap of the shot was drowned out by all the commotion, and the largest monkey pitched backward, limbs akimbo. The other looked down with an amazed expression, then tore off into the tree. There was a stampede, and within fifteen seconds there wasn't a monkey left in the neighborhood.

A thin wisp of smoke curled from the end of the sound suppressor. "Damn," Welsh said. "They were really wild. Protecting their territory, aggressive as shit. Probably never saw a human before." He turned to Scanlan. "Any objection to saving the plantains for dessert?"

"Are you kidding?" she replied, with a look of pure bloodthirstiness. "I've had snake and iguana so far. Why not monkey?"

"Why not?" Welsh asked.

"You could pass me one of those plantains now."

"Have you had dysentery yet?" Welsh asked.

She gave him a look. "I think I would have known."

"You haven't because we've cooked everything. We'll boil the plantains. And they're better that way. Really."

She said it with great forbearance. "Yes, I'm sure they are."

They decided to move out of the area before stopping to cook. If they were attracted to the plantains, someone else might be too. Scanlan carried the monkey, tied to a stick, so he could walk point with the pistol.

There was still the matter of water. And as usual, Welsh heard it running before he saw it. But as he slowly pushed through the leaves, he also heard something unusual. He held up a hand and Scanlan froze behind him. It wasn't the unnatural sound of human movement; softer, though still out of the ordinary. And it was right in front of them.

Welsh didn't know if they could back away without making noise. If they hadn't been out of water he might have tried. And if it had sounded like someone shifting around in an ambush position. Or bees. But something made him move forward. He brought his pistol up, took two steps forward, slid under a branch, and there was the stream.

Welsh literally felt the hair go up on the back of his neck. It was an instinctive, primitive reaction. Standing on the edge of the stream, halfway in the water, was a jaguar. The big cat, a female, had one protective paw atop the carcass of a wild pig. The light came through the canopy and caught the black rosettes blending hypnotically down her yellow sides. Temple art, Welsh thought.

He was transfixed. The jaguar was still breathing hard

from the hunt. Her tail waved languorously, and then stiffened as Scanlan made a tiny noise coming up. The cat's black-tipped ears twitched, she dropped to a crouch, and the head turned quickly. Welsh found himself gazing into two sublime pale yellow eyes. He and the jaguar stared at each other, and then the cat picked up the pig in its mouth, cleared the stream in a single powerful bound, and plunged into the trees on the opposite side. The movement and disappearance were so fast Welsh though he might have had a hallucination.

"Did you see that?" he whispered.

"Yes, I'm sorry I scared it."

"The breeze must have been blowing toward us; she didn't get our scent. Don't worry, she's the dominant predator in this jungle, and we were just an annoyance." He sat down beside the stream, the pistol in his lap. "No wonder the Indians worshipped them. Did you ever see anything more magnificent in your life?"

"It was beautiful, but I thought you were going to shoot it."

Welsh shook his head vehemently. He was facing the opposite side of the stream, and Scanlan saw him bring his sleeve up to his face. "Are you okay?" she asked.

Welsh turned to her, his eyes shining. "Do you know how lucky we were to see her out here? Free? What a gift!"

She smiled warmly. "So there's a spiritual side too."

The male in Welsh only shrugged. "So how do we interpret such a powerful omen?"

"I'll leave that to you. I'm still trying to decide whether we have good karma because we got out of the hotel and lived through that ambush, or bad because we have to eat bugs in the jungle."

"You'll never let me forget about those termites, will you?" They'd come across the distinctive aboveground nest mounds in the course of an otherwise food-less day.

Welsh smashed the nests with a rock and quickly shoveled the pieces into their mosquito head nets. He dunked them in the nearest stream, dissolving the nests. The occupants were de-winged and roasted in the embers of a fire. Scanlan apologized yet again for being ungrateful, but said that she would still hold it against him.

The thought of it made Welsh smile as he looked around the stream. It was only a foot wide, shaded by the trees and dappled by sunlight, so shallow and clear that the gravel bed was visible. "This is beautiful, isn't it?"

She sat down beside him so they could speak very softly. "What my dad used to call a good medicine place."

Welsh slipped off his pack and began filling the water bottles. He shook them vigorously to dissolve the iodine.

"I suppose in another few years the chainsaws will take care of it," Scanlan said.

"Careful," he warned. "People will start calling you a cynic like me. Don't worry about the jungle. They can cut the hardwoods, slash and burn, run cattle in for American fast food. But the soil isn't Iowa, pretty soon the cattle have no graze, and within a generation the jungle is back. A few jaguars will come out of hiding, and all the get-rich schemes of twenty-first-century man will look like the Maya temples you find around here with the vines growing over them."

"I suppose that's a hopeful thought."

"As hopeful as you can get with Homo sapiens running around loose."

"I don't know. If people are educated, they can change things."

Welsh smiled sadly and shook his head again. "I know my species." He passed her a water bottle. "And now we've got to get hydrated and find a spot to cook some monkey."

Scanlan sighed. "There's your realistic side taking over again. You notice I didn't say cynical."

"I appreciate that."

Later, hunched over the fire, he said, "Arm or a leg?"

"Whatever's medium-rare."

"Well-done," said Welsh. "I'll give you the long reason again. We were talking about what humans are doing to the tropical forest. Well, the forest has its own defenses. Out here there are viruses we've never encountered, just waiting to hop aboard. Mr. Spider Monkey may be immune, but our DNA is uncomfortably similar. Both HIV and the Ebola virus got loose when some Africans decided to snack on raw chimpanzee. So we'll have our monkey well-done."

"You know, if you just gave arbitrary orders I could enjoy being resentful. Well, I'm glad you cut his little hands and feet off anyway. I think I've dealt with things pretty well, but I'd have trouble with fingers and toes."

After they finished it was still light, so they kept walking. They were halted by a river more than fifty yards wide with a very fast current. "The good news," he said, "is that this is the Belize River, and they don't name things after Belize in Guatemala. The bad news is that we have to cross it to get anywhere."

"And I suppose the risk of drowning is the bad news."

"I couldn't have put it any better. I'll throw my trotline in the water tonight, and maybe we'll have fish for breakfast before we drown."

"I wouldn't have put it like that," she said.

Chapter Thirty-one

In the morning there were two peacock bass high up on the trotline, and a catfish near the bottom.

After breakfast Welsh showed Scanlan how to make a raft. He spread the nylon tarp on the ground and placed both their packs side by side in the center. Then he rolled the tarp around them like a cigar. He tied one end off with parachute cord. He put his mouth over the other, blew the package up like a balloon, and tied that end tightly.

He braided the remaining parachute cord into a triple thickness, tying one end around her waist with a bowline knot, the other around his.

"Whatever happens," he said, "happens to both of us."

"That could be good or bad. We just float across?"

"Actually, we kick like maniacs. And whatever happens, don't let go of the raft."

"Don't worry about that."

They went across at first light, when there was less

chance of being observed. A running start and a hard leap off the bank onto the river. The water was freezing, and the current took hold of them. They kicked hard, but made more progress downstream than across. As they finally got close to the opposite bank, it looked like they'd made a major miscalculation. The bank was high and undercut, with no place to get a handhold and pull themselves up.

Welsh was starting to get both tired and concerned when he saw it. The river had eroded the bank and dropped a tree into the water. The trunk had snagged a lot of other floating branches. At least the raft was out in front of them so it would get impaled by a branch first.

They hit the tree trunk so hard it slid a little deeper into the water. Now Welsh was really concerned. If the trunk came off the bank they were going downstream with it. He hooked one arm around the trunk, pulled the folding knife from his pocket, and cut the parachute cord linking them. "Pull yourself up," he shouted over the roaring water.

Scanlan went first, inching up the trunk and snapping off branches. The trunk was saturated with water. The bark slid off at every touch, and the underlying wood was slick as glass. Welsh pushed from behind, and Scanlan scrambled onto the bank. The trunk slid a little bit more. She reached out her hand for his; he gave her the raft instead.

A foot from the bank, both Scanlan's hands grabbed the back of his shirt collar in a death grip, and he half pushed, half flipped onto the bank. As he was lying there gasping for breath, he could see that only a few inches of the mushroomed root system was still on the bank. Then he rolled over and Scanlan's face was right in front of him.

"*That* was fun," she said.

"Funny you should say that," said Welsh. "*I* didn't like it at all."

"Next time bring a rubber raft and an outboard."

"I'll make a note of that."

When he got his wind back, they carried the raft intact to the high ground overlooking the stream-valley. Since they'd floated more than a quarter mile downstream from where they'd initially crossed, Welsh had to do another map resection to determine where they were.

After he got that done, he pulled out the binoculars to check the other side of the river.

Scanlan dragged the packs over to where he was glassing the surrounding area.

Welsh said, "I think I have the answer to that omen."

"What do you mean."

"Someone is following us."

"Who's following us?" Scanlan said quickly. "The same ones as before?"

Welsh was still lying on his belly looking through the binoculars. "One guy, dressed like a peasant, a *campesino*. He's carrying a civilian rifle or a shotgun."

"Couldn't he just be out hunting?"

"Hunting us. When I first caught sight of him, he was running down the bank from upstream, trying to see where we came ashore. He's right on our track. I imagine there's quite a bounty on our heads."

"But how did he find us?"

"He could have just stumbled across our trail."

"What are we going to do?"

"Let's see if he has any friends with him."

Welsh kept watching. Scanlan found herself fidgeting, and sat down on her pack.

"No," Welsh said after a few minutes. "A loner. He's chopping trees and making a raft. Must not have wanted to share the reward. A little greedy, if you ask me."

"So what does that mean?"

Welsh kept his eyes on the river bank as he talked. "He may try to sneak up on us while we're sleeping, or he may just follow us and go for help as soon as we get near a populated area."

"Are we going to hide again?"

"In a way. We'll hide while we wait for him to show up, and when he does I'm going to kill him."

"Is that our only option?"

Welsh turned to look at her. "If you can think of a way around it, you've got the floor."

She surprised him by saying, very coldly and clinically, "How will you do it?"

Welsh recited, " 'If somebody's trailing you, make a circle, come back onto your tracks, and ambush the folks that aim to ambush you.' "

"That doesn't sound like one of the classics."

"Ah, but it is. The Standing Orders of Rogers' Rangers, written in 1759 and still relevant. As a matter of fact, we've already followed most of them."

"Then I'm glad you remembered them."

"By the way, how do you feel about being the bait?"

"I figured it would be something like that. All right."

"All right?"

"Yes, all right," she said impatiently. "I suppose you were waiting for me to say, 'Rich, why do I have to be the bait?' so you could say, 'Okay, Maggie, you take the gun and shoot him.' Well, I'm filthy and hungry and tired, and more than a little mad about being chased through this stinking jungle. Right now I'd love to shoot the fucking asshole, but I couldn't do it as well as you. So I'll be the bait."

Welsh was starting to grasp why throughout history warriors feared death in battle less than being taken alive and turned over to the women.

They left the high ground before the *campesino* put his raft in the water. Welsh guessed that, wherever the guy came ashore, he'd just work his way up the bank until he picked up their trail again.

Just as the pace count from the stream reached one thousand, one hundred meters, a beautiful dense thicket appeared before them. And right on their route of march, so it would look like a natural obstacle they'd been forced to go through.

He led the way with his staff, and Scanlan followed. Birds were screaming at them, but that was what Welsh wanted. He only hoped they didn't bump into a snake, or another beehive.

They'd crawled about forty yards when he stopped and took off his pack. "I want you to stay here and make noise," he said. "Nothing obvious. Every once in a while rattle the packs, break a stick. You'll be holding his attention to his front, and I'll be off to one side."

"Don't take this wrong, but what happens if everything doesn't go according to plan?"

He handed her the map and compass. "Now aren't you glad you learned how to use these? If he gets me, leave your pack here and take mine. Follow the route and compass bearings on the map and you'll eventually run into civilization. From there you're on your own. If I don't make it, good luck. I think you're really special."

Before she could say anything else, Welsh slithered back into the thick vegetation. Scanlan looked around for a moment, then picked up a stick and with great concentration began breaking it into small pieces.

Welsh crawled slowly. The jumble of branches and twigs made it impossible to move very quietly, but that was what he wanted. When he thought he was nearing the end of the semi-circle, he periodically raised up to look for the wide groove they'd made passing through the brush. When he saw it he backed off until he was positioned beside the thin trunk of a sapling, with its branches spread out over him. He cleared the area of twigs and anything else that might make a noise, then got down on his stomach with the pistol extended before him and his elbows braced on the ground. He was between ten and fifteen feet from the original trail, and at a right angle. When he was settled he took the Beretta off safe, keeping his index finger alongside the trigger guard.

If he listened carefully, he could occasionally hear Scanlan off to his right. He concentrated on slowing his breathing. There would be just one chance to do everything right. It was easy to hit a target on a sunny day at a well-organized shooting range, but conditions were never so pleasant when it was for real.

Hours passed, and it was afternoon. Welsh refused to move even to look at his watch. His thighs and chest felt on fire. He had to piss, and would have gone in his pants if he hadn't been afraid the smell would give him away. At least the discomfort made him concentrate. Bugs crawled over him and bit him relentlessly. But still he didn't move.

More time passed. How much he didn't know, though the light changed as the sun continued its leisurely movement. Then Welsh heard a very subtle noise off to his left. Come on, he thought. Come right ahead. He felt excited, but not at all frightened. That worried him a little.

An occasional sound grew closer. Very careful, Welsh thought, very deliberate. Like a good hunter. What was that short story: *The Most Dangerous Game*? Hunting man for sport. He thought he remembered an old movie too. Forget that, he told himself. Concentrate.

The sounds became a gentle rustling, noticeable only from a short distance. It started and stopped in a regular rhythm. His opponent was halting every few feet to listen.

When the sound of movement was almost opposite

him, Welsh slid his finger onto the trigger, and popped up on his knees. He raised the pistol until the sights settled on the human shape in the path, then smoothly squeezed the trigger. The hammer fell, but there was only a dull click as the cartridge refused to fire.

The *campesino* whirled about; Welsh launched himself like a sprinter out of the blocks and charged. He let out a wild yell to tamp down his fear. The branches snagged and cut him like little whips as he tore through. It was only ten feet, but it seemed he'd never get there.

The *campesino* rose from the ground and brought his weapon up. He was also hindered by the thick brush.

A flash and thunderclap blew up in Welsh's face and blinded him for a moment. His right arm took a tremendous blow, but his momentum carried him on. Welsh hit the *campesino* at full stride, leading with the shoulder, and felt all the air go out of him. They rolled, Welsh lashing out with his elbows and knees, both of them grunting like wild animals. The secret of hand-to-hand combat wasn't fancy moves, but ceaseless aggression. In the tangle something steel hit Welsh hard on the jaw, but he didn't stop. Welsh finally got his left arm under the *campesino*'s chin and yanked back. He had a height and weight advantage, but the smaller man was hard and wiry. Welsh grabbed his left wrist with his right hand and squeezed as hard as he could. The body in his grasp scratched and kicked and thrashed wildly. Welsh held on, driving with his legs to keep the other man's arms pinned against the ground. The body relaxed slightly, and Welsh squeezed even harder. He kept on until he couldn't feel his arm anymore and didn't even know if he was still squeezing.

He finally let go. The limp body dropped from his grasp and rolled over. The man was at least part Indian; Welsh guessed a professional hunter. The eyes were half open and dead, the face horribly contorted. Welsh felt for a pulse at the wrist, since the carotid arteries in the neck were probably ruptured. Nothing.

Then he realized that Scanlan must have heard the shot. If she started running he might not be able to catch her. "Maggie!" he shouted, disregarding the danger. "Maggie!"

"Rich?" It came through the wall of branches.

"It's all right," Welsh shouted. "It's over. Come here." He felt a little woozy, and put his head between his knees for a moment. Then it occurred to him that he might be wounded and pumping blood and not even know it.

He was bleeding. His right shirt sleeve was ripped to pieces, and blood was flowing down his arm. There was a lot of blood but Welsh didn't panic, knowing that even small wounds bled excessively. There was none of the powerful spurting that would come from a punctured artery. He felt along the arm until he found the wound, then applied hard direct pressure to it with his left hand. Shit, it really felt big. He called out, "Maggie, bring my pack." The blood was slippery, and it was hard to get a good grip on the arm. He held it over his head to further slow the bleeding.

There was a crashing in the brush. "Over here," he kept saying, to give her something to home in on.

Scanlan appeared, fighting through the branches. She glanced first at the body, then him. "Oh, my God."

Welsh had a feeling he didn't look so good; she seemed more horrified at the sight of him than the dead man. "I think it might have gone better if I'd let you shoot the son of a bitch," he said. "Would you take out my first-aid kit?"

"Are you badly hurt?"

"I don't know," he said, trying to sound calm. "You're going to have to check."

Scanlan pulled out the Unit-1 medical bag and un-zipped the pockets.

"There's a syringe in there," he said. "No needle on it, just a catheter tip. We also need a tweezers, a couple of gauze pads, and a tube of antibiotic ointment."

Scanlan got everything out. She wiped back her hair with a dirty hand, and despite his anxiety Welsh had to smile at her face, so determined to be strong. He said, "I'm going to take my hand off, tell me how it looks."

The wound was bleeding much less now. Scanlan examined it closely, wiping the blood and gore away with the gauze. "It looks like slices cut across your upper arm," she said. "Not very deep, but the flesh is all torn up."

"Any holes, like a slug or a pellet?"

She probed with the tweezers, and he winced from the shivering pain. "No, whatever it was went across, not in. But there are little black spots all around."

"Powder burns," said Welsh. "They'll work their way out on their own. Take a look around for anything else."

She wiped his face with another gauze pad. "You're bleeding from little cuts all over your hands and face, and there's a big lump on your jaw, but that's it."

Welsh was overcome by a rush of pure relief. "If you can't be good, be lucky." He felt sick to his stomach, and knew the arm was going to hurt like a bastard as soon as the nerves woke up. "Maggie, there's a bottle of Tylenol with codeine in the bag."

"Tylenol with codeine?"

"That's right. Please get it."

She found the bottle, but Welsh's hands were shaking so bad she had to pop a tablet in his mouth and hold the water bottle so he could wash it down.

"A little shock and a lot of hyperadrenia," he said. "Load the syringe up with iodized water from the bottles.

271

Use it like a squirt gun to blast the dirt out of the wound."

Scanlan cleaned it out thoroughly. "How do you happen to have Tylenol with codeine?" she asked, if only to keep his mind on something else while she worked.

"You recall I mentioned I was a Winter Mountain Leader Instructor? The school is in Bridgeport, California, up in the Sierras. We were on what they call expedition week, coming down off a ten-thousand-foot ridgeline on skis, and one of the guys broke his leg and couldn't be moved."

"Was it that bad a fracture?"

"No, but the strongest painkiller the medical corpsman carried was aspirin."

"Good Lord, why?"

"Rear-echelon asshole military doctors. Better to let someone suffer than take the responsibility for letting their corpsmen carry narcotics like morphine in peacetime. A medevac helicopter showed up eventually, but it taught me a real lesson. Ordinarily, I'd have my doctor prescribe me a painkiller strong enough to get me out of the bush if I broke something. But the DEA monitors doctors so tightly, they won't hardly prescribe narcotics for pain, let alone backpacking or backcountry skiing."

"So where did you get it?"

Welsh smiled. "They sell it over the counter in Canada."

"Smuggler."

"I confess. And I always bring the first-aid kit when I travel."

"Very prudent, as usual."

Welsh looked down at his arm. "Okay, the wound's too ripped up to close, and I don't have a non-stick dressing that big. Unfold a fresh gauze pad to the right size, spread a layer of antibiotic ointment all over one side, then slap it on." She did it. "Okay, let's wrap it up.

We're going to need to check it every day, so we'd better use the ace bandage."

The small cuts on his face were from the branches and vines he'd run through. Scanlan washed them out and only applied antibiotic ointment, since in that climate Band-Aids wouldn't adhere. While she worked, he told her what happened. She finished and asked solicitously, "Did that hurt?"

"Yes," Welsh replied with a smile, "very much. And thank you." The trembling in his arms had stopped; he took the bag and brought out a bottle of his other prescription drug, an antibiotic for the inevitable infection.

The Tylenol began to hit with a soothing warmth. Even so, it was a while before he felt like getting up, and the arm was very stiff. He had to poke through the brush until he found the Beretta. He racked the slide back and examined the ejected round. There was no pit in the primer, which meant that the firing pin either hadn't hit it at all, or too lightly. He thumbed down the lever to release the slide and chamber a new round, aimed at the brush, and squeezed the trigger. This time the pistol fired.

Scanlan had been watching. "I think there was some rust accumulation around the firing pin," he said.

"But you clean it every day."

"I know, but this climate is hard on metal, and hair oil isn't a manufacturer's recommended lubricant. I suppose I could have tried to chamber another round, but if that one had misfired I would have been dead."

"So it was just as well you did what you did."

"Probably. Sometimes giving in to that old fight-or-flight instinct isn't the wrong thing to do."

Welsh went over to the Indian's body. Jeans, check shirt, straw hat; it was hard to find someone in rural Guatemala who wasn't wearing that combination. The man had been carrying a single-shot 12-gauge shotgun.

273

Holding it Welsh felt a sudden chill, and his whole body began shaking so badly he had to sit down. He'd only been hit by the very edge of the pattern of shot, which must have been supertight at such close range. A few pellets had grazed his arm as they went by, and the rest had chewed up his shirt sleeve. A small error in aim was the only reason his arm was still attached to his body. The shotgun action was open; the Indian had been trying to get another round in the chamber.

The ants had already discovered the corpse. In the pockets Welsh found a Guatemalan national identity card, some papers, and a few *quetzal* coins and small-denomination notes. The Indian had a machete, a skinning knife, and a shoulder bag made from a flour sack that held shotgun shells and a stack of flour tortillas wrapped in newspaper.

Welsh replaced everything but the tortillas and one of the papers. He handed it to Scanlan. "Ever been wanted dead or alive?"

The paper was a sort of wanted poster, with brief descriptions of Welsh and Scanlan in Spanish. But it had nothing at all to do with the Guatemalan government. There was a telephone number to call and give information or claim the reward.

Scanlan did the currency conversion in her head. "Fifty thousand dollars. It doesn't say dead or alive."

"It doesn't have to," said Welsh. "Nobody's going to risk having all that money run away from him."

"That's like a million bucks to the average Guatemalan."

"It means every asshole who can pick up a machete is going to be beating the brush for us. You notice the reward won't be paid without our bodies and all belongings. They want what's in that ammo can very badly."

Scanlan motioned toward the body. "What do we do with him?"

Now his voice was cold enough to make her shudder. "Fuck him. The jungle will take care of everything."

"Are you going to take the shotgun?"

"No. It would make too much noise to hunt with, and I wouldn't want to run into anyone who might recognize it." He held out the tortillas. "We do have dinner, though."

"A year ago I never would have thought that I'd help kill a man and then eat his food. Now I'm so hungry I don't care."

"It'll do that to you," said Welsh.

Chapter Thirty-two

"You told me we were going to San Ignacio," Margaret Scanlan said accusingly. "Now I'd like you to explain to me why I can't go into town and take a shower. And, yes, the *really* long explanation this time."

"Take a look at the map and imagine you're the bad guys. We missed the two gringos, Welsh and Scanlan, on the road. Then we lost them in the jungle, and it's a damn big jungle. So let's say no one sees them or collects the bounty on them, and they actually make it out of the jungle. Where's the one place we look for them to show up?"

"San Ignacio," Scanlan replied in defeat. "The biggest town close to the border, on the single highway into Belize City. No matter where the gringos come out of the jungle, they're still going to have to go through San Ignacio."

"A brilliant deduction," said Welsh. "So since we're Guatemalans and can't dump a million hit men into Belize, all we have to do is stake out the bus station in San Ignacio. Town of eight thousand people, a couple of strange gringos are really going to stand out."

"But they could just as well stake out the bus stop in some other town along the highway."

"Why bother? San Ignacio, the bus stations in Belize City, and you're covered. Just sit back and wait for the gringos to show up."

"So I don't get a shower."

"How about a bath instead?"

"I have been traveling with you *way* too long not to think there's going to be a catch."

It was just after sunrise, and they were standing by a branch of the Belize River that was much calmer than its source. The stream had an exposed sandbar along one bank. Welsh dug a large hole in the bar with the machete and lined it with their nylon tarp. He dumped out his pack and used it to fill the tarp with water. Then he tossed Scanlan the bar of soap he'd been hoarding. "Scrub a-dub-dub."

"I knew there was a catch," she said confidently.

"I'm going to go take a walk," said Welsh. "Enjoy."

When he returned, Scanlan was sitting on the sandbar sunning herself in bra and panties. Her clothes were drying on a branch. "God, it feels good to be clean," she exclaimed. "But just look at me. I'm a mass of insect bites, scratches, pimples, and peeling skin."

"You look great," said Welsh.

"I changed the water," she said, motioning toward the tarp. "Twice."

Two hours later they were sitting beside an asphalt highway, waiting for a bus to come along. Welsh was checking down the road with his binoculars.

"Okay," he said. "There's the seven A.M. bus from Benque Viejo."

"But is it the right one? There's a bunch of different bus lines."

"Belize City, right on the front."

"How do I look?" Scanlan asked.

Welsh's eyes didn't move from his binoculars. "You look great."

"Are you sure I look all right? We want them to stop."

"You look fine," Welsh repeated. "I'm the one who looks like Hogan's goat." He was referring to his shotgun-shredded right sleeve roughly patched and stitched together. He put the binoculars back in his pack. "At least people won't be bailing out the windows at the smell of us."

As the bus wheezed up, Welsh used a little trick he'd picked up trying to hail Tokyo taxi cabs. Simply stand in the middle of the road. It had always worked so far.

Like most buses in South America, it was a former U.S. school bus. It might even have had the original brakes, because when they were applied, the squealing had the same effect as fingernails on a blackboard.

The driver yanked the door open. "What the hell you doin', mon?" he demanded.

"Thanks for stopping, captain," said Welsh, already on the bus. "Visiting some friends, had trouble with their car." He passed the driver a U.S. $10 bill, more than enough for two fares. U.S. dollars were as commonly used in the country as Belize dollars. "Going to Belize City, appreciate you stopping, saved us a walk to the next town. Why don't you hang onto all of that?"

The bill disappeared. Mollified, the driver shrugged his head toward the back of the bus. "Ain' no seats." There were about a hundred people already on the bus.

"No problem," Welsh assured him. He and Scanlan flopped down on their packs, in the aisle.

It was about a three-hour trip to Belize City, and forty

minutes before enough people got off so they could sit down. Which was a mixed blessing.

"There was more legroom on the floor," said Welsh, trying to wedge himself into the seat. He leaned forward to examine the metal back of the seat in front of him.

"What are you looking for?" Scanlan asked.

"My initials. Could have sworn I rode this baby to school in 1972."

"I'll just say one thing: It's better than walking."

"I don't know about that," said Welsh, sitting with his knees up around his ears.

On the outskirts of Belize City, Welsh went forward and slipped the driver a couple of bucks to drop them off before the bus station.

That was on the cheerfully named Cemetery Road in western Belize City. They stepped off on the curb, and Welsh did a few knee bends to get the blood back into his legs.

Scanlan took a deep breath of fresh air. "The bath was great, but with all the BO on that bus, I don't think it was necessary."

"Deodorant is a luxury of the rich," Welsh replied. He was looking for a cab, and instead saw two serious locals step from a doorway and head right for them. One had a blade cupped in his hand, but wasn't making a show of it.

"Do you fucking believe this?" Welsh said out loud. He was wearing his pack so it hung under his left armpit. He reached in for the Beretta.

But Scanlan already had her pistol out. "Okay, which one of you wants to die first?" she shouted. "C'mon, raise your hand."

Before she finished the two were running the other way down the street.

"You get extra points for style on that one," Welsh complimented. He'd almost forgotten she still had her piece. "Just try not to shoot anyone you don't have to."

"I'll see what I can do," she replied.

They only had to walk half a block before a cab happened by. It had the green license plate and driver ID card, as recommended by Welsh's guidebook. There was no meter, so they negotiated the fare before getting in.

"We're looking for lunch," said Welsh. "Not at one of the hotels."

"A big lunch," Scanlan broke in. "A really big lunch."

"Dit's," was all the driver said. And then in that wonderful Belizean lilt, "That's the place for ya."

"Let's roll then," said Welsh, getting in.

Dit's turned out to be the name of the restaurant. The waitress set two colas down on the table, and Welsh and Scanlan contemplated the frosty glasses in respectful silence. Scanlan brought hers up to her mouth, took a sip, and her eyeballs bulged slightly. "It has been a while since I had any sugar, hasn't it?" she said. Then she drained the glass while simultaneously waving for a refill.

Then the waitress delivered two enormous plates of rice and beans with chicken. There was a big lunch crowd, but rising above the din in the direction of Welsh and Scanlan's table was the sound of metal utensils scraping plates at an extremely rapid rate. Very similar to machine-gun fire.

When the waitress ambled back to see if the meals were all right, she was confronted by two immaculately clean plates.

"Hamburger?" Welsh asked Scanlan.

She only nodded, being in the process of finishing up the last of the bread.

"One?" the waitress asked, a little uneasily.

"Two, please," said Welsh.

"And some more bread, when you get the chance," Scanlan added politely.

After the hamburger platter, Welsh finished up with a piece of cake, with ice cream, and felt quite full. Scanlan had the same, and a piece of pie on top of that for variety. He had no idea where she fit it.

By then they were on a first-name basis—made-up first names on their part—with the restaurant staff and most of the locals having lunch. Getting a little nervous about the attention they'd called to themselves already, Welsh insisted on leaving before anyone could act on the suggestion of having commemorative T-shirts printed up.

"That wasn't so bright," he said when they emerged from the restaurant out on King Street. "We'll be lucky if we don't spend the rest of the afternoon puking it up."

Scanlan startled him by grabbing his arm for support and ripping off a belch that must have registered on the Richter Scale.

"Oh, I beg your pardon!" she exclaimed, a red wave of embarrassment forming around her cheekbones.

"It was the beans," said Welsh. "You would have hurt yourself if you tried to hold that baby in."

"I feel great now. Let's go do some shopping."

On Regent Street they bought clothes, toilet articles, and small duffels to replace their battered and stained packs. The ammo can, ideal protection from the jungle elements, would no longer serve to carry the tapes across international borders. For camouflage Welsh decided on a leatherette cassette case and another portable tape player.

It was not yet 2:00 in the afternoon, and they engaged another cab to drive them to the town of Ladyville, just north of Belize City. After a short wait, the scheduled northbound Batty Company bus pulled up, and they wedged themselves inside. The destination was Chetumal, Mexico.

"After this, I'll never get on another bus in my life," Scanlan announced.

"Just remember the iron rule of South American bus travel," said Welsh. "As long as there aren't any pigs aboard, it's a good trip."

"Pigs? You mean the four-legged kind? As cargo?"

"Yeah, and you can take my word for it, pigs don't travel well."

The trip north took almost five hours. There were quite a few stops, which wasn't the disadvantage it might have seemed since the unaccustomed quantity of food had put their formerly underworked bowels on overtime. There were no facilities on the bus, and it was an agonizing wait between stops, followed by a hobbling run out the door.

The border guards at Santa Elena, the last stop in Belize, paid no attention to anyone leaving the country, so the absence of a Belize visitor permit stamp in Welsh's and Scanlan's passports was no problem.

Then there was Subteniente López, the Mexican crossing point. And, to Welsh's knowledge, the only place in the world ever named after a second lieutenant.

Entering a country by bus through a sleepy border post could be easier than arriving at an international airport, if a few simple rules were observed. It was not a good idea to wear cut-off jeans or a Grateful Dead T-shirt, or carry a backpack with peace signs and marijuana leaf patches sewed onto it. And if retaining a jungle beard for purposes of disguise, as was Welsh, it needed to be well-trimmed.

And when handing over $5 for a visitor's card, it helped if a larger-denomination banknote was inserted into the first page of your passport.

"That always pisses me off," Scanlan said after they got back on the bus. "I hate getting held up like that."

"Think of it as a simple service gratuity," Welsh said

calmly. The bus had to wait while two righteously principled German tourists had their belongings ripped apart and faced the prospect of flashlights shined up their colons before finally coughing up a contribution to the Border Police retirement fund. "You paid to avoid a lot of time-consuming formalities."

"I still don't like it. The corruption is what's holding these countries down."

Welsh laughed loudly.

"What's so funny?" she demanded.

"Just a memory from my college days. I went to school in Philadelphia. One day a guy I played rugby with asked me to fill in for him at a local bar, checking IDs at the door. Back then Pennsylvania was the only state with a drinking age of twenty one. But to get into this bar all you had to show was college ID. They always knew in advance when the inspectors would show up, and on those nights everyone had to be twenty one.

"My first night, after last call, one of the bartenders gives me a big paper bag and tells me to take it outside. There's at least a case of beer in the bag. I ask what's going on, and he smiles and tells me I'll know when I get outside. It's after two in the morning, I go out on the street, and I swear to God there were four police cruisers and a van lined up.

"Well, I may be a hick but I'm not that slow, so I walk up to the first cruiser. The window rolls down, I hand over the bag, and start walking back. This hardass cop voice goes, 'Hey, kid.' I turn around, very polite, and say, 'Yes, sir?' because in those days in Philly it didn't take much lip for the cops to haul out their nightsticks and give you the old wood shampoo. Anyway, the cop hands me back the bag and says, 'It's not cold enough.' "

"I don't believe it!" Scanlan exclaimed.

"I take the bag back into the bar, and the bartender

says, 'What's the problem?' I tell him, he gets pissed and says, 'For Christ's sake, we had a busy night, we don't have anything colder.' He went out to explain it personally."

Scanlan shook her head.

"So much for a middle-class upbringing and all those 'Policeman Bill' booklets," said Welsh.

"And the moral of the story is?"

Welsh thought about that before answering. "The more you're told about the way things are *supposed* to be, the more you can be sure they're not. And for most people, why they do what they do is pretty simple. Good, evil, right, and wrong are just words. When push comes to shove, they act according to their desires and what they perceive to be their own self-interest."

"Do I act that way?" she asked, an edge to her voice.

"Well, I haven't known you all that long," Welsh said reasonably. "So far, taking your revenge and getting out of Guatemala alive has been in your own self-interest."

Scanlan was looking at him through narrowed eyes. "You're a . . . you're a very unsettling person, Welsh. *You* certainly haven't acted in your own self-interest."

"And you can just see what kind of trouble it's gotten me into so far," he said ruefully.

It was getting dark as the bus arrived in Chetumal, on the southwestern edge of the Yucatán Peninsula. Scanlan had been reading Welsh's guidebook for diversion, and it provoked a small disagreement.

"There's an airport *here*," she said. "As much as I'd like to go to Cancún, I'd rather fly out of here than spend seven more hours on a bus."

"Let me ask you this," he said. "Would you rather be one of the few well-remembered gringos to fly out of the little airport at Chetumal, and maybe have a Guatemalan or two waiting when we get off the plane, or be one of the thousands of tourists to fly out of Cancún on a given day?"

"Welsh, this whole 'being right' thing is getting old."

"Feel free to secretly resent me—I can take it. We've done well so far, be a shame to screw it up now."

At Chetumal they changed over to a Mexican bus line, and it was quite a change for the better. The Mexicans took their bus travel seriously. First-class bus travel in Mexico left the big U.S. lines in the dust. And no live-stock allowed.

Chapter Thirty-three

Welsh glanced over at the clock radio. It looked as though Scanlan was going to be spending the rest of the night in the shower. He flicked through the TV channels, but after ten days in the jungle the Latin soaps and screeching game shows were unbearable.

Their Cancún hotel was right across the street from the bus station. Which was just as well, since they hadn't been in the mood for much more traveling.

Welsh clicked off the TV and began thumbing through the newspaper he'd snagged in the lobby, pausing occasionally to scratch the chigger bites on his ankles.

Scanlan finally emerged from the shower wearing a hotel bathrobe and vigorously toweling her hair. "I never thought I'd be clean again," she said. "I almost started crying."

"Nothing like a little hardship to make you appreciate all the basic comforts you used to take for granted."

She was smiling at him.

"What?" Welsh asked.

"Why are we still whispering?"

He chuckled. "Hard to break those jungle habits."

Before he went into the shower Scanlan insisted on examining his wounded arm. "Healing nicely," she said, "but it looks like you got branded with a waffle iron."

"It'll make a good conversation piece."

"Your beard covers the bruise and scratches pretty well."

"Itches like crazy. I can wait for this to be over so I can shave."

"It doesn't look that bad," she said appraisingly.

Welsh just grinned foolishly and headed into the bathroom. But he stopped abruptly when something occurred to him. "Maggie, don't make any phone calls."

"What do you mean?"

"I mean I'd like to let my mom know I'm alive too. But we have to worry about my crooked CIA buddy Thomas Kohl and an organization called the National Security Agency."

"What about them?"

"What if I told you they can intercept any telephone call made anywhere in the world?"

"I'd say that was a little hard to believe. Not to mention physically impossible."

"Believe it. There are satellites orbiting the planet vacuuming up phone calls twenty-four hours a day. Listening posts all over the world doing the same thing. Everything they pick up is downlinked through other satellites to NSA headquarters at Fort Meade, Maryland. And there it's run through supercomputers, which NSA has more of than any other organization or country on earth."

"But I thought computers had trouble recognizing and interpreting human speech. How could they handle telephone conversations, not to mention trillions of calls every day?"

"The NSA uses the same basic technology as a digital phone to convert a tape of the human voice to computer language: ones and zeros. And speech in numerical form can be scanned at supercomputer speeds. All they do is program the computer to identify trigger words or phrases, like Rich, Richard, Maggie, Margaret, Welsh, and Scanlan. Whenever the computer runs across one of them, it spits out the complete transcript of the call for a human being to evaluate."

"So the only limitation on what they can listen to is the capacity of the computers?"

"Exactly. In the old days the NSA could only target a limited amount of voice communication, because no matter what all the antennas were able to suck in, someone still had to physically listen to the tape and type out a transcript. Now computers can scan every phone conversation in an entire country and pick out the ones you might be interested in. Ironically enough, because of advances in cryptography, most governments, terrorists, and criminals have access to unbreakable code systems. Just like Corporal Richardson provided for the Guatemalans. Nowadays the NSA mostly listens in to regular Joes talking on the phone."

"I know I sound like a real innocent, but isn't any of that against the law?"

"If you're overseas, or your call or data goes across the border, you have no right to privacy. In the U.S., all they need is the approval of a special federal judge, which they always get."

"And Thomas Kohl can get all this information just by asking for it?"

"He can put us on what's called a watch list, but that would mean going on record with his interest in us. But he won't have to do that. By now Senator Anderson wants to know what's going on, and probably asked the intelligence community to help out. So the NSA will be listening for any mention of us."

"And if we make any phone calls, they find us. And that means Thomas Kohl knows where we are. And he calls the Guatemalans and lets them know. And they try to kill us."

"I think that pretty well sums it up. Oh, and the same goes for credit cards. Even easier to trace. Cash only."

"That's a problem. Not money, but cash."

"I think we can squeak by. I took advances on my credit cards before all this started."

"Being prepared again?"

"I enjoy it. And my two visitors back at the hotel in Santa Elena made a donation to our escape fund."

"No calls," said Scanlan. And then: "Why are you taking your pistol into the bathroom with you?"

"Marine Officer Candidate School," Welsh said sheepishly. "You never separate yourself from your weapon because, the way life works, whenever you don't have it with you is when you'll need it."

He set the pistol on the toilet tank and cranked on the shower. With any luck the hotel had a little hot water left.

Welsh was soaping himself up when he heard the bathroom door open. She must have forgotten something.

Then the curtain opened and Margaret Scanlan stepped naked into the shower with him. Welsh was so utterly stunned that he almost swallowed his tongue. He opened his mouth and couldn't get any sound to come out.

"I just didn't feel clean enough," Scanlan announced calmly. "Hope you don't mind."

Welsh blinked hard, the way fighter pilots pulling a lot of Gs do to keep from passing out. He decided that saying absolutely anything right then would be unforgivably stupid. Instead, he very gently put his arms around her waist, drew her close, and kissed her deeply. She wrapped her arms around his neck.

It went on for some time, and Welsh thought he felt his brain melting. He was leaning against the back of the shower, her weight on him and the water beating down. When Scanlan released his tongue, he said, "I have to warn you. I'm very dirty."

She smiled like the Mona Lisa. "I'm counting on it."

They continued their embrace. One of Scanlan's thighs moved slowly between his. Welsh was massaging her neck with one hand and lightly stroking the small of her back with the other, the water lubricating their contact.

They laughed softly whenever their lack of sexual familiarity broke up the rhythm of the kissing. Scanlan took up the soap and began lathering him up, a little too vigorously from his perspective.

Welsh was tracing small wet circles around her breasts. "Easy there, ma'am. I've been in the jungle a long time."

"We wouldn't want the shower to be over while you're still dirty," she said, her breath running short.

Welsh paused to nuzzle her neck, then claimed the soap and dropped to his knees. "Do you usually wash from the top down, or the bottom up?"

Perhaps it was the location of his head, but every word he said made her jump. "I usually start at the top, but since you're already down there . . ."

Without moving his head, very much that is, Welsh began to slowly soap her calves.

Chapter Thirty-four

Welsh woke up the next morning feeling as if he'd been beaten with a baseball bat, but pleasantly so. He had woken up, so even though it seemed unlikely, he must have gotten some sleep.

Scanlan was sitting naked at the desk, looking through the newspaper. Welsh tried to raise himself off the bed, and his vertebrae popped like castanets. He groaned and fell back.

Scanlan bounced up, leaped onto the bed, and landed on top of him. Welsh wrapped his arms around her in an embrace that was both genuine affection and an attempt to minimize injury. He'd encountered this phenomena before. After making love all night she was full of piss and vinegar, ready to go out and hang new gutters on the hotel. He, on the other hand, felt as if it was going to take a couple of bellboys and a hand truck just to get him to the bathroom.

Scanlan kissed him and said, "Good morning."

"Good morning," Welsh replied. She shifted her weight on him, and he groaned again.

"Are you all right?" she asked, patting his chest sympathetically, as if he were damaged goods.

"I'm ruined," he declared with a smile. "But in a good cause. As far as epics go, last night made the *Odyssey* seem like a road trip to the nearest Wal-Mart."

Scanlan laughed so hard she fell off him. Welsh found the strength to lunge over and plant a kiss on one buttock.

That warmed up his muscles to the point where he felt limited movement might be safe. He limped across the room to visit the bathroom and brush his teeth.

When he returned he crawled back on the bed and kissed her again.

She ran her hand through his hair. "I know what you want to ask me, but won't."

"What's that?"

"Why I jumped your bones in the shower."

"Sure, go ahead and objectify me," Welsh exclaimed in mock dismay. "Like I was a piece of meat or something."

She smiled and tugged on his hair in reproach. "A woman knows when a man finds her attractive. I was ready to handle that at all the worst times, but you were always very proper and gallant."

"Thanks. You make me sound like a real mouse."

Scanlan yanked his hair again. "No, it was the right thing to do. And you've done everything exactly right. And unless someone forces you to be otherwise, you're very gentle and sweet."

"Sweet?" Welsh said skeptically, interrupting her.

She kissed him hard and nibbled his lower lip on the way out. "Yes, very sweet. A lot of men try to act dangerous. You don't. But you're the most dangerous man I've ever met."

"Strictly by necessity. After all, look how dangerous you've become."

"The attraction was mutual, and this seemed as good a time as any. I hope you weren't shocked."

"No, actually, I was aroused. I'd been thinking along similar lines, though I have to admit nothing so spectacularly direct. But I knew that while we were in the jungle sex would be the last thing on your mind."

"Of course, it was so hot and filthy. Didn't you feel the same way?"

"Oh, no. Guys can get horny standing in a pile of garbage."

Scanlan shook her head fondly.

Welsh lay back on the pillow with his forearms over his eyes. "I feel so used."

"I'm sure you're already over it."

They laughed together, and kissed again. She laid her head on his chest, and he put his arms around her again.

"You're a very strange man, Mr. Welsh, and I'm very glad I met you."

"The feeling is mutual, Ms. Scanlan." Then Welsh found himself kissing the pillow as she sprang out of his embrace.

"We have to get moving and make arrangements to get out of here," she said.

"This is payback for the jungle, right?" Welsh said into the pillow. "I knew it would happen sooner or later."

"I'll go down and see about the plane tickets. You try and get your strength back." She slapped him on the fanny and got dressed.

"I knew this was going to happen," Welsh repeated into the pillow.

Scanlan took the elevator down to the lobby, to the little travel agency office there. She had her story ready. She needed two one-way tickets to Mexico City, the first available flight out. Some friends were sick, the vacation had to be cut short. The credit cards were maxed out, so she had to pay in cash. There was no problem. And dollars were accepted everywhere in Cancún.

When Scanlan returned to the room with the tickets, Welsh was showered, dressed, and packed.

The desk had an orange and beige Transporte Terrestre airport van waiting outside for them.

The international airport was south of the city. Welsh persuaded the driver to make a brief stop near a secluded stretch of beach. He ran down to the water and scattered a paper bag full of pistol and suppressor parts and bullets into the surf. Then they continued on to the airport.

The Aerocaribe jet took off on schedule, and as it gained altitude over the pure blue ocean, the knot in Welsh's stomach began to straighten out. As soon as the seat-belt sign went off, a pair of screaming children began running up and down the aisle, watched by smiling indulgent adults.

"Too bad you threw the guns away," Scanlan murmured in his ear.

He almost came out then and there and told her he loved her. But he didn't have the guts. Physical courage was easy. He pretended to doze off.

All of a sudden they were moving with unimaginable speed compared to the previous week and a half on the run.

When they landed at Mexico City, Welsh went into the men's room and shaved off his beard, leaving behind only a vacation mustache. While he was doing that Scanlan did some comparison pricing before going to the airport bank to change sufficient dollars into pesos. Then she stopped by the Aero California desk and purchased two more tickets.

By late afternoon they touched down in Tijuana, just across the border from the United States of America.

Chapter Thirty-five

In the Tijuana terminal they dumped their duffels in an airport locker and tossed the key into a trash can. They'd already transferred the cassette tapes to her shoulder bag. American citizens crossing the border for a day didn't usually return to the U.S. carrying suitcases. At least not if they wanted to avoid being examined by Customs.

Now unencumbered, they left the terminal and hailed a cab. "San Ysidro," Welsh said to the driver. It took them a minute to haggle over the price of the ride.

Welsh had the driver stop a short distance from the San Ysidro border crossing. It was a sandstone-colored building on a palm-tree-lined road. The pedestrian crossing was a bridge over the traffic gates.

As soon as she saw the building, Scanlan grabbed hold of his arm. "I'm having second thoughts. Are you sure it's such a great idea to cross the legitimate way?"

"Maggie, this is the U.S. border, not the Iron Curtain. We don't need to work up any James Bond scenarios.

Besides, it gets damn cold sneaking around the desert at night, and you never know who you might bump into."

"Okay, okay."

They started walking. Welsh said, "Don't worry, this is the last hurdle."

"What?"

"Okay, the last big one."

"That's more like it. I think I've got my courage back up; how are you feeling?"

"I think I've been scared shitless so much lately that I'm not noticing it anymore."

They fell in at the rear of a fairly long queue waiting in the Nothing to Declare line. The crossing had all the charm of a cattle chute; just the United States of America's way of saying that no one really asked you to come.

Scanlan slung the shoulder bag casually under her arm. Welsh had the tape player clipped to his belt and the headphones around his neck. They chatted casually, in good American English, a clean-cut young couple wondering if they'd get back to San Diego in time to make their dinner reservations. The line moved steadily forward.

They approached the Customs agent. "Are you folks American citizens?" the agent asked.

"Yes, sir," Welsh replied, displaying the first page of his passport.

"Thank you," the agent replied, glancing at it. "Did you make any purchases in Tijuana, ma'am?" he asked Scanlan.

"No, I didn't," she said, smiling brightly and showing her passport. "I really wanted to get one of those stuffed armadillos, but my boyfriend talked me out of it. He said I ought to—"

Welsh nearly swallowed his tongue.

"Thank you," the agent said, probably wanting to forestall a lengthy conversation.

"Thank you so much," said Scanlan. She took Welsh's arm, and had to give it a little tug to get him moving toward the turnstile. Then they passed through it, into the United States of America.

Outside the building they kept walking, as if not knowing what else to do.

"I don't believe it," Scanlan whispered. "I feel like crying."

Welsh was breathing normally for the first time in several minutes. "I've really got to hand it to you, Maggie, you've got solid-brass balls. When you started talking about freaking armadillos I almost blacked out."

"It seemed like the thing to do at the time," she said sweetly.

"You shouldn't put that kind of stress on my adrenal gland."

"Oh, don't be such a worrywart."

Welsh wrapped his arms around her and kissed her.

"Now why did you do that?" she asked, smiling.

"Well, I didn't think it would be a good idea to kiss the *ground*."

She hit him on the chest. "You know, I never realized the border was so open," she exclaimed, just like an aggrieved taxpayer. "We could have been international terrorists."

"Now, Maggie, don't you think it's just a little ungrateful to complain about something so damn convenient?"

"I suppose you're right."

A hundred feet from the border they climbed aboard the San Diego Trolley, which left for the city every fifteen minutes.

Scanlan nestled up against Welsh and used him as a pillow. "What's next on the agenda?"

Welsh put his arm around her. "A couple of bus tickets to L.A., and a pizza."

She looked up at him. "How did you know I wanted a pizza more than anything?"

"Are you kidding? It was written all over your face. Besides, after I pay for the bus tickets that's all we can afford."

"What do you like on your pizza?"

"Everything or nothing; I'm easy."

"Hmmm. Let me ask you something. Do you like anchovies? Careful now, this is one of those crucial relationship questions."

"I know, I know," said Welsh, with appropriate gravity. "Now, I realize this is a minority viewpoint, but the answer is yes."

"Damn. I do too. I've always relied on them to keep other people away from my pizza."

"That's just another risk you're going to have to take."

"Are you going to call your friend when we get to San Diego?"

Welsh nodded. "I know he'll come through; he's an old Marine Corps buddy. I just hope he's home."

At the Santa Fe Depot in San Diego, Welsh went off to make a telephone call and returned smiling. "Our luck is holding up just fine," he said.

A cab driver took them to a pizza place he personally recommended. Welsh and Scanlan celebrated their safe return to the United States with a pizza with everything on it, including anchovies, and a couple of beers. Then they caught a bus to Los Angeles.

Chapter Thirty-six

"At first the newspapers and TV said you'd been kidnapped," said Nelson Albertson as they relaxed over drinks in the living room of his apartment in Studio City. "They had all these pictures of your car burned to a crisp, Guatemalan soldiers and police running around saying you'd been ambushed by guerrillas. The Ambassador made sure everyone knew he was awfully sorry, and that it wasn't his fault. Back here, your Senator threw himself in front of the cameras to say what a great guy and a dedicated son of a bitch you were. It was all very touching."

"You know," Welsh mused, "I always had the feeling that a lot of people would like me better if I was dead."

"And rightly so," Albertson replied. He was a native Californian madman with brown hair and classic Celtic features. Welsh could hardly recall him without a smile on his face, even when complaining about the ways of the Marine Corps, which he'd done with both operatic brilliance and no regard for who in authority might be listening. The classic aviator, who put up with the military in exchange for those glorious times the canopy snapped shut and everyone left him alone to fly the jet.

"Thanks, Nelson," said Welsh. "But I can see why people would buy the story. It does look as if we were stopped on the road and grabbed, then the bad guys pushed the jeep down the hill and torched it."

Albertson leaned over to talk to Scanlan. "When there were no ransom demands, everyone figured you were dead. Our friends called to cry about it, but I told them not to bother. Being dead would be too *easy* for Rich. No, he'd have to walk his butt out of the jungle. So my phone rings, and there's Rich going, 'Hey, Nelson, come pick me up at the bus station.' You're such a dick," he said to Welsh.

"I know," Welsh replied. "But thanks for the ride anyway."

"It was worth it just to hear the story."

"Rich tells me you fly for the airlines," Scanlan said.

"I'm a flight engineer, which means that when you tell the attendant you're too cold, I'm the one who turns on the heat. Then ten minutes later when you're too hot, I turn up the air. Then when you complain it's too cold again, I snap out and start screaming that the 727 is twenty years old so get off my back. But I do get to operate the flaps."

"The way you describe it, I can almost feel the romance of flight," said Welsh.

Nelson's wife Donna, a beautiful, willowy strawberry blonde, had been listening tolerantly to the exchange. "This is the usual Nelson and Rich Show, if you hadn't guessed," she told Scanlan.

A copper-colored cat stopped the conversation by springing up onto the couch, settling in Welsh's lap, and immediately falling asleep. The expression on Welsh's face caused Nelson to break up in the middle of a slug of beer. He left the room before it began spewing from his nose.

"Cats instinctively know I don't care for them," said Welsh. "They do this just to screw with me." He turned to Donna. "Do you still have the other one?"

"Nickels is around somewhere," said Donna.

"You'll never see it," said Nelson, returning from the kitchen. "Animal's seriously neurotic, hides from strangers. Pretty amazing actually, when you consider it's the size of a small bear. A small *fat* bear."

"We've talked about this," Donna warned him. Then, to the rest of the room: "Nelson tried to kill Penny the other day."

"The animal *fell* off the balcony," Nelson protested vehemently. "Why would I throw a cat off a balcony when I know it's just going to land on its damned feet anyway?"

"Stick to that story, slick," said Donna.

"Rich tells me you were in the Marines together," Scanlan said diplomatically to Nelson.

"We were roommates at the Basic School," said Nelson.

"Which is something in the Marine Corps?" said Scanlan.

"They send every brand-new second lieutenant to the Basic Officer Course at Quantico," Albertson explained. "It lasts about six months, and it's called the Basic School. So you get prospective aviators, such as myself, and prospective grunts, like Rich, all lumped together."

"What exactly do they teach you?" Scanlan asked.

"Applied chickenshit and how to be miserable in the woods," said Nelson.

"Every Marine officer gets basic instruction in infantry tactics," Welsh explained. "The aviators think getting sweaty and rained on is beneath them."

"It is beneath us," said Nelson.

"You sound as if you didn't like it much," said Scanlan.

Nelson got up from the couch. "I'll be right back."

"And you're getting your MBA?" Scanlan said to Donna.

"Next year," Donna replied. "Right now I'm an accountant at a computer-software company."

"Where are you going to school?"

"I haven't decided yet. Nelson wants it to be somewhere with good hunting and fishing. I think he mentioned the University of Wyoming." Donna gave them a sweet, when-Hell-freezes-over smile.

Nelson bounded back into the room carrying a framed three-and-a-half-by-five photograph. He handed it to Scanlan, and she burst into laughter. Welsh looked over her shoulder and groaned. The photo had been taken at night. The flash captured several Marine Corps second lieutenants, wearing full-dress white uniforms, in the process of urinating on a large granite stone inscribed: *Camp Barrett, The Basic School.* Albertson was among them. Rich Welsh was the solitary figure perched unsteadily atop the stone, straining to direct his stream away from the surrounding throng.

"It was after a mess night or something," said Nelson. "I think we *were* a little drunk."

"I fly here for this guy's wedding," said Welsh. "I'd never met Donna. So I get here, and whenever I'm introduced to her friends and family, the first thing everyone says is: 'Oh, you're the guy in the picture!' Couldn't ask for a better first impression."

"It was the only snap I had that showed the real you," Nelson said innocently.

"I don't suppose this sort of behavior was encouraged," Scanlan said between giggles.

"If they'd heard about it, they would have thrown the book at us," said Albertson.

"They wouldn't have thrown it at us," said Welsh. "They'd have beaten us to death with it."

Scanlan was still studying the picture.

"It was a cold night," Nelson said defensively.

"That's our story," said Welsh. "And we're sticking to it. The guy shows this picture to everyone, and I still haven't gotten a wedding photo from him."

"You haven't sent Rich a wedding picture yet?" Donna said to Nelson.

Welsh smiled at Nelson's guilty expression.

"I've been meaning to get around to it," Nelson sputtered. "I wouldn't think he wanted one—we both look drunk in every frame."

"The fact that we *were* drunk probably accounts for that," Welsh replied.

"Well, what was there to do in that hotel room all day except drink beer and watch USC lose at football?" said Nelson, the loyal alumnus.

"The best man," Donna said to Scanlan, aiming her thumb at Welsh. "Nelson's exaggerating their condition. It was probably better he was a little tranquilized anyway."

"He kept trying to make a move for the door," Welsh volunteered. "But Donna wouldn't go for the fake."

Scanlan yawned abruptly.

"I guess you had to be there," Welsh said to Nelson.

"You're boring her," Albertson said. "You've always had that problem with women."

"No, you're not," Scanlan insisted, blushing. "I'm just so tired."

"Why don't you get some sleep?" said Welsh. "Nelson and I have to get caught up."

"I'll get you some bedding," said Donna. She and Scanlan went off.

303

Nelson and Welsh took their beers into the spare bedroom, which had no bed. One wall was occupied by a machine that wrapped guides on fishing-rod blanks. Nelson was an artist whose métier was custom-fishing-rod design. Another wall held a desk and computer. The third wall was all fishing rods and graphite blanks. The rest of the space in the room was taken up by fishing, hunting, and camping gear, and cardboard boxes.

"She's really something," Albertson said.

"No, she's not," said Welsh. "She's incredible."

Albertson gave him an appraising look, and then began to pantomime landing a large fish on a rod and reel, even providing the whirring sound effect of the line running out. "He's hooked!" he called over his shoulder to an unseen crew. "They said no one could do it, but he's hooked!"

Welsh turned bright red, and looked into the doorway to see if Scanlan had heard. "Quiet there, you."

"Just like a mackerel," Albertson sang.

"I'll smack you one," Welsh warned halfheartedly.

"There's just one thing I can't get a handle on," Albertson said with a grin. "Are you trying to say that she was better than me in the bush?"

Welsh started laughing again. "You never would have made it, old buddy. We didn't have jungle hammocks, Top Ramen noodles, or one of those little backpacker espresso machines."

"I've got one of those around here someplace."

"I'm sure you do. Actually, to be fair, you making it through the jungle wouldn't have been the problem. A day or two of listening to you bellyache about the conditions and I would've had to shoot you."

"Oh, now that really hurts." Albertson turned serious. "Speaking of shooting, you want a piece?"

Welsh smiled. "Are you sure you can spare one?" It had taken both of them several trips to move just a small part of Albertson's personal collection of rifles, pistols, and shotguns into the Basic School armory.

"Well, maybe *one*."

"No, thanks, pal. The way things have been going I might have to use it, and I wouldn't want the serial number coming back to you."

"It won't."

"You've got something unregistered?"

"Gun-show piece. A .45."

"You can never have enough .45's," said Welsh. It was the answer Nelson had given years before, when another Marine, looking through the collection, had asked why anyone would need more than one Model 1911A1 automatic pistol. "But unregistered?"

"In L.A. criminals might as well be an endangered species. They catch you shooting one and you have to spend every dollar you'll ever make on lawyers."

"You've always been broad-minded," Welsh observed. "But I will take you up on it."

Chapter Thirty-seven

Welsh woke up, and the moonlight was shining through the sliding glass windows to the balcony. Scanlan was snoring quietly on the smaller couch, diagonal to the one he was lying on. Penny the cat was sitting attentively on the coffee table, no doubt waiting for him to fall deeper asleep and then curl up on his face.

Welsh eased himself off the couch and tiptoed to the bathroom. Long time between beers. It was the second bathroom in the apartment, across the hall from Nelson and Donna's bedroom. A half bath, but only because the tub was being used as an overflow storage area. Not wanting to wake himself up, Welsh shut the door and prepared to take care of business by the small night light.

He'd just begun when something shot by his legs, crashed into the closed door, and began to howl.

If he'd been a little more awake Welsh would have pissed all over himself and the bathroom. It was Nickels, the neurotic cat. With characteristic intelligence, it had picked a rarely used location like the bathroom to hide in. Now, trapped inside with Welsh, the hysterical beast was howling like a mountain lion and trying to claw its way through the door.

The whole apartment building was going to be up in a second. Welsh was in mid-stream; it was no time for sudden movement. He couldn't reach the door. And throwing something would only make it worse. "Shut up!" he hissed. "Shut the fuck up!"

That only made Nickels howl louder and tear at the door like a demented weed-whacker. The noise was unbelievable; Welsh had never heard anything like it. He was finally able to stop, lunge across the room, and wrench the door open. Moving deceptively fast for its size, Nickels shot out before Welsh could launch the kick he was thinking about.

Welsh stuck his head out, expecting to see Maggie, Nelson, and Donna arrayed before him in the hall, demanding an explanation. But the hall was empty. He went back in the bathroom and sat down, seriously stressed out. Fucking cats. They did it just to screw with him.

He told the story in the morning, and got a big laugh.

Donna went to work. Welsh and Nelson left on errands; Scanlan settled down to watch TV. The two men returned with shopping bags. Nelson changed into his pilot's uniform, kissed Scanlan, shook hands with Welsh, and left again.

Welsh unpacked the boxes of blank cassettes and began setting up the dual tape deck to make copies.

"You've got some friends," Scanlan said.

"Marine Corps buddies. Most people never know if their friends are really going to be there for them when it's needed. In the military you do dangerous stuff all the time, and you find out about people pretty quick. If I was in a Guatemalan prison, one day the wall would

307

blow in and the boys would be standing there, looking at their watches, going, 'Hey, Rich, any day.' And I'd do the same for them."

"I don't have any friends like that."

"Yes, you do," said Welsh.

The next thing he knew he was being pinned to the floor and kissed. He almost passed out before she let him get some air.

When the embrace ended, Scanlan took charge of the taping while Welsh fired up the Albertsons' computer and composed a memorandum to go along with the tapes.

Scanlan came in the spare bedroom while he was working. "Just listening to these thugs is making me sick," she said. "I'm trying to figure out the Marine who did the taping, Corporal Richardson."

"Don't bother," said Welsh. "Something like this, it's hard enough to figure out *what* happened, let alone *why*."

"But that's what I want," Scanlan said, in a fake whiny voice.

"Everyone wants to know why someone does something. The truth is, people do what they want to do, and only after do they sit down and think up a reason, or an excuse. Why did Corporal Richardson get involved with the Guatemalans? Because he was typical for the age in having no sense of right and wrong? Because of his father? Was he just another innocent abroad? Or did he just want to?"

"Like my brother."

"Richardson wasn't trying to help anyone but himself. He fell in with the sharks, thought he was smart enough to run his own game on them, and they had him for breakfast."

"What are your motives for doing all this, Rich?"

"Not to die of a well-deserved heart attack after forty uneventful years behind a desk."

"That doesn't sound like the real reason."

"There you go," said Welsh.

Scanlan smiled and shook her head. "I wonder how much money it took to buy him."

"Richardson? Booker said it was a nice piece of change. You know, Maggie, the one thing they didn't do was try to get me to take a payoff. I wonder why."

"In Guatemala their first instinct is always to kill you. It's a lot cheaper too. By the way, after we get done with the taping, how are we going to overcome our cash problem and get out of here?"

"I'm just going to say what's on my mind right now," Welsh told her. "I have to get back to Washington to finish this and see what's hanging over our heads from Guatemala. I'd really love to have you come along; I think we've got the beginning of a beautiful friendship here. But if you want to head back home and close out this portion of your life, I understand. No hard feelings."

Scanlan was waving her hand like a propeller, as if trying to find the words she needed. "Do you always just—"

"Yeah," Welsh replied, nodding. "I say how I feel about something, you say how you feel, and we try to find some common ground. Saves a lot of misunderstanding. And hopefully no one ends up feeling resentful, the way we would if we were silently working off different assumptions."

"You're a very strange guy, Rich."

"Yeah, I know."

"I want to go to Washington with you. I think this is the beginning of a beautiful friendship too—Louis."

Welsh leaned over and kissed her. "I love it when you quote from *Casablanca*. And now that we're across the border, the rules have changed. If you buy an airline ticket with cash, whoever sold it to you turns you in to the nearest anti-drug task force to collect the reward, since of course you've got to be a dealer. You also have to show ID to get on a plane. So we can use our credit and ATM cards. We just have to get out of town as soon as we do."

"Great, I'll pay for the plane tickets."

"That's right, you are a millionaire, aren't you?"

"Yes," said Scanlan. He was staring at her. "What?"

"If it's at all possible," he said, voice low and mock-romantic, gazing deeply into her eyes, "you've become even more gorgeous since you reminded me of that."

Scanlan's mouth dropped open. Welsh rolled off the chair onto the carpet, shaking with laughter. She leaped on him and began pummeling him. Welsh covered up and rode it out, and soon they were both weak from laughter.

The copies of the tapes were just good tactics. Welsh kept the originals and mailed the copies and explanatory memorandum to the home of Supervisory Special Agent James MacNeil of the Federal Bureau of Investigation.

"Another buddy of yours?" Scanlan inquired.

"Sort of," said Welsh. "It's every career-minded bureaucrat's worst nightmare to regularly have to do business with a non-career-minded loose cannon. A bastard like that is liable to do anything, guaranteed to get you in trouble sooner or later. To MacNeil, I *am* that bastard."

"All right," Scanlan said slowly.

"He's also a pro. And the FBI has never had any qualms about jamming it to the CIA."

Chapter Thirty-eight

The plane landed in Philadelphia on a Friday afternoon. A light rain was falling, and the sky was an angry pewter. They were shivering as soon as they stepped out of the terminal.

"Good grief," Scanlan moaned, digging in her suitcase for a sweater. "My blood must have gotten thin."

Welsh had his collar up and his hands in his pockets. "Not very inviting, is it?"

"Whatever you do, don't bring up omens again."

Just like San Ignacio and the bus stations in Belize City, Washington, D.C., was where the Guatemalans would expect Welsh to eventually show up. If they hadn't abandoned the chase. But it would be reckless to assume they hadn't. So Dulles and National Airports, and Union Station, were out as arrival points.

The rental car was waiting for them. Before they started driving, Welsh removed Nelson Albertson's parting gift from the bag he'd checked at LAX to keep from having it X-rayed. It was a Springfield Arms copy of the Model 1911A1 .45 automatic pistol.

The pistol had Nelson's firearms-loving touches all over it. The feed ramp and barrel throat were polished. The trigger was set at about 4.5 pounds, and smooth as silk. The issue plastic handgrips had been replaced by a wraparound neoprene rubber model made by Pachmayr.

Nelson had included three top-of-the-line Wilson/Rogers seven-round magazines, a concealment holster for the pistol and double pouch for the magazines, and two boxes of Winchester's now-discontinued Black Talon hollow-point ammunition. Nelson probably had a storage locker full of it.

As they turned onto Route 95 South, the pistol was riding on Welsh's hip in Condition One: a round in the chamber, hammer fully cocked, and the thumb safety engaged. He was going to be keeping his jacket on.

Almost every national chain motel was clustered around the Springfield Mall in Springfield, Virginia. How to pay for a room by credit card and not be registered under that name? Scanlan paid for the room. Her husband was going to be getting a lot of business calls. Could they put his name on the room? As long as they had an approved credit card slip, the motel didn't care. Scanlan made up a name.

Once they got up to the room, he laid out his plans.

"I understand you wanting to cache the tapes in a safe place," she said. "Am I coming along, or do you still not trust me?"

Ah, a test, Welsh thought. "You can come along and hold the flashlight while I dig the hole, or you can stay here and watch TV and when I get back I'll tell you where I buried them."

The cloud passed away from her face and the sun

came out. Then she thought about it. "You're going to bury the tapes in the woods?"

"I'll buy another ammo can in the Army-Navy store in the mall."

"I'm all wooded out. I'll hold down the fort here."

"Whatever," said Welsh.

Chapter Thirty-nine

Welsh had chosen the motel because it was laid out so that guests didn't have to go through the lobby, as long as they had a plastic key card. On his way back to the room, up the first-floor stairway, he ran into a maintenance man coming out of a storage closet. He said hello as they passed, but the guy said, "Hey, wait a minute."

Puzzled, Welsh stopped.

"The cops were looking for you," the maintenance man said quietly.

Stunned, Welsh demanded, "What was that?"

"They had your picture, man. Be careful." The maintenance man continued down the stairs.

Welsh's stomach clenched up. He quickly put the "how" out of his mind and started concentrating on what to do. He'd be lucky if they were really cops. He had to get up to the room, get Maggie, and get the hell out of there.

"Oh, fuck!" Welsh muttered fiercely. He drew the .45

and held it at his side, under the edge of his jacket. Then, very carefully, he started up the stairs.

The hallway of his floor was empty. Welsh had the key card in his left hand; the pistol stayed in his right. He went down the hall quickly, turning and looking.

When nothing happened he allowed himself an optimistic thought. Maybe they didn't want another firefight in a hotel, and were waiting for the two of them to come outside together. If that were the case, he and Scanlan could barricade themselves in the room and call the FBI to get them out.

Welsh reached the room. He wasn't going to duplicate the mistake those two guys in Santa Elena made. He'd go in fast; Maggie was young, her heart could take it. Don't stand in front of that door when you open it, he told himself. Wood didn't stop bullets very well.

When he slipped the key card into the lock Welsh heard a muffled female scream that was immediately cut off. He pushed the door open and dropped to one knee: They wouldn't be looking low. With the frame protecting his body, he exposed just one eye and the .45 into the doorway. Then across the hall a door swung open very fast. Welsh whirled, there was a loud hollow pop, and an unbelievably powerful blow hit him in the side, took him clean off his feet, and threw him against the wall. He blacked out.

Chapter Forty

Welsh came to in a haze. His head felt thick and congested. His mouth was tacky and parched, and he knew he'd been drugged. As his senses slowly cleared, he felt himself sitting in a chair, and without any clothes on. His arms were secured behind his back with what he thought were handcuffs. His ankles were fastened to the legs of the chair. Voices behind him were speaking Spanish.

The terror came on like a wave of sickness, and he had to consciously tighten his muscles to keep his sphincter from opening.

It took every bit of concentration to regain control. Welsh opened his eyes a slit to try and see where he was, and was shocked to find himself in his own apartment. He wondered how they'd gotten him in, then saw the answer: a hand truck and a large cardboard box with the name of an appliance manufacturer on the side.

They'd stuck him inside and delivered him to his own apartment.

It wasn't like coming out of anesthesia in a hospital. Fear and adrenaline had already woken him up. He tried to focus on what being in his apartment meant.

After they found out where the tapes were, he was either going to commit suicide or get killed during a burglary. It could be the only reason he was there, and still alive.

The drapes were closed, and his belongings littered the floor. They'd made a search to pass the time. The only thing he could see in his favor was that they couldn't mark him up too badly if they wanted it to look like an accident.

"He's awake," a voice behind him said in Spanish.

Welsh kept his eyes closed. Then someone grabbed his hair and yanked his head up. Something metal hit him on the side of the face. Welsh opened his eyes and looked at the small man standing before him.

"I told you to be careful," Lieutenant Colonel Armando Gutierrez said reproachfully. "You see what happens?" He was speaking English for Welsh's benefit. Nelson's .45 was stuck in his belt.

Despite the example of the movies, engaging in witty banter with a stone killer who had his merit badge in torture wasn't prudent. Especially when stripped naked and tied to a chair.

Gutierrez held up a thick metal tube for Welsh to see. It had a smaller straight handle on one end, like a billy club. "We been waiting a long time for you to show up. We want to talk, so we use this. You know what it is?"

Welsh knew. It was a stun-bag projector. Compressed air cartridges fired a heavy cloth bag filled with metal shot. When it came out of the tube, the bag expanded and hit like the proverbial ton of bricks, but non-lethal and quiet.

"We couldn't take chances," Gutierrez said in an ingratiating tone. "You showed us in Santa Elena. Very smart, very tough. Kill two men with their own guns, you with just bare hands. Through the jungle with nothing, even the Indians can't find you. Very good. Now, you could be dead, but you still got a chance to make a deal. You tell me what I need to know, give me what I need to have, we let you go. No hard feelings. What do you say?"

Welsh didn't say anything.

"Okay," said Gutierrez. "Just one question, you tell me the truth. Where are the tapes?"

If Scanlan had told Gutierrez that a copy of the tapes had been mailed to the FBI, Welsh knew he wouldn't be alive. He felt both fury and pride. Somehow she'd managed to outwit them. He stared at Gutierrez, and didn't say anything.

"Booker is dead," Gutierrez said. "You don't owe him nothing."

Welsh looked at him as if he didn't understand.

"You worried about your woman?" Gutierrez inquired. "She's okay. I knew. A real man never tell a woman his business."

So that was it. She knew these macho sons of bitches cold, and had used their own prejudices against them. Though he knew he'd soon be dead, it gave Welsh heart.

"You don't want to tell me?" Gutierrez sounded hurt. Receiving no response, he said, "Tino."

Another man filled Welsh's peripheral vision. Welsh had to turn his head to take it all in. Tino was definitely over six feet, considerably more than 250 pounds, and didn't look like he'd gone to college.

Gutierrez held out his hand, and Tino put something into it. Gutierrez flicked the switchblade open and whipped it down into Welsh's lap. It struck the wood chair seat, uncomfortably close to Welsh's genitals. Welsh flinched, but knowing Gutierrez wanted him to, he didn't look down.

Gutierrez pulled the knife from the wood and laid the blade across Welsh's penis. "Where is it?" he asked, tapping the blade.

Welsh just stared at him.

Gutierrez sighed. "Okay," he said. "You're tough." He left Welsh's field of view, and Welsh's stereo came on, loud. Welsh had a brief hope that the neighbors would complain. No, they'd think it was the usual shit from Tom and Lois, the assholes who lived upstairs.

Welsh readied himself as best he could. Everyone talked eventually; that was a given. He was trying, but couldn't think.

Gutierrez came back in front of him. "You're tough, so I have to be tough with you," he said. He nodded, and a clear plastic bag came down over Welsh's head. From behind Tino twisted it tight at Welsh's neck to make a seal.

Welsh's breath steamed up the bag. Soon the air was replaced by carbon dioxide, and his lungs began working faster and faster to try and get oxygen. It was a terrible sensation of breathing hard but yet not breathing. His brain felt itself dying, and to preserve itself began hurting the body to it make take in air. The pain came in the lungs, the head, the eyes. Welsh was thrashing wildly in his bonds, trying to escape it.

The pain went on a long time before he started to black out. As his struggling decreased, the bag came off. Welsh drank in the cool air with huge shuddering gasps, unable to get it fast enough. Then the bag went back on.

Sounding anxious to leave, Tino asked in Spanish, "Why don't you ask him the question?"

"He's not ready yet," Gutierrez replied softly.

The second time the bag came off, Gutierrez asked, "Where is it?"

Welsh didn't have to fake it; his mouth was dry as wood. He rasped, "Can't talk, water."

Gutierrez snapped his fingers, and Tino went to the kitchen for a glass of water. Welsh took advantage of the respite to breathe. Then in the midst of everything it hit him, how to save his life. But an incredible long shot.

Gutierrez held the glass up to his mouth, and Welsh drank it down. "Now," Gutierrez said.

Welsh shrugged.

"Stupid."

The bag came back down, and it all happened again. "The *capucha*," Gutierrez said, making conversation. "They say it is like drowning. They say to drown is easy, but this is not easy. Every time you die, and every time we bring you back. If you want, we do this all night."

It was worse each time, and each time Gutierrez spoke to Welsh in the tender, empathetic voice of the professional torturer. If Welsh would only cooperate he would stop doing what was paining them both, what Welsh in his obstinacy was making him do. Giving Welsh in his pain and disorientation something to latch onto.

And Gutierrez was having a wonderful time. Tino was just a big piece of meat who did what he was told.

When the bag came off again, Welsh knew he couldn't take any more and still function. After he got enough air to speak, he managed to croak out, "The safe."

Gutierrez leaned forward. "Is it in the safe?" he asked eagerly.

Welsh nodded.

"Where is the safe?"

Welsh was groggy. "Bedroom."

"The bedroom here?" Gutierrez demanded.

"Hidden. Show you."

They dragged Welsh into the bedroom, still bound to the chair. He told them about his safe, slowly enough to get them frustrated, but not so much they'd take it out on him.

In their zeal they threw everything out of the closet and nearly broke down the wall.

Gutierrez came out of the closet. He yanked on Welsh's hair again. "Tell me the combination."

"Right 24, left 14, right 5."

Gutierrez sprang back into the closet. A minute later he came out and slapped Welsh's face. "Give me the right fucking combination." For emphasis he held up the bag.

"It is the right one," Welsh insisted desperately. "Why would I tell you about the safe and give you the wrong combination? It's just sticking."

"It better be." Gutierrez went to try again. When he came back he had Tino put the bag on again. When it came off he said, "Tell me the combination."

"It is the right combination," Welsh gasped. "You just have to play with it."

Gutierrez made him repeat the number over and over again. He tried one more time, then, at the end of his patience, said, "You do it." He gagged Welsh with tape, and used the switchblade to slit the tape holding his legs. Tino unlocked one of the handcuff rings, brought Welsh's hands around to the front, and relocked the cuffs.

"Don't fuck with me," Gutierrez warned. "I show you how stupid it would be."

Welsh heard a crackling sound, and then a lightning bolt struck him on the shoulder. Every muscle in his body contracted; his jaw slammed shut hard enough to chip teeth. He fell to the floor, curled up in a ball like a worm exposed to a flame. He was wracked with con-

321

vulsions, and it felt as though the flesh was coming off his bones.

After the agony finally passed, Gutierrez ripped off the tape gag and showed him the plastic box with the two metal poles on one end. A line of blue electricity crackled between the poles. A stun gun gave off around 100,000 volts, but the very low amperage wouldn't kill or cause permanent injury. "Now you know what it feels like," said Gutierrez. "Go open the safe."

Supporting himself with his handcuffed hands in front of him, Welsh crawled on his knees toward the closet. Gutierrez poked the toe of his shoe in Welsh's ass to urge him on. Welsh could hear Tino laughing.

There was only room for one in the closet, so when Welsh crawled in Gutierrez crouched behind him. Welsh was drenched with sweat and sick to his stomach. The electricity had drained away all his strength, and his head still felt like it was clamped in a vise.

Welsh was on his knees and bent over the safe. He could feel Gutierrez's breath against his neck, the warning hand dug into the tendons of his shoulder, the stun gun so near his left ear that all he could hear was its crackling.

Welsh concentrated on the dial, blinking rapidly to focus his eyes. The muscles in his arms were still dancing from the electricity. He spun the dial slowly and carefully, knowing there would be only one chance and afraid it wouldn't open. The combination he'd given Gutierrez was two numbers off at each place, not enough that he'd notice now from behind. Gutierrez was brushing Welsh's ear with the plastic body of the stun gun. Welsh knew he'd be hit with the electricity again as soon as he got the door open.

Inside the safe was the Ruger .357 Magnum revolver he'd put there for safekeeping the morning he'd left for Guatemala. It seemed like a hundred years ago. The

Ruger's five-round cylinder was loaded with Glaser Safety Slugs: a light copper case filled with thirty-two pellets of #6 birdshot and tipped with a plastic cap. After the slug penetrated an inch or so of solid flesh, it opened up and the birdshot literally shredded everything in an ever-widening path, producing massive hydrostatic shock. It was as guaranteed a one-shot stop as could be found in pistol ammunition. But only if he could get the pistol out and use it.

"Hurry up," Gutierrez said from behind, his voice harsher than before.

"I want to be sure I get it right," Welsh said quickly. "I can't take any more."

"Open it up," Gutierrez said, more soothing this time, "and you won't have to worry."

Welsh knew Gutierrez was leaning forward off balance. He was careful not to tense up and give himself away. He set the dial on the last number, then dropped his hands to the locking lever and twisted it violently. As the door came open he exploded into movement, using every last bit of his strength to drive himself backward into Gutierrez.

The top of Welsh's head caught Gutierrez flush under the chin. The hand holding the stun gun flashed past Welsh's face, and Gutierrez was knocked back onto the floor. Welsh scrambled forward and thrust his hands into the open safe. He touched the Ruger, but his hands were clumsy in the handcuffs, and he knocked the pistol from the shelf onto the floor. He fumbled for the weapon, picked it up, and then almost dropped it again when right behind him Gutierrez screamed in Spanish for Tino to help.

Over his back Welsh saw Gutierrez lunging with the stun gun. He pulled the trigger while he was still turning, and the muzzle flash from the short barrel nearly blinded him. Gutierrez screamed. The impact of the slug drove him back down to the floor, giving Tino a clear shot at Welsh from across the bedroom.

Tino's first shot was high. He kept firing and missing, and then, frustrated by his marksmanship, charged, firing wildly as he came on.

Welsh fell back against the safe and braced the pistol against the sides of his upraised knees. He aimed at the huge chest of the screaming man and fired twice.

Tino jerked violently at the impacts, halting in midstride. Awed by the effect of the Glasers, Welsh stopped and watched as Tino's hands fell to his sides and he dropped his pistol. He began to sway gently back and forth, moaning in a dialect Welsh could not understand. Snapping out of it, Welsh fired again. Tino let out a deep animal grunt and collapsed to the floor.

Welsh swung the pistol back to Gutierrez. There was a dark stain at his left collarbone, and the left arm hung limply. Gutierrez was trying to get Nelson's .45 out of his belt with the other hand, but the shock of the Glaser had him moving in slow motion.

It took all of Welsh's willpower to keep from passing out. He cocked the Ruger's hammer with his thumb, aimed carefully at Gutierrez's head four feet away, and fired. The force of the Glaser opening up in Gutierrez's brain blew both eyeballs out of their sockets, and Welsh was drenched with the bloody brain matter that sprayed from the empty holes. He collapsed onto his side and vomited.

Chapter Forty-one

Only the animal compulsion to survive got Rich Welsh up off that floor. But a few seconds on his feet made him so lightheaded that he had to sit down on the bed. He looked down at the revolver in his clasped hands and swung the cylinder out, ejecting the empty cartridges. Inside the safe were three speed loaders, one filled with five more .357 Magnum Glaser Silvers, the other two with 125-grain jacketed hollow points. Welsh grabbed one and reloaded the pistol. Then he went over to Tino, made sure he was dead, and searched his pockets for the handcuff keys. He found them and got the cuffs off his wrists.

He had no idea who the shots would attract, but felt that if he didn't get the blood and brains and puke off his body that second he was going to start screaming.

It was enough to get him moving. Shuffling about like a zombie, he threw the dead bolt on his apartment door and jammed a chair under the knob. Then he took an ice-cold shower with the pistol on the soap dish and the bathroom door open. Standing up was too hard; Welsh soaped himself leaning against the tile wall, quenching his overpowering thirst right from the shower head. It revived him slightly.

Each new task was a test of will. He didn't want to go back into his bedroom, which now resembled a slaughterhouse, but did long enough to get dressed in a pair of jeans, a sweater, sneakers, a jacket, and a baseball cap. He filled a Marine Corps nylon seabag with more clothes, all his spare ammunition, and his other pistol, a Glock 21. Not knowing what other shooting he'd have to do, he'd use Nelson's unregistered .45 and then throw it away.

Welsh couldn't believe that neither the cops nor Gutierrez's compatriots had shown up yet. Or that his neighbors hadn't heard the gunfire.

He wouldn't call the cops. Welsh had a vision of Thomas Kohl as the administrator, calmly assembling the relevant information from all his powerful sources and then calling in the executioners to finish the job. Welsh was sure he'd screwed up somehow. Was it the motel?

The clock read 3:12, and it was light outside. Gutierrez had kept him doped up for quite a while.

As he stopped in the kitchen for his spare set of car keys, Welsh realized that he had to put something in his stomach. He'd gotten rid of all the perishables before leaving for Guatemala. The prospect of canned beans made the bile rise again, so he chugged an unopened two-quart bottle of cranberry juice he found sitting in the cabinet. First it made him sick, then it made him feel better.

He went back out into the living room. As he turned off the stereo, he saw Gutierrez's briefcase lying on the couch. It was big, like a pilot's chart case. There were interesting things inside, but Welsh didn't feel he had time to examine them. He searched Gutierrez and Tino thoroughly, and threw everything in their pockets into the case.

Besides Nelson's .45 and spare magazines, Gutierrez had been carrying a compact .22-caliber Beretta automatic pistol, one of the trademarks of Israeli training. Welsh left it behind. He left the apartment with the duffel bag slung over his back, the Ruger in his belt, and the case in his left hand. He carried the .45 in his right, a raincoat draped over the arm to conceal it.

The hall was deserted. He stopped on the stairway to peek out the window overlooking the parking lot. There was a van with a rental logo parked there that matched the receipt in Gutierrez's wallet.

Only the chance that Scanlan was inside that van kept him from running in the opposite direction.

Back in the apartment all he'd wanted to do was collapse. Now he felt jittery and alert, though distanced from his senses and dangerously immortal.

He went out the back of the building with the raincoat on and the bill of the baseball cap pulled over his eyes. He walked all the way around to the parking lot. The van was parked in the row closest to the street, and he approached it from the sidewalk outside the lot. The man in the driver's seat had his head back as if he was sleeping. Seeing that, Welsh angled into the lot, walking just behind the front row of cars. That way he could come up from behind but stay out of view of the rear windows.

He set the duffel bag and case down quietly, walked up to the driver's window, and thrust Nelson's .45 inside. He blew the driver's brains out, point-blank, and then the passenger's. Most of the sound was muffled inside the van.

Welsh ripped open the door and aimed over the seat, but the back was empty. He locked the door and threw the case and duffel into his own car. After all the time it had been sitting there, it amazed him by starting on the first try.

There was something he had to do. He had to do it even if it cost him his life, because he knew he couldn't live with himself otherwise.

He drove back to the motel. The room key card had been in Gutierrez's pocket.

A Do Not Disturb sign hung from the doorknob. The .45 was out and ready as Welsh slid the card into the lock. The green light blinked and he made a good tactical entry. He was halfway across the room before the door bounced against the wall and slammed shut behind him.

Their clothes were still there, the bed unmade, and no signs of any struggle. Welsh went back down the alcove to the bathroom, moving one quiet step at a time. All the time he was pleading with God not to let her be in there. He'd do anything, just don't let her be in there. He opened the door and turned on the light.

The bathroom was spotlessly clean. And empty.

Standing there in the bathroom, after the ordeal of the past hours, his emotions as brittle as glass, Rich Welsh finally broke. He began to cry and couldn't stop. He didn't see how she could still be alive. And everyone who could have told him where she was or what happened to her was dead by his hand. His hand. Rich Welsh had never felt so isolated in his life. He had no idea what to do.

Chapter Forty-two

After the indulgence of tears, there was nothing for Rich Welsh to do but ratchet his emotions back down and deal with the situation. He searched the room for any signs of Maggie or her fate, and found nothing.

No one at the motel paid any notice to the man in the raincoat with one hand in his pocket and a stricken look on his haggard face.

Welsh got in his car and drove blindly. The Springfield Mall came up in his field of view, and he cut across two lanes of honking traffic to make the entrance. He parked in the crowded lot, nicely hidden, and afterwards couldn't for the life of him remember any details of the trip from the motel.

Another eruption of emotion brought him out of the trance, and he pounded on the steering wheel in his rage. It was not supposed to happen like that. He thought he'd done everything right. He'd been prepared for violence and risk, even welcomed them like a fool. But he hadn't been prepared for loss. Welsh only stopped pounding when the muscles in his arm gave out. He opened Gutierrez's case for something to do, some hint to his next step.

There were Tino and Gutierrez's wallets, with fake Virginia driver's licenses. Guatemalan diplomatic passports, but not in their own names. Room keys from a number of hotels, where Welsh assumed they'd been staying. Welsh's own wallet. Two Washington, D.C., Metropolitan Police detective badges and IDs that looked genuine. Margaret Scanlan's wallet. Welsh tenderly moved that off to one side. A black leather-bound appointment book that had to have belonged to Gutierrez.

Then the toys. A matched pair of Israeli Mini-Uzi 9mm submachine guns; only fourteen inches long with the stock folded and 1,200 rounds per minute at the cyclic rate. Eight twenty-five-round magazines. Two short sound suppressors with all the manufacturer's markings removed. No problem getting them into the U.S. if you had a diplomatic passport. A cellular phone, which Welsh assumed was the means of keeping in touch with the lookouts in the van. The switchblade, a roll of duct tape, and two pairs of handcuffs. A set of lock picks. The stun gun. The stun bag projector, two bags, and a box of CO_2 propellant cartridges. A box of surgical rubber gloves, and another of large gauze pads. Finally, a zippered leather case like a shaving kit. Welsh opened it up and found ampules of sodium pentathol, a can of chloroform, a bag of sterile disposable syringes, and a surgical scalpel handle and a box of blades. He could still feel the two small welts on his thigh where he'd been injected. There were also bags of white powder; either cocaine or heroin, Welsh couldn't tell which. The taste test only worked on TV; neither cocaine nor heroin had any taste. But perfect for leaving at the scene of an overdose.

"Jesus Christ!" Welsh exclaimed out loud when he reached the bottom of the case. Two Vietnam-era M26A2 fragmentation hand grenades, with Israel Military Industries markings in English. He immediately ripped off two pieces of duct tape to wrap around the pins. With the car bouncing around, if a pin fell out there would be a dandy explosion.

There was nothing else of any interest except a little over twenty-five thousand dollars in cash. Expense and escape fund. Welsh transferred the money to his pockets.

He returned to the appointment book. All the pages up to that day had been neatly ripped out. Gutierrez had probably been unprofessional enough to record his movements, but professional enough to destroy the record when it was no longer needed. There was a single entry for that day: "K at 8." The meaning presented itself immediately. But where?

He set the book down and double-checked the wallets for anything he might have missed, using the switchblade to cut the stitching and rip the leather open. Nothing. He slashed open the lining and bottom of the case itself. Still nothing. He went back to the appointment book, checking each page for any more writing. Still nothing.

In his frustration he sliced off the binding, and inside the back cover was a photograph. Folded around it was a piece of a Washington street map. The section was of The Mall, and an X was marked on the opposite side of the reflecting pool from the Vietnam War Memorial. The photo showed a park bench, circled in magic marker, along a path at the very same spot.

It was the sort of thing an intelligence officer sometimes had to resort to when a contact either didn't know an area or couldn't be relied upon to remember details.

Even with everything else flooding his mind, the plan fell into place like a straight line to a certain destination. Welsh closed his eyes and went over every possible thing that could go wrong.

In the mall he purchased a pad of paper, pens, a padded envelope, a nylon jogging suit, a scarf, and a bottle of aspirin for his crushing headache.

Back in the car he wrote Special Agent MacNeil of the FBI another memo. He didn't mention Maggie or the two guys in the van, but added a postscript to expect the package of tapes in the mail. The memo went into the envelope along the Guatemalans' wallets, passports, and hotel room keys.

A twenty-four-hour courier service on North 19th Street in Arlington promised to deliver the envelope to MacNeil at his home, at exactly 7:00 A.M. the next morning.

Welsh drove around to kill time. Thinking about her was driving him crazy. All that held him together was the certainty that at eight o'clock that night someone was either going to tell him everything, or pay the whole price.

Chapter Forty-three

Welsh was careful not to show up until only a few minutes before 8:00. He knew that the other party attending the meeting would make very sure the area was completely clear before committing himself.

His train pulled in to the Metro station on The Mall, and he came up on the escalator. He was wearing the nylon jogging suit, sneakers, baseball cap, and the scarf wrapped around his nose and mouth. There was an early cold snap and everyone on the street was dressed too lightly for it. It made them walk fast and keep their heads down. Welsh broke into a slow jog, heading toward the Lincoln Memorial on the sidewalk bordering Constitution Avenue.

The Lincoln Memorial was haloed in its usual warm blue light. Near the Vietnam War Memorial, Welsh took out the cellular phone, dialed 911, and reported a man with a gun near the Department of Agriculture building on the far side of The Mall past the Washington Monument. A minute later he watched two police officers run past him in that direction.

It was 8:02. He pulled the scarf over his face and tugged the long sleeve of the nylon jacket over the Ruger revolver in his hand. He started jogging again, crossing over the front of the Lincoln Memorial onto the path on the other side of the reflecting pool. He couldn't see the bench from there; it was in a good spot, well screened.

Nothing succeeded like simplicity. As he ran down the path Welsh casually looked over at the bench, and saw Thomas Kohl sitting there with his right hand inside his jacket.

Welsh decided to stop a little short so he'd have a better angle if Kohl got the pistol out or decided to try and shoot through the jacket. He halted abruptly, dropped into a crouch, and thrust his arm out so the pistol came clear. "Pull that hand out and you're dead," he barked.

Kohl froze.

"Let go of the piece," Welsh commanded, "and spread your fingers out so I can see them through the jacket."

Kohl thought about it for a short second. Then Welsh could see his hand relax.

"Now take the hand out real fucking slow," said Welsh. "Don't fuck around, I'd just as soon blow you away."

Kohl did it in slow motion.

"Drape it on top of the bench, just like the other one."

Once Kohl had done as Welsh directed, he said very calmly, "Listen, I think—"

"Shut up," said Welsh. "Don't say another fucking word." Keeping the pistol aimed at Kohl's chest, he very carefully circled around to the back of the bench. As he left Kohl's view, he said, "Don't even think about it."

Welsh jammed the barrel of the Ruger in Kohl's neck and reached into the jacket with his free hand, bringing out a SIG-Sauer P-228 9mm automatic. He pressed the decocking lever to drop the hammer, and put the pistol in his pocket. Then he patted down Kohl's front and belt area.

When he was done, Welsh said, "Skid forward on your ass and drop to your knees. Keep your arms spread out from your body, like Christ on the cross."

As Kohl moved, Welsh could see him weighing his chances at each step, waiting for an opening.

Welsh edged around the bench. "Move forward on your knees, into the middle of the path." Then: "Okay, flat on your stomach, keep the arms spread."

Kohl dropped smoothly onto his outstretched hands.

Welsh could see that Kohl was braced on his palms, ready to spring if he got the chance. "Get those palms up in the air, and spread the legs wide," said Welsh. He knelt down, jamming the pistol barrel into the base of Kohl's skull, one knee hard in the small of Kohl's back.

Welsh heard footsteps and voices. A man and a woman were coming down the path. They saw the scene and screeched to a halt. "Hey," the man said tentatively.

Welsh dug the barrel harder into Kohl's neck. He had Gutierrez's badge out, and waved it at them. "Police officer," he announced. "I'm making an arrest, move on."

"Oh, yes, sir," the man said, tremendous relief in his voice. They both shot past and disappeared down the path.

"You're no cop," Kohl said into the ground.

Welsh pushed his face into the asphalt. "I thought I told you to shut up." He began a frisk, starting at the arms, then the hair and collar, then down the back. Taped to the inside of Kohl's belt, at the small of his back, was a handcuff key. Welsh threw it onto the grass. "Cute." Most cops got shot because routine made them careless.

Welsh repositioned the Ruger to the base of Kohl's spine and went down the legs. He found a small Walther .380 automatic in an ankle holster.

"Put your left hand on the back of your head," said Welsh. He snapped on one handcuff bracelet, then wrenched the arm around into a lock. "Right hand behind your back." He jammed his left knee into the back of Kohl's neck, pinned Kohl's left arm with his right knee and all his weight, and cinched on the other bracelet. Just as the chief had taught him that week in Shore Patrol School at Norfolk Navy Base.

Welsh had Kohl roll over. He frisked his front thoroughly, including the crotch. It was the best place to conceal a weapon, because even the hardest guys got timid feeling around there.

Welsh dragged Kohl to his knees, then told him to get on his feet himself. They began moving: Kohl out in front and Welsh behind, out of kicking range. He gave directions, and the caveat "Run and you're dead."

They cut across the grass to Welsh's car on Independence Avenue. He'd parked it there four hours earlier. The minute he found the right spot he'd locked up the car and taken the subway out of Washington entirely. No matter how much prior surveillance Kohl had done, it was just an empty car that had been sitting there for hours.

Welsh put Kohl on his knees again while he unlocked the car door. Then he grabbed the handcuff chain and yanked Kohl into the backseat. His arms level with his neck, Kohl had no choice but to go along, and no time to try anything.

Kohl was face-down on the seat with Welsh sitting on top of him. Welsh grabbed a plastic bag from the floorboard, opened the twist tie, and stuck the bag over Kohl's nose and mouth. In the bag was a handful of gauze pads soaked in Gutierrez's chloroform. Kohl struggled fiercely, but was still within a minute. Welsh kept the bag on a little longer just to be sure.

The smell was making him sick. He sealed up the bag and threw it and the rubber gloves he'd been wearing into a larger bag, knotting the top. He rolled Kohl onto the floorboard and covered him with a blanket.

With a feeling of grim satisfaction, Rich Welsh climbed into the front seat, opened all the windows, and drove off.

Chapter Forty-four

Thomas Kohl sat propped up against the trunk of a large oak tree. His arms were straight over his head, duct tape banding them to the trunk. There was more tape circling his torso. His legs were spread and extended on the ground, his ankles tied to the ends of sticks that had been sharpened and pounded into the earth like tent pegs. He was dressed only in shirt and pants. His bulletproof vest and other clothes lay in a neat pile beside him. A big nine-volt flashlight was on the ground between his legs, the beam shining into his eyes. But Kohl was still unconscious.

It was night and clear, with bright stars and a half-moon. The temperature was near freezing, and Rich Welsh's breath steamed around his head. He was nearby sitting on a blanket, taking in the smell of the woods and waiting patiently. They were in the Quantico Marine Base, the land navigation test area, to be precise, about two hundred yards from a dirt trail where Welsh's car was parked.

Kohl groaned loudly, and began to stir. He came around, and flinched at the light. His eyes were wide and helpless, like a deer frozen in a poacher's jacklight. Finally he said in a rasping voice, "Listen, I think you're making a mistake here. Whatever the problem is, you've got the wrong man."

Without a word, Welsh sat down in front of him and turned the light on himself. Then he took off the scarf covering his face.

Kohl recoiled. "Welsh!"

"Kind of like Banquo's Ghost, aren't I?" Welsh asked with false cheer. "Always turning up where I'm not wanted. I guess you didn't recognize my voice through the scarf."

Kohl recovered impressively and turned authoritarian. "Welsh, do you have any idea what kind of trouble you're getting yourself into?"

Welsh jumped to his feet and kicked Kohl twice in the ribs. Hard, and it felt good. Harsh exhaled grunts came out of Kohl at each blow. "Gutierrez is dead," Welsh said flatly. "Him and three of his boys. And by the way, he also tortured me. I'm feeling a little emotionally fragile right now, so you'd be well advised not to fuck around."

Kohl then took what Welsh thought was a desperate shot, perhaps thinking that Welsh had only gotten lucky and followed him to the Mall. "You can't think I was involved with that?"

Welsh kicked him in the ribs one more time, then reached down and turned on a portable tape player. They listened to Kohl's Guatemala conversation with Lieutenant Colonel Armando Gutierrez, and when it was done Welsh shut the machine off. He showed Kohl the page from Gutierrez's appointment book, the photo of the park bench, and the map.

Listening to the tape, Kohl had seemed to visibly shrink. Quite understandably, he changed his approach. "What do you want?"

"What makes you think I want anything?" Welsh replied casually.

He must have broken a rib, because Kohl had to force the words out. "I'm sitting here with you in the woods. You didn't call the cops; you grabbed me all by yourself. What do you want?"

There was a lot of ego there. Welsh could hear the humiliation of being trapped and taken. "You're going to answer some questions. If you don't want to, we'll see how much you remember from the CIA resistance-to-interrogation course. I'll be honest with you, Tom, I've got a lot of issues to work out. I guarantee there's no one around for miles. Now, what happens afterward is going to depend on how cooperative you are. But I can tell you that if you don't help me out, you'll end up in here." Welsh swung the light over to reveal a freshly dug grave. The dirt was piled on the old green tarpaulin from the trunk of his car.

"You wouldn't dare."

Welsh laughed again; it had a brittle, high-pitched edge to it. "Hey, asshole, I've already got a body count of nine, starting in Guatemala. And as far as I'm concerned you're more responsible than any of them." He paused. "Shit, it might happen anyway. Unlike yourself, no doubt, I'm an amateur at field interrogation. I might get too rough and waste you by accident."

Kohl didn't have anything to say.

"I'm in a bit of a hurry," said Welsh, picking up the Mini-Uzi, "so I'm going to ask you some questions and zero this weapon at the same time."

He extended the single-strut folding stock and

screwed the sound suppressor can onto the barrel. "How did you find us?" He wanted to know if it had been his fault.

"It was a fluke," Kohl said quickly. "One of the Guatemalans was out shopping at the Springfield Mall. He saw the girl, Scanlan, and followed her back to the motel. Then he called Gutierrez."

Welsh inserted a magazine into the pistol grip and cocked the action. He placed the stock into the pocket between his shoulder and collarbone and peered through the sights. "Why did you go to work for the Guatemalans?"

Kohl was getting his second wind. "What difference does it make?"

That arrogant tone helped Welsh squeeze the trigger. A single shot. It was a good suppressor; the only sound was the metallic clacking of the bolt moving forward and back. "I was using one of your fingers for an aiming point, but the sights were off. About two clicks to the right and one down." He adjusted the front and rear sights.

Kohl tried to pull his fingers down into a fist, but found they were taped upright to the trunk. The fear rose in his voice. "It was a dirty war, but what the hell do you think the country would have been like if the Communists took over? We didn't make up our missions, we were given them. Then when the missions went public, the people who gave the orders got amnesia. A lot of good loyal men got fired for only doing what they'd been told. And the rest of us? Just twist there in the wind until it's time to dump you too!" He was shouting now. "I was not going to be one of the Company's human sacrifices! I gave them half my life, two marriages, and some of my blood. I owed the Guatemalans more than I owed *them*."

All those years of dirty deals with the little devils in

order to fight that big Russian devil, Welsh thought. Then one day all that was left were the little devils and a very bad smell in the room. And everyone who'd looked the other way now wanted to know who made it.

A spy's job was to lie, cheat, steal, manipulate, and even kill, all in a good cause—for country. Welsh could understand the effort to keep what the job demanded from turning you around. Loyalty to the organization and the cause had to be a big part of it. And then one day they tell you: Yes, you've been a good soldier, but now you have to fall on your sword for the sins of your masters.

"And what about the dead?" Welsh asked. "The Marines, and how many others? Everyone who got in the way of your comfortable retirement." There was no answer for that, so he moved on to a more pertinent question. "Where is Margaret Scanlan?"

"I don't know," said Kohl.

Welsh aimed carefully and fired again.

Kohl screamed. The bullet had taken off the forefinger of his left hand.

"Sights are dead-on now," said Welsh. "Hope you aren't left-handed." Seeing the look on Kohl's face, he said, "Yeah, you all did a hell of a job, put me right in the mood. So," he asked, in a voice as cold as the night air, "where is Margaret Scanlan?"

He took aim again, and Kohl, sobbing from the pain, said, "They're keeping her at a house in Woodbridge."

"Is she alive?" Welsh demanded, still looking at him through the sights.

"As far as I know."

"Give me the address."

Kohl said it; Welsh wrote it down. "Gutierrez had a cellular," said Welsh. "Give me the number at the house. Don't even dream of telling me you don't know it."

Kohl gave him the number.

Now Welsh really had a reason to hurry, but there was one more thing. "Where is your protection?" he asked.

Kohl had sweated though his shirt, in spite of the cold. "I don't know what you mean."

"You've got your own stuff stashed away. For protection. So if they ever caught you and thought about putting you on trial, it would be like a cesspool backing up all over the government. You're going to give it to me."

Kohl spoke much too fast. "It's in a bank vault in Europe."

Welsh fired again, and there was another scream. Kohl thrashed against the tree trunk, and then threw up on himself. A thin trickle of vomit hung from the corner of his mouth, and he couldn't move his shoulder over far enough to wipe it off. He tried to spit the taste out of his mouth, but the saliva wouldn't come.

Welsh was unmoved. "The human capacity for deception is infinite. You're a pro, Tom, and the stuff is where you can put your hands on it within an hour, twenty-four hours a day. You're going to tell me eventually, so why not make it now. If not . . ."

It took Kohl two tries to get it out. "If not what?"

"You've got eight more fingers, to start with."

Kohl told him. And then: "Okay. A million dollars. I'll get you the girl and you let me go."

"Is that what your ass is worth?"

If he'd been able, Kohl would have screamed it out. "Then what do you want?"

"Nothing," Welsh said calmly. "I think I understand everything now. I haven't got any evidence against you that would stand up in a court of law. Even the world's worst lawyer could get Corporal Richardson's tapes declared inadmissible. The CIA would say you'd been a rogue, a bad apple, and any incriminating documents would either disappear or be withheld on national security grounds. All your years of honorable service to your country? Shit, you were probably even an abused child.

"So it's on me. What do you think I ought to do, Tom? Let you go, or put a bullet in your brain? Take your money? Forgive you, or make sure you never hurt anyone ever again? What would the parents of those Marines want me to do? What would Maggie Scanlan want me to do?"

Kohl was looking at him like an animal in a trap.

"It's a moral quandary, to be sure," said Welsh, rising to his feet.

Chapter Forty-five

Welsh managed to convince himself he wasn't handling it on his own just because it was his nature, nor was it a typical case of testosterone poisoning.

He was certain the Guatemalans wouldn't act like terrorists or criminals holding a hostage. As soon as they heard a police bullhorn, they would shoot Maggie in the head and try to make a run for it.

He was equally certain that would already have happened by the time the Woodbridge, Virginia, Police Department, the Prince William County Sheriff's Department, and FBI finished arguing over jurisdiction.

The house had been chosen well. A sparsely populated, heavily wooded street bordered in three directions by Route 95, the massive Potomac Mills shopping mall, and the site for a commuter rail station that would probably be under construction for the next ten years. Perfect escape routes in every direction.

Welsh very slowly and quietly circled the house, trying

to figure out what to do. There were lights on, and people inside, but since all the blinds were shut tightly, he couldn't figure out who was in which room. And more important, which room they were holding Maggie in.

If he tried to sneak in quietly and was discovered, it was all over. If he tried to crash in and picked the wrong part of the house, she'd be dead before he could find her.

He was going to have to make them bring her outside to him. Pretty simple plan, and if it didn't work, he'd be able to hear the shots that killed her. How much easier to put the responsibility on the police.

Welsh crawled up to the car parked in the driveway. It was between him and the house. He prepared the Mini-Uzi and set it down on the asphalt driveway. He turned on the cellular phone and dialed the number Kohl had given him.

"Yes?" was the greeting.

Welsh had practiced the low raspy voice, and repeated his trick of scratching the mouthpiece to produce static. "This is Kohl, put Gutierrez on the line. Quick."

"He's not back yet," said the Spanish-accented voice.

"The police know about the house," said Welsh. "You've got to get out of there fast. Take the girl with you, get in your car, drive to the mall, and wait there. I'll call you back in about fifteen minutes. Do you understand?"

"Yes."

"Get moving." Welsh broke the connection. He put the phone in his pocket and picked up the submachine gun. He concentrated on controlling his breathing.

The back door slammed shut. Welsh got on his stomach and peeked around the front tire without exposing his head. Scanlan, handcuffed and with a hood over her head, flanked by two Guatemalans holding her arms. Neither had their guns out.

From underneath the car, Welsh watched their feet.

He pulled back on the Mini-Uzi pistol grip, locking the stock into his shoulder. When they were at point-blank range, Welsh sprang up and leaned over the hood. He squeezed the trigger twice and one startled face blossomed red.

But the other one had lightning reflexes, and dove to put the car between them. Welsh lunged across the top of the hood, flicking the selector switch to full-auto. The Guatemalan's hand was coming out of his jacket. Welsh pushed the Mini-Uzi over the side and emptied half the magazine into him.

Welsh rolled and landed on the body. Scanlan was still standing upright, hooded and shaking like a leaf.

Breathing so hard he couldn't speak, Welsh yanked the hood off her head, hooked his arm under her armpit, and dragged her back around the car.

Scanlan blinked her eyes to focus them. "Rich?" Then louder: "Rich!"

A window shattered in the house, immediately followed by a tearing burst of automatic fire. Bullets thudded into the car. Another Mini-Uzi from the sound. He pushed Maggie up against the wheel for protection and pressed the handcuff key into her hand. "Stay down!" he shouted. For a split second he thought about giving her a pistol, but she'd just get up and start shooting and he wanted her safe.

The low-powered 9mm ammunition wouldn't penetrate the car body, but they were still pinned down. Any move in any direction and they were easy targets. One guy was in the house firing. And maybe another maneuvering outside while they were pinned down? That wasn't a vote in favor of staying put and waiting for a neighbor to call the cops.

The Guatemalan in the house was a sprayer, ripping off an entire magazine in a single burst and then taking a few seconds to reload. In each lull Welsh risked a look, and located the broken window he was firing from. Welsh stuck his hand in his jacket pocket and found the hand grenade.

It was a drill. Spoon against the web of the hand. A really hard yank, because the pin never came out easily. A steady grip—if you milked it the spoon could slip, the cap could ignite, and 4.5 seconds later it blew up in your hand.

When the next burst stopped Welsh rolled the smooth metal grenade from his palm to his fingers, flipping off the spoon with a backhand motion. Thousand-one, thousand-two; he reared up and whipped the grenade at the window. He ducked back down; if he missed the window or the grenade hit a screen it could bounce right back at them.

The blast was deafening. It was always amazing how a little palm-sized egg could make so much noise. Welsh looked up, and smoke was pouring from the window.

Scanlan had the cuffs off. "Can you run?" he shouted. "Yes!"

Welsh pulled the pin on the second grenade and lobbed it at the back door of the house. It blew.

He grabbed her hand. "Come on!"

They ran across the backyard, screened from the house by the acrid black high-explosive smoke. Inside the tree line Welsh dumped the Mini-Uzi and magazines. No fingerprints, he was wearing gloves. Sirens wailed in the distance.

They walked quickly through the woods, following the rings of white medical tape Welsh had left on the trees on his way in. It brought them to the side street on the opposite side of the mall, where his car was parked.

His embrace lifted her off her feet. He buried his face in her neck and felt her lips against his ear.

"Rescued from the jaws of death in a shoot-out," she whispered. "Who the hell said men can't make a commitment?"

Chapter Forty-six

Driving south on Interstate 95, Welsh decided that, no matter what they'd done to her, he'd make sure she knew that his feelings were unchanged and he'd be there for her. But she didn't seem traumatized. Unlike the big tough Marine.

He was just about to ask, as gently as he could, when Scanlan said, "Tell me what happened to you."

Welsh told her everything except the location where he and Thomas Kohl had had their discussion. He was immediately ashamed, but it was the difference between trusting someone with your life, and trusting someone with your life in prison. Then it was Scanlan's turn.

"A little while after you left the motel they crashed into the room. Except they had a key, and the only thing that crashed was the chain. Six of them were all over me before I could even get off the bed. I tried to yell when you came back, but I was gagged and one of them chloroformed me. When I woke up I was in a house with no furniture except the chair I was tied to." She paused. "Gutierrez introduced himself. Did you ever notice how sadists are such genial fellows?"

"Getting to practice their hobby puts them in a good mood," Welsh said grimly.

"They threatened to rape me," she said.

Welsh put his hand on her knee.

"I told them to go right ahead: I was HIV positive."

Welsh's mouth flopped open at the sheer audacity of it.

"That took the wind out of their sails," she said. "After that, all they had the nerve to do was . . ." She hesitated, as if searching for the right word, and her tone was cold and clinical. "I guess molested would be the right word. Can you handle that?"

"The way I feel about you? I can handle that," Welsh replied. Scanlan was wearing a satisfied little smile, as if he'd passed another test.

"But I'm glad I killed the sons of bitches," he growled.

"After that," she said, "Gutierrez used this electric shock machine on me."

"Did the same to me," Welsh said tightly.

"The first thing—boom!—he wanted to know where the tapes were. I didn't know. You went off on your own, you wouldn't take me with you, you wouldn't tell me your plans, you didn't trust me."

"He bought it," said Welsh.

"Play the stupid woman and they go for it every time," she said contemptuously. "But anyway, they couldn't wait to get to you. I was going to be the dessert after they made you give them everything."

She said it without batting an eye; it was Welsh who shivered.

"Gutierrez and three of the others left," she said. "The three who stayed were just ignorant little thugs; they thought they could get AIDS if I breathed on them. And you wouldn't believe how scared one of them was of you. He was a real backcountry boy, and he knew all about the hotel at Santa Elena and the jungle. He thought you had to be some kind of witchman who carried invincible magic. Then they got a phone call and all hell broke loose. They dragged me outside, and there you were."

"Do you know how lucky we were?" said Welsh.

"You still haven't told me where we're driving."

"Spotsylvania Battlefield National Park."

"That's nice. Why?"

"We have to dig something up."

"That's nice. What?"

A stainless-steel case. Buried beside a boulder near a road intersection and the shallow remains of a Civil War trench system.

Now Scanlan was driving and Welsh was examining the thick stack of CIA cables by flashlight. They were evenly divided between Kohl's communications with CIA headquarters and theirs to him as Chief of Station Guatemala. All were stamped TOP SECRET, along with the Sensitive Compartmented Information code word for the operation involved. NOFORN, meaning that the material could not be viewed by foreign nationals or intelligence services, and NOCONTRACT, denying access to contract agents or consultants.

"Everything is here," he told her. "Guatemalan generals in negotiations with representatives of the Cali drug cartel in 1988. A Canadian labor activist kidnapped and executed by a death squad linked to the Esteban family manufacturing interests. It's documented. The CIA knew everything that happened in Guatemala. They told everything to headquarters in Langley. And Langley didn't give a flying shit." He kept leafing through the papers. "There's a whole set on your brother, Maggie."

"What does it say?"

Welsh skimmed them. "You killed the right guy."

They both fell silent. Then Scanlan said, "We're coming up on the Capital Beltway."

"Take the 495 exit."

"Where are we going now?"

"Chevy Chase, Maryland."

She looked at the clock on the dashboard. "It's late."

"I'll call ahead," said Welsh.

Chapter Forty-seven

It was a large country house on at least five wooded acres. Swimming pool, tennis court, the whole nine yards. But the white plantation house only dated back to the 1960's, so the ambiance could be achieved without having to deal with rotting timbers and plumbing that had to be rammed into spaces never meant for plumbing. Like all rich Eastern houses, it was screened from the road by tall trees. You had to deserve to see it.

The house was in darkness, and Rich Welsh was sitting in the living room, which bore all the trademarks of Mrs. Senator Anderson. He called her that, out of earshot, because he'd always imagined the title was the most important thing to her, like all the Mrs. Colonels in the Marine Corps. Mrs. Anderson was Kentucky horse-rich, but even though the Senator had climbed all the way up from the bottom, he was the trophy spouse: the gold entry card into the top ranks of the Washington social scene. Welsh had never cared for her. Unlike his late predecessor, Senator Anderson didn't need to hire a dominatrix—he'd married one. She didn't care for Welsh either; he was help, and didn't suck up to her the way help was supposed to.

The living room was her territory, with the early Picasso, the Dürer engraving, the Bokhara rugs, and the silk upholstered furniture that took real nerve to sit down on. The manly Remington bronze, golf clubs, gun case, and elk head had all been exiled to the Senator's mahogany study.

A few minutes earlier a car had come up the drive, and now the front door was being unlocked. Footsteps came down the hallway, and the lights in the living room snapped on. Welsh remained motionless.

Senator Warren Anderson tossed his tuxedo jacket over the back of the couch and headed straight for the antique cherry-wood liquor caddy. He mixed himself a highball in a crystal glass. It must have been a real tough night for the Senator not to wait to go into his study and use his beloved set of glasses with the country club seal on them.

The Senator had a welcome taste of his drink, then turned and realized that someone else was sitting in the room. He froze, and when nothing bad happened he leaned forward, squinting as if trying to make out what he was dealing with. When he recognized Welsh, the heavy glass dropped from his hand.

"My God," the Senator exclaimed. "My God, Rich!"

Welsh had to fight against a middle-class instinct to dive for the carpet and start wiping up the spill. Instead he got up and directed the Senator to the couch. "Sorry about startling you, sir. Let me get you another drink." The Senator was quite pale, so Welsh made him a stiff one.

The Senator snatched the glass back and took a large gulp. He slumped onto the couch. "I can't believe it.

Rich, I'm so glad to see you alive I'm not even mad about scaring me out of ten years I can't afford." He paused. "No doubt there's a reason for the dramatic entrance?"

"I'm afraid so, sir."

"How in the world did you know I was going to be here?"

"A couple of phone calls and I found out that you were at the Kennedy Center and Mrs. Anderson was back in Kentucky."

The Senator was returning to his normal ruddy color, and his habit of becoming sidetracked by minutiae once again came to the fore. "With all the money I spent on a security system, I would have thought I'd be seeing you first at the police station."

Welsh indulged him. "Well, sir, when the alarm is tripped, the signal goes out to the security company over the phone line. I disconnected that outside."

The Senator blinked, and took another gulp from his drink. "But what about the siren that's supposed to be loud enough to raise the dead, not to mention all the damned floodlights?"

"They run on electricity, sir. Before I came in the window I pulled the electric meter to kill the power. Then I went down to the basement and followed the alarm system wires to the breaker box. I tripped the appropriate circuit breakers, then went outside and plugged the meter back in."

The Senator shook his head. "Why did I even bother to buy an alarm system?"

"For peace of mind, sir?" Welsh suggested.

The Senator chuckled. "I've missed you, Rich. You never told me about your criminal tendencies."

"When I tell you the story, sir, you'll understand why I did it this way."

The Senator held out his empty glass. "I have a feeling

I'm going to need another of these before you start."

Welsh poured. The Senator made himself comfortable, and then Welsh, pacing back and forth in front of the couch, began his story.

It took over an hour to tell the edited version without any of the incriminating details. When it was over, the Senator got up from the couch and went to the bar. He held up a glass, but Welsh shook his head.

"Incredible," the Senator said quietly. "Absolutely incredible. Are you sure you're all right?"

"I'm fine, sir, but I feel a little like Alice after she went through the looking glass. I'm having to run as fast as I can just to stay in the same place."

"I can understand why."

Now the Senator was looking uncomfortable, and Welsh knew why. The essence of politics was to never commit to a course of action unless absolutely necessary, and maybe not even then. Welsh didn't want the Senator comfortable, so he shut right up. The best way to get a born talker to talk was to stay quiet; they could abide anything but silence.

The Senator brooded over it for a while. "Hell, Rich," he said finally. "When I sent you down there, I didn't expect you to actually find out anything."

Welsh thought he ought to mix the Senator doubles more often. It wasn't often he heard frankness of that magnitude. "Sorry about that, sir. I didn't plan on it."

"We'll get you FBI protection," the Senator decided. "Turn the whole thing over to them. I'll speak to the Director personally."

"Sir."

"Yes, Rich," he said cautiously, keying on Welsh's tone.

"Sir, if these documents get back in the hands of any government agency, with their classification they're going to disappear back into the black world forever."

The Senator didn't seem to think that would be such a tragedy. "You don't know where this guy Kohl is?"

"No, sir."

"What do you want me to do, Rich?"

"Sir, if there was ever a reason to hold some hearings, this is it."

The Senator thought that over. "Holding hearings and grandstanding at the CIA's expense is one thing," he said. "Being the one who damaged the CIA beyond repair—that's another thing entirely. Do you realize how many constituencies would come marching on my office with torches and pitchforks? Even worse is putting yourself in the position where you're the one who's expected to identify what's wrong and make changes."

In wine there is truth, Welsh quoted to himself. You'd never hear all that at a Rotary Club banquet. It was a cold day in Hell when you got a chance to step inside a politician's head and watch the political math being done.

He also had a feeling that Senator Anderson had grasped the one essential point of the whole business. The big boys of the CIA didn't hang out in a room full of beer cans and empty pizza boxes and throw darts at a map of the world to see which country they'd fuck with next. When you worked for the government, the first thing you learned is that no one ever did anything their boss didn't want them to do. Every President of the United States sent the CIA off to do the dirty work he wanted done and didn't want the American people to know about. The cables in Welsh's possession covered three different Administrations of two different parties, which meant bipartisan interest in covering ass.

"So what you're trying to tell me is that you've decided it's a losing hand."

"There's no need for that, Rich."

There were always such excellent reasons for chickening out, Welsh thought. The right thing had a consistent way of being too expensive a proposition.

The Senator seemed about to say something more, but instead got up and walked all the way over to the phone before he remembered that the line was dead. His leather briefcase sat on one of the end tables. He opened it up and took out a cellular phone. "I'll call the FBI right now."

Welsh stood up. "Sir, would you give me that phone?"

"Believe me, Rich, this is the best way to handle it." The Senator switched on the phone.

"Sir, would you please put that phone down."

Senator Anderson wasn't one to be told what to do.

Welsh pulled out Nelson's .45 and fired a shot into the wall. Touching off a .45 in an enclosed room was a major attention-getter. The Senator dropped the phone and found a chair so he could take a load off those rubbery legs.

"One time I asked a gunnery sergeant about Vietnam," Welsh said conversationally. "He said the only way I'd really understand was if he shot at me while he was telling the story." He bent down and picked up the ejected shell casing, then walked over to the cellular. There was a satisfying sound of crunching plastic when he stamped on it.

"Rich . . ."

"Yeah, I know," said Welsh. "You can consider this my resignation. Well, we all have defining moments in our lives. You had your chance to be Sam Ervin, but you showed what you were really made of." He turned to leave, stopped, and turned back around. "We'd both better forget this meeting took place. Because if I get any blow-back from the story I told, or my expenses don't get approved in full, you'll see first-hand just what I'm capable of. Sorry about the hole in the wall. A little spackle will cover that up."

Welsh went out the back door, through the garden, past the pool, and over the security fence. Scanlan had the car door open and the engine running.

"Where to now?" she asked.

"Back to the interstate."

Chapter Forty-eight

There was one hotel in Richmond with twenty-four-hour room service, and they took advantage of it.

"God, I loved the look on the desk clerk's face," Scanlan said, "when he asked you if we had any baggage. And you said, 'A lot, but no luggage.' " She almost choked on her shrimp cocktail.

"It wasn't that funny," said Welsh.

"Yeah, but at the time." She paused. "Why are you so glum? You knew the Senator probably wouldn't go for it."

Welsh wiped his mouth and set his napkin back in his lap. "You're right. A politician being a politician? I'm more upset than I have a right to be."

"Well?"

"Well, when your dad has a night out with the boys, and the next morning he tells you to wash the car, and you find dainty little footprints on the inside windshield, then you're either going to develop a real tolerance for hypocrisy or a real resentment for it."

"You ever tell anyone about that?"

"Not before today."

"Rich, you are either the most open guy I ever met, or the slickest dog who ever walked the face of the earth."

"You figure out which, let me know."

She shook her head fondly. "What's our next move?"

"Tomorrow we'll drop by a copy center. We'll send one copy of the cables to the *New York Times*, and another to a producer I know at *60 Minutes*."

"Why both?"

"Free market competition. If each knows the other has the story, then even if they wanted to, they'd be too afraid to sit on it. Besides, more people watch TV than read nowadays. We'll send another copy to Nordstrom, that ex-State Department guy the CIA got fired for passing classified material on your brother to the Congressman. He's working for the Congressman now, and he deserves it."

"I feel good about that. And then what?"

"Not only could I use a vacation, but I think getting out of the neighborhood is a good idea. What about you?"

"Are you kidding? I've been dreaming about a warm beach and blue water. Let's go to Hawaii."

"Hawaii it is. Gutierrez made a cash contribution to the vacation fund."

Scanlan was grinning at him across the room service table.

"What?" Welsh demanded.

"I forgot to tell you. While you were in talking with the Senator, I was looking through Kohl's case. There was a waterproof pouch taped to the lining on the bottom. Inside it were three different passports and sets of identification, and fifty thousand dollars in cash."

"That was his escape kit," said Welsh. "Classic intelligence tradecraft."

"Wait. There was another envelope in there, filled with information about a numbered account in a bank in Liechtenstein. There's three million dollars in the account."

"Crime does pay, doesn't it?"

Scanlan leaned over the table and slapped him on the side of the head.

"Hey! What did you do that for, Maggie?"

"Don't you get it? It's a numbered account. Whoever has the transaction codes and procedures, which were inside the envelope, can transfer that money into any account, under any name, in any bank in the world. Congratulations, Rich, you're now a millionaire too."

"Quite a world, isn't it?" said Welsh, almost lost for a moment in bitterness. "You get screwed for doing the right thing, but killing is always profitable."

"Rich . . ."

Welsh went off in deep thought, then brightened up a bit. "Remember Raul the professor, back at the Embassy party? I'll give him a call, I'm sure he knows a bunch of worthy Guatemalan charities that could use some blood money."

"Rich, you are *not* giving that money away. At least not all of it."

"We'll see," he said unconvincingly. "As far as Washington is concerned, I might as well be a leper. Is there a job open as your boy toy?"

She smiled lasciviously. "You meet all the qualifications."

"I always knew I'd find my niche eventually."

"Rich, I'm worried about something. Our relationship has been fantastic, but you've got to admit it's been based on running for our lives and pretty continuous action and adventure. In everyday life are we going to do that couple thing and drive each other crazy?"

"We rolled up in the same tarpaulin in the middle of the fucking jungle," Welsh almost bellowed. "Just what annoying little personal quirks do you think are going to crop up at this stage of the game?"

"Point taken," Scanlan said, laughing again. "It was just in the back of my mind, though. You've got to admit nothing about us has been normal thus far."

"*Anyone* can be normal," said Richard Welsh.

SILENT DOOMSDAY

ROBERT PAYTON MOORE

The U.S. military has developed a new technology so effective it will render modern weapons of destruction totally useless. But the dream turns deadly when a mole in the lab leaks the technology to a Libyan despot with dreams of a unified Middle East under his iron rule, with no country able to stand between him and his terrifying goal. Suddenly the U.S. is confronted with their own super-weapon, and a total, all-out war to save the world from a silent doomsday.

___4395-5 $5.99 US/$6.99 CAN

BROTHER'S KEEPER

JIM DeFELICE

F.B.I. agent Jack Ferico has never gotten along with his estranged older brother, Daniel. But now their father is dying and he wants to see Danny before he goes. The trouble is, when Jack tries to contact Danny, he finds he's disappeared—without a trace. The search that Jack begins simply for his father's sake soon uncovers secrets, hidden agendas, and a danger far more serious than he ever imagined. Danny—Dr. Daniel Ferico—is working with an international think tank as a specialist in stealth technologies, and his disappearance raises some major red flags. If any of the classified technologies were to fall into the wrong hands, national security would be threatened and the balance of power could shift. Suddenly Jack's not the only one looking for Danny. But if he wants to save his brother and end an international crisis, he'd better be the one who finds him . . . and fast.

RED SKIES

KARL LARGENT

"A writer to watch!" —*Publishers Weekly*

The cutting-edge Russian SU-39-Covert stealth bomber, with fighter capabilities years beyond anything the U.S. can produce, has vanished while on a test run over the Gobi Desert. But it is no accident—the super weapon was plucked from the skies by Russian military leaders with their own private agenda—global power.

Half a world away, a dissident faction of the Chinese Red Army engineers the brutal abduction of a top scientist visiting Washington from under the noses of his U.S. guardians. And with him goes the secrets of his most recent triumph—the development of the SU-39.

Commander T.C. Bogner has his orders: Retrieve the fighter and its designer within seventy-two hours, or the die will be cast for a high-tech war, the likes of which the world has never known.

_4117-0 $6.99 US/$7.99 CAN